T0363664

DESTINATION:
Paradise

CARA COLTER &
ANDREA BOLTER

MILLS & BOON

CONTENTS

Second Chance Hawaiian Honeymoon

Cara Colter

Cara Colter shares her home in beautiful British Columbia, Canada, with her husband of more than thirty years, an ancient, crabby cat and several horses. She has three grown children and two grandsons.

Books by Cara Colter

Cinderellas in the Palace

His Convenient Royal Bride
One Night with Her Brooding Bodyguard

Matchmaker and the Manhattan Millionaire His Cinderella Next Door
The Wedding Planner's Christmas Wish
Snowbound with the Prince
Bahamas Escape with the Best Man
Snowed In with the Billionaire

Visit the Author Profile page
at millsandboon.com.au for more titles.

Dear Reader,

I first visited the Hawaiian Islands when I was sixteen years old. I have been under the spell of that warm, exotic land ever since.

In the past few years, I have had the opportunity (and the privilege) of escaping the coldest months of Canadian winter and spending that time on the Big Island of Hawaii.

I do not think, in just one lifetime, it is possible to capture the essence of this mystical, sacred island, but I hope to have at least given you a tantalizing taste of its beauty and magic. I hope, too, I have captured at least some of the warmth and welcome—the spirit of aloha—that lives in the people of Hawaii.

I cannot think of a more remarkable background for the hero and heroine of this story, Joe and Blossom, to explore their enchantment for each other, and to rediscover the depths and healing power of love.

Hawaii will also be the setting for the second book in this duo, where Blossom's twin sister, Bliss, finally meets her match!

Mahalo for sharing this journey with me.

A hui hou!

Cara

Mahalo to my Hawaiian *ohana*,
the Woodwards and the Carters.

Praise for
Cara Colter

"Ms. Colter's writing style is one you will want to continue to read. Her descriptions place you there.... This story does have a HEA but leaves you wanting more."

CHAPTER ONE

BLOSSOM DUPONT made her way through the late spring crowds in the historic Gastown area of Vancouver. It was just one of those perfect days: the sun out; the leaves on the trees unfurling, fresh and green; something vibrant in the air.

Spring did this, didn't it? Made the whole world light up with a kind of hopeful energy.

She was not unaware of eyes on her, as she walked to her destination. She could feel a shimmer, deep in her belly. She wondered if it was that same aura of expectation that was in the warm spring day.

But somehow she doubted that it was anticipation and happiness shimmering in her.

It was that darned anxiety that she was trying so hard not to acknowledge.

Life's too good. The other shoe is going to drop.

Of course, that disturbing encounter with Joe's father hadn't helped.

Stop it, she ordered herself. Just stop it.

In a little over two weeks, she was going to be married!

She was well aware being loved had given her this newfound sense of coming into herself, so much so that most days she could ignore that little voice saying *Don't get your hopes up.*

Blossom didn't consider herself beautiful—though oddly she considered her identical twin sister, Bliss, exactly that.

And maybe Bliss, living up to her name, was beautiful because she had always radiated exactly the kind of energy Blossom was brand-new to.

Well, that and Bliss was way better with makeup, and hair, and clothes. Blossom liked as little fuss as possible. Before she'd begun dating Joseph Blackwell, makeup was a time-consuming nuisance. She rarely curled her long, dark brown hair or put it up. She'd had an absolute aversion to dressing up ever since her senior high school prom.

But as soon as Joe had asked her out, Bliss had placed herself in charge of the management of all things Blossom. Really? She should have appreciated having a private consultant making her look her best every day. The man was a billionaire! As Bliss had pointed out, you didn't go on a date with a man like that in wrinkled khakis and with a sunburned nose.

Blossom did appreciate her sister's efforts. Of course she did!

How convenient was it to have your identical twin sister's rather extensive wardrobe open to you? How wonderful was it to have your fashion-savvy sibling putting together outfits for you?

Right now, Blossom was wearing a short, black, flirty pleated skirt that swished around her thighs, slender boots with a skinny heel that added two inches to her height, and a filmy, pink pastel blouse, the lacy red camisole underneath just peeking through.

Bliss had pronounced, with satisfaction, that the outfit was sexy as hell and then she'd gone to work to make the rest of Blossom match. So, her abundance of hair was held loosely up in a clip, giving her a casual I-don't-care-what-my-hair-looks-like look that was devilishly hard to achieve. The dark suede brown of her eyes had been accentuated with artfully placed smudges of shadow. Her cheekbones looked high and her cheeks looked hollow. Bliss had declared Blossom's faintly glossed lips *kissable.*

"Who needs to have kissable lips to go out for lunch?" Blossom had asked.

"Lunch with Joe Blackwell," Bliss had reminded her.

Unfortunately, that reminder, and the faintly incredulous note in her sister's tone, brought out the very voice Blossom was trying to silence.

The voice that was asking her if Joe had fallen for *her* or for Bliss's creation. Because she'd been down this road before, hadn't she? Pretending to be something she was not. With catastrophic results.

Bliss's creation was attracting quite a bit of attention. It was a bit of a marvel, because, with one notable exception in her past, Blossom had never really been the woman who garnered male attention, and yet she could feel eyes following her with interest. A construction worker, uncaring of political correctness, bless his heart, wolf-whistled his appreciation.

She stopped in front of Essence, the new *it* restaurant in Vancouver. The restaurant did not take reservations, and hopefuls were lined up to the corner and beyond.

But those hopefuls weren't engaged to Joseph Blackwell. When he'd suggested lunch here, Blossom had said she didn't have time to wait in the line. Truth be told, she barely had time for lunch.

She had a wedding to get ready for.

A wedding in the final countdown. Sixteen days.

Of course, that was her job. She always had a wedding to get ready for. She and Bliss had started their wedding planning company, Blossoms and Bliss, three years ago. They liked to joke that their weird names, bestowed on them by their wildly eccentric artist mother, had finally paid off.

The company had taken all their money, all their heart, and every ounce of their courage. Several times they had thought it was over, that they were going to go under, that the dream was dead.

But then they had been hired by Vancouver real estate phenom, Harold Lee, to do his daughter's wedding. The Cinderella-themed, over-the-top wedding had moved their company into the awareness of people in entirely different circles. They were now fielding requests from dream clientele.

And, of course, it was because of the Lee wedding that Blossom had been introduced to Joe Blackwell, the groom's best friend and best man.

Nobody could have been more surprised than her when, at the end of the evening, he had asked for her—not Bliss, who was usually the one who was swarmed with the attention of any available male who had attended the wedding—if she would like to dance.

Normally, she would have said no. Normally, she would have considered it unprofessional.

And yet that night, the last dance of the night had been to the song "Hunger." The waltz, with its haunting melody, was about passion. Longing. And, finally, fulfillment.

And when Joe Blackwell had held out his hand to her, she had taken it, unable to resist. Since that first electrical touch, Blossom had known exactly what hunger, on every level, meant.

Now, all these months later, she was still unable to resist him, still hungry for his touch, his gaze, his slow, sexy smile.

After a whirlwind romance, she was about to marry a man who had actually laughed when she mentioned the line-up at Essence. He and the owner were old college buddies. There wouldn't be any line for them.

Of course there wouldn't, because Joe lived in *that* world.

And now, she thought with a tiny shiver, so did she.

But again, that shiver was nebulous. It could equally be happiness or bad nerves because Joe so obviously belonged in a world that she was still finding her way in, like a tourist lost in the mazelike streets of Paris.

Again, she remembered that stunning encounter with his father, James. The Blackwells were a well-known and well-heeled Vancouver family, what people often called *old money.* That evening, not even a week ago, Blossom and Joe had been invited for dinner at the Blackwell senior's estate in the tony British Properties in West Vancouver.

Joe's parents, James and Celia, had always *seemed* to like her.

And yet James had been standing outside of the bathroom door when she had come out, as if he'd been waiting for her.

I know what you're up to.

She had been stunned, but when she had pressed James for clarity, he had given her a dark look, gone in the bathroom and shut the door in her face.

Blossom shook it off as she stepped past the first people

in line, ignoring their annoyed looks as she went out of the brightness of the day into the restaurant.

The woman at the front hostess station was one of those intimidating types. She was regal, all in black, with a string of tasteful pearls at her neck. She looked more like a member of an exclusive country club than a hostess at a restaurant, even a posh one.

She raised a perfectly shaped eyebrow at Blossom, asking, without saying a single word, who did she think she was? Hadn't she seen the line-up outside?

At least Blossom was finally able to identify the shiver within her. Nope. Not happiness. That voice.

"Not good enough."

"Imposter."

"Hopelessly out of her depth."

Joe's father's words had brought each of those insecurities she'd thought long buried rushing to the surface.

Without warning, she was once again the girl at the senior high school prom, the one who had the date with the star of the high school football team, whose mother had been so excited to find a Jacob Minstrel original gown at the secondhand store.

For once, Blossom had been the fairy-tale princess.

Until it had all fallen apart. She shivered. She did not want to think of that now. But because she had allowed it to creep into her thoughts, she had a sudden fear that maybe Joe—who had never stood her up or let her down—wasn't here, that this, too, was going to all fall apart.

She could almost hear her mother, always quick with the New Age advice—and also, ironically, the source of that fear that you could always count on things to go sideways—saying, *Fear is like saying a prayer for what you don't want.*

She took a deep breath and shook off the feelings. Instead of trying to tug the skirt down to cover an extra inch of her thigh, Blossom raised her eyebrow back at the hostess. "I'm Blossom DuPont."

There was that subtle sneer at her name—as if it was a stripper name—just the faintest lifting of a red-painted lip.

"I'm meeting Joseph Blackwell." She could not resist adding, "My fiancé."

The sneer disappeared as if the woman had tried to swallow her lips. Before her expression smoothed over completely, Blossom caught a flicker of envy, that look that said, *Why you?*

A question she had asked herself a hundred—no, a thousand—times over the last action-packed months of romance.

"I'll show you—"

"It's okay, thanks, I see him," Blossom said, moving past the woman. She paused before she went into the main area of the restaurant. She understood that woman's envy completely.

When she saw Joe, she always had this sensation.

Pinch me. I must be dreaming.

Today, it was even more intense, a sensation of wanting, accompanied by a delicious flutter in her heart. In sixteen days, *this* sophisticated, handsome billionaire was going to be her husband.

Blossom admired Joe even more because he had not been satisfied to rest on his family's laurels. He had cut his own swathe to fortune with hard work and savvy, creating one of the most well-known software design companies in the world.

He wore his success with the confident ease of a man who had never expected anything less of his life than the lofty place he had arrived at. Whereas Blossom had to *work* at looking a certain way, elegance and good taste came to Joe as naturally as breathing.

Today, he had on jeans and a deep gray suit jacket, a crisp white linen shirt, undone at the throat. Even without a hint of a label showing anywhere, the cut and quality of that clothing screamed the expense and classiness of the very best men's designers in the world. He could leave lunch and be on for the cover of *Trends*, the men's lifestyle magazine that always had a hot, hot model on the cover.

Joe had all those cover-ready qualities: absolutely masculine, stunningly gorgeous, radiating masculine self-assurance.

The subtle restaurant light was playing with his perfectly cut light brown hair, spinning strands of gold into it. The soft glow showed his features to advantage, the beautiful nose, sculpted cheekbones, the faintest cleft to that strong chin, all of it with just a hint of whisker shadowing.

He had been studying the menu, but as if he sensed himself being watched, he suddenly glanced up. A smile touched his full, sensual lips, and revealed straight, even, beautifully white teeth. Blossom felt that familiar melting sensation.

Her fiancé. In sixteen days, she would be Mrs. Blackwell.

She savored the impact of those eyes that were taking her in with grave male appreciation. Joe's eyes were a shade of green deeper than the most valuable jade, and like valuable jade, seemed to spark from within.

She was pretty sure that was what she had loved about him first, how the light in his eyes deepened whenever he looked at her. Suddenly, Blossom was nothing but grateful for the outfit Bliss had selected.

Joe rose from the table as she arrived, took her shoulders and kissed her on both cheeks.

"You look gorgeous," he said, his voice so deep, so familiar, so sensual. His eyes lingered on those *kissable* lips.

And then he gave in and kissed them, the kiss lingering.

Blossom turned to liquid, hot and melting. He broke the kiss, but reluctantly, and she slid into the chair he held out for her, boneless.

"Sorry," he said. "I can't resist you."

There was just a tiny smudge of her gloss on his lips that she wanted to remove. Those green eyes sparked with something so hot, she considered suggesting they skip lunch.

Which, of course, would be *trashy*, a word that had haunted Blossom for nearly five years.

"Thank you," she managed to stammer. "You're looking pretty irresistible yourself. The hostess has the hots for you."

The hostess, me, any female breathing within a hundred yards or so...

He glanced over at the hostess station, lifted a shoulder, dismissing the compliment, looking back at her as if she was the only woman in his world worthy of note.

Something in Blossom sighed. He was so *perfect*.

"So, how's your day been?" he asked. His hand closed over hers and squeezed, and she squeezed back, marveling at the small intimacies that love imbued with the light of the spectacular.

"Busy!"

"You said today was busy, so I've been studying the menu trying to decide what you might like. I guessed the pear and brie croissant. What do you think?"

In what world was one of Vancouver's richest men trying to decipher what she might like for lunch? *Her world.*

But there was that cloud again. Pressing at her world of sunshine and blue sky, telling her, *Watch out. There's a storm brewing.*

"That sounds perfect," she said, hoping her tone was bright and chipper and not faintly uneasy. "Just like you."

He smiled at her, but, always hyperalert, Blossom thought she noticed something in his smile. Was he tired? So was she. Exhausted. But it would all be worth it soon.

"Can you believe we're in the final stretch? Sixteen days," she said to Joe, brightly. Again, she could feel something forced in her deliberately cheery tone.

He lifted his water glass to her. "I can't wait," he said.

Some intuition insisted on tickling along her spine. It felt as if he had left the sentence unfinished. As if what he wanted to say was, *I can't wait for it to be over.*

Well, she did this for a living. She knew, at this stage, everyone—but particularly the groom, it seemed—was exhausted with the inevitable minutiae of a wedding, especially an extravagant one.

"Just think, in seventeen days," he said, "we'll be on the Big Island."

Blossom had learned the island they were flying to—on Joe's company's private jet—the day after their wedding, actually bore the name Hawaii, but it was called the Big Island to distinguish it from the chain of islands that made up the State of Hawaii.

"Mr. and Mrs. Blackwell," Joe said. "On our honeymoon."

Again, there was a wistful, almost weary note, as if he would like to just skip over the whole wedding and get to the good part.

Not that the honeymoon wasn't going to be a good part—

the Blackwells had friends who had turned over their entire Hawaiian estate for the enjoyment of the newlyweds—but Blossom had to stay focused on the tasks right in front of her.

For her, right now, the *good* part was the wedding, everything under control, a plan being skillfully executed, so that she and Joe and their guests could enjoy an absolutely amazing day.

"Speaking of the wedding," she said, though technically they had been speaking about the honeymoon, "I think we need to make a change to the menu. We should tweak dessert."

She had hung her bag over the back of the chair and twisted to get in the main pocket for the menu. "Here it is. I just scratched out the first choice and wrote in the other. I caught it before they were printed, thank goodness, and before the caterer carved it in stone."

She slid the sample menu across the table.

He took it and glanced at it, set it down and rubbed a hand over his face. He *was* tired. But her intuition was nagging at her. It was something more. Her hinky sense went on high alert. There was that shimmer.

Becoming uncomfortably electrical, and not in the good way, like when Joe claimed her lips with his own.

"Is everything okay?" she asked him.

"Sure."

But there was something in his tone that didn't sound *sure*.

"Is something wrong with the menu?"

He glanced at it again.

"I guess I was just wondering," he said, after a moment, "what a different kind of wedding would have looked like."

Blossom felt everything in her freeze, as if she had stopped breathing and turned to stone. As she looked across the table at her fiancé, she felt her intuitive sense crow, *Aha! This is the moment you've been waiting for.*

Bracing herself for, really, with her senior prom disaster history, and even more so since Joe's father had said those words.

Ever so carefully, she unfroze herself. She forced herself to take a sip of her water. Ever so carefully, she said, "Sixteen days out, and you're wondering what a different kind of wedding would have looked like?"

Inwardly, she wondered how far that was from Joe wondering what a different kind of bride would have looked like.

Joe lifted a broad shoulder, clearly uncomfortable. He met her eyes, and then looked away. "Forget I said it."

As if that wasn't impossible!

"But what exactly does that mean? A different kind of wedding?" she asked, unable to let it go. Despite trying to strip the note of hysteria from her voice, she could hear the brittleness in her tone.

This is what she *did*.

Weddings. Perfect weddings.

And hers was going to be the most perfect of them all. Everything was in place. A venue to die for. The best catering in Vancouver. A live band to dance the night away to. The most incredible wedding gown ever…she was going to be a princess. And this time, no clock was going to go off at midnight to return her to the scullery.

"What does that mean?" she asked, again, when Joe didn't answer right away.

He met her gaze. This time he didn't look away. "Do you remember that time we went camping?" he asked her.

"Camping?" she stammered.

"Maybe we should have done something like that."

For a moment, Blossom really didn't understand what he was saying. But her heart was beating hard, the fear beat, as if a bear was hiding in some bushes waiting to eat her, which she had wondered about quite a bit on that camping trip that he was remembering so fondly!

"I'm not quite following," she admitted, nervously twisting her beautiful solitaire diamond engagement ring around her finger.

"You know. Something less formal. For the wedding."

Blossom stared at Joe, trying to comprehend what he was saying.

"Are you actually suggesting we change the wedding plans?"

"Do you think it's too late? Just us and our families and a few friends," he said, expanding a little too enthusiastically on the idea of switching out *her* wedding for camping.

She stared at him, feeling as if the man she loved so completely had morphed into a stranger before her very eyes.

Hundreds of hours of planning.

Thousands of dollars already spent on dresses and flowers, deposits and venues, catering and live music.

"The wedding is sixteen days away," Blossom said. It sounded like her voice was being delivered in a bubble from the bottom of a well.

"I know. I'm just thinking out loud. I'm sorry."

Sorry? Had a word ever seemed so puny?

"You don't like the plan for the wedding?" she said. Did her voice sound a wee bit shrill? There was that hand rub again. This time the back of his neck. "It's a little late for that."

"I was just thinking out loud," he said, his tone aggravatingly mild.

"How can you not get this?" she asked. "It's not just a wedding. It's who I am."

He looked at the menu she had passed him.

"This is who you are?" Joe asked, picking it up and studying where she had scratched out one dessert and written in another.

CHAPTER TWO

"YES!" BLOSSOM SAID, desperately, "that's exactly who I am."

But, of course, in the back of her mind, she wasn't that at all. She was the girl standing in Ryan Paulson's living room waiting to have prom pictures done by a professional photographer.

She was the girl trying not to gawk at how gorgeous his house was.

And she was the girl trying not to notice how Ryan's mother and sister had stared at her, before disappearing, making a sense of foreboding snake across her spine.

And then she'd seen the picture on the mantel of Ryan's floor-to-ceiling granite fireplace. His sister's prom from last year. And she had been wearing the very same dress that Blossom now had on.

Feeling suddenly sick, she'd asked directions to the restroom.

On her way there, past a closed door, the voices drifting out of it. His mother and sister, distressed about the photos, about the same dress appearing on two different girls in the proudly displayed photos. His sister, her voice a bray of pure malice.

She's making that dress look trashy.

Blossom stared at Joe, feeling as if he had morphed into a stranger before her very eyes, feeling as if he had morphed into Ryan Paulson.

Or, maybe more accurately, that she had morphed into her former self: just a trashy girl pretending to be a princess.

He looked back at her steadily. "I think you're a little more than table-fired crème brûlée, or lemon chiffon cake with a blueberry reduction."

I'm not, she cried silently, though a smug voice inside her asked her if maybe she wasn't a little *less*, the girl who had grown up thinking a fancy dessert was a chocolate pudding in a packaged cup with a squirt of canned whipped cream on top.

She could feel a slow-burning fury that he—the man of her dreams—so didn't get it. The anger shocked her. Over the course of their entire relationship, she'd never been mad at Joe.

Out loud, her voice surprisingly controlled, she said, "You're trivializing what I do. It's not about brulée or chiffon cake. It's about the details. I'm extraordinary with the kind of details that move an event from mundane to magnificent. You've seen how I am about my work."

He sighed. "Right. Work."

As if she'd turned everything about their wedding into work. How could Joe not see that this wedding, her wedding—their wedding—had to be the best she had ever done, an absolute testament to her love for him?

She could feel that confident woman she had been just

moments ago—or pretended to be—deflating, like a balloon with a hole in it.

The little voice was winning. *Too good to be true.*

"Sixteen days before our wedding, you decide you don't like anything about it?"

There was his opening. To tell her all the things he *loved* about their plans. Instead, he was silent.

He didn't even say he liked the *bride*.

Don't cry, she told herself.

"Maybe we should postpone," Blossom said. She didn't mean it, of course. She expected him to disagree and adamantly. Instead, he looked pensive. Her heart felt as if it was going to beat right out of her chest.

"Maybe we should cancel," Blossom said. Was that her voice? Laying down that gauntlet so cavalierly?

She saw just a flicker of something in the deep green of his beautiful eyes.

And no matter what he said next, she could never unsee that.

Relief.

He didn't want to marry her.

It felt as if everything froze around her, except the wild beating of her heart. One completely crystallized thought came out of the deep freeze.

Blossom knew what she had to do. Who wanted a reluctant groom? She had to salvage a tiny scrap of her pride.

Just as all those years ago, when she'd never found the restroom in Ryan's house, had slipped down that hallway, found the back door and walked home in those flimsy shoes.

"Consider it canceled," she said, her voice oddly firm.

Joe stared at her, stunned. "Look, that's not what I—"

"In fact—" she twisted the ring off her finger and placed it carefully in front of him "—consider *us* canceled."

Distressingly, Blossom could feel the anxiety that had plagued her for days easing. The worst had happened, right on cue. The waiting was over. Hadn't she always known good things didn't really happen to people like her?

Hadn't she always known it was like throwing a gauntlet before the gods to think she could belong in a world like Joe's?

Fear, Blossom could almost hear her mother's voice, *is like saying a prayer for what you don't want.*

Touché, Mom, touché.

A part of her, naturally, inwardly begged him to give her back the ring, stand up and cross the distance between them, gather her in his arms, beg her not to mean it.

Just as she had hoped Ryan would come looking for her. Would call. Would *care*.

Instead, Joe, like Ryan, disappointed. He looked at the ring, astonished, and then at her.

"Are you breaking up with me?" he asked.

Did he sound faintly incredulous that *she* would be the one breaking up with *him?*

No, part of her screamed, *of course I'm not breaking up with you. I can't. You are the other half of my heart. You have made my days worth living. You are the prince I have waited all my life for.*

But it was the part of her that knew never to get her hopes up, that knew she was not princess material, that answered.

And that voice said, "Yes, I'm breaking up with you. It's over."

It was the most ridiculous impulse! And yet now she felt as if she couldn't back down. Before she could take it back, before she cried, before she threw herself upon him and pleaded with him to love her, she gathered her things—crumpled those menus and stuffed them back in her purse—and walked quickly from the restaurant, her spine straight and proud.

Part of her hoped he would come after her. Part of her hoped he would be the one who begged.

But he didn't come after her.

She wished, if she had to give in to impulses, she had given in to the one she'd had after Joe had kissed her, the one to suggest they skip lunch. It might have been trashy, the thing she always guarded against. But she would probably still be engaged! It was probably the first of many regrets her next weeks and months and years were going to be filled with.

She went right by that same construction worker. This time, he didn't even notice her. Because it was the love of an incredible man—not Bliss's outfit—that had made her beautiful. And that was lost.

Blossom DuPont was invisible again.

It was pitch-black, but when Joe touched the keypad, it lit up. In the faint illumination he could see that a hibiscus beside the door, drooping under the weight of heavy blooms, was the source of the fragrance that had been tickling at his nose.

He checked his phone for the code, punched it in, and heard the click of the door unlocking.

The keypad was a very modern addition to the door, carved of ancient, deeply grained mango wood. At his touch, the heavy door swung inward silently.

The fragrance of frangipani overtook the scent of the

hibiscus and welcomed him as he stepped through into the space inside. The moon came out from behind the clouds that had turned the night to pitch, shining through an entire wall of floor-to-ceiling French-paned doors at the back of the house. Dancing shadows were cast on a room that was distinctly Old Hawaii.

Woven bamboo cloth was behind the heavy wooden beams of the high vaulted ceiling. Huge brass-and-wood ceiling fans, the blades leaf-shaped, silently cooled a space furnished in deeply cushioned antique pieces. Scattered casually about were ancient and contemporary Hawaiian art and carvings, probably priceless.

The moonlight made the wide-plank wood floors—Joe knew it be koa, which grew nowhere else in the world—glow as if they held a light. Indeed the wood was known for its chatoyancy, a property usually attributed to rare gems.

Hale Alana.

Joe had been here, to this beautiful estate, owned by his parents' oldest friends, Dave and Becky Windstorm, every single year for ten years, since his parents' twenty-fifth wedding anniversary had been held here. He'd been nineteen the first time he'd come here and the mystical allure of the Big Island had held him in its thrall ever since.

Even at the time, at only nineteen, he had known that somehow the deep enchantment of the setting had contributed to his parents' extraordinary celebration of lasting love.

Now, Joe's own celebration of love had been abruptly called off.

Dave had come down with a sudden illness while the couple had been visiting Patagonia. When Joe had received a note from Becky saying they would not make the wedding, he had not had the heart to add to their problems by telling them there would be no wedding. He was sure, in time, his parents would break the news to them.

Both pieces of news.

A canceled wedding. A devastating diagnosis.

Would his parents celebrate their own thirty-fifth anniversary? Things that had once seemed like constants now seemed horribly fragile.

"They think it's a rare kind of dementia," Joe's mother had told him, not an hour before he had met Blossom for lunch that awful, awful day just a little over two weeks ago.

They think.

Joe clung to those words. "They" had to be wrong. His dad. The most brilliant man he had ever known. The man who had always been his number one supporter, who had encouraged him to believe he could do anything. Be anything.

And then there was the other question, like a hum in the background, from the second Joe had heard the news.

Was it hereditary?

When Blossom had suggested postponing the wedding, he'd felt nothing but relief. He needed time to find answers.

You didn't knowingly subject someone you loved to a horrible future. And, if it was hereditary, what about children? What about *their* children?

His losses felt unbearable at the moment. His dad. Blossom. Their future children. Was that why Joe had come here to Hawaii? Obviously Hale Alana had been still available. Had he been thinking he would find something in this powerful, beautiful land, where *ohana*—family—was sacred, that could reassure him about the abiding power of love?

Every single thing Joe thought about love had been tested in the last weeks and days. If his assumption was that he would find something here to bring him clarity, he could already, despite the quiet feeling of sanctuary in this room, feel the error of it.

He and Blossom had chosen Hawaii for their honeymoon because she had never been anywhere tropical. He had so looked forward to being the one to introduce her to Hawaii, and particularly the Big Island, a place of so many stunning contrasts.

On any given day, molten lava could be spilling from Kilauea, and snow falling on Mauna Kea. This island was a whole world unto itself that begged discovery, that opened the senses.

Some landscapes were dense with lush greenery threaded through with unbelievable flowers, while others were stark with the black endless seas of old lava flows.

The ocean delighted with dolphins dancing and whales breaching above water, the secret and enchanting worlds of the coral reefs below the surface.

Now, without her, without Blossom to show it to, to discover it anew with, Hawaii, that place that demanded every sense be opened, felt as empty as a yawning cavern.

Just like his life.

It occurred to Joe he wasn't going to find what he was looking for here. Or probably anywhere, for that matter. Maybe he'd just stay the night and then go home. Work had been his balm over the last two weeks. Okay, work and hanging out with his best friend, Lance, who was supposed to have been his best man.

Joe wondered what moment of madness had made him decide to trade work and those surprisingly satisfying, if somewhat drunken all-women-are-evil-so-let's-stay-single-forever discussions with Lance, for this—

The moon disappeared back behind clouds, and the room was plunged again into a darkness that matched the bleakness of his soul.

A movement, just caught out of the corner of his eye, startled him. Too late, he realized he was not alone.

A figure, possibly taking advantage of the return to darkness, burst from behind a tall hutch in the corner of the room behind the door.

Intruder.

It seemed impossible, incongruous with the scent of frangipani and the lush, old-world serenity of the room, but Joe was being attacked.

Someone, baseball cap pulled low, charged out of the darkness toward him, a weaponized object held high. A vase?

Just before collision, Joe registered, with some relief, the slightness of frame of his attacker. A teenager, then. He caught a tiny wrist and forced release of the weapon. But his attacker managed to propel it rather than drop it. The vase narrowly missed his head, before falling to the floor and shattering. He tightened his grip on that surprisingly small wrist and heard a yelp of pain and distress.

A girl teenager.

The realization tempered his instinctive response. She was trying, with the desperation of a trapped animal, to yank her hand out of his grasp.

Thankfully, she had no hope against his far superior strength. But when escape failed, she turned and, with a warrior shout, tucked her chin, her face completely hidden by the murky darkness of the room and the ball cap. She rammed into him with surprising might.

The momentum carried them both to the ground, his

hand still locked around her wrist, carrying her with him as his back hit the unforgiving, glass-covered floor. As her weight fell full on top of him, he felt the shards of glass grind into him.

Oddly, despite the shock and pain, he noted he could read her ball cap, her face completely shadowed by the brim: *True North*.

There was no accounting for minds in these situations, because his pointed out to him, with a certain languid interest, that it was a Canadian ball cap and what were the chances of a Canadian being attacked in Hawaii by someone wearing a Canadian ball cap?

For a blessed second his attacker was still, almost limp.

He thought he'd won, that she had surrendered.

But no, she'd just been gathering herself, or trying to lull him into a sense of security, or maybe some combination of both.

With the desperate strength of a wild thing, she exploded. She tried to free her hand again, and with her other she reached up and attempted to scratch his face. He closed his eyes against fingers that seemed intent on removing an eyeball, found her other wrist and held tight, thankfully before she made contact.

"Let...me...go."

She squirmed hard against him. He was still trying to temper his reaction despite the fact he was pretty sure he was now bleeding from his glass-embedded backside. His mind felt super alert and sluggish at the same time, laser-focused and yet also roaming over a large radius.

And then suddenly the scent of her hair rose above the scent of the frangipani that filled the room.

It was full seconds since she had spoken, but suddenly he registered her voice.

Something clicked.

No.

It. Was. Not. Possible.

It was just because he had been thinking about her when all this happened. It was just because it should have been him and her, Mr. and Mrs. Blackwell, coming through that door. Would he have carried her?

Thank goodness she *wasn't* here. What a terrible start to a honeymoon this would have made! To be carrying her over the threshold when a stranger came at them out of the dark.

Still, with mind both roaming and focused, Joe contemplated the ancient role of warrior protector, as *that* scent tickled his nose again.

He knew only one person whose hair had the exotic and unusual combination of lavender and lemongrass. He opened his eyes. He let go of one wrist, flicked the brim of the cap, and her face came out of the shadow.

She managed to stop her momentum midswing, which was good because she obviously fully intended to hit him with that freed hand.

They stared at each other, completely shocked.

Completely frozen.

"Blossom."

Really? A man should not say a woman's name like that. Especially a woman who had just attacked him. Especially a woman who had basically left him at the altar. Especially a woman who had challenged every single thing he thought he knew about love.

A man should not say her name as if it was a blessing

that had been bestowed upon him, a blessing that turned a world black-and-white back to color.

"Joe."

A man had to remember who had turned that world black-and-white in the first place.

So he stripped the tenderness from his voice, hoping in her shock, with her adrenaline running on high, that she had not heard what he so did not want her to hear.

"What the hell are *you* doing here?" he growled, letting go of her wrists.

She scrambled off him, stood up and took off her baseball cap. Her hair, which she had rarely worn loose in the course of their relationship, cascaded over slender shoulders in a luxurious, shiny dark wave.

Joe extinguished the unexpected longing of having her familiar curves pressed against him, that the simple cascade of her hair falling over her shoulder caused in him. Too easy to imagine his fingers combing through it.

Slowly, he found his feet and stood glaring down at his ex-fiancée, Blossom DuPont.

"What the hell are *you* doing here?" she shot back at him.

CHAPTER THREE

"I'M ENJOYING THE home of *my* family's friends," Joe told Blossom, heavy emphasis on whose friends they were.

In the dimness of the room, he could still barely make out her features, but he was pretty sure she was paler than usual. He reached along the wall behind him and found the light switch. He threw it.

Blossom was indeed pale. Her eyes looked huge and brown, though there was a hint of tired circles underneath them. But maybe that was noticeable because she didn't have on any makeup. Had she lost weight?

"How could you have not known it was me?" she demanded.

This seemed unreasonable, indeed. The furthest thing from his mind would have been the possibility that Blossom would arrive at their honeymoon destination on her own.

But even aside from that, he would never have recognized her dressed the way she was. Though, like most men, he was no women's fashion aficionado, he'd always appreciated the way Blossom put together an outfit. She had an unconventional flair that made him—most men, he'd noticed—want to look at her and not stop.

But her outfit, at the moment, could be described only one way. It was hideous. The baggy sweatpants were the color of a popular remedy for upset stomachs. The T-shirt was too big, and solid black, which might be why she looked so pale. The ball cap was also too large, settling around her ears. He could see why he had mistaken her for a teenager.

Despite the outfit and the lack of makeup, he was aware he still found her cute—very cute, in a new and different way, like a little waif who needed a warrior protector. He was intensely aware of the danger of these kinds of thoughts toward a woman who had broken his heart. These were feelings he needed to fight as if he was fighting for his life.

Which he was.

"How could you have not known it was me?" he asked her back.

"I just wasn't expecting *you*."

"Ditto," he snapped.

"I thought you were an intruder," she said. Despite her attempt at bravado, he could tell she was well and truly shaken, and he had to fight an intense desire to gather her in his arms and stroke her hair.

There was that hair thing again. Geez, he loved her hair. It was what he had noticed first about her.

"I thought *you* were an intruder," he shot back the same words at her. "In the dark, it just looked like some young hooligan coming at me."

"Hooligan?" She looked down at herself and then tossed her hair. "This is what I really look like. When I'm not trying to impress anyone."

With hair like that, she could wear a sackcloth and still

impress. Actually, a sackcloth might be an improvement over her getup.

Was there an underlying message there? That she had been trying to impress him? Their entire relationship?

If that had been her goal, she had succeeded in spades. But here they were, with her not trying to impress at all, and he was still feeling the same thing he had felt when they had danced to "Hunger" all those months ago.

It was a weakness that had to be tamed. Obviously.

"I could have killed you," Blossom offered, faintly contrite.

Her concern was hardly a declaration of love, he warned himself. People who loved you did not cancel your planned nuptials with them on the flimsiest of premises.

"There's not the slightest chance of that," he told her. "With a vase? Seriously?"

"You probably could have killed me," she decided. "By accident."

He debated telling her that his desire to kill her was so last week. But even if he said it kiddingly, she would know something of his fury and frustration with her, how her sudden ending of their relationship had devastated him.

He wasn't giving her that kind of power over him.

"Killing seems a bit extreme, but I could have hurt you very badly," he said. "What were you thinking?"

"I didn't really think. I had just gotten here when I heard someone at the door."

"It could have been the estate manager!" he admonished her.

"No, I spoke to him last week. He'd told me we would be completely alone. All the staff were given time off so that you and I..." Her cheeks flushed.

Because of what he and she might have been doing on the estate alone? On their honeymoon. That familiar heat was rising in him.

But maybe her cheeks were flushed because she had obviously misled the manager.

Whatever the reason, she attempted to cover up her embarrassment by snapping at him. "Besides, I don't think the estate manager would be creeping around in the dark. Like a creeper!"

His honeymoon night—that wasn't his honeymoon night—seemed to be deteriorating even more. A creeper?

"Look, it appears to be you who was creeping around in the dark," he said sternly, and then could not stop himself from giving her a few instructions. For future reference. So she could protect herself in the life she had chosen. Without him.

He told himself it wasn't his job to be protective of her anymore. Instructions for how to live her life were someone else's job.

And yet Joe could not stop himself.

"Why didn't you have some lights on, for pity's sake? And why didn't you hide in a closet and dial 911 if you thought there was an intruder?"

"I didn't get an international phone plan," she said haughtily. "And how would I know if they have the same emergency numbers in Hawaii as we have? How would *you* know?"

"I've been here before."

She lifted an eyebrow at him. "And your past visits necessitated a call to 911? You killed an intruder by mistake?"

He frowned at Blossom.

They had seen each other for only two months when

he had known, beyond a shadow of a doubt, that she was the one.

He had never felt as alive as he felt with Blossom. The chemistry of that first night simply didn't quit. They had such incredible fun together.

He had asked her to marry him. They had been engaged for another nine months after that. Never once, in that nearly yearlong courtship, had she been like *this*. Dressed down. Sarcastic. Spoiling for a fight.

"I'm unlikely to kill a teenage girl under any circumstances, past or present."

"Trust you to be a perfect gentleman during a mugging."

She said that as if being a "perfect gentleman" was somehow a bad thing. It seemed like a flimsy reason for a breakup, but how many little irritations had to build up in a person for them to call off a wedding? Had she been stifling herself around him? She'd insinuated she had felt a need to dress to impress him. He hated it that maybe she had thought she had to change who she was for him.

He hated it that maybe calling off the wedding had been the right thing. They didn't, it appeared, really know each other at all.

"I think of a mugging as more of a street crime," he informed her.

"Let's not do semantics right now."

"Suggesting that I *do* semantics at inappropriate times? Two flaws thrown at me in two seconds. I'm glad this isn't our honeymoon."

Did she flinch ever so slightly? No, she folded her arms over her chest. "Me, too," she said.

"As lovely as this reunion is, I have—"

"To be somewhere else?" she asked hopefully.

"Uh, I have a pain in my backside."

"Are you suggesting I'm a pain in your backside?" she huffed.

"The cause of it," he said. He reached back and ran his hand carefully over a buttock. He flinched. "I'm pretty sure there's glass in me."

"You're hurt?"

He looked at her. The sarcasm was gone. She looked genuinely distressed. Easy to mistake pity for love.

"I think it's just a scratch," he said.

She was staring at his hand. "It's not. You're bleeding. A lot. Your hand is covered in blood."

He followed her gaze to his hand. It was not exactly *covered*, but he wasn't going to point that out and hear the semantics complaint again.

Before he could properly prepare himself, she had darted behind him and was inspecting his backside.

"There's quite a bit of blood," she said. "I wonder if there's more glass embedded?"

"Get your hands off my shorts!" he said tersely.

He was thinking this could only happen to him. Glass in the ass instead of a blissful honeymoon in Hawaii. The woman who used to be his fiancée trying to get his shorts off for all the wrong reasons.

"Oh, don't be a baby," she said.

A baby?

He liked the old Blossom—the one who constantly told him how perfect he was—much better.

Without warning, she yanked at his waistband. He felt air on his rear. He pushed her hands away and pulled his shorts back up.

"Let me look."

"No," he said through clenched teeth.

"I got a quick look, and it looks quite bad," she said.

His ass looked bad. Just what every man wanted to hear on his honeymoon. Except it wasn't his honeymoon.

Which did not make his ass looking bad feel any better. At all.

"You're going to have to let me look at it," she told him.

"No."

"For first aid purposes!"

"You are not going to administer first aid to my backside," he said brusquely.

Especially not on the night that they should have been in each other's arms exploring the complete world of being husband and wife.

"Oh, stop," Blossom said. "It's not like it's something I haven't seen before. And I think it's going to be hard for you to administer to that area yourself. Unless you want to go to the hospital?"

"It's just a scratch."

"I looked at it, and I'm telling you, no, it isn't. Multiple punctures. How are you going to pluck glass out of your own ass?"

When Joe had woken up this morning, it never occurred to him he might be contemplating such a question before the end of the day. And never in a million years would he have thought that question would be coming from his ex.

He did not like surprises.

He did not like things out of his control. No wonder the last two weeks had been so utterly miserable! It wasn't just the loss of Blossom…it was also the loss of feeling as if the world was a predictable place.

"I'll look after it," Blossom said soothingly, "and then

you can go, though I think you're going to have an uncomfortable trip home."

Trip home? Considering that just seconds ago Joe had decided he would probably only stay the night, he suddenly felt as if a stick of dynamite couldn't remove him from Hale Alana.

"I'm not leaving," he said coolly, making a manly effort not to reach back and see if he couldn't staunch the pain with a bit of a rub. "I think you're the one who is going to have to leave."

He folded his arms in front of him.

"Well, I can't."

She folded her arms in front of her.

He lifted an eyebrow at her.

"Unlike some of us," she said, "I live in the real world."

"What's that supposed to mean?"

"I don't have access to your company's private jet. I can't flit around the world at will."

Now would be a nice time to deny he had come on the jet, but she knew they had booked it to bring them to Hawaii. He thought of how different that lonely flight would have been if their world had not blown apart. If they had been together. It was possible the honeymoon would have started at twenty thousand feet.

Do not go there, he ordered himself. *And do not look at her hair.*

"I flew economy," she said.

"I don't know what that means."

"You wouldn't."

"I know what flying economy means," he said with elaborate patience, "I don't know what it means in terms of your leaving."

"In the real world, you can't just rebook tickets without paying a financial penalty. It's usually worth more than the original flight, which was worth plenty booked on such short notice. So, I'm staying."

"You're going to have a honeymoon by yourself?" he asked incredulously.

"Is that what you're doing? Having a honeymoon?" she shot back. "Because I wouldn't call it that. After the wedding has been called off. By the way, canceling a wedding is just as much work as having it in the first place. Maybe more. I'm exhausted and I need a rest. I deserve a rest, in fact."

Was she actually acting resentful of *him?*

"You're saying that as if I called off the wedding," he said, his voice tight. "And that's not how I recall it. At all."

"Funny. I don't remember you voicing any objections."

Joe thought again, astounded in the worst possible way, that they had been together eleven months, most of those as an engaged couple. In that time, they had never—not even once—raised their voices to each other. This woman with the snapping eyes and *that* tone was a complete stranger to him.

Why did this new side of Blossom seem like a rather intriguing development?

Not that he'd ever let her know that.

"Okay," he said, with what he could muster for dignity and because the pain was becoming quite acute. "You can look."

"This isn't quite the introduction I was expecting to paradise," Blossom said to Joe, joining him as they searched Hale Alana for a first aid kit.

There was no doubt in her mind that this *was* paradise. Though the Big Island had been mostly wrapped in darkness as she was whisked to the estate in a cab, and she'd been totally exhausted from her travels, Hale Alana had pierced that exhaustion.

It was part of why she had not turned on the lights after she had stepped in the door, letting the feel of the place soak into her.

Fragrant, silent, calm, and yet oddly and beautifully *sensual*. She was aware of that now, as they went through the magnificent house. The very air around her soft and warm and moist, like a kiss.

Or maybe it was her close proximity to Joe that was making her every sense feel alive and tingly.

And also way too aware of how she looked.

She had left all those incredible honeymoon outfits that she and Bliss had chosen together behind. Just looking at them had been too painful. Well, almost all of them. She had packed a few bikinis.

And then dressed sensibly for her travels. Who needed to impress a bunch of strangers? And so she had arrived in Hawaii rumpled and wrinkled, her messy hair hidden by a ball cap. She had seen the shock in Joe's face when he had taken in that outfit.

Blossom realized it was the first time he had actually seen her, not her dressed up the way Bliss thought she should dress for him.

Joe, naturally, looked amazing. No dressed-down, travel-weary look for him. In fact, he looked, as always, totally ready for a men's magazine cover shoot.

This evening, fresh off his jet, he was modeling tropical casual. He was wearing pressed khaki shorts and a solid navy blue shirt. The shorts showed off the long length of powerful legs, and the shirt molded his chest and the swell of bicep muscles. She felt a renegade longing to lay her hand on that familiar chest, to feel his heart beating beneath her fingertips.

His feet were in sandals, and she refused to look at them, in case she remembered kissing each of those toes individually.

His hair was only ever so faintly ruffled from his travels and he had more beard than normal, but even that was becoming on him.

Blossom surreptitiously studied his face for signs of heartbreak—bags under his eyes, worry wrinkles in his forehead, et cetera—but sadly, she could see nothing. Unless the grim line around his mouth counted.

When she looked at her own face over the last two weeks, she had seen utter devastation in it.

Her mother might be inclined to see Joe arriving here in Hawaii at the same time as Blossom as a gift from the Universe.

Blossom, however, thought she needed to see it as a *test*.

She could not entertain thoughts of reconciling with Joe.

The differences in their appearances or their travel wear choices might be a small thing, but for Blossom it accentuated the disparity in their worlds. Would she have been able to navigate his world at all without Bliss's help?

And if calling off the wedding had left her this devastated, barely eating, barely sleeping, barely functioning, what would it do to her if her marriage—that Cinderella fantasy she had nursed her whole life—didn't work out?

Not survivable, she told herself, and steeled herself anew to the shocking reentrance of Joe into her life on the night that should have marked the beginning of their honeymoon.

After a lengthy search for a first aid kit, they finally found it prominently displayed in a white cabinet with a red cross on it by the backyard pool.

If it could be called a backyard. Blossom recalled that Celia referred to the senior Blackwells' backyard as "the garden."

The Blackwells also had a pool, but nothing this spectacular.

The whole area was not like anything Blossom had ever seen before, even making Blackwell seniors' back garden and pool seem modest in comparison.

The entire wall of windows on the back of the house folded back, accordion style, so that the inside of the house suddenly and seamlessly blended into this magical grotto.

The pool was gorgeous, pond-shaped, in the middle of black lava rock. Lights under the water turned it to sapphire. Above the main pool was a smaller one, which she assumed was a hot tub. She could not imagine anyone using a hot tub in Hawaii, but still the mist rising off it added to the ambience, and for some reason reminded her she was on an island with an active volcano.

A waterfall tumbled between the two pools. More lights winked in thick green foliage and showed off the native hibiscus rioting with colors. The scent of flowers was absolutely heavenly.

"Let's get on with it," Joe snapped.

He threw himself down, belly first, across a large round glass table, his legs spread, his hands gripping the edges.

Blossom dragged her eyes from paradise, bit her tongue between her teeth and yanked down his shorts.

Now she was looking at him in such a different context from what she had once dreamed of for tonight—nearly her wedding night—that she had to bite back a laugh.

If anyone's life had taught them to expect the unexpected, it was hers. And always with the bizarre twist.

CHAPTER FOUR

"ARE YOU LAUGHING?" Joe asked Blossom dangerously.

Had she ever heard that dangerous edge to his voice before?

"No," she said.

"Because it sounds as if you are."

"It's not a *Gee, is this ever fun?* kind of laugh, if that's what you're worried about."

"I was more worried about a mocking of my undignified position."

That did make her giggle. Or maybe that baleful tone to his voice was making her feel edgy, and the giggle was a nervous one. "Now that you mention it—"

"Stop it."

"I can't."

"There's a difference between can't and won't."

"You've always had the cutest derriere," she said. The words were out before she could stop them.

"Not now, Blossom, I'm warning you." Joe's voice had a rasp to it that sent a shiver down her spine. It was unfair that that rasp—that danger—was so sexy.

The words had come out before she could think them through. Who was she kidding? The air wasn't sensual! It was her nearness to *this* that was sensual.

Her awareness of him was suddenly so acute if was painful.

"You'll be happy to know, it looks to be surface wounds," she told him, trying for an indifferent tone that denied the tingling sensation that was singing through her veins. The universe, for whatever reason, was upping the level of the test!

"I don't want to know what it looks like. Get on with it," he bit out.

Maybe he was just a little more aware of her than he wanted to be, too?

She found a pair of tweezers in the kit, placed her fingers carefully on his cheek to steady herself, and then dispensed with the first tiny shard of glass that was embedded. She should not have enjoyed his yelp nearly as much as she did.

"That hurt," he told her.

"Just pretend we're camping," she suggested sweetly. "You've landed in bramble bush."

"I had no idea you didn't like that camping trip we went on."

"There were things I liked about it," she said carefully.

Sharing a double sleeping bag with Joe, for one. Being snuggled against him, under a blanket, a campfire going and the stars coming out, for another.

"But?"

"There were things that scared me, too." It occurred to her she was not used to being this honest with him.

"Like?" he prodded her.

"Having to get out of the tent to go pee in the middle

of the night when there could have been bears out there. Thinking it felt kind of isolated, like an ax murderer could be hiding in the trees watching us."

He was silent for a long moment. "Why didn't you tell me you were scared?"

She was too busy trying to impress the billionaire, that's why. Because she had wanted desperately—pathetically, now that she thought about it—to like what he liked.

Which was really quite deplorably phony, and which had led him to believe she might be willing to trade out her dream day for a camping-themed wedding, instead!

"I thought you would think less of me."

If I showed you who I really was.

"Oh," he said, miffed, "thanks for the vote of confidence."

"I think it's about me."

"Yeah, right, not trusting me with your fears. Geez. No wonder I was attacked with a vase, with you thinking those kinds of threats are lurking in the darkness."

"See? There's the proof! You do think less of me."

"I don't," he said stubbornly, but she couldn't accept it.

"You do. You think I overreacted. You want a woman who is bold, not scared of everything."

"You don't have a clue what I want," he snapped. "And I'm not sure it comes much bolder than rushing out of the darkness to clobber a suspected intruder with a vase."

She was silent.

"I've always thought of you as bold," he said. "From the way you dress, to your willingness to try new things."

Now did not feel like the right time to confess Bliss had dressed her. And her readiness to try new things had been driven largely by a desire to please him.

"This is going to hurt," she warned him. She was *not* happy to be hurting him. She was *not* getting back at him for the sting of his comment that she didn't have a clue what he wanted. She was *not* angry because he had believed the illusion Bliss had created.

"The last thing didn't hurt?"

"This is going to hurt more. It's a bigger one. And more deeply embedded. I have to dig."

"Argh!"

"Be brave. Outdoorsy people put up with this sort of thing all the time."

"How would you—secretly scared of the great out-doors—know what outdoorsy types put up with?" She could tell his teeth were gritted.

Well, so were hers. That *secretly scared* was a judgment against the real her.

"There's this series on television where they drop people off in a remote location. It's called *That's Wild*. Last season a woman put a stick right through her foot. Now, *that* was a puncture wound."

As she had hoped, her chattering seemed to take his mind off the uncharted territory their conversation was moving them in, and what she was actually doing.

"Spare me the details," he moaned. And then, after a moment, "We didn't watch that together."

We.

A terrible pain filled Blossom. There was no more *we*. And there never was going to be again.

Because she wasn't brave enough to face all the daggers hidden in the cloak of love.

"Well, I watched it," Blossom said, as if she had a whole

secret life Joe knew nothing about. Which, come to think of it, she did.

"When?"

He was right. If they had watched television—and they hadn't very much—it had been together. She certainly had not had time to indulge in the entire ten hour-long episodes of a series on her own.

Because last year, little old Blossom DuPont had had a super-sexy boyfriend and then a supernaturally exciting fiancé. Her time had been jam-packed with exquisitely romantic activities, and all the bold adventures he had encouraged her to go on with him.

And then her time had become jam-packed with planning a wedding.

No, it was since the breakup that Blossom had binge-watched every episode of the survival in the wilderness program *and* considered putting her name in for casting. Why not, now that she had nothing to live for? Now that she had thrown away her chance at happily-ever-after?

Over nothing, as Bliss had informed her.

Bliss who was so mad at her she could barely speak to her.

Because her sister felt she had tossed away the world's best guy. Because she was useless at work and could not handle the cancellations without crying. Because they had been planning a very expensive wedding, and Blossoms and Bliss was now scrambling to find money for it. Because of the late cancellation, very little of what had been put in place had been refundable.

"You have to tell Joe how much money we owe," Bliss had pleaded with her. "You have to."

Joe's mom and dad had graciously offered to pay for the

wedding. But Blossom couldn't bring herself to call him—
or them—and remind them. In her mind it would amount
to begging for money.

In her mind, it would have just confirmed James Blackwell's *I know what you're up to.*

So, instead, Blossom had drained her own personal ac-
counts and was waiting for loan approval. She shouldn't
have come to Hawaii, but, on the other hand, she felt com-
pelled to take a break from all the pressure her life was suddenly filled with. Except for the flight, there was no cost.

Well, the cab to Hale Alana, which was a long way from
the airport, had added up to a fare that had nearly stolen
her breath.

Hence no phone plan, an economy flight to get here, a
sense that an expensive rebooking was not an option.

Not that Blossom had ever been anything but an economy flight kind of person, anyway.

Yes, being marooned in the wilderness with a single
match—despite Blossom's former dislike of camping—
now seemed like a viable option for her miserable life.

"That seems like a strange entertainment choice for
someone who doesn't like camping," Joe said.

"There's a lot you don't know about me," she told him.

"Apparently."

"For instance," she said, "Bliss and Mom and I once lived
in a car for three months."

Why was she telling him that *now* when it—her secret
life—had never come up when they were a couple? She'd
been so thankful for that.

He went very still and then twisted his neck to look back
at her.

"What?" he said.

Her heart was beating way too hard.

From her proximity to his adorable butt, obviously!

"Nothing," she snapped.

"Blossom—"

"Nearly done!" She sponged on antiseptic with a little more enthusiasm than was necessary and made a note to herself that inflicting pain was a pretty good way to stop an uncomfortable conversation.

She patched up the little glass scratches with Band-Aids and gauze until his butt didn't look sexy at all.

"There," she said with satisfaction. "You look just like a grandma's quilt."

Then she gave his butt a little slap, like a football player might give a teammate on the field, snapped his shorts back up into place, and moved back so he could get up from the table.

He did, swinging around to look at her. "Thanks for the patch-up job. Even if I do look like a quilt."

His eyes really were unfairly beautiful. The greens in the grotto intensified their depth and spark.

Blossom was suddenly aware her comfy travel clothes were way too hot for this environment. He'd been here before. That was why he'd arrived dressed as he had, in shorts, ready for the warmth and humidity.

She told herself her sudden heat, and her desire to get naked and plunge in that pool, had nothing to do with Joe, his incredible eyes, and her recent close encounter with his naked bits.

"It's b-been a very long day," she stammered.

This would have been her wedding day.

She should have been married to this beautiful man with his gorgeous butt. Just touching him, no matter how hard she had tried to remain clinical, had filled her with the most unbearable longing.

Heat.

Not at all helped by the warmth of the tropical evening.

Well, she could put a lid on that. The hard truth was she wasn't married, she wasn't on her honeymoon, and even her sister—the other half of her soul—the one who should have been propping her up through this travesty, was barely speaking to her.

Her life, quite frankly, was a mess, a mess not in the least helped by Joe's sudden, unexpected appearance in the place she had hoped she could regroup. Pull herself back together.

Find clarity.

Grieve her loss and move on. Heavy emphasis on the "moving on" part.

But none of that seemed possible now that he'd arrived.

Joe had suggested Blossom leave, but she felt a strange sense—or maybe a familiar one—of not knowing where home was.

"I don't know what to do," she admitted. "Obviously, it's going to be unacceptably awkward with both of us here."

He had an odd look on his face. *Sympathy?* Maybe patching him up hadn't gotten his mind off her spilled confession as much as she thought it had.

"I don't know," he said slowly. "Maybe we can make it work. I think we just passed the awkwardness test. I mean, could it get any worse than that?"

"That was worse for you than for me."

"Obviously."

And then they were both laughing. It was just a moment, until they realized they were laughing together, and that it felt good and familiar and that maybe it shouldn't.

"We could both stay," he said, looking at her. "It is a very large place. I'm sure we can keep out of each other's way, blood-drawing attacks notwithstanding."

From engaged to staying out of each other's way. Was he telling her she could stay because he felt sorry for her? Or because he was grateful that she had rendered first aid? Or just because, innately, he was a good guy?

Whichever of those it was, it was a long way to fall from wildly and madly in love.

"I'll clean up the vase, then I'm going to bed." Blossom did a quick calculation of the time difference. It was 2 a.m. in Vancouver.

A time when people could become very vulnerable. And chatty. And say all manner of stupid things that they didn't intend to say, like *I lived in a car once.*

Why had she said that to him? No one knew about that. Except her. And Bliss. And their mom.

She was lucky she'd said that. And not *I love you. I miss you so much I feel like I can't breathe.*

"I'll clean up the vase," he said.

Joe! Quit being decent and nice!

Despite being very tired, not to mention totally discom-bobulated by his presence, she had a sudden quiver of ap-prehension. "What do you suppose it's worth? The vase?"

"No doubt it's Ming."

"Please say you're kidding."

"Okay, I'm kidding."

But she couldn't tell if he was or wasn't.

"But expensive," she said dolefully.

He raised an eyebrow at her. That raised eyebrow said more clearly than if he had spoken that *his* people did not furnish their homes with dollar-store finds.

"Geez, Blossom, are you going to faint over the value of a vase?"

"Possibly."

"Go to bed," he said, gruffly. "Don't give it another thought. I'll look after it."

Of course, she couldn't let him look after the expense of replacing the vase. She would add it to her crushing debt. But now was not the time to address it. He was right. Her legs were wobbly with exhaustion.

"Is there a bedroom I should take?" she asked him.

"Anything on this floor. I think the upstairs will be locked off. That's Becky and Dave's private sanctuary. When they're here. They have several houses around the world."

Uh-huh.

Those were his people. When she had told him about the car, he'd probably thought, *Whew, near miss. I almost married a girl who once lived in a car.*

She found her way to an opulent bedroom and threw open the windows to the night sounds. The scent of hibiscus floated in. She brushed her teeth and put on her pajamas, and then slid between cool, crisp sheets.

Blossom told herself she was never going to be able to sleep. Strange place. Strange bed. Adrenaline incident. The man who had almost been her husband unexpectedly sharing accommodations with her, but not her bed.

The ceiling fan made a distracting clicking sound, and in the distance, she could hear waves crashing.

She fell asleep as soon as her head hit the pillow.

CHAPTER FIVE

BLOSSOM AWOKE IN the morning to a riot of bird sound. It was what she imagined a jungle would sound like. One kind of bird was particularly loud, announcing the new day with a repetitive and insistent enthusiasm.

It was all quite exotic, light throwing palm frond shadows on the bedroom wall, a delightful breeze stirring the curtains, the sounds of the waves, more gentle than last night, the tantalizing smell of coffee brewing.

Considering the crazy events of the previous evening—and considering this should have been the morning after the night of her wedding—Blossom had an unexpectedly light feeling of well-being, certainly the first time she had felt that since her disastrous breakup lunch with Joe.

She told herself it was the magic of Hawaii, and not the fact that those rustling sounds in the kitchen would be coming from Joe.

The man who had almost been her husband.

She shouldn't really want to see him. But she did. She looked down at her pajamas. They were what Bliss might call frumpa-lumpa—comfy, plaid cotton pants and a matching button-up top.

Changing would not be that helpful, since regrettably, every single thing she'd thrown in the carry-on—no paid luggage for her—reflected the wardrobe of a woman done with love.

But the decision what to wear turned out not to be necessary, because as Blossom lay in bed contemplating her options, she heard the front door open and then close.

She got up and went to her window, which looked out through fronded palms to the curved black driveway. Joe was leaving!

Today he was dressed in another pair of nice shorts, a crisp white, short-sleeved button-up shirt.

He was wearing sunglasses that made him look rather movie star-ish, and he had a bag slung over his shoulder. For a moment she thought he might be leaving Hawaii.

Considering how wise that would be if he left, and took all that tension with him, she contemplated the downward fall of her heart.

This was what she had to guard against: falling under his spell. She had to remember two of the words from the song "Hunger"—*love hurts*.

She would deliberately not think of the next line, which said it was worth all the pain.

She had admitted to Joe last night she was not the bold woman she might have presented herself as over the course of their relationship. Scared of everything, in fact.

But what she had not admitted was that she was most afraid of that.

Love.

Squinting at Joe's bag, she realized she could see a towel protruding from the top of it, and a tube of sunscreen.

He was just leaving for the day. Not forever.

But lest she give in to the flutter of her heart, Blossom reminded herself he was leaving *her* for the day. Making good on his pledge of avoidance. He got into a silver open-air four-wheel drive, backed up and pulled out of the driveway.

She watched him go and then noticed the view, which was almost good enough to take away the feeling of disappointment—that she didn't want to have—that Joe had abandoned her for the day.

The view was truly glorious. Hale Alana, and its substantial grounds, had been cut into the side of a hill, and the front-facing view was lush, ending in the ocean she had heard last night. In the distance, she could see a windsurfer dancing in turquoise waters, leaping in and out of white waves. Beyond the break, boats bobbed.

Something in Blossom sighed.

She went down the hall to the open living space and crossed it into the modern, very upscale kitchen. The space looked even more inviting in the bright morning light than it had last evening.

A huge vase of bird-of-paradise—that she hadn't even noticed in last night's excitement—was at the center of the island. There was also a bottle of what looked to be very expensive champagne. Beside that was a basket with a bow on it, overflowing with exotic fruits: pineapples, papayas, mangoes, avocados, passion fruit, tiny bananas.

In it was a white square card, addressed to Mr. and Mrs. Blackwell. She picked it up and ran her fingers over the cursive.

It was obvious, from the heft of the envelope, there was something inside it.

The estate manager had called her a few days ago. She recalled the conversation.

"Miss DuPont! Awakening House is ready for you."

"Awakening House?"

There was gentle laughter. "That's the translation for Hale Alana."

Awakening.

"All the staff has taken leave," Kalani had told her. "To guarantee your complete privacy. Complete."

Blossom had felt herself blushing. Geez, did he think people ran around naked on their honeymoons?

Would they have? She couldn't go there!

"The fridge is completely stocked, and the chef put meals in the freezer. Everyone here is so excited that a honeymoon is happening. They have gone out of their way to make sure everything is in readiness, everything is perfect."

Blossom had opened her mouth to tell him there would be no honeymoon. She had! But the words got stuck in her throat.

No one was going to be at Hale Alana.

No one would ever know if she went there. By herself. She could go there and nurse her wounds. She loved her sister, but she'd never dealt with anything entirely on her own.

She had done the kind of thing that Bliss did on a regular basis, but that she did not. Blossom had given in to an impulse.

Maybe she had even told herself it would be a shame to let all the work the staff had done go to waste.

Still, she had not considered the complication of a *gift*. Who should open that? Her or Joe? Should they open it at all? Of course they had to open it! And it would probably require some kind of response, but Blossom just didn't want to think about that right now.

She turned quickly from that display. Joe had made coffee, the bag that the freshly ground Kona beans had come from put away neatly beside the coffee maker.

She poured herself a cup and a little moan of pure delight escaped her at her first sip of what was arguably the best coffee in the world.

There was a note beside the coffee maker and she recognized his strong handwriting.

You could spend a lifetime exploring the Big Island and still not know it completely, but there are three must-sees: Hapuna beach (careful, big waves), the volcano (currently erupting), and the Hawaiian Tropical Botanical Garden.

The first two she got, completely. Joe would be a bigwave kind of guy. And as red hot as that volcano.

But a garden?

See? They didn't really know each other at all.

He'd very considerately left her a map, marked, and she gave it a quick perusal. She hadn't known the island was this big! The volcano was hours away. So was the garden, in the city of Hilo, on the northeastern side of the island when she was, according to the map, on the Kohala Coast. The closest attraction to her was the beach, which might be within walking distance if she felt energetic.

Which she did not.

With the price of cabs she wouldn't be doing too much exploring. Long, leisurely days by the pool were her idea of the best holiday, anyway. It was Joe who had been dragging her out of her comfort zone for all these months.

She turned and took in her surroundings and felt a tickle of delight. Aside from the awkwardness of both her and Joe showing up at the honeymoon accommodations, could there be a more perfect place to rediscover who she really was? Blossom loved the idea of holing up here for her entire stay.

The estate manager had promised everything at Hale Alana was in readiness to meet every need of honeymooners—though she was not going to let her mind go to what she and Joe might be doing if they were holed up here.

She saw that beside the big basket of fruit with the card was a plate with muffins and cheeses.

Joe had taken one pineapple out and cut it, and when she went over to the counter, the smell of that was nearly as heavenly as the coffee.

She picked up a slice and bit into it. She had never tasted anything so exquisite. What passed itself off as pineapple in Canada was not remotely the same fruit as this Maui-produced one was.

Of course it would taste delicious! It was practically the first food she'd noticed eating since the breakup.

"I am going to have the best day ever," Blossom told herself with determination.

Joe pulled up in front of Hale Alana. He had left in his rented four-wheel drive first thing this morning, grateful that Blossom had not been up yet. He had come here to get away from the flurry of feelings Blossom was one hundred per cent responsible for.

And yet here she was, and that flurry of feelings was worse than ever!

And so he had spent the whole day exploring out-of-the-way spots, trying with furious determination to enjoy Hawaii.

Unfortunately, the thought that he was supposed to be doing all this with *her* stayed with him stubbornly. It seemed each blossom he saw—and there were thousands of them—called her name.

If he was going to rate his enjoyment, so far, of the Big Island, it would be a perfect one on a scale of ten.

Because of *her*.

Thankfully, there was no sign of another vehicle in the palm-tree-shaded parking area in front of the estate house, so Joe presumed that Blossom must have found his note and decided to go exploring. As uncharitable as it was, he hoped she had, like him, had a disappointing time.

But was she being careful?

When he'd been here last, he'd benefited from Dave and Becky's long experience with the islands. For the uninitiated, however, this could be a dangerous place.

He'd been warned about the aa lava, responsible for thousands of cuts, sprained and broken ankles of the unwary every year.

He'd been warned that the ocean, in particular, could take a greenhorn completely by surprise. Those towering waves on some of the beaches along the Kohala Coast were awe-inspiring and also unbelievably powerful.

Joe realized he should have waited this morning and shared some of those safety insights with Blossom.

On the other hand, hopefully she had decided on a beach day and found her way to Hapuna, as he had recommended. It was the closest beach to Hale Alana and it had lifeguards to educate the unsuspecting.

But there were lots of secluded beaches you could find your way on to, and find yourself in trouble before you knew it, dragged out to sea by an undertow.

And the danger on the beaches wasn't just from waves.

A woman alone. Somewhat—at least he assumed—vulnerable after their called off wedding. With those big dark eyes, that gorgeous hair flowing down her back, and that air of crushed innocence, she could be targeted by a *real* creeper.

He realized he couldn't separate from his concerns for her, much as he wanted to. You didn't just turn off caring about someone as if it was a water faucet.

How could he possibly share a house with her under these circumstances, send her off to explore on her own, and not worry about her?

He'd come here with the express goal of getting away from all his Blossom-related thoughts!

I'm going to have to leave Hawaii, Joe thought, *and the sooner the better.*

It was the first peaceful thought he'd had since being attacked with a vase and then allowing Blossom to be his rump doctor.

Exiting his vehicle, he went into Hale Alana with a plan. He'd change into his swim trunks, grab a beer and a quick swim. From the pool, he'd call and make arrangements for the jet, and be on his way.

Relief swept him.

Maybe he should just skip the swim so he could be gone by the time Blossom got back. But the lure of the pool was too great. Besides, he still had to make arrangements with the pilot, and it was only early in the afternoon. If she'd made her way to Volcano National Park or Hilo he wouldn't be seeing her anytime soon.

He went and changed, slung a towel around his neck and picked up a beer. He noticed the back wall to the pool was wide open.

That was strange. Despite the fact Hale Alana seemed like an enclave of complete safety and serenity in the world, Blossom had known last night, as she jumped to the conclusion of an intruder invading, that it was still part of a larger world. Surely she knew it needed to be locked up when they left?

If Blossom couldn't even do that, how could she possibly take proper precautions to protect herself as she explored the islands?

He stepped through the open doors and onto the deck around the pool.

Blossom was there.

His first reaction at seeing her was relief. She was safe! She'd navigated the hazards of the Big Island.

By herself.

Without any help from him.

In fact, she wasn't just safe. Joe was not sure he'd ever seen such a complete picture of relaxation.

Blossom was lying facedown on a lounge recliner on the other side of the pool, her fingertips resting lightly on a book that had slid off the lounger onto the deck beside her.

Joe gulped.

Her bikini bottoms were tiny and her back was naked, her hair pulled over her shoulder, the strings of her bathing suit open so that she would not get tan lines.

Okay, so no swim for him. When had she come back? It

must have been while he was changing, though he hadn't heard a car.

Curious, he went back to the front door, opened it and looked out. No vehicle. Except his.

He ordered himself to change his plan. Skip the beer. Skip the swim. Skip the heartache. Go home.

But he was drawn to her as a magnet is drawn to steel, and he went back to the doorway and gazed at her, unable to resist the opportunity to look at her when she didn't know. Even if that did make him a creeper.

She appeared to be fast asleep, a danger in and of itself, as her skin was very pale, just coming off a Canadian winter.

Joe greedily took in the roundness of her shoulders, the slender curve of her back, the way her shiny hair, exactly the same color as that Kona coffee he had brewed this morning, had been pulled off her back and cascaded over her shoulder, her bikini-clad bottom, her shapely legs.

Just a few weeks ago, she had been his to touch, to explore.

The chemistry between them had always been off the charts.

Who could have believed that all that could end, and be replaced by this: the sensation of empty longing that he had been experiencing since she had plunked that ring back on the table?

A new thought occurred to him, and it was not a happy one. Maybe the chemistry between them, that compelling electrical force, had been so strong it had nearly obliterated everything else.

Including good communication.

Go, he told himself.

He had to go before he went too far down that rabbit hole. What had gone wrong? Could it be fixed? Was there hope?

Hope. Wasn't that the most dangerous thing of all?

He could leave her a short note.

Still, he took in the delicacy of her skin again. What kind of person would leave her to get sunburned?

He took a fortifying swig of the beer and strode out onto the deck.

"Hey," he called, since he didn't have any intention of being accused of being a creeper again. Even if he just had been.

Blossom startled awake and flipped over, blinking. When she saw him she gave an adorable little shriek and scrambled to cover herself. With the book! Which she had to reach for, and which was barely any cover at all.

Had he hoped that would happen? After her inspection of his bottom yesterday, yes, indeed he had!

She seemed to realize the book was not exactly covering anything. Holding it in place with one hand, she reached around with her other until she found her towel. Glaring at him, she flipped it over herself. Damn her for looking gorgeous when she blushed!

CHAPTER SIX

OR MAYBE, JOE THOUGHT, it wasn't a blush. Maybe Blossom was just getting way too much sun.

The protective feeling she had always aroused in him was still there, just as if he had not been buffeted by Hurricane Blossom for the past two weeks.

Pretending as if being exposed to her familiar lovely curves and the cascade of all that luscious hair hadn't bothered him at all, he strode across the deck and took the deeply cushioned lounge chair beside her.

"Have a good day?" he asked her. He took a swig of beer.

"Excellent," she said, adjusting her towel primly. "You?"

"Excellent, as well." He took another swig.

"Good," she said. "I'm glad for you."

He was having this stilted, horrible conversation with the woman, whom just a few short weeks ago he'd chased around his bedroom until they both couldn't breathe.

"How's your...er...injuries?" she asked, her tone still maddeningly formal.

He should have made his escape while he had the chance.

"I'm sitting down, aren't I?"

Why did every word between them have this faintly abrasive feeling? He hated it. And he knew exactly where it was coming from.

"We have to talk about the elephant in the room. Are we going to talk about what happened?" he asked her quietly.

"What happened?" she asked, deliberately obtuse. "To your behind?"

"To the wedding. To us."

Blossom went very still. Joe noticed she wouldn't look at him. She was staring at the pool as if the secrets of the universe were about to be unveiled in those blue depths.

"This conversation seems at odds with staying out of each other's way," she decided, as if it was her decision alone to make.

"I think we need to talk about it, Blossom."

"I thought that was the line every guy dreaded. *I think we need to talk.*"

"I always liked talking to you," he said.

"Unless it was about crème brûlée," she countered.

"I want to understand what happened." There he was, going down the rabbit hole. Why hadn't he left when he had the chance? "I think it was about a little more than a stupid dessert choice."

He shouldn't have said *stupid* because she flinched, and then that remote look was on her face again.

"Humph," Blossom said. "If you were so desperate to know what happened, you could have called. Anytime in the last two weeks. And I hope that doesn't make it sound like I was waiting by the phone because I wasn't!"

That was said fairly defensively. As if she had, indeed, been waiting.

Joe looked at Blossom closely. She tilted her nose up,

daring him to guess she'd been waiting for *him* to bridge the gap between them.

"I was supposed to call you?" he asked, his surprise and annoyance genuine. "You're the one who threw the ring at me."

A fact he had gone over, ad nauseam with Lance, who had confessed the other DuPont twin had also thrown something at him, once.

They had decided, between them, speech only slightly slurred, that a propensity to throw things no doubt ran in the DuPont family, and that Joe had had a lucky miss. And so, Lance had confided, had he, with Bliss, though he'd never even had a date with her.

"And not for lack of trying, either," he'd confessed glumly.

His glum tone indicated that, like Joe, he really wasn't that convinced of their good fortune.

"I didn't throw the ring at you," Blossom said.

"Semantics," he said, ridiculously satisfied to get in that dig.

She was quiet for a long time. He thought she wasn't going to answer.

"You seemed to have lost your enthusiasm for me," she told him, her tone controlled, "No girl, not even one who once lived in a car, wants a reluctant groom."

Lost his enthusiasm. For her? A reluctant groom. Him? Could she possibly believe that?

"You never said that before. About living in a car," he said. Now she had mentioned it twice in less than twenty-four hours.

"It's just not the type of thing a planner of exclusive weddings wants to get out."

"You think I would have told someone?" he said, stung.

"You wouldn't have told anyone? You wouldn't have been ashamed of me?"

"I don't recall you twisting things like this before," Joe said, and then quietly, "Blossom, I didn't lose my enthusiasm for *you*."

"That's how it felt to me," Blossom said. She tucked her towel in a little closer around her, as if to let Joe know how thoroughly he could not be trusted by her.

"At Essence that day, I was thinking out loud," he said, "about the wedding. I wasn't expecting a bomb to go off over sharing a thought with you."

Somehow, with that statement, he hoped he conveyed just how thoroughly *she* could not be trusted by *him*!

"It wasn't just *the* wedding. It was *our* wedding that I had put my whole heart and soul into."

"I know," he said, genuinely contrite over that part.

"Well, if you knew, how could you suddenly be wanting a change of plans? Quite a drastic change of plans, I might add."

He sighed heavily, gazed out over the pool.

"The wedding just seemed like…"

"The wedding just seemed like?" she prodded him.

"I don't want another bomb to go off."

"Bombs away," she challenged him.

"Okay. It felt as if the wedding was changing you."

There was the Blossom he'd fallen in love with—real, earthy, funny—and then there was the wedding planner Blossom.

At first Joe felt indulgent of her excitement and so happy to be the source of it. But then the wedding had seemed to become her obsession, bringing out perfectionism and a preoccupation with minutiae.

As if choosing between crème brûlée and cheesecake was a decision with earth-shattering consequences.

It was partly his fault, he thought. He had made romancing Blossom his mission. It had given him incredible joy to see her wide-eyed wonder as she embraced the experiences he presented her with.

They had seen the famous rocker EJ in concert, had front row seats at the World Cup. They had schmoozed on the red carpet and eaten at exclusive restaurants. They had taken whirlwind trips to New York and Paris.

So, why did he remember that camping trip with such longing?

Because, of all the things they had done together in his mad pursuit of romancing her, somehow that stood out.

As real. Pure. Uncomplicated.

He'd been so intent on winning Blossom he'd bombarded her with all the experiences and gifts his money could buy. And when he wasn't doing that, he was exploring that electrical, all-encompassing energy between them. He should have left room to breathe.

After he had proposed, it seemed to Joe the level of complication had increased. As he watched, with a certain horrified fascination, Blossom had made it more and more about the wedding and less and less about them celebrating this crazy, wonderful gift called love.

And still, none of that had made him suggest she rethink the wedding.

And for some reason he didn't feel ready to reveal that. At all. Because the trust between them had become such a fragile thing?

His mother's voice played again in his mind. *"Under the circumstances, we can't come to the wedding."*

* * *

Blossom thought it was unfairly hard to think straight with a nearly naked Joe on the lounge chair beside her. He was simply incredibly and beautifully made. Broad-shouldered, long-legged, deep-chested, and narrow-waisted. This time his delectable behind was covered, but her mind could not forget, from her life before the bomb had gone off, what touching him felt like.

Tasting him.

Sheesh. And here she was clutching a towel to her own nakedness!

This could have been so much fun if it was a honeymoon. So much of their relationship had been pure sizzle.

But she couldn't let her thoughts go there. She couldn't. Because it was hard enough to keep her head on straight, even when she reminded herself Joe had just said very hurtful things to her! Blossom contemplated Joe's words.

The wedding just seemed like it was changing you.

She wanted to angrily dismiss those words, but in fact Bliss had said almost the same thing.

Blossom remembered that day she had stormed out of Essence. She had managed to somehow get back to the Blossoms and Bliss storefront without distractedly walking in front of a bus, though a cab had honked at her once, and not, she'd suspected, because of her cute skirt.

Seeing their storefront was like seeing a place of refuge from the battlefield. Blossoms and Bliss was a narrow, one-story building on a downtown Vancouver side street. It was crammed between two much larger buildings. It had been dilapidated, but they had nursed it along, seeing its potential and putting money into it.

Now it looked extraordinary. Their mother had done one

of her famous murals on the outside of it, a huge cherry tree in full blossom, with blissful-looking birds sitting on the branches. The building looked like a sanctuary from the business of the city that swarmed around it, and that was how it felt, with their business downstairs and their cozy apartment upstairs.

She had gone in the door, and as soon as she was inside, she'd felt safe, as if someone had been chasing her. She recalled she'd shut the door behind her. And locked it.

And then taken it all in: the subtle pink cloud patterns painted on the walls, the walls covered in huge black-and-white photos of brides on their wedding days.

She and Bliss made dreams come true.

Except their own, apparently.

Bliss had been at her desk, and she'd looked up and frowned at the locked door, at Blossom leaning against it.

The frown was quickly replaced with alarm, her twin's intuition kicking in. She came around her desk and as she did, Blossom noted that they might be identical twins, but her sister looked—as she always did—ravishing.

The things a person remembered were silly, but Blossom remembered that day, Bliss had on false eyelashes. Blossom thought they looked ridiculous on most people, but her sister, naturally, had been rocking them. They made her eyes look smoky and sensual and full of mystery.

Bliss wouldn't have had to be in love for a construction worker to whistle at her.

It was when her cat, Bartholomew, had come and rubbed against her legs, that a little sob had escaped Blossom. Bliss had put her arms around her and leaned their foreheads together. Bartholomew, twisting in and out of their legs, had meowed as if the world was ending.

"There, there," Bliss had said. "Tell me what's wrong, Blossom."

"The wedding is off," Blossom had whispered.

"What? Your wedding?" Bliss had pulled back from her.

"I called it off."

"*You* did?"

Her sister was unaware it was vaguely insulting that she could see Joe calling it off, but not Blossom.

"I did."

"But why?" Bliss had wailed.

"All of a sudden he didn't like anything about the wedding. He wanted to go camping, instead."

Her sister had been silent. "You called off the wedding over that? He's just being a guy, Blossom. What guy wouldn't want to go camping instead of to a wedding?"

Her sister, much more successful with the opposite sex, would know about the behavioral patterns of men. Her, not so much.

"His *own* wedding. To me," Blossom had explained. "He was having cold feet. I could tell."

Her sister had taken a step back from her and studied her, tapping her own cheek with a fake fingernail. Like the lashes, Blossom didn't generally like them. Naturally, Bliss made the look ultra-sexy.

"But *you* called it off?"

"Because *he* was having cold feet!"

"Maybe it's you having cold feet."

Maybe it had been her! Trust her twin to know.

Bliss had pulled her phone from the back pocket of her pants. She'd thrust the phone at Blossom. Every word of that conversation was etched in Blossom's mind.

"You phone him right now," Bliss had said. "Get this

straightened out before it becomes something that can't be straightened out. That happens more easily than you think."

Blossom had slid sideways, away from the phone.

"No," she'd said, suddenly feeling a sudden need to resist her sister's direction of her life. "I'm not calling him. I don't want to marry him."

"You're being crazy!"

She'd known that. But she'd still had to rationalize it for her sister.

"I just knew it wasn't the wedding he had doubts about. It was *everything*."

Bliss had looked strangely pensive, not at all as sharing in her outrage as Blossom might have expected.

"You're not taking his side!" Blossom had said accusingly.

"Does there have to be a side?"

"Yes!"

"Blossom, he got cold feet. Or you got cold feet. We're in this business. We've seen it happen a hundred times. Did you ask him why he was feeling that way? Why he felt as if, all of a sudden, he wasn't on board for a big wedding?"

"I did not," she had said firmly. "Stop looking at me like that. As if I'm the problem."

Her sister had sighed.

"You think I'm the problem?" Blossom had breathed.

It wasn't enough that her dream wedding had been snatched from her? Now her sister, the other half of her soul, the one who knew her so well they finished each other's sentences—was not getting this?

"No," Bliss said, but with just enough hesitation that Blossom felt sick.

"That wasn't a very emphatic no!"

"It's just this wedding, Blossom. It's changed you."

Now Joe was saying exactly the same thing!

"In what way?" Blossom had asked her sister.

"Weddings have always charged us up. Filled us with joy. For some reason, your own seems to be dragging you down."

"Being the bride is different than being the wedding planner."

Bliss had bitten her lip.

"Are you saying I was turning into a Bridezilla?"

"No, of course not, but I always felt the growing success of our business was because of your ability to care about people. You almost have a sixth sense about their hopes and dreams. You're the most caring person I know. And yet you didn't even ask Joe, the man you love, why he had this sudden change of heart about the wedding plans."

"It's too late for him to have a change of heart!"

"Well, you seem to have had one! This is exactly what I mean. Suddenly it's all about you."

Blossom had felt stunned by her sister's insensitive assessment of the situation. She wished Bliss would be quiet.

But none of her wishes had come true that day.

"There just seems to be this sense of urgency about you. Obsession. Panic to make everything perfect."

"Before it disappears like every other good thing that ever happened to me!" Blossom had wailed.

"Aw, sweetie, maybe this is for the best."

"Now you sound like Mom. *Everything happens for a reason.*"

"Maybe it does," Bliss had said, with a hint of stubbornness.

"It's way too soon for a philosophical take on it," Blossom had retorted. "My heart is broken."

"Hey, earth to Blossom!"

Blossom came back from that memory of her sister agreeing with what Joe had just said.

Joe was looking at her sympathetically. The last thing she wanted was his sympathy!

"Okay," she said, "so maybe the wedding was changing me. Not a problem now. Moving on."

"Agreed," he said. "Let's call a truce. I want you to enjoy your time here."

She hated it that he was insisting on being so decent. She was well aware she could get rid of that *I'm a perfect gentleman* countenance in a second. What would he do if she dropped the towel, reached over and touched his chest?

"I plan to enjoy my time here," she said stubbornly. "And I don't need you to do it."

CHAPTER SEVEN

THE LOOK JOE gave Blossom was aggravatingly level.

"Okay," he said, "you might not need me—"

Yes, I do need you, everything inside Blossom screamed, but she would not let him see that weakness, or any other, ever.

"No, I won't."

"The Big Island of Hawaii doesn't have many faults," he told her, "but this is one of them—you cannot go anywhere on this island without a vehicle. There's no good island-wide public transportation system. Cabs and rideshares are not abundant and not reliable."

"Cabs are expensive," she said. "I took one from the airport."

"Anyway, you should rent a car."

"Oh, I'm just going to hang out here," she said. "This is pretty much my idea of a perfect vacation. Sunshine, a book and a pool."

"You're not going to explore the island?"

"Maybe later."

He glanced over at her. He looked as if he could tell from

her tone she had no intention of leaving the sanctuary of Hale Alana.

"You know, you could have rented a hotel room in Vancouver if you just wanted to sit by the pool with a book."

"No sunshine," she said to him.

He narrowed his eyes. She could tell things started to click in his mind. The economy flight. The worry about the cost of the vase. The noticing the cab had been expensive. No rental car.

"Look," he said, "you can't come to Hawaii and not *do* things."

"I might take a bus tour," Blossom said. She was pretty sure even a bus tour was way out of her budget for this trip, which was pretty much zero, but so far he didn't seem to have registered she was destitute. That was a weakness he didn't have to know about. She could still cling to her little sliver of pride.

"A bus tour," he repeated slowly, as if she had said something in a foreign language that he did not quite understand.

"There's nothing wrong with a bus tour!"

"I didn't say there was. Spare me another lecture about the real world."

"Consider yourself spared," she said, snippily.

"You at least have to get in the ocean."

Was he now suggesting *free* stuff on purpose?

"You can't come all this way and not at least get in the ocean. Boogie board. Snorkel."

Both of which, she was pretty sure, required expensive gear.

"Sharks," she said. It was not a weakness to be afraid of sharks, and lest he thought it was, she said, "Haven't you ever watched *Shark Week* on cable?"

"The woods are full of bears and ax murderers and the ocean is full of sharks?"

"Don't forget intruders creeping around in the dark."

"I'm not likely to forget that."

"Being cautious could be seen as a strength, not a weakness," she told him proudly.

"Uh-huh," he said, not convinced. "I hate to break it to you, but the biggest danger you're in—"

Is her poor heart, from being around him, obviously.

"Is getting a sunburn. Are you wearing sunscreen?"

Thank goodness he hadn't seen what the biggest danger really was. But then, Joe had proven himself to be colossally insensitive.

When it mattered.

"I'm good," she said. "I put it on where I could reach. I'm in the shade."

"Lots of people wreck their whole holiday here because they do not understand the power of the sun, here, even in the shade."

"There's a fine line," Blossom told him, "between caring and being controlling."

He glared at her. "Let me see your back."

"No."

"You saw my heinie."

"For medical purposes only!"

"This is the same."

Why allow him to think she thought it was a big deal?

"Fine." Still clutching her towel to her, she turned her back to him. She felt him reach around her to get the sunscreen.

And then Blossom felt Joe's hands on her back. They were warm and strong as he applied sunscreen, unhurried, his movements slow and tantalizing. On purpose? She ached for where it all could go. She felt as if she couldn't breathe.

"How much are we out for the wedding?" he asked her.

Blossom realized Joe *had* figured out why she was pinching pennies. Probably all her efforts to hide weakness from him had been futile.

After eleven months he *knew* her. At least in some ways. Certainly, in *that* way, that his touch on her back, so familiar, reminded her of.

His rubbing sunscreen on her back was just a sneaky way of bringing up the finances casually, while distracting her.

As if he had figured out, and rather quickly, too, that a discussion of money with someone who had once lived in a car was going to be somewhat sensitive.

"Lots," she said. "We're out lots of money on the wedding."

"My parents wanted to pay for it. They wanted to give that to us, as a gift."

"I'm not accepting a gift for a wedding that didn't happen."

"Under the circumstances, I think they'd still want to pay for it."

"I don't need their pity."

"That's the wrong way to see it."

"Don't tell me how to see things."

"Holy moly, you're prickly."

Just what every woman wanted to hear from the man who used to love her and was currently rubbing sunscreen on her back in a manner that was criminally sexy.

"I'll pay for it," Joe said, as if that decided it, "if you don't want my parents to."

For the briefest second she felt so relieved, she thought she might start crying.

But then she had the most horrible thought. What if she had loved Joe not just for Joe? But because of this, too? And not just the way his hands felt on her back.

Bur for his ability to wave the magic wand of money and make problems disappear? His ability to go anywhere, do anything, buy anything.

If she had married him, she would have never had to worry about money, again, ever. That little girl inside her, who was so terrified of not having enough, had finally felt safe.

He and Bliss had both been right. Planning the wedding had changed her. Being engaged to Joe had changed her.

And not in a nice way, at all.

Having enough wasn't a substitute for being enough, she realized sadly.

Blossom pulled away from his hands, readjusted the towel and leaned back on her chair. She picked up her book and pretended to read.

It was never too late to do the right thing. She waved a hand at him as if he was a pesky fly.

"No, don't give paying for the wedding another thought," she said loftily, her tone haughty with pride. "Apparently it was all about me, so I'll accept responsibility for it."

"I don't know when talking to you became like navigating a minefield," he said to her, tersely.

Her sister had indicated Blossom was a problem. Joe seemed determined to see her as a problem.

Blossom was not going to be anybody's problem, except her own!

"Oh, well," she said, "Minefields. Weddings. Sunburns.

Transportation troubles in paradise. Not your problems any-more."

"You're right," he said.

"If you're looking for something to be in charge of—"

"I'm not!"

"But if you were, you could deal with the card addressed to Mr. and Mrs. Blackwell that's on the counter. It feels fat, as if it's got something other than a card in it. No doubt, a wedding gift that has to be returned. You can deal with that since I've dealt with everything else."

"Whatever," he said.

He got up, took the towel from around his neck, and the phone from his pocket. He strode to the edge of the pool.

Blossom did not want to look at the beautiful, perfect lines of his back! She'd done a pretty good job of being strong so far, of driving him away, of killing any remain-ing affection he had for her.

But, she discovered, she wasn't that strong! She looked. She felt that awful ache of wanting him.

But she wasn't sure she deserved him.

In fact, Blossom wasn't even sure who she was anymore. This time in Hawaii was supposed to have been her time to figure all that out. It was going to be impossible with him here. Should she bite the financial bullet and book a trip home?

Before Joe surfaced, she fastened her bathing suit top, picked up her book and marched away.

In the safety of her room, she looked up flights leaving Kailua-Kona.

The soonest one was a week away. She was only here for a total of ten days, anyway. Nine now.

She was just going to have to suck it up.

* * *

Joe felt so angry with her he was pretty sure his skin sizzled when he got in that pool. When had Blossom become so unreasonable?

Some of his anger was with himself: he knew at least part of the sensation of his skin sizzling had nothing to do with anger and everything to do with touching her back.

He thought the swim would cool him off, but it didn't. He felt as aggravated when he finally pulled himself from the water as he had when he got in.

She had disappeared, thank goodness. It was very hard to think straight with Blossom around, especially a scantily clad Blossom, whom he had made the mistake of touching!

Obviously sharing space, even a place as spacious as Hale Alana, was unworkable. He picked up his phone and went into the house. A quick call to the pilot and his imminent departure would be in play.

He grabbed an apple banana from the fruit basket and then saw the envelope she'd been talking about.

When she'd first mentioned it was addressed to Mr. and Mrs. Blackwell, he'd thought it must be for his parents! He was glad he hadn't blurted that out to the porcupine he was sharing space with. He was pretty sure Blossom would have had something to say about the idea of them—as in him and her—as Mr. and Mrs. Blackwell.

"Because we aren't," he said out loud. She wasn't even in the room and he was defensive.

He ate the banana—a quarter the size of a regular banana, and a hundred times as delicious—in one bite. He tore open the envelope.

Blossom had been correct. It contained a card, which he

put aside. Who wanted to read well wishes for an event—a life—that hadn't happened?

Vouchers and coupons, tucked inside that card, spilled all over the counter. He couldn't help but notice what they were as he tried to stuff them back in the envelope. Gate passes for Volcano National Park. Entry to the tropical gardens by Hilo. Admission to Hulihe'e Palace in Kona. A night swim with manta rays.

What was the best way to deal with it? He realized he had buffered himself from a lot of the pain involved in calling this thing off. He'd had his personal assistant go through the guest list and notify people on his side. He and Lance had had way too much to drink in the last two weeks.

He realized how hard it must have been for Blossom, canceling everything. No wonder she seemed edgy. Exhausted.

Well, one thing she was not doing, on top of having shouldered a hundred per cent of what was involved in canceling? She wasn't paying for it.

He picked up his phone.

"Blossoms and Bliss," a voice answered on the other side. A voice like Blossom's and not like hers at the very same time.

He was not sure how two identical twins could be so different.

"Hi, Bliss, it's Joe."

Silence.

Of course she was going to side with her sister! She was, after all, the other DuPont twin who threw things.

He felt a little embarrassed knowing that about her.

"Don't hang up," he said.

"Joe! I wasn't going to hang up! I'm just shocked, but in the nicest way. I'm glad to hear from you."

"Look, I've had a discussion with Blossom—"

"Has she come to her senses?"

"In what way?" he asked carefully.

"Has she realized she tossed away the best thing that ever happened to her?"

As nice as it was to have someone see things his way, he felt a little taken aback that Bliss seemed to be on his side.

Because she and Blossom were extremely close, the way twins were. Somehow, he had thought the twins would be shoring each other up, the way he and Lance had been doing. But if Bliss was on his side, who was on Blossom's side? As unreasonable as Blossom was being, she would need her sister right now. Wouldn't she?

"She hasn't come to that realization, no."

"I've tried to talk some sense into her, but she's not listening. In fact, she went to Hawaii, anyway. And didn't get a phone plan. I think she didn't get the plan so she didn't have to talk to me. Or Mom." Bliss paused. "How is it you've had a discussion with her?"

"Um, I ran into her."

"Ran into her? She's in Hawaii."

"I happen to…er…be in Hawaii, too."

"You're in Hawaii together?" Bliss breathed.

"No. Not really. Not together. I mean it was an accident. We're in the same place, but—"

"She can't see that's Fate?"

"Apparently not," he said, a little dryly.

"She's being unreasonable!"

He realized he was not the least bit comfortable discussing Blossom behind her back, with her sister. Though it had been another matter with Lance, now he felt guilty about that. As if he'd betrayed Blossom, and not the other way around.

How had everything Blossom become so complicated?

"I just called because Blossom kind of indicated the wedding had some outstanding items."

Bliss sighed heavily. "You're not kidding."

"I want to pay for those."

"Thank goodness!" Bliss said.

At least someone appreciated him. Bliss seemed so reasonable. It was too bad he knew she liked to throw things.

"That wasn't exactly Blossom's reaction," he admitted, "but I'm going to give you my assistant's number, and you can give her the details. I want to pay for the whole thing. Whatever's left owing and a reimbursement of whatever your business has into it."

Joe realized this—solving financial problems, doing business—was exactly in his wheelhouse. After feeling off balance ever since running into Blossom last night, it felt good to take charge.

"I can't thank you enough. I wasn't sure what we were going to do. She's waiting for loan approval, but..."

Loan approval? Joe closed his eyes. Really? Blossom was that stubborn that she'd ruin herself to make a point?

"Don't tell Blossom," he warned Bliss.

"A secret," she said gleefully, and then became somber. "Secrets don't make for very good relationships."

"We aren't in one anymore, so that's not a problem. Plus, I'm sure she's going to find out eventually, but hopefully I'll be out of range when she does."

"Joe?"

"Yeah?"

"I think Blossom might sabotage things when they're

going too well. She doesn't believe good things can happen to her," Bliss told him softly. "She's afraid to hope."

Joe let that sink in. Blossom was afraid to hope.

"Anyway, thanks again, Joe. You're a really good guy."

Leave it at that, he thought, but then he didn't. "You know who else is a really good guy?"

"No," Bliss said lightly. "Who?"

"Lance."

Why had he said that? No one would appreciate it less than Lance. They had already decided, between the two of them, that women who threw things were bad news.

Even though, as Blossom had pointed out, she hadn't really *thrown* the ring at him. It had just felt as if she had, as if that returned ring had hit him with the force of a ninety-mile-an-hour baseball straight to the chest.

Then he realized why he had entered the cringe-worthy arena of standing up for his friend to the woman who had spurned him.

Because, unlike Blossom, and with all the evidence pointing in the direction of it being a foolish belief, Joe Blackwell still thought maybe people should give love a chance.

Not him, naturally.

Other people.

CHAPTER EIGHT

NOT JOE, THOUGH. For himself, he had come to the realization that hope was the most dangerous thing. Yet still—

He mulled over Bliss's final words long after he had hung up the phone and eaten several more apple bananas.

All this time together and he hadn't known that?

Call the pilot, he ordered himself.

But he didn't. He contemplated Bliss's revelation that Blossom did not believe good things could happen to her. That she *sabotaged* things when life was going too well.

His attention was drawn back to the card. It was a reproduction of a painting of a silhouette of a man and a woman sitting side by side on a beach, looking over the waves, bathed in the light of the setting sun.

It was a perfect card for honeymooners.

But it also reminded Joe of the time he and Blossom had gone camping. Reluctantly, he opened the card, bracing himself for the pain of the well wishes.

Inside was a message, hand-done in calligraphy. It was signed by Kalani and all the staff of Hale Alana. Joe read the message, and then read it again, slowly.

Maybe Blossom didn't want to marry him anymore, this woman whom he had loved, who had morphed into a stranger.

But he suddenly had a feeling it had less to do with him suggesting they rethink the wedding and more to do with a history she had hinted at and that Bliss had also just alluded to.

So, maybe, despite his own misgivings about getting married because of his fears over his father's diagnosis, he wouldn't leave. He'd take the words in the card as an invitation to see differently, to be better. He looked at the card again.

Bliss had asked if Blossom couldn't see Fate might have had a hand in both Joe and Blossom ending up in Hawaii.

He was not sure he believed in Fate, but he was not sure it was something you wanted to scoff at, either.

Joe considered the message of the card. He could delay leaving by a day, couldn't he? Just to make sure Blossom didn't hide out here the entire time and never saw Hawaii at all?

Volcano National Park and the Tropical Garden on the other side of Hilo would make a nice day trip. They could stop at Punalu'u, the most famous of the island's black sand beaches, on the way there. There were almost always turtles on that beach. He had a feeling turtles would delight her. In some small way, he could show Blossom that good things could happen to her.

And just to show himself that guess what? It wasn't always all about him. He could be a better man.

He put the bottle of champagne in the fridge. He didn't think they were quite ready to toast a truce—if she agreed to one—with that. He really needed to keep his wits about him. Besides, champagne was horrible warm.

Joe picked up the coupons and the card. Feeling like a warrior heading into battle, he strode down the hall and stopped at the door of the room Blossom had chosen. He took a deep breath and knocked.

"Yes?"

Blossom, already in her hideous pajamas, plumped a pillow behind her back, tucked the sheet under her armpits, picked up the book and pretended total engagement in it.

In fact, she had not absorbed a single word since Joe had shown up at the pool.

Joe opened the door and came in. Blossom frowned at him. Her room, which had seemed very spacious, suddenly seemed too small, as if his presence was taking up all the space and all the air.

He was still damp from the pool. He also hadn't put a shirt on.

"I opened the envelope," he said.

"What envelope?" she stammered.

"The one you told me to deal with?"

Oh. That one. The Mr. and Mrs. Blackwell one. If they were Mr. and Mrs. Blackwell, they'd be in this bed together. That delicious expanse of beautiful male body would be hers to explore, to taste, to touch.

Blossom felt almost dizzy with longing.

"It had coupons in it," Joe said, as if he had no idea how distracting he was.

"Coupons?"

"Like vouchers. For all the must-sees on the island."

He came over and dropped the vouchers on her lap.

She looked through them, trying not to let what she was feeling show on her face. Which was first of all, Joe was in her bedroom, so close his shadow was falling on her. And, a very distant second, maybe she could see Hawaii after all.

"It's not from Becky and Dave, my parents' friends," he said, "it's from the staff. Some—like that night swim with manta rays—have a date on them. And they're non-refundable."

"Oh."

"We have to go."

"We?" she squeaked. She had thought he was giving the coupons and vouchers to her, the destitute person who couldn't afford to see Hawaii. "We, as in you and me?"

There was no *you and me*. She shouldn't have to remind him of that.

Joe, uninvited, took a seat on the edge of the bed. So close! His scent—unique to him, not diminished by his swim—engulfed her, warmly masculine.

Without warning, she was swamped with memories. Of the first night they had spent together. Of his tenderness. And of her surrender.

Of a sense of being part of a force so mighty it had created the universe, possibly out of a big bang—an explosion of energy—not so different than the one they had just experienced together.

She deliberately slid away from the temptation of all that damp skin and eyed him warily.

"This is what we have to understand," he said, apparently not being rocked by memories at all, "I'm sure Becky and Dave pay the staff well, but people who work here probably still make very modest incomes. And yet they spent their money on us. Every one of these gifts is intended to deepen our enjoyment of their home, these islands."

Blossom realized her memories had left her defenseless, weak with wanting him, exhausted from trying to keep her walls up high. It was impossible with Joe sitting on the edge of the bed. Anything he asked of her right now, she would give him. Anything.

"These people," he told her, "complete strangers to us, have extended us a welcome, an invitation to enjoy their land."

It was just wrong to be disappointed that Joe was obviously intent on sharing this gift with her, nothing more.

"I don't think you want to make Madame Pele angry by refusing such a gift."

"Who is Madame Pele?" she asked.

"She's the goddess of volcanoes. The ancient belief is that she is the creator of the Hawaiian Islands. I'd like to go to Kilauea tomorrow and see her fire." His voice dropped. "With you."

"I—"

"Before you say no, I want to read the card to you."

She was astounded that he hadn't figured out she could not say no to him, not right now.

"Aloha," Joe read, his voice even more sensual for the softness in it, "in Hawaiian means both hello and goodbye.

"But it is so much more than that. The Hawaiian people consider aloha to be a spirit that asks people to coordinate heart and mind, to come back to self-knowledge in order to *always* have good feelings toward others.

"Aloha means you treat your fellow travelers on the life journey with regard and affection, that you extend warmth and caring to each person you meet."

The beauty of what he was saying, and the way he was saying it, intensified Blossom's feelings of weakness.

"I would say that's exactly what the staff has done that for us," Joe said, "Extended aloha, by getting this place ready for us, by offering us these gifts."

She gulped, humbled, as Joe continued to read.

"Aloha recognizes people are intertwined and need each other to exist."

Intertwined, she thought, stealing another glance at his very attractive, naked chest.

He seemed oblivious to her rising temperature. "Aloha also conveys the ability to hear what is not said, to see what is not seen, and to know the unknowable."

"That is a lot for one word," she said. Her voice felt like a croak.

"Isn't it?" Joe agreed. "Finally, it says, to extend aloha also means there is no expectation or obligation for a return."

She was silent. The words touched her unbelievably. She could feel something hard around her heart break open just a tiny crack.

"I cannot refuse this gift," Joe said. "Are you with me?"

At the moment if he had asked her to bungee jump from Navajo Bridge, she would have followed him, willingly, over the edge. She swallowed hard.

His eyes met hers. "If complete strangers can offer us the gift of aloha, maybe we can be open to offering that to each other."

"Maybe we can," she agreed softly, when she found her voice. "But it seems so complicated between us."

His sitting on her bed was proving that in spades!

"What if we don't try to deal with the complications?

What if we just take it day by day, and see what happens? At the end of our time here, maybe we'll have a clearer idea what needs to be dealt with and what comes next."

He was offering her the remaining time here—nine days—together. It was an unbelievable reprieve from what she had thought would be a life without him. She was not strong enough to say no to that.

"Aloha, Blossom," he said softly.

"Aloha, Joe," she responded, knowing it could mean both hello and goodbye.

And so much in between.

For one second, she leaned toward that *in between*, wanting, almost desperately, to deepen the meaning. With—

Joe jumped off the bed, as if he'd read her intent. She looked at him sourly. He'd never been the one to back away from *that* before.

Still, Blossom could barely sleep thinking of spending the day tomorrow, together, and all the days after that.

Was it a second chance for them? Or were they literally, on this island famous for eruptions, playing with fire?

Before she finally slept, she realized if this was a second chance—or even if it wasn't—she had to make an effort to fix one of the places she knew she had gone wrong.

In the morning, she was up before Joe. She put the coffee on, and as the kitchen filled with that rich scent, Blossom did a quick perusal of the cupboards to see what kind of supplies they had and if they would need anything to get them through the next days.

The house, not surprisingly, was extremely well stocked. A person could live quite comfortably here for months. She felt a familiar sense of reassurance when she found a large jar of peanut butter among the more exotic tinned and dried offerings.

Joe came into the kitchen, looking so sexy, his hair still wet from the shower. They had never lived together, and he had never stayed overnight at her place because she shared the apartment over their business with Bliss.

But Blossom had stayed at his upscale, waterfront Vancouver condo many, many times. When she thought of what she missed about that, it wasn't the granite, or the floor-to-ceiling windows with their views, the extraordinary quality of the furniture, the floor coverings, the art, or that sense of luxury and arrival.

It was the lovemaking, of course, but beyond that it was this more ordinary thing. A man in the morning, his wet hair, his scent, his freshly shaved face, the way he slid a look at her, the way he sighed with simple pleasure after that first sip of coffee.

He had on gray shorts and a navy blue shirt with subtle gray palm trees in the pattern. It was an outfit any well-heeled, eighty-year-old tourist would be quite happy to wear.

It seemed really unfair that Joe rocked it. Particularly since her own wardrobe was so limited by the fact she had refused to pay extra for checked bags.

She had on a T-shirt and shorts that could be safely rolled into a tight ball. Neither of them looked *crisp*. And certainly not sexy. That look he'd slid her way must have disappointed him.

"You're up early," he commented. If he'd even noticed her outfit was somewhat lackluster, he didn't let on.

"Who can sleep? That bird! *Ooh-hoo, ooh-hoo!* Like an excited Tigger talking to Pooh."

He smiled at her description. And she missed that, too,

his smile in the morning, the memory of his mouth on hers fresh, invigorating, making the coming day seem splendid with possibility.

"It's a mynah bird," Joe told her.

"Well, I can't decide if I love it or hate it."

"Me, either," he agreed, his smile deepening. "What are you doing?"

"I'm packing us lunch."

"What? Why?"

"I had this thought. That we shouldn't spend any money. Well, not *we*. You. You shouldn't spend any money."

"Why?"

"I don't know. An experiment. See what it feels like without that. I'll pay for what we need. You've always paid."

"But I liked that."

So had she, admittedly. And, sensibly, now was not the time for her to be putting out a pile of money. *Any* money. She wasn't even confident her credit card would clear.

But they had the coupons and vouchers, and she had easily put together lunch and snack items from things in the fridge. Really, if her childhood had given her any gifts, Blossom knew how to do things on a shoestring.

She wanted—needed—to know what she and Joe were if you took away the money factor? The lavishness? The luxuries? The never having to think about money?

"Okay," Joe agreed thoughtfully. "I've been giving it some thought, too."

His eyes trailed to her lips.

"I think," he said huskily, "some perimeters would be good. For instance, we should avoid sunscreen application and backside inspections."

She understood immediately what he was saying.

They needed to avoid the kind of contacts that were bound to remind them of past intimacies. Just looking at his smile in the morning, breathing in his scent, filled her with a kind of desperate longing. Last night she had almost given in to the temptation to taste the familiar tang of those full, sensual lips.

He took her silence to mean he needed to convince her.

"Don't you think it clouded everything? That fact that we couldn't keep our hands off each other?"

She was not sure *cloudy* described how she felt, at all. In fact, it seemed to her Joe's touch had always given her great clarity, a sense of being able to see into a brilliant future.

Perhaps the very fact they saw it so differently made it a wise—if annoying—suggestion. It would keep the complications between them to a minimum.

But his suggesting that touching was now off limits made a white-hot longing leap up in her. She understood Eve gazing at the apple, the lure of forbidden fruit. Not that she'd let on.

"Got it," she said casually, as if it didn't matter one little bit to her that she had to keep her hands off him. "So, let me make sure I understand the rules—no money, no touchy."

"Do you have to make it sound as if we're in a cheap bordello?"

She giggled. He chortled. And then they were both laughing, as if nothing had ever gone wrong between them.

An hour later, the tension between them still felt eased by that moment of shared laughter. With a cooler packed with all the food they would need for the day, and beach bags packed with everything else, they were in his four-wheel drive and on the highway. Beyond what she could see from

Hale Alana, this was her first real glimpse of Hawaii, since it had been dark when she'd arrived.

Blossom could not believe she had nearly chosen to miss this! Her every sense was on high alert as she drank in the new and exotic sights. On one side of the highway was the ocean, and on the other, the mountains rose, spectacular, in the distance.

"In Hawaii," Joe told her, "in the context of directions, there is the *mauka* side of the road, which means the mountain side, and the *makai* side, which means the ocean side."

Blossom was astonished by both the *mauka* and *makai* sides of the landscape. Before coming here, she had pictured only lush, tropical greenery, the Hawaii of television shows and the movies, and certainly the Hawaii of Hale Alana.

On the *makai* side of the highway she caught glimpses of postcard-pretty Hawaii, beautiful oases of green palm fronds dancing with the sky, surrounding bays of turquoise water.

On the *mauka* side, Blossom could see steep, dramatic-looking mountains that looked green and jungle-like.

But in between both the sea and the mountains, the near landscape was quite astonishingly stark.

"The lava," she said, awed. "It's everywhere. It's like driving through endless fields of charcoal."

"These are old flows, actually. Eruptions created these islands. This is the youngest of the Hawaiian island chain, which is why so much of the lava has not broken down yet. It can take thousands of years for it to become the soil that creates so much lush greenery.

"Because of continuous eruptions the Big Island grows a little bigger every year. Madame Pele at work."

Blossom had always enjoyed this about Joe. He was curious and had enjoyed so many unique experiences. But he was never satisfied with superficial explorations. He always had to dig deeper. It made him interesting and knowledge-able. In this instance, it was like having a personal tour guide. She could feel something relax in her as she remembered how easy it had always been to spend time with him.

"Do you want to stop and look at it?" he asked her.

"Oh, yes!"

He pulled over as soon as it was safe to do so, and he and Blossom got out and walked out onto the lava. The black surface was attracting astonishing heat. She bent and ran her hand over the surface.

"There are two kinds of lava," Joe told her. "This kind is called pahoehoe, and it's smooth and billowy. Sometimes it looks like big lengths of giant rope. The other kind is called ah-ah. The locals joke that *ah-ah* is the sound you make if you step on it. It's very jagged. It can be extremely danger-ous, and rip through skin, or even footwear."

They were soon back in the vehicle, welcoming the breeze after the heat of the lava.

"I've never been in a roofless vehicle before," Blossom admitted. "It's exhilarating."

"And here I was just thinking of putting the roof up to protect your head from the sun."

"Please don't."

"Where's your ball cap?"

"I never thought of it this morning."

He handed her his. "We'll have to get another one."

There was that ache of missing him again. Joe was al-ways casually chivalrous. But today, Blossom told herself, she would not dwell on what they had once been.

Her New Age mother would be so proud of her.

Blossom intended to embrace every moment as if there was no past, as if there was no future.

She put his hat on her head. "Okay, we'll get a new one, but I'm buying it."

He smiled at her indulgently. "If that's the hill you want to die on."

She enjoyed the drive immensely, admitting her focus felt sharpened by her vow to be in the moment. She was feeling as if she was soaking up the warmth and the wind, the colors and sounds, through her skin. They went by Ellison Onizuka Kona International Airport, where she had arrived so late the other night. Joe told her it was named after an astronaut, who had died in the Space Shuttle Challenger.

Onizuka, he said, was from Kealakekua, a village they would pass by today. "I'm hoping we'll snorkel in Kealakekua Bay."

She loved his ease of pronunciation, the sensual sound of the Hawaiian words coming off his tongue. A few minutes later they were entering the outskirts of the town of Kailua-Kona.

"I'm a little disappointed," she said. "A strip mall?"

He laughed. "Even in Hawaii. I'll make sure you see the downtown before you go. It's a historic village and really pretty."

But then there was the advantage of strip malls, practically right in front of her.

"Look," Blossom said, pointing, "there's exactly the place to get cheap hats. On the *mauka* side. Wally Wiggles!"

"What?"

"Turn left at these lights. That's what Bliss and I call that big-chain box store that sells everything, including the kitchen sink, and cheap."

"Everything?" he said. "We should see if we can pick up some snorkels there. Do you think they'll have that?"

"Oh, I'm pretty sure."

They pulled into a packed parking lot, and Joe secured the vehicle by putting the roof up. They got out, and Blossom stared, open-mouthed, away from the store.

"Look at the view!"

"Spectacular," he agreed, and they took a moment to stand side by side appreciating it together.

The store was perched high on the slopes of the coffee-growing mountains that surrounded the village of Kailua-Kona, which they could see below them. The view was of church spires, palms, hotels, and then the endless blue of the ocean, dotted with paddle-boarders, kayakers and pleasure craft.

She sighed. "Okay. Even the strip malls in Hawaii are beautiful."

She turned to the store and glanced at Joe. Was he eyeing it with a certain wary curiosity?

"Have you ever been in one of these before?" Blossom asked him.

"I think I've been in this chain store before," Joe said.

But that answer, and his slightly dubious tone, told Blossom a great deal. A famous celebrity had once been asked about this very store, and had giggled and said, "What do they sell there? Walls?"

Joe was closer to that world than Blossom's. He had to think about it. He wasn't quite sure. He didn't even know they would have a huge sporting goods section.

This was one of the big differences between them and their worlds. In his world, shopping meant high-end stores and exclusive websites. In his world, if he needed something, he probably sent his assistant out to get it.

In her world, you stretched pennies and found bargains and made do.

But today, Blossom was determined to treat their different worlds as a wonderful thing.

Joe could share his extensive knowledge of one of the most beautiful places in the world, knowledge born of being well-traveled and wealthy.

She could share her knowledge of Wally Wiggles.

She had never invited him into this part of her life before. Strangely, maybe because there was no longer any pressure on her to be the perfect billionaire's wife, it felt like it just could be fun!

"We'll be on a strict budget," she told him. "Fifty dollars."

"Fifty dollars?" he said, aghast, "What can you get for that? A pair of socks?"

Again, there was the difference between their worlds.

"You'll be amazed," she promised him.

CHAPTER NINE

THE TRUTH WAS Joe was already amazed. Not by Wally Wiggles, but by the light in Blossom's face as she drank in the morning on the Big Island of Hawaii.

He was reminded of what he had first loved about her, beyond the exquisite chemistry. It was her incredible sense of wonder, like the look on her face when she had run her hand over the smooth surface of the lava this morning.

He'd done the right thing by staying. By embracing the message of that card and the spirit of aloha, by stepping up to be the better man.

He watched now as she paused at a dress rack under the harsh glare of the lighting in the store. Extremely colorful sundresses were on display, with elastic bodices and skinny shoulder straps and wide skirts.

But what he really noticed was that they were ten dollars, and she was hesitating.

"This one," he said, reaching by her and plucking a dress off. It was white with bold pink hibiscus blooms all over it. "Aw, what the heck. This one, too." It was yellow, covered in white frangipani flowers.

"That's almost our whole budget," she said, but she was hugging those dresses to her, like Cinderella with a choice of ball gowns.

"Let's up the budget," he suggested.

"We're barely an hour in, and you already want to up the budget?"

"Seventy-five bucks?"

She considered this solemnly.

"Okay," she finally said, as if she was signing a million-dollar real estate deal. "On one condition."

He cocked his head at her.

"I get to pick out something for you."

Joe would not have agreed to that so readily if he'd known she was going to find a five-dollar pair of shorts for him on the sales rack. They were black with pink flamingos on them. The thing was, they made her laugh, which made it five bucks well spent, even if his dignity was going to take a bit of a hit.

She went and found a change room, came out in the pink-and-white hibiscus dress.

Joe's mouth fell open. She was making that ten-dollar dress look as if it was haute couture!

She did a little twirl in front of him and her cheap dress hugged her in all the right places and swirled around slender legs.

Joe could feel his mouth going dry.

"Is it too short?" she asked pensively.

Was there any such thing?

"Uh, no, I think it's just right."

"It's not trashy?"

"Trashy? Blossom, you couldn't look trashy if you were wearing a garbage bag."

Why was she looking at him like that? As if he'd drawn down the moon and presented it to her as a gift?

"Do you think it would be okay if I left it on?" she asked. "I'd like to wear it today."

Oh, sure, be a temptress in your ten-dollar dress all day.

He wanted to tell her that volcano might be colder, that the thin cotton dress might not be the *sensible* choice. On the other hand, look where being sensible all the time had gotten them.

Not that what had gone on between them at an intimate level could ever be described as *sensible*.

He had to get his mind off *that*, a mission made harder by the dress.

"What do you think? Should I just leave it on?"

He could hardly tell her to take it off to aid him in his mission of being sensible. In what world did telling someone to take off their dress add up to being sensible?

In a change room in a public store, he reminded himself. He had to keep his head on straight. He had to keep things in context.

To her, he said, "Sure, just leave the tag on it. They can scan you at the till."

"If you're sure," she said. "What if I forget? I don't want to get arrested for shoplifting at Wally Wiggles in Hawaii."

He wasn't likely to forget she was in that dress!

"If you get arrested," he teased her, "we could just consider it part of the adventure. Though, according to the rules, I'm not sure I'd be allowed to spend money on bail."

Joe realized it felt good to tease her, it felt good for things to be lighthearted and not so purpose-driven as they had become toward all things wedding.

"Isn't that bail bondsman on television from here?" Blossom asked. "I could bypass you. I might even be on an episode!"

He snickered at the ludicrous thought. She giggled. And then something cracked open between them and they laughed together for the second time that day. But as it turned out, it was only just the beginning of the laughter.

Because next, they found the hat section.

"How about this one?" she said, picking the most absurdly large sunhat she could find. She put it on her head and sauntered by him with a hand on her hip. She winked when she went by.

"Do I look ready for my cameo on *Jails Away*?" she asked earnestly.

"Your cameo relies on you stealing a dress," he reminded her.

"Forgetting to pay for it!"

He found himself laughing, again, which was a mistake, because, encouraged into further silliness, she found a fedora-style hat for him. Instead of handing it to him, she leaned in. She stood up on her tiptoes, one leg straight, the other bent behind her, and plopped the hat on his head.

For one breathless moment, her chest brushed his chest. Really, it seemed as if it would be petty to mention the no-touch rule over such a small thing, even if it had raised havoc with his senses.

That was the problem, he reminded himself sternly, *the smallest touch from her raised havoc with him.*

Therefore the no-touch rule, a return to sanity, a backing off from that crazy-making chemistry between them.

To hide the disturbance that smallest touch had caused in him, he turned and looked in the mirror. "I think I look like a movie star."

"Which one?"

"You guess. Just a sec," he said, "I'm going to look up a quote to go with this hat."

He found one, lowered the phone, squinted at her and deepened his voice.

"A hot dog at the game beats roast beef at the Ritz," he said. "Who am I?"

She looked at him thoughtfully. She tapped her finger on her lip. "Rodney Dangerfield?"

"Ouch! That hurt!"

"Mr. Bean?"

"Mr. Bean doesn't talk!"

"Indiana Jones?"

"That's better, even if it is because of the hat and not my innate masculinity, charm and sexiness. I'll give you one more chance."

"Okay," she said with entirely false contriteness.

"Things are never so bad they can't be made worse," he intoned, tipping the brim of his hat over his eyes.

She did that tapping thing with her finger on her lip again.

"If you don't guess right this time, we get to up the budget by twenty-five bucks."

"Humphrey Bogart!" she spat out between giggling fits.

He tilted his hat at her and drawled dangerously, "You knew all along."

She actually squealed with delighted laughter. And then they were both howling with laughter, and other shoppers moving by looked at them indulgently.

"Hand me your phone." She looked something up, then handed it back. She found another wide-brimmed hat. She bent over, as if she was holding down her skirt, half-lidded her eyes and made a cute little pucker. Despite the fact there was no hat in that famous subway grate scene, of course, he knew who it was before she said a single word.

"It's someone intensely glamorous," she told him, as if he needed a hint.

And then she said, her voice extraordinarily husky, as if she was channeling Marilyn Monroe, "A wise girl knows her limits...a smart girl knows she has none."

"Huh. Mayim Bialik?"

"Who's that?" she asked, annoyed, straightening and smoothing down her skirt.

"Sheldon's girlfriend. A very smart girl in real life. Some kind of scientist."

"You guess correctly, right now, or I'm deducting twenty-five dollars from our budget!"

He crooned softly, "Happy birthday, Mr. President," and they both had fits of laughter again.

Joe realized how strangely nice it felt to just be two anonymous tourists being silly in a big chain store in Hawaii.

By the time Blossom finally chose a five-dollar white straw sunhat, they had tried on every hat in the section, done imitations of many, many celebrities and their stomachs hurt from laughing.

Moving on from the hats, she found a shelf full of reef-safe sunscreens.

She held up one that was a spray bottle for his inspection. "I can apply this myself, in accordance with the no-touchy rule."

Looking at her in that dress, her face glowing with good humor, recalling their contact earlier when she had set the hat on his head, Joe congratulated himself for coming up with that rule!

They made their way to sporting goods. There were walls of snorkels. Joe drifted, wistfully, to the better-quality ones. He picked one out and was studying it when she came over, squinted at the price on it and gasped indignantly.

She then held up one that was half the price. "Does this seem any different to you?"

"I think in some ways you get what you pay for."

"Nonsense. This is not rocket science. Two pieces—a mask and a breathing tube."

"Generally called a snorkel?" he suggested dryly.

"This is the one I got!"

He glanced at it. It was bright pink. "Is that a kids' snorkel?"

"Yes! I have a small head. I'm sure it will fit. If I get this one and you get this one—" she wagged her choice at him "—we'll still be five dollars under budget, according to my calculations."

He gave in good-naturedly and put the more expensive snorkel back.

"We need this, then, with our extra five bucks." He plucked a plasticized chart off a rack. "It shows all the fish you'll see snorkeling in Hawaii."

She definitely had to have the chart!

"What about boogie boards?" he asked, stopping to look at a few as they passed them.

"That one board is nearly our whole budget!"

"Come to think of it, they have them at Hale Alana. I've used them before. They're stored in the garage."

She beamed at him as if he had saved the world by not spending sixty bucks on a new board.

With taxes, at the checkout, they were nearly six dollars over budget. Joe actually held his breath for a moment when Blossom saw the total, wondering if she was going to put something back. He hoped it wouldn't be the other dress, since the first time in his life that he could recall, he was looking forward to seeing what a dress looked like *on*.

Blossom didn't put anything back but gathered up their purchases with glee. No single-use plastic bags were allowed in Hawaii, and she had refused a reusable one to save seventy-five cents.

"I'm starving," she told him as they made their way out of the store, and he had to keep catching items that were falling out of her overloaded arms.

He eyed the chain hamburger joint at the front of the store with longing. "I bet we could have lunch for under ten bucks."

He should have known better.

"But I brought food! Look, there's a picnic table over there, against that wall."

He fished through their purchases for his new shorts and changed into them tucked behind the door of the jeep.

Somehow he had not seen this coming: Joe Blackwell changing clothes in a bargain store parking lot. And yet, breaking out of his long-held habits made him feel curiously alive.

Or was he kidding himself? Being with Blossom made him feel alive.

A fact confirmed by her smile when she saw the shorts.

Joe said with pretend grumpiness, "I feel as if we're getting ready for a tacky tourist party."

"We are tourists," she reminded him. "I don't think you look tacky. I think you look really—" she blushed "—cute. Do you think I look tacky?"

He gulped. "No."

He didn't expand, because she didn't look cute, either. She looked damned sexy.

He grabbed the cooler and, at the last moment, the fish chart they had bought, and followed her over to the table.

And so they sat at a picnic table at the very edge of the Wally Wiggles parking lot. Blossom handed him a sandwich and he unwrapped it.

"What is this?" he asked, prying the bread apart and looking inside.

"Peanut butter."

He wasn't aware of making a face, but he must have been, because Blossom said to him, "Oh, for heaven's sake, don't be such a snob."

"Snob or not, I'm not eating peanut butter. I'm going to get a hamburger. And don't even suggest a hamburger from Mickey D's makes me a snob."

In five minutes he was back at the picnic table with his hamburger and a large fries. Blossom eyed him balefully as he bit into his burger.

"I'm not sure I've ever tasted anything so good," he decided.

"Oh, sure. You're just trying not to be a snob. You've eaten at some of the best restaurants in the world."

He held out the burger to her. "Taste it. You tell me."

She leaned over the table and took a bite. He watched her lips touch the very place his lips had just touched and wondered how something so very simple could seem so intimate.

She tried—and not very successfully—to act like it wasn't good.

"Want me to go get you one?"

"No! It's breaking the rules," she said.

"It is, but in a very budget-friendly way."

"That's how it starts. Then next thing you know, we're five-star dining our way across Hawaii."

"We can only hope."

"We're only a few hours in. What if I started breaking your rule?"

"Oh, good," he said. "I can hardly wait."

"In fact," she said, "you've broken my rule once, so I get a free one. To break your rule."

If he mentioned she already had when she had reached up to put that hat on his head, it would seem like he'd attached way too much importance to that.

She gave his lips a look so heated he nearly choked on his hamburger.

"Okay," he said, his voice raw. "Get it over with."

CHAPTER TEN

BLOSSOM SMILED SWEETLY at Joe. "Get it over with? Nope. My rule break could come out of nowhere. Anytime. Anyplace."

He could feel tension—delicious—shivering across his spine.

"Here," he croaked, "have the French fries."

"It's okay. I really like peanut butter." She hesitated, and then she said, "When we were kids, we didn't always have much, but if there was a jar of peanut butter in our lives, I just had this lovely feeling that things would be okay."

He was silent for a minute. "I don't get why I'm just hearing stuff like this now. Living in the car. Seeing peanut butter as a lifeline."

"I got my prom dress at a secondhand store. It was such a find. Jacob Minstrel."

Something in her tone warned him this was a big deal to her. "And?"

"It turned out my date's sister was the one who had donated it to the store. Her mother and her agreed that I managed to make it look trashy."

So, that was where the concern about the sundress came from. Joe was stunned by the flash of rage he felt. "They told you that?"

"I overheard them."

"You know what that really means?"

"No. What's it really mean?"

"It looked better on you. I'm going to guess way better. You were Cinderella, she was the ugly stepsister."

"Funny you should word it like that," she said, with a small smile that lit up his whole world.

"Why's that?"

She wrinkled her nose. "Me and my princess dreams. Blossoms and Bliss is really about fairy tales."

He considered that, the underlying tone, which seemed to imply dreams came true for other people, but not for her.

"Why didn't you ever tell me these things before?"

She lifted her slender shoulder. He noticed it was turning a little pink. She needed some of that spray-on sunscreen.

"I don't like it when I hear other people talk about their bad childhoods," Blossom said, squinting into the distance, not looking at him. "Or that they grew up poor. Sometimes it seems exaggerated. It seems everybody has their poor-me story."

"I don't," Joe said. But then he thought, *didn't*. Because, suddenly, he did have challenges of the sort he had not experienced before. A broken engagement. A sick father. His perfect world coming apart at the seams.

"I know," she said, and he heard something distinctly wistful in her tone. "You know what I really longed for, growing up? A dad. I don't even know who my dad is."

Again, Joe felt as if he should have known this. On the very odd occasion Blossom had said anything about her childhood journey, she had made it sound like a fun adventure with her wildly eccentric mother.

What a sad thing it would be not to know who your father—half of you—was. He thought again of his own dad, and how, so many times in his life, he had *needed* that firm hand guiding him through the tumultuous temptations of youth, veering him away from all the traps that awaited young men.

Somehow, as he had become immersed in his own business, his dad had always been there in the background, although not playing such a big role in his life. Joe had assumed there would be time later—maybe when the grandkids came along—for the fishing trips and baseball games and holidays together.

Now, in the blink of an eye, the possibility of children, at least anywhere in the near future, had been swept from his life, and the window of opportunity to bond with his dad had been slammed shut.

Three staff members, a man and two women, arrived at the table, cutting off their conversation. Joe was not sure if he was thankful or distressed by the interruption as he and Blossom were navigating such personal territory.

"There goes your chance," he said, and she looked relieved, as if he had expected more confessions from her. He deliberately lightened the conversation up between them.

"My chance?"

"To break the rule. I was bracing myself in case when you finished eating your sandwich, you leaped across the table and attacked me. Peanut butter kisses. Ick."

She squinted at him, a look that clearly said if she decided to kiss him, peanut butter or no, the last thing on his mind would be *ick*.

"I think I'll be more subtle than that," she decided.

The anticipation tingled again.

What exactly did that mean?

Blossom turned her attention quickly to the staff, scooting down to the end of the table. He did the same. He pointed out a little sign to her that he hadn't seen before: Staff Table.

"I'm sorry," she said. "We didn't mean to take your break spot."

But in the spirit of Hawaii, the woman laughed. "Oh, no, there's room for everyone. Where are you from?"

When Blossom said Canada, they all shivered, as if on cue.

Joe noticed Blossom seemed more the way she had seemed when he first met her. She was totally engaged with the people, her interest in them entirely genuine. Five minutes in, she knew the names and ages of all their children!

This, he thought watching her, was why Blossom DuPont was a phenomenal success in the highly competitive wedding market in Vancouver.

A quieter voice said, *And this, along with all that wonder, is why you fell for her.*

She shared the pineapple spears and cookies that she had packed for their lunch. And the locals offered them *poke*, a diced raw fish that was a mainstay of Hawaiian cuisine.

Everybody laughed at the face Blossom made when she tasted it.

The chart Joe and Blossom had bought to help them identify tropical fish was noticed lying out on the table—somehow they had never gotten around to that in their heated exchange about sneak kiss attacks and there was much good-natured discussion about the best snorkeling spots on the island.

When Blossom admitted she had never snorkeled before, one of the young men pointed below them, to the downtown area.

"Some of the best snorkeling on the island is right there in Kailua Bay," he said. "The little beach in front of the King Kamehameha Hotel is a great place to learn. There's lots of fish there."

"Are there sharks?" Blossom asked.

"We do have sharks here, but shark attacks are very rare. And in that particular place? Impossible. The water's shallow, and there's a man-made rock wall at the mouth. The smaller fish can get through but nothing big ever has that I know of."

After their new friends had left, Blossom gathered up their things. She looked wistfully down at the sparkling waters of the bay.

"Should we change plans?" she suggested.

Joe considered Blossom's suggestion with some surprise.

Blossom was not really what he would call spontaneous—she liked everything pretty carefully controlled.

Of course, that was part of what had blown up their world. A suggestion of change. The merest hint of it!

To be perfectly honest, he wasn't averse to controlled circumstances, either. In fact, he'd seen both their aversions to the unexpected as a good thing between them, a shared common value.

That was the nature of being two businesspeople. They were both successful in their fields because of their ability to be highly structured.

But suddenly he recognized that their common liking for security had morphed into rigidity. When had they allowed life to become so predictable? Where had all the fun gone between them?

Maybe it was never too late to find it.

Really, it was something of a miracle that both of them had decided, spontaneously, to come to Hawaii.

"What do you suggest?" he said.

"I'm hot now. I'd love to get in the water."

"Especially with no sharks?" he asked, dryly.

"Especially that," she agreed.

Joe realized, with some amazement, that they had just picnicked in a parking lot. And had a really fun time in a chain store. That Blossom was wearing a ten-dollar dress and a five-dollar hat.

How was it possible this morning shone as brightly— maybe even more so—than all the awesome things they had done together: the concerts, the sporting events, the exclusive restaurants, the whirlwind weekend trips?

"Here's to spontaneity," Joe said, even as he wondered how far you had to stray from the plan before you entered uncharted waters.

"Here's to no sharks!" she said.

The danger zone.

He glanced at her pulling her hat low over her eyes, adjusting a falling strap on her new dress.

He realized he was tense, in the best possible way, in anticipation of when she was going to break his rule. About touching.

Who was he kidding? They were already in the danger zone. And it had nothing to do with sharks.

His vow to be a better man was less than twenty-four hours old. And already it was wavering like a mirage on a hot desert day.

* * *

As they drove down into Historic Kailua Village, Blossom thought about their conversation. She had told him about her awful prom dress. And instead of thinking less of her, he had thought less of *them*.

It was so endearing!

"It seems everybody has their poor-me story," she had said.

"I don't," Joe had said.

And that was so true, and also endearing. That was part of what she loved so much about him. Joe seemed so normal. It felt as if he could lead her there, to that place she had always longed for.

Even now, sitting beside her in the vehicle, those crazy shorts couldn't even touch how normal he was.

Calm and in control.

"The traffic is insane," she said.

"Nothing driving in Vancouver hasn't prepared me for. You have to remember this was once just a quaint and sleepy fishing village, and a summer retreat for Hawaiian royalty. This main road, Ali'i Drive, despite lots of upgrades, just wasn't originally designed to handle the huge amount of traffic it now gets."

A tiny car shot out of a parking spot and would have hit them if Joe was not so alert. He calmly put his arm out the window, folded three fingers down, and with his thumb and pinky up, wagged his wrist at the other driver.

"What's that mean?" Blossom asked.

"It's the *shaka* sign. Sometimes called *hang loose*. You'll see it's a pretty common gesture on the islands. It kind of means, we're all friends, take it easy, all's good."

"Very different than the one-fingered salutes you get

while driving in Vancouver, and that you'd especially get after nearly smashing into someone!"

"The *shaka* is just part of that aloha attitude. Look how congested it is, and yet the only agitation you see is from the tourists. And they generally calm down, become more live-and-let-live, after the islands have worked their magic on them for a few days. Besides, we got left a parking spot!"

Blossom would have passed on the slot they'd been left as too challenging to get the larger vehicle into. But Joe maneuvered into the tiny parking stall with that easy confidence he did everything with.

Again, it reminded her it wasn't necessarily the big things—fancy dinners and extraordinary travels and lifestyles of the rich and famous—that she missed about having Joe in her life. It was the little things. A man fresh out of the shower in the morning. His attitude in traffic.

His innate confidence that things, large and small, would just go his way.

She hardly knew where to look first, as they got out of the vehicle on Ali'i Drive. A steady stream of both locals and tourists moved down the sidewalks. She and Joe, in outfits that had seemed wild just a few minutes ago, were now only part of a moving river of color and energy.

"This is Moku'aikaua Church," Joe told her of the enormous structure beside them, the stones black with age. There was something about Joe's easy pronunciation of the difficult and exotic Hawaiian names that was alarmingly sensual. She turned her attention, quickly, to the plaque on the gate. It was Hawaii's earliest Christian church and had been built in 1820.

As amazing as the church was, her eyes were drawn

across the street from it. A building slumbered under the canopy of the biggest tree she'd ever seen.

"It's a banyan tree," Joe said, following her gaze and smiling at her. There was something so appreciative of her in that gaze. "And that's Hulihe'e Palace."

It didn't look anything like what Blossom would have pictured a palace to be. It was a large, square cream-colored building with green shutters. It kind of reminded her of Joe's parents' house, which most people would call a mansion.

A group of people sat in a circle on the lush front lawn in the shade of the banyan tree, strumming away on ukuleles. The music floated out over the street.

"The palace is one of the things we were given vouchers to see," Joe said. "Would you like to? Since we're right here?"

She felt like laughing out loud at how the day kept defying their efforts to tame it and kept escaping their plans. She loved how it seemed as if Hawaii was taking them where it wanted them to go.

Or maybe it was just exactly as Joe had said: Hawaii itself invited you to be more laid-back, to *hang loose…*

"Of course," she said. "And then I want to see the church."

It was two hours before they finally made it to the beach after their sightseeing exploration of the downtown. Blossom felt as if she was overflowing with newfound knowledge of Hawaiian culture and history.

They walked north from the church and palace, along a sidewalk beside a stone seawall. They avoided a wave that lapped over the wall and doused an unsuspecting tourist with sea foam.

"Blessed by the sea," a local called cheerfully.

They passed under a banyan even larger than the one at the palace.

Blossom could not resist stopping and gazing up at it.

"It reminds me of an elephant," she said, as cars drove under the thick curving gray branches that canopied Ali'i Drive.

Joe paused with her. "There's an even bigger one in Maui. The canopy is said to span nearly two acres, a whole city block."

"It's incredible." Would discovering something so magnificent be just as incredible without Joe at her side? She doubted it.

"Listen," he said, cocking his head. "We've found the home to all those mynah birds."

And then he lifted his hands to the branches and clapped them loudly. The mynah birds fell silent, and she couldn't help but laugh.

"Can you do that in the morning, please?"

The mynah birds started chattering again. "As you can see, it's a temporary fix."

He turned from her just as a boy on a skateboard barreled toward them. He took her shoulder and spun her out of the way.

The boy shot them a nonchalant *shaka* over his shoulder and Blossom glanced up at Joe's face and shivered at the look on it. A warrior called to protect. He'd only been out of her life for a little over two weeks, but of all the things she missed, this was one of them. That feeling of being protected.

"That counts as your touch," Joe said, letting go of her shoulder.

"It doesn't. You instigated it."

"Show a little gratitude," he said. "I saved your life."

She smiled at the overstatement. He smiled, too.

"I remember a time you did save a life," she said.

"What? No, I haven't."

"It was the fourth time we'd gone out." That made it sound as if she'd been taking notes of every single date! Which she practically had been.

"Is that the time we started to go to the Broadway show at the Queen Elizabeth Theatre? The night you got Bartholomew?"

Such a relief, somehow, that it had meant enough to him to remember it, too. He was smiling now.

"The night you saved Bartholomew. We were walking by a grate in the street," she recalled. "And I heard that sound."

"I still don't know how you heard it. That poor kitten."

It had been pouring rain, and the water had been sluicing into that grate. When they had peered inside, a little orange kitten, drenched and shaking, had stared up at them imploringly.

Somehow, in an act of superhuman strength, Joe had wrestled the grate off and, not giving one single thought to his expensive jacket or pants, knelt down on the ground, reached down into that sewer and plucked the tiny kitten out.

He was a mess.

They'd never made it to the theatre. Joe had tucked the soaked kitten inside his jacket next to his heart, and they had run back to her and Bliss's place, dried the kitten and given it warm milk, and it had curled up on Joe's chest and gone to sleep, purring heavily.

It was the first night Joe had kissed her. *Really* kissed her. Not a polite good-night peck.

He was smiling, his smile so warm, so tender, with the same remembrance as her, that it made her unable to resist what she did next.

She stepped into him. She twined her arms around his neck. And under the banyan tree, she kissed him on the lips.

She didn't care if it was a mistake.

She didn't care if it made things complicated.

But in fact, it didn't feel complicated at all. It felt as if all the traffic noises faded. Everything faded, the crowds parted around them, waves parting on the sea. What could be simpler than a world of the two of them?

She drank in the familiar taste of his lips. She drank in his scent. She drank in the texture of him where their bodies touched.

For the first time since she had given him back his ring, the empty spot within her felt filled up. She felt complete.

She stepped back from him, savoring his taste on her lips, the stunned look on his face.

"Thank you," she said, "for saving my life. And Bartholomew's. And *that* counts as my touch."

"I thought you were going to be subtle," he croaked. And then quickly tried to recover himself. "You know what that calls for?" he asked.

"What?"

"Spending some more money."

"Don't you dare!"

"But there's shave ice right over there. You can't come to Hawaii and not have shave ice."

"I don't even know what shave ice is."

"Well, then, you're about to find out."

"Okay, but I'm paying for it!" As long as her credit card wasn't refused, that was.

Why be stubborn? If he paid for it, according to the rules of their game, she would get to touch him again.

Too dangerous.

Still, when he took her hand and tugged her across the street to the shave ice stand, she didn't even try to pull away. Somehow that—his hand in hers—felt as good as the kiss. It felt so right. It felt like homecoming. For the first time since their breakup, her world felt as if she had come into possession of a jar of peanut butter. It felt like maybe, just maybe, everything was going to be okay.

That feeling, of the whole world being right, only intensified as they sat on a bench thigh to thigh under the banyan tree, enjoying their unexpected treat.

"It's delicious," Blossom decided, licking her baseball-sized shave ice. "I don't think there could be a more perfect treat than this for a hot day."

Unless you counted that kiss. That had been more perfect than this.

"I thought you were never going to pick a flavor," Joe groused good-naturedly.

"Seventy to choose from!"

"And then you choose strawberry," he said. "Really?"

"Volcano Lava is not a flavor!"

"Apparently it is and a delicious one, too." She watched his tongue do a tantalizingly slow exploration of his orange-and-black shave ice. She suddenly felt like volcano lava, as if heat was moving through her whole body in a slow wave!

Well, two could play that game. She deliberately did something with her tongue that made him draw in a deep breath. Touching wasn't the only thing that could make the awareness between them flow red hot!

He gobbled down the rest of his shave ice without looking at her again. When they disposed of their paper cones, he put his hands in the pockets of those silly shorts. He distanced himself from the growing intimacy between them by acting like a tour guide again.

"The swimming section of the Ironman starts right here," Joe told her, pointing at a narrow band of sand on the left side of the Kona Pier. "The cruise ships anchor out there and run shuttles in."

Blossom ducked into a nearby change room, and felt both self-conscious of her bathing suit and pleased about it. She was pretty sure the minuscule black bikini—that Bliss had encouraged her to buy for her honeymoon—was going to make Joe realize the no-touchy rule was going to be pretty much unworkable between them, even if he had chosen not to hold her hand again after the shave ice.

Still, at the last moment, she couldn't be bold enough to just walk out there in that. She was shy enough to wrap a towel around herself until they got to the beach. Joe was waiting for her and they walked the few steps to the beach on the right side of the pier.

He didn't offer his hand, even when they came to the railing-free steps that led to the beach.

Apparently he'd had enough of playing with volcano lava for one day.

But then, for Blossom, the pure awareness of where they were crowded out even Joe's substantial presence.

She felt the sun on her face and a gentle breeze stir her hair. Was it possible it was this beautiful land that somehow stoked a sense of sensuality and awareness?

CHAPTER ELEVEN

"IT'S QUINTESSENTIAL HAWAII," Blossom breathed, taking in the outrigger canoes lined up in neat rows above the small crescent of umbrella-dotted, white sand, and the little grass hut that rented kayaks and paddle boards.

But all that was only a backdrop to a grass structure that sat on a peninsula of rock at the mouth of the tiny, sheltered bay they were on.

"What is that?" she asked, awed.

"It's a reproduction of King Kamehameha's personal Ahu'ena Heiau, or temple," Joe told her. "He lived out his final days in this bay."

Again, Blossom was impressed with his substantial knowledge of Hawaii, and how his familiarity was adding to her enjoyment, even if he was choosing, since that kiss, to hide behind the tour guide persona.

"It's a National Historic Landmark, actually."

It added to Blossom's sense of wonder and her growing appreciation of Hawaii, that she was going to learn something totally new—snorkeling—in the shadow of something so old and so obviously sacred.

They laid out towels, and then Joe sat and invited her, with a gesture, to do the same. He slipped off his shirt. She was pretty sure every female sunbather on the beach suddenly went on high alert.

He took out the spray bottle of sunscreen.

"Let me do your back."

She was very sorry she'd found the spray variety, because he was able to do her whole back without a single touch. After he'd finished doing her back, he did his own, reaching over his shoulders with the spray can all by himself.

Unfortunately, that particular stretch flexed the gorgeous muscles in his arms, broadened his chest and likely made every female on the beach go from high alert to red alert in the blink of an eye.

Unaware that he was causing quite a flutter among the female hearts on the beach—and Blossom's—Joe took their snorkels from the bag and did a manly struggle with the packaging.

"Does nobody get the irony that we can't get a plastic bag to carry this out of the store, but we can have all this to dispose of?" he said, holding up the now mutilated packaging that he had freed the snorkels from.

He handed her the pink one. "Just slip the goggles on over your head. You're going to have to stretch the band. They're tight."

She did as he asked, and the goggles snapped into place. Joe moved in close to her. "Let me adjust it a bit. It's too tight. That's what you get for buying the children's one."

She shouldn't have insisted on paying for the shave ice! Because if she had let him break that rule, then she would have another rule break available and she badly wanted one right now. The scent of him, of the sun in his hair, already turning it a lighter shade of gold, the nearness of his body to her own, was mesmerizing. It begged her to just take advantage of his closeness, to just lay her hand over his heart, rediscover the warmth of him, the silky texture of his skin.

She didn't want to admit it, but maybe his no-touch rule wasn't unworkable. She had to fight these temptations. Wanting to touch him—and badly—changed the whole feeling of the day, added an unexpected tension to it.

No, wait, that had happened when she had foolishly given in to the impulse to kiss him!

Meanwhile, Joe seemed totally unaware of the war going on in her.

"You want to tug all this hair out of the way, or the goggles won't seal properly. Now, this piece goes in your mouth, and you've got it!"

She stared out from behind her goggles, as he put his own on. He looked hilarious, like a cartoon bug. She must look the same. But for some reason, while she was pretty sure the snorkel made her less sexy, it wasn't having that effect on him.

In defense of not looking sexy, Blossom dropped the towel she had been clutching to her up until this point.

Even behind the goggles, she could see the green of his eyes turn very dark. He ran a hand through his hair, and she was pretty sure it wasn't so that the goggles would seal properly.

"Follow me," he said, put the snorkel in his mouth and waded into the water, the muscle in his thighs rippling. He turned and waved her forward.

Even with all that had passed between them, her heart sighed. Her heart said it would follow him anywhere. She did not come from the same world as him—which had probably involved swim lessons and swim team—so she was not a great swimmer. But it didn't feel as if it mattered.

In fact, even if this water had been infested with sharks, she had a feeling that if Joe would have said *Follow me*, she would have gone, trusting him to know the path through the danger.

The water felt extraordinarily sensual as she entered it, warm, lapping at her gently. Was it because her senses were heightened by awareness of him that she felt so wide-open?

"That's it," he said, his tone gentle and encouraging.

What was wrong with her? If this man wanted to change their marriage plans to a chicken coop on a farm, she should have just said yes!

"Come all the way in," he said persuasively. "Perfect. Just push yourself out, now, let go of the bottom. Lie flat, like a starfish. It's salt water, so you'll be very buoyant. You can just put your face down. Okay, now bring your arms in beside you. Just flutter kick your legs."

He rolled over and showed her.

She hesitated, feeling a reluctance to put her face in the water. But then she made a decision to give herself entirely to this experience.

Blossom was not sure she'd even known how cautiously she approached most things until that caution was gone.

She laid herself out on the water and found herself floating weightlessly. The goggles allowed her to see below the surface, and the snorkel allowed her to breathe, even if her breath suddenly had the hollow sound of a space creature testing air for the first time.

She gazed, astounded, into the depths of a watery world tinged with turquoise. It was astonishingly clear. The sun filtered through it. And then she saw her first fish!

She had never seen anything like it, ever. It was perhaps the size of her fist, boxlike in shape, navy blue on the bottom, its flat top black with white dots on it. The black section was rimmed in bright yellow.

If she had not had the snorkel clamped firmly in her mouth, she would have cried a delighted and astonished *oh* at this world that lay completely hidden right beneath the calm surface of the ocean.

A school of bright yellow fish darted underneath her. She realized that Joe was right beside her, they were moving deeper, shoulder to shoulder, his skin occasionally brushing hers, reassuring, connected.

He tapped her arm and pointed. "The state fish of Hawaii, a reef triggerfish."

He must have lifted his head out of the water and removed the snorkel to shout it at her loud enough that she could hear him even with her ears partially under the water. "It's called *humuhumunukunukuapua'a.*"

The word was a tongue twister, and his voice sounded as if he was gargling. She wanted to tell him not to make her laugh, but she would have had to remove the snorkel to do so. Instead she thumped his arm warningly. He laughed, but then surrendered his duties as narrator, and they just swam side by side, utterly engrossed in the incredible experience. Sometimes he would nudge her arm to point something out to her, and sometimes she would nudge his.

The fish came in the most amazing array of colors she had ever seen. In light blue and turquoise, in purple, in pink. Some had stripes. Some had polka dots. Some had neon lines. Some were tiny, and others were quite large.

She had no idea how much time had gone by. They made

several circuits of the small bay, but each time it looked different to her, and each time they saw entirely different fish.

Finally, she had to give in to the pleasant exhaustion that was making her limbs feel heavy, the faint sensation of cold that had begun to seep into her.

The warmth of the sun felt incredible as they lay side by side on their tummies on their towels on the beach.

Propped up on their elbows, they studied the plastic Hawaiian reef fish card they had purchased, their heads close together, pointing out the fish they had seen. Parrot fish. Trunk fish. Several varieties of tangs. Moorish idols. Butterfly fish.

Joe tried, several times, to teach her to say *humuhumunukunukuapua'a*, but each time it just ended up with both of them in gales of laughter.

Finally, pretending total exasperation, he gave up and laid his head on the towel, his arms splayed out from his shoulders on the sand.

He closed his eyes, and Blossom took in the sweep of his lashes, the beautiful curve of his back, the strong length of his legs.

It occurred to her she had only ever done one other thing that made her feel as exquisitely and fully alive as snorkeling did.

And that was making love to Joe.

They snorkeled again and again, until it was late in the afternoon.

"Let's just have dinner down here," Joe suggested to Blossom. "There's so many great seaside restaurants where you can watch the sunset."

Why was he doing this?

Playing with fire? Acting as if it was their honeymoon!

Without the benefits, he reminded himself sourly, *because of your own stupid rules.*

But the truth was, he just liked being with her. Blossom's wonder—her absolute delight in everything—felt like a reprieve from the life of abject loneliness he thought he had been sentenced to the day she had given him back his ring.

And now, of course, they had to contend with her stupid rule: no money. Which, he could tell just by the look on her face, she was going to bring up.

"There's a sandwich left!" she said.

"And there goes the perfect day," he muttered. "Could I at least buy some dry shorts to put on?"

She contemplated that. "If I get to pick them."

And so a few minutes later, they were settled on the wide ledge of the seawall, with what was left of the contents of the cooler for their supper. She had changed back into the cute sundress, and he was wearing a pair of bright blue shorts gaudily decorated with illustrations of nearly every fish they had seen today.

The sense of the perfect day didn't go away but deepened, as they split the sandwich, and not in a civilized way. She took a bite and then he took a bite, passing it back and forth until it was gone.

Until that very moment, Joe might have said peanut butter was one of his least favorite foods. But somehow, with her passing him the sandwich, and the sun going down, it tasted like ambrosia.

"Look," Blossom said, nodding to her left and right.

The whole world stopped when the sun went down in Hawaii. It was like a ceremony in reverence as every single person paused, gazing as the huge orb disappearing into clouds that rode the edge of the horizon. The sky turned pink and orange, and the clouds were briefly gilded in brilliant gold. The sun wallowed briefly behind them, and then seemed to plunge into the sea. In a matter of minutes, the world was plunged into darkness.

The tiki torches began to sputter to life all around them, and they packed up the remains of their picnic and put it back in the vehicle.

Then they strolled around downtown. Somehow, their hands found each other, and that increased his enjoyment of the music and laughter spilling out of the bars and restaurants on the *mauka* side of Ali'i Drive, and how the waves, silver-capped as the moon came up, sang the song of the sea on the *makai* side.

The air, soft, warm, salty, intensified the enchantment of Hawaii.

Finally, almost reluctantly, they made their way back to the vehicle. He had a parking ticket, which he swept quickly off the windshield before she noticed it and complained about spending money.

As they took the highway back toward Hale Alana, Joe contemplated how not one single thing about the day had gone as he had planned it. They had not made it to the Black Sands Beach, the volcano, or the gardens at Hilo.

Despite his no-touch rule, they had kissed. And held hands.

Despite her no-money rule, they had spent a little bit.

It was like the islands were mocking his efforts—both their efforts—to get things under control.

When they got back to Hale Alana, he forced himself to say a very circumspect good-night, with absolutely no touching!

Because if he touched her now, their worlds would ignite, and melt together, and he would take those lips that she had teased him with this afternoon. Once he gave in to that temptation, would they ever emerge for air again?

Doubtful. He reminded himself, sternly, of his mission. To discover what they had, beyond chemistry. And on a deeper level, to protect her.

What if his dad's disease was hereditary?

The next morning, he found her sitting out by the pool, drinking coffee. What was she wearing? It looked to be one of his T-shirts.

Her hair was still ruffled from sleep, and she looked really sexy in that shirt. He felt the sharp pang of memory of what it had been like waking up to her.

A man could be swamped by those kinds of memories. A man could lose all sight of his mission, his need to protect.

"You're up early," he said, joining her.

"Mynah birds. What's on our agenda for today?"

Our. Agenda.

With those big brown eyes fastened on him, he realized it was a chance to start again. They'd gotten off course yesterday, but he could do a correction today. He didn't want Blossom to miss some of the highlights of the island because he was finding her so distracting. He needed to summon his discipline. It had always been legendary.

How could it be fading in light of something as simple as Blossom in a T-shirt, even if it was his T-shirt.

She couldn't wear that T-shirt all day!

"I was thinking we could do the circle I had planned for yesterday. Black Sands Beach, Volcano National Park, the gardens at Hilo."

"That sounds amazing," she said.

"I'll look up the weather. To see how we should dress." He secretly hoped it was going to be really cold on the volcano and really rainy at Hilo so he could avoid an outfit more tempting than the T-shirt, like her other ten-dollar sundress.

He frowned at the phone.

"Bad weather?" she asked, disappointed.

"Uh, no, another glorious day in paradise."

"Then?"

"In Hawaii, the surf report comes up with the weather report. They're expecting really high surf on the west and north shores, starting tomorrow."

"I'm not following."

"Well, if we wanted to boogie board at Hapuna, today would probably be the day to do that."

"We can do the other things tomorrow."

Something in him surrendered. Maybe a life entirely out of one's control was not going to be as bad as he thought it was.

CHAPTER TWELVE

"SHOULD I PACK a cooler?" Blossom asked. She had gone and changed out of Joe's T-shirt. Which should have been a blessing! But naturally, she was wearing the new sundress. The yellow made him aware that her skin tone was changing, kissed by the Hawaiian sun, turning to an extraordinary shade of light gold.

He did not want to think of her skin in terms of anything kissing it.

This was how far a man could fall: jealous of the sun. It sounded like the name of a song.

"It's a fair distance from the parking lot to the beach at Hapuna," he told her, trying to focus on the issue at hand, which was whether or not they were going to pack a lunch. "We'll already have the boogie boards to carry."

She tapped her finger on her lip, drawing his attention to the fullness of it. Now, he had thought of kissing her twice in as many minutes! He was determined to exert his control, at least over this.

Joe had not seen the tapping-lips thing over the length

over of their entire engagement. Because she pretty much had gone along with him!

When he contemplated that, he realized surprisingly that he did not miss her being agreeable as much as he might have thought he would.

"There's a great food concession there," he said persuasively.

"Oh."

She did not look persuaded. He could sense her tipping away from him.

"Maybe we could have a small daily budget," he suggested, "just twenty bucks or so."

Furious tapping on her lip.

"You know," he elaborated, "so we're not chained to a cooler."

Filled with peanut butter sandwiches. On the beach. Ugh. If there was anything worse than a peanut butter sandwich, it was probably a sandy peanut butter sandwich.

Though in fairness, he had quite enjoyed their shared sandwich on the seawall last evening.

"Okay," Blossom finally said, moving her finger, blessedly, from her lip. "But I'll pay. Not you."

"I think it's my turn. You bought everything yesterday."

"Huh. We've had eleven months of your turn. I think it's my turn."

"I didn't realize it was such a burden for you," he said.

"It wasn't a burden. It was wonderful. Like a fairy tale. But life isn't a fairy tale."

There it was again. That insinuation that somehow what they had experienced during their engagement wasn't quite real.

Well, what would it hurt to do things her way? For a few days? Why not see what Blossom thought was real?

Hapuna Beach was exactly as Joe remembered it—simply breathtaking. The half-mile crescent of pure white sand was consistently ranked the best beach in the United States—and in the top ten beaches of the world.

Joe was actually glad life was a bit out of his control. If they had not had this change of plan, he might have missed seeing Blossom experiencing this place for the first time.

As he drank in her wonder, he felt like it was a life-giving nectar.

The waves were absolutely perfect—three-to-four-foot swells—for a novice boogie boarder. Though it was early, the water was already filled with people, young and old, enjoying the thrill of riding a wave into shore.

They placed their things on towels in the fine sand and Blossom wiggled out of the dress. What she had on underneath it was a thousand times more beguiling than the dress! A little white-and-yellow bikini that, if he didn't know better, he could have sworn had been purchased to match the dress.

It now seemed imperative to get into the water. Fast!

But there was the whole sunscreen thing they had to get through. He, congratulating himself on his wisdom, handed her the spray bottle to do her own…which was not so wise after all. Those contortions were delectable!

"The waves seem quite high," she said with a bit of trepidation, when the sunscreen ritual was finally, mercifully, finished.

"Don't worry. We'll stay shallow. See where those kids are playing? We'll go right there."

Joe showed Blossom how to strap the board lines to her ankle, and then holding the boards in front of them, they waded out into the crashing surf.

They were soaked in seconds from the foam exploding off the waves. She looked like a model for one of those swimsuit-edition sports magazines! When they were in up to their thighs, he turned around, putting his back to the ocean, his boogie board in front of him. He gestured for her to do the same.

"Look over your shoulder," he called to her. "When you see a good wave, grab it! Right on the break. There it is!"

He held his board out in front of him, felt the wave lifting him up and at exactly the right moment, threw himself onto the board. Out of the corner of his eye, he saw Blossom doing the same thing.

She was on her belly, leaning on her elbows, her fingertips in a death grip on the front of the board.

The white crest of the wave caught her and propelled her forward.

Her mouth formed a tiny O of astonishment at the speed of the wave. And then, she was in the shallow water, tumbling off the board, laughing and swallowing seawater.

He went and plucked her out of the sand before the next wave hit her and smacked the board into her.

She didn't seem to notice she was practically melted against him in that very scanty outfit.

"How can I have lived this long and missed out on this experience?" she asked him breathlessly. Her trepidation had completely melted away. And then with a squeal of delight, she was out of his arms in a flash, running back into the waves, waiting eagerly, in the line of children, for the next wave.

Joe just watched, intensely enjoying her enjoyment. She took a wave, but grabbed it just a bit too late, and it fizzled.

She caught the next one, and rode it all the way into the sand, where she was unceremoniously dumped.

She howled with laughter as he plucked her from the sand, rescuing her from getting pummeled by the incoming wave.

"Ah," he adjusted the strap on her bathing suit. "You're losing your top."

"I think my britches nearly got yanked off, too."

He gaped at her. And then she laughed. Her laughter was amazing.

And totally contagious.

In all the time they had been together, Joe was not sure he had seen this in her. A complete letting go. A surrender to joy.

He was suddenly aware that everyone seemed to be laughing. The children. Her. Him. They had entered the zone of pure happiness.

He ran back to where their stuff was on the beach and extracted his T-shirt for her.

"Sunburn," he said gruffly, handing it to her.

"Oh," she said, pulling it over her head, "who are you trying to kid? You're protecting me from wardrobe malfunctions."

Either way, he was protecting her, and it felt, dangerously, like the job he'd been born to do.

They went back out into the waves and waited, side by side, watching for just the right one. They played relentlessly, giving themselves over to being the biggest kids on the beach. Their bliss blended into the shrieks and laughter of the children around them. The whole experience—the waves, the sun, the sand—all seemed to shimmer with an uncanny light.

They gave themselves over, completely, to the ocean.

They played and played and played. His stomach actually hurt, not from the bruising activity, but from the laughter.

Finally, exhausted, legs rubbery from exertion, they exited the water. She looked as sexy in that sopping, clinging shirt as she had looked in just the bathing suit!

She stripped it off and threw herself on her towel, still panting with exertion. He lay down beside her.

The happiness continued to shimmer in the air between them as the warm air and sea breezes dried them.

"Let's get out of the sun for a bit. We'll go get something to eat," he suggested after a while. He slipped on his shirt and she pulled her sundress back over her head. Her wet bathing suit showed through it.

He was not sure Blossom had ever looked more beautiful: her hair soaked, her face sandy, her dress transparent, her feet bare. She looked like a creature of the sea, a mermaid who had been granted a day to be human.

They walked up the hill above the beach on a paved pathway. Somehow, she was holding his hand. Joe felt so light, so carefree, from what they had just experienced he wasn't even sure holding hands would qualify for the no-touch rule. Somehow, it just seemed as if it would be petty to mention it. Somehow it didn't seem like a day for rules. At all.

At the concession stand they ordered the famous fish tacos and then sat at a picnic table in the shade to eat them. Blossom said what he was thinking.

"I think I'm in heaven." She bit into her taco, drinking in the incredible view.

Joe, so magnificently male, was part of that view. Part of

the great sense of exhilaration unfurling in her like a sail catching the wind.

At first, she noticed that a noisy group of young girls and a few mothers had taken a table not far away, only on her periphery. But she focused more on them as their exuberance increased. The table they were at was festooned with balloons and the girls were wearing party hats. Her feeling of happiness was suddenly tempered with an odd wistfulness.

"Birthday party," Joe said, following her gaze. "Do you think this would be the best place ever to have a party?"

The perfection of the day was suddenly marred. She had thought they would have children, someday. Stockings on the fireplace at Christmastime. Birthday parties. A dog.

A *normal* life.

"What was your best birthday party?" Blossom asked.

"Hard to pick just one. I remember being really young and going through a pirate phase. My mom had a themed birthday party for me. There was a couple of pirates there who had a sword fight. There was a cake shaped like a treasure chest, spilling gummy candies out of it.

"When I was ten, the folks rented a whole paintball place for the party. Fourteen ten-year-olds trying to murder each other. You would think it doesn't get any better than that, but the next year my dad got us tickets for the World Series."

Was that what his father had seen in her when he'd said *"I know what you're up to"*?

That she was the girl desperate to belong to a world where someone had trouble picking their favorite birthday party out of their memory box?

"Your birthdays must have been different?"

She started. How did he know?

"Sharing it with a twin?"

"Oh, that wasn't the only way they were different."

"What do you mean?"

Blossom said, "I don't remember a best one. Maybe a most memorable one."

"Okay, tell me about that one."

She considered this. She thought of how she had given him carefully edited versions of her life, making growing up with an eccentric mother seem as if it had been only fun, an endless adventure in unpredictability.

"I know what you're up to."

As if Joe's father knew she was an imposter. As if he was aware that there were things she had deliberately not said, and that she was just trying to use his family to improve her position in life. As if he thought she could never quite belong.

If this was going anywhere—their faux honeymoon—maybe it was time for a little more honesty.

Was it going anywhere? For as lovely as Joe was being, this man who had almost been her husband, protective and attentive, he certainly had not indicated there was a future for them beyond these few days.

"Bliss and I were turning seven," Blossom said slowly, her eyes on those carefree girls at the table next to them. "We were living in the Okanagan Valley. My mom had gotten a job painting sets for a theatre company run by hippies. We were new in town, as always, and she promised us a birthday party that would make everyone want to be friends with us. She promised us ponies at the party.

"We even advertised them on the birthday invitations. Everybody in our whole class came. That was a first.

"And then the pony lady showed up. She rattled up in a rusted trailer that looked like the wheels were going to fall off. She had eight ponies, but she was drunk before they were all saddled. And then the ponies revolted and all got away. While she threw beer bottles at them and cursed, the ponies dodged her, drank out of the wading pool and ate the birthday cake.

"One of the ponies—a little black one with a white mane and tail—knocked over a snooty girl named Beth-Anne. She had mud all over her dress."

She snuck him a look. She'd kept her tone light, as if it had all been quite hilarious.

But Joe did not look the least bit fooled. "Aw, Blossom, I'm sorry. I really am."

She smiled shakily. "You know what's funny?"

His look told her there was nothing funny about what she had just told him.

"You know how close Bliss and I are?" she pressed on.

"Of course. You finish each other's sentences. You scrunch up your noses the same. You dress the same."

She considered telling him she hadn't dressed the same as Bliss before she'd met him and Bliss had appointed herself the fashion police, but one confession at a time seemed like more than enough.

"I mean, we are different in some ways. Bliss is way more extroverted than I am. Although usually we're so much on the same wavelength that we have the same dreams at night. But you know what Bliss says when that party comes up?"

"What?"

"'*Best birthday party ever.*' She's particularly gleeful about Beth-Anne and her frilly party dress."

"And you?" he asked quietly.

"Definitely not the best birthday party ever. Not even close. What I remember is that, after that, Beth-Anne slid us looks and the other kids in the class seemed standoffish. I usually wasn't glad when my mother announced another move, but I was that time."

"I'm really sorry," he said again. As if he meant it. It didn't seem as if he pitied her. The look in his green eyes was purely empathetic.

And yet she felt that familiar need to minimize.

"Life with Mom," she said lightly, making a concerted effort to drag her eyes away from that oh-so-normal birth-day party. "Always unpredictable. However, it gave me a lot of tools for dealing with the unexpected."

She could tell Joe didn't fall for her light tone, or her dec-laration of lessons-learned. He looked pensive. He didn't say a single word. But when he covered her hand with his own, there was no pity in the small gesture.

In fact, what was in that gesture, and in his eyes when he looked at her, was the greatest gift of all.

Acceptance.

The gift she had never been able to totally give herself.

It occurred to her she had done Joe a disservice by not trusting him earlier with some of the details of her life. She'd done a disservice to him, and to herself, as well.

Because this moment with Joe, his hand on top of hers, felt like one of the most intimate they had ever shared.

CHAPTER THIRTEEN

THAT MOMENT OF Blossom telling Joe about her seventh birthday party—and his reaction to it—gave her courage.

Not just to tackle waves and a possibly shark-infested ocean, and all manner of things unknown, but to reveal herself. To be herself in ways she had not allowed herself to be before.

"Hey," he said that night, after they had returned from Hapuna, exhausted and exhilarated. "I have another beach I want to show you."

"I can't ride one more wave. Okay. Maybe one."

"This is a different kind of beach. I thought we could get supper down there. There's a couple of restaurants nearby."

"We already bought food today."

"Yeah, but we're under our twenty-dollar budget."

"*Your* twenty-dollar budget."

"You're splitting hairs."

"We're only six dollars under."

"I'll buy us supper. Something simple. I promise."

"No," Blossom said firmly. "It's a slippery slope. It starts with something simple, and then we're dining on lobster tails, with white linen, candles and a bottle of wine that costs more than I make in a year."

"One can only hope," he said, and then, "I didn't realize that was such a hardship for you."

She didn't know how to explain to him that it was not that it was a hardship to be wined and dined and treated like a princess. But in the last little while, she'd become very aware that all of that got in the way of *this*.

An intense kind of togetherness.

"Can we just try it my way?" she asked.

"If we must," he said, pretending to grouse, but looking pretty indulgent.

"You know what? When you were pulling the boogie boards out of the shed, I think I saw a little barbecue in there."

"I love it," he said. "Barbecued steaks on the beach. Maybe lobster?"

"We're having steaks, all right," she promised him. "But with a twist. My way."

They found the barbecue and some propane, packed it into the vehicle. She made him stop at a mom-and-pop grocery store she had seen earlier.

"No, you stay here," she said. "I'm surprising you."

She came out of the store a few minutes later, with a bag full of goodies and a thankful heart. For some reason, her credit card was still working.

"I don't think you got steaks in that store," he said, sending her a sideways look.

"Define steak."

He gave her a look. "Define steak? That's kind of like saying define dog. It just is."

"No, it isn't. There are lots of different kind of dogs."

This kind of discussion was new for them. Blossom was increasingly aware she'd always just gone along with him. She was finding she *liked* sparring. She *liked* expressing her own ideas. She *liked* not always acquiescing, not always being pleasing, not always being agreeable.

"You're going to love this beach," he said. Joe didn't seem to mind her sparring with him at all. "The locals call it the Sixty-Nine."

She would not give him the satisfaction of blushing. "They do not!"

"They do." He wagged his eyebrows at her.

"You have a dirty mind."

"No," he said, "*you* have a dirty mind. Look over there."

"I don't see anything."

He was turning off the highway.

"Look at the mile marker."

She burst out laughing. The mile marker they turned at read 69.

"The actual name of the beach is Waialea. It's only just a few minutes from Hapuna, but it's totally different."

They got out at the parking area. Joe carried the barbecue down and Blossom carried the grocery bag. She stopped as they arrived at the beach.

Given its close proximity to Hapuna, it might have been in a different world. The bay was sheltered, so the waves were gentle, not powerful and white-capped and frothy as they had been at Hapuna. A large rock rose out of the center of the bay. Huge trees lined the edges of the fine sand beach.

But what was most different was the energy. Hapuna generated the same kind of energy as the waves that landed there.

Waialea was quiet, but not just because there were fewer people. It offered calm, respite from activity, a place to rest.

"I think this may be the most beautiful beach I've ever seen," Blossom breathed. She glanced at Joe's face.

He was so happy to show this to her, like a gift.

He set up the barbecue and lit it while she emptied the bag.

"Where are the steaks?" he asked, coming over and peering over her shoulder. "Blossom! Those look suspiciously like hot dogs."

"Don't say it like that!"

"Like what?"

"Like a snob! When we were growing up, we called them tube steaks. They were a mainstay in our house."

"Kind of like peanut butter?"

Again, she took that opportunity to reveal something of herself. "Hot dogs were more of a treat than peanut butter. I still love them."

This, she realized, as they sat side by side munching their hot dogs as the sun went down, was exactly what they had missed.

They'd had a whirlwind romance. Joe had treated her to the best of everything. He had given her entry to a world she had only dreamed existed. She had been swept off her feet.

But except for that one time camping, and maybe the evening that they had found Bartholomew, it suddenly felt as if there had not been nearly enough of *this*.

Just simple moments. Ordinary, and yet beyond ordinary. A blanket in the sand. A charred hot dog. Low music playing on Joe's cell phone. The last rays of the day's sun on their faces. The mynah birds singing out the day.

All of it raised up, somehow, with togetherness. With connection. With banter. With stories exchanged.

The next few days were crammed with new things and discoveries. She saw huge turtles resting in the charcoal-colored sand of Punalu'u; she saw and smelled steam vents in Volcano National Park; she walked in Nahuku, a five-hundred-year-old lava tube. She saw Kilauea's lava lake filling the crater, Halema'uma'u.

Everything was so new and exciting. Everything vibrated with a light. Because Joe was at her side.

But her favorite moments remained the quiet ones, where nothing appeared to be happening and everything that was life hummed just below the surface of that nothingness.

They spent every evening now at Waialea. They made it *their* thing to take dinner to the beach and watch the sun go down.

They watched children reluctant to get out of the water as their mothers packed up their things, they watched locals come down for an evening swim, they watched young men tossing a Frisbee as the day died behind them, they watched young couples stroll the beach, hand in hand.

It felt to Blossom as if everything was deepening between her and Joe, intensifying, just as the sunset deepened and intensified everything around it for that brief moment in time.

That intensity was in the way they enjoyed each other. In how the conversations were so easy. But that intensity also lived in the deep and comfortable silences. It was in the laughter they shared. It was in Blossom recognizing Joe had so many strengths completely unrelated to the fact he was wealthy.

Her sense of coming into herself just continued to deepen.

Whereas she had always held a part of herself back from Joe, always been *on* in some way, trying to win him, trying to be what Bliss had created instead of who and what she really was, now she felt herself relaxing.

Revealing who she really was.

She realized she had done them both a disservice by thinking she was not equal to him, that somehow she had to be forever grateful that a man like him could ever see anything in a girl like her.

She had brought those insecurities to the table, not him.

So, now they ate hot dogs—food of her childhood—at the beach. They were in the water so often she stopped wearing makeup altogether.

She lovingly wore one of her ten-dollar dresses every day, while the other dried from being washed in her bathroom sink the night before.

Joe seemed more relaxed, too.

He put his phone away. He didn't take calls or answer emails. He didn't seem quite so driven—as if he was managing to squeeze time together into his busy schedule.

"You know who was happy about the wedding being canceled?" she asked him one evening as they sat in the splendor of the setting sun in what had become their favorite place on Waialea.

He sighed. He looked at his watch. "We have four more days before we need to talk about the past. But don't say it was me who was happy about it, because it wasn't."

She could see how wise it was to have postponed this discussion. Because as soon as he said that, the hurt part of her wanted to say, *Why didn't you fight harder, then?*

Instead, Blossom said, "I wasn't going to say you."

"Who, then?" he asked with genuine surprise.

So, he didn't know his father had his doubts about her.

But it wasn't his father who came to mind.

"My mom," she said.

"That's not possible," Joe scoffed. "Sahara loves me."

"Her real name is Sheila."

"Your mom has a real name?"

"Yes, the only person you will ever meet with an 'also known as' who does not have a criminal record. Or at least not one I know of."

Again, there was a sense of stripping away the pretense around her family.

This is who we really are. What do you think?

"She gave herself a name that she thought suited her better."

"Interesting. It doesn't really suit her at all. I mean it's exotic sounding, but the Sahara is a desert, and your mom is lively and full of life."

"She is that," Blossom said. "Some people would say kooky."

"Kooky in a cookie-cutter world. I've always loved that about her."

It felt as if he had passed a test Blossom was not aware she was giving. He *liked* her mom, kookiness and all.

"Well, my kooky mother was happy the wedding was called off, not because of you. She adores you. Which should give any sane person pause."

He laughed.

"Maybe *happy* is the wrong word, but there's nothing my mom loves more than an unexpected change of plans."

"That's pretty much the opposite of you."

"Mom didn't like the wedding. She looked at everything about it with increasing horror. I thought she'd be over the moon with excitement, overjoyed for me, but nope. The wedding plans seemed to cause her hand-wringing moments of aggravation.

"She actually hasn't ever expressed approval for any of the Blossoms and Bliss weddings, so far, even though she'll offer up her artistic skills in a pinch."

"Your mom isn't proud of you?" he asked with such genuine indignation Blossom wanted to kiss him. "That's just wrong. What is she thinking?"

"She thinks it's all too extravagant. She likes to remind us we weren't raised that way."

In fact, their mother was so lost in her artsy world she had barely raised them at all.

"The truth is, Bliss and I raised each other," Blossom confided in Joe, "living in that *twin* world of shared thoughts and dreams. We read each other fairy tales, built castles out of blankets and became the princesses in our own made-up worlds."

The truth was she and Bliss had longed for every value their fiercely single mother had eschewed: stability, family, home, romance and glamour.

Blossom had found them all with Joe.

She had almost become Mrs. Blackwell.

Before she had thrown it all away.

And yet, now it felt as though she were getting a second chance, and this time she was being given an opportunity to build a foundation based in honesty.

In who she authentically was.

But could Joe still possibly love her?

Over the last few days, it felt as if he could. The future was shimmering with possibility again.

She was endlessly trying to quell that part of her, but it

felt like a bird beating its wings against a cage, wanting out, wanting to be free.

That part of her was hope. She could feel herself, ever so tentatively, opening the cage door.

And despite so much evidence in her life of how wrong things could go, it felt as if setting hope free made her braver than she had ever been.

"You know what?" Joe said as they finished another sunset supper at Waialea and packed away the remains of cold cuts and buns. "We need to book that night snorkel with manta rays if we're going to make that happen before we go."

Before we go.

That reminder that their time together in paradise was nearly done.

Of all the vouchers they had been given, that one made Blossom the most nervous. Getting in the ocean at night to swim with gigantic rays?

Any sensible person would say no.

But the brave person said yes.

He picked up his phone, which had been playing music, and looked up the excursion. "It's done," he said, pressing a button. "Tomorrow night. No going back now."

No going back now.

His phone returned to playing music. Recognition tickled along her spine.

"That just randomly appeared?" she asked him.

"It did."

It was a sign, she thought. *Their song.*

He pushed the volume button and the haunting opening notes of "Hunger" filled the air. The beach was nearly dark now and had emptied out. But it wouldn't have mattered if they were in a stadium with twenty thousand people looking on, she still would have said *yes* when he asked her to dance.

The distinctive voice of KaJee, the singer, swept across the beach and through her heart.

One of Joe's hands found its way to hers, and the other found the small of her back. Blossom felt the very same way she had felt when he had asked her to dance at the Lee wedding all those months ago.

As if she had been sleeping, and he would show her what it was to be awake.

As if she had been thirsty, and he would help her find her way to water and a long, cool drink.

As if she had been hungry, and he alone knew the way to a banquet hall rich with the kind of delights she had never even imagined.

They danced slowly, sinking into sand that still held the warmth of the day in their bare feet. They swayed together as if they were the only two people in the world.

They danced as if nothing had ever gone wrong between them.

They danced lost in the sensations of their closeness, the look in each other's eyes.

Blossom was aware, even as her focus on Joe was intense, she was hearing the song in a different way.

It was a musically complex song that required KaJee to use his complete range of vocals. The lyrics were unabashedly sexual. It was a song about need. About passion. About longing. About the fire that could ignite unexpectedly between two people.

But for the first time, Blossom was aware the song was unfolding on several different levels at once.

It seemed it was about physical intimacy, but dancing with Joe on the beach, she heard another layer.

The song was about a longing for connection, not just a physical one, but also a soul connection.

Maybe she was hearing it in a different way because she was a different person than she had been just a short few days ago.

He held her long after the last notes of the song faded, until the only sound on the beach was the sound of the waves and their breathing.

And then he dropped his mouth over hers and kissed her. Maybe because she was such a different person than she had been, it felt like it was the first time his lips were claiming hers.

It was exhilarating, and also the most natural thing in the world.

It felt physical, but the other connection was there, too.

It was literally breathtaking, as if he was taking the breath from her mouth. As she melted into him, Blossom had the sensation of melting into everything.

She and Joe and the world—sand beneath their feet, lapping waves, crying birds, the leathery whisper of the breeze in the palm fronds, the incredible light—all became one.

It was completely dark when he lifted his lips from hers. He traced them with his thumb and a sigh escaped him.

"Sorry," he said.

"Sorry?"

"Because I made a vow that we would see how it went for just a little while—a few days—without *this* changing everything, altering everything, becoming everything."

And then he stepped back from her, ran a hand through

his hair and said, "It crowds out every other thing. That makes it so I can't think straight."

She wanted Joe with an ache so deep she did not feel as if she could survive without his touch, his lips, culmination.

"Joe," he said to himself, his tone wry, "you only had one mission. And you have failed."

He saw kissing her as a failure of his strength?

In this moment, love and hate warred within her. Because she actually hated him for having the discipline she did not possess.

He gathered up their things and headed off the beach. Back at Hale Alana, he said a crisp good-night to her.

It wasn't until she was lying in bed that Blossom recognized her final disservice to Joe and to herself.

Because she had never been completely authentic with him, she had not recognized her power.

But she recognized it now. She chuckled to herself, and said out loud, "Oh, Joe, you are in for a very rough day tomorrow."

That particular force, what they had felt while they danced when their lips had met, did not want to be put back in the box.

And Blossom was suddenly as intent on letting it out as he was on keeping it in!

"What's on the agenda today?" she asked him the next morning, plunking herself down at the kitchen table. She was wearing only a T-shirt as she sipped her coffee. He wouldn't look at her.

"I thought we'd go up Mauna Kea. It's a dormant volcano and the world's largest astronomical observatory is up there."

That sounded perfectly dull. She saw Joe was retreating to the safety of being her Hawaiian tour guide.

She looked at him over the rim of her coffee cup. She stretched a leg and smiled to herself when she caught him sneaking a peek.

"You'll have to dress warmly," he said gruffly. "It can be really cold up there."

Aha! There was the Mauna Kea motivation! Keep them both dressed! But coming into her power gave Blossom the loveliest realization that she did not need to wear a bikini to be sexy.

And so she spent a delightful time tormenting him and teasing him, exploring what it meant to be a woman in ways she had not done before.

Flirting came naturally to other people.

Her sister had been born knowing how to use a glance, a provocative gnaw on her own lip, a hand on the hip, to send a message that she knew she had power and that she was not afraid to use it.

Blossom, for the first time in her life, was looking forward to practicing the age-old art of being a woman.

Letting out her new self—temptress!

It was cold at the visitor center—the first time Blossom had been cold since arriving in Hawaii. She used it as an excuse to tuck herself into Joe and wrap her arms around his waist.

Underneath his jacket, she could feel the hard beating of his heart.

"I know a way to warm up," she murmured, looking at his lips.

The look he returned to her was scorching. But then he

moved away from her, determined, apparently to adhere to his no-touch rule.

"So do I!" And he broke away from her and did jumping jacks. It was really a measure of his desperation that the normally dignified Joe was doing jumping jacks!

"I was thinking more of the hot tub. When we get back to Hale Alana."

He frowned. He looked at his watch. "We won't have time," he decided. "Before the manta rays."

After that, Blossom took advantage of every opportunity to draw his attention to her lips, and her hips. Just like she didn't have to wear a bikini to be sexy, she realized *not* touching him was building the tension between them. She found that tension delightful.

She played word games, pretending innocence when some of what she said had double meanings.

She knew Joe had always adored her hair, and so she played with it unabashedly, running her hands through it, tossing it over her shoulder, gathering it up and twisting it into a rope that she stroked.

When they finally came down the mountain, he asked if she had packed a lunch.

"Not today. You can buy me lunch. There's supposed to be a really good restaurant in Waimea."

He mulled that over silently. "What about the money rule?" he asked.

"Rules are meant to be broken." She didn't have to say that meant she fully intended to break his rules, too.

"I know what you're up to," he said.

And the wind went out of her sails, a bit. Why had he chosen the exact words his father had said to her?

The tiniest bit of doubt crept into her. Was she being manipulative to get what she wanted?

As it turned out, Joe made sure there was no time for the hot tub. After the Mauna Kea visit, they had a quick lunch—he didn't even offer to buy, so she had to hold her breath to see if her credit card would go through—and then he insisted on a tour of a coffee farm.

By the time they returned to Hale Alana they were pushing it to be on time for the manta ray swim.

Still, Joe was doing such a good job of resisting her that she decided it was time to haul out her teensiest bikini.

Joe actually looked smug when at the dock on Keauhou Bay, a crew member from the manta ray swim charter gave them both wetsuit shirts to zip on!

As he zipped his up it molded to him, from the broad sweep of his shoulders to the washboard perfection of his abs.

"It looks good on you," she told him throatily. How many days had they been together now, so much of it half-clad, as they went in and out of the ocean. She felt as if she could just never get enough of looking at him, and it felt wonderful to not be scared to let him know.

With a certain reluctance, he took her in.

"It looks good on you, too," he admitted, huskily.

It felt as if he had given a bit of ground.

She realized suddenly that she was really nervous. Because he'd given ground?

"I feel as if I can barely breathe," she confided in Joe.

But whether it was because of their upcoming swim with manta rays or because of that delicious tension between them—the silent scream for fulfillment—she was not sure.

He looked at her, deep into her eyes, for what felt like the first time today.

"Now you know how I've been feeling all day," he admitted.

CHAPTER FOURTEEN

"WHAT HAPPENED TO that woman who was afraid of sharks?"

Did Joe say that with a certain longing?

It was a legitimate question, Blossom thought. The truth was she did not feel anything like the woman who had arrived on Hawaii: defeated, hopeless, afraid.

She was now the antithesis of all those things. She had never embraced life as fully as she had over the last few days. And today, it felt as if she had entered a whole new level of boldness.

This was what she realized: the more she embraced life—the more she hoped—the more fearless she seemed to become.

And with that fearlessness came a sense of being alive.

That courage was flowing in her veins now. Here she was, Blossom DuPont, getting ready to go night snorkeling with manta rays.

Here she was, Blossom DuPont, sharing Hawaii with the man she—

"Mr. and Mrs. Blackwell?"

She started at being called that. Joe shot her a dark look that said, *Do not play with this.*

Of course, then she couldn't resist playing with it! Plus, it helped her with her nerves.

"That's us," she said, taking Joe's hand and leaning into him. "Newlyweds. This is our honeymoon, actually."

Joe broke away from her, shot her a warning look and stepped forward, his hand extended. "I'm Joe. This is Blossom."

Obviously wanting to avoid being called Mr. and Mrs. Blackwell again!

"I'm Gary, your captain tonight. I saw from the info card this private charter was a wedding gift. Are you enjoying your Hawaiian honeymoon?"

"Absolutely," Blossom said, and then mischievously, "What do you think, honey? Are you pleased with the honeymoon?"

He squinted at her. She should have taken that as a warning that she was playing a dangerous game.

But the new her seemed to enjoy flirting of all kinds, even with danger.

"The honeymoon has been completely unexpected," Joe said, watching her narrowly.

"Well, this is going to be the best part," Captain Gary told them, and then looked back and forth between them, embarrassed.

"Maybe not the *best* part," Joe said. "Right, *honey*?"

Blossom felt her cheeks catch fire. Well, she'd been playing with this all day. It was exciting that he was firing back.

She touched his arm, ran her fingers possessively over the muscle encased in that wet suit fabric. It was surprisingly erotic. "Right," she said.

Instead of backing away, he took her hand, kissed the fingertips, lingering. His gaze rested on her.

And there was no pretense in it. None at all.

He was warning her he was all done backing away. Blossom had been warned all her life about playing with fire. What no one ever told you was how completely exhilarating it was.

Captain Gary introduced them to the crew, went over a few safety rules and then they boarded the boat.

Captain Gary handed them snorkels.

"Oh, what do you know?" Joe said dryly, looking at his. "Real snorkels, not toys."

The sun set around them, absolutely stunning, as the boat headed out into ink-dark waters.

She shivered, and Joe, the perfect Mr. Blackwell, put his arm around her shoulder. It felt as if it belonged there. It felt, for a suspended moment, as if they really were Mr. and Mrs. Blackwell.

It didn't feel like a charade they were playing out for the captain and crew. It felt *real*. It was just one more perfect moment to add to her collection of perfect Hawaii moments.

And then what?

They had not once discussed what the future held.

And she was not, Blossom told herself with determination, going to ruin this moment by thinking of it now.

The boat cut its engine only a few minutes out of the bay. As always in the tropics, darkness had fallen with astonishing abruptness. The stars winked on above them. The lights of a hotel, sitting on a cliff not far away, twinkled in the water below it.

A crew member, Sara, went down a ladder and got into

the water. Joe adjusted his snorkel and followed. Blossom hesitated on top of the ladder.

The water was as dark as ebony. For a moment, it felt as if her new boldness was going to flee her.

Who did she think she was? The *real* Blossom DuPont would never jump into a dark ocean at night. The *real* Blossom DuPont would never want to swim with fish that could weigh a thousand pounds or more!

A thousand pounds! Blossom thought. *That was—*

"Hey, Mrs. Blackwell! Jump," Joe called to her, the lights from the boat illuminating him against the darkness of the ocean.

His look was completely unguarded, and he was looking at her as if he believed she could do anything. He held out his arms, and she pulled on the snorkel and went off the ladder. The water closed around her, and for a moment she felt primal terror.

But then Joe found her, and his arms closed around her, and through those crazy goggles, she could see the deep green of his eyes.

Blossom saw her real self reflected there. Her best self. She realized, astounded, she was in the ocean at night, about to swim with fish approximately the size of baby elephants, and she felt safe.

The lights on the boat turned off. Though the running lights remained on, the sensation of darkness was complete.

She, who had never felt truly safe in her whole life, felt safe in the black, shockingly cold waters of the ocean on a charcoal-dark night.

Because Joe's arms were around her. Because his eyes were taking her in so deeply, as if he could see straight to her soul. As if he saw the real her, and always had.

"So, nothing to it," Sara, the crew member, said. "Just follow me."

Her voice actually startled Blossom, because she had felt so totally alone with Joe, as if this whole watery world was just him and her.

They swam together holding hands, as Sara guided them a few yards from the boat to where a large flotation device—probably eight feet long and two feet wide—awaited them.

"Just lie flat on the water and look down through your goggles," Sara said.

Joe was right about the snorkel. The quality of it was evident. Blossom was thankful she was now quite familiar with snorkeling, and that she wasn't just learning it at this very moment. She was thankful for Joe at her side, making every experience an experiment in boldness.

"Hold on to this rung around the board. I'm going to turn on the lights now. The lights illuminate the plankton, which the rays eat," Sara explained. "It's against the law for you to deliberately touch a ray, but don't be alarmed if they touch you. There's no stinger in their tail. They're very gentle and very sensitive. They can actually feel the vibration from the beat of your heart."

When Sara said that, Blossom became aware of the beat of her heart, and was also electrically aware of her shoulder touching Joe's through the fabric of the wetsuits.

Was she imagining things, or could she feel the beat of his heart, too?

Strong and steady like him, something you could rely on in an uncertain world. She could definitely feel faint warmth coming off him, which she was grateful for, because even with the wetsuit top, she could feel how much colder the water felt at night.

Sara turned the lights on the board, and suddenly the inky ocean was illuminated below them. Joe let go of the board for a moment and gave Blossom a thumbs-up below the surface of the water, before grasping the rung again.

There was an incredible amount of plankton in the water, invisible to the eye during the day. Now Blossom could see hundreds of thousands of tiny dots floating upward, illuminated by the light. It felt as if they had been dropped inside a giant snow globe.

To her grave disappointment, nothing happened.

But then, Joe nudged her shoulder with his own, released one hand and pointed to the dark depths below them. Holding her breath, she looked where he indicated and spied a shadow emerging just out of range of the lights.

Suddenly she didn't know if the thrumming through her veins was excitement or terror. She was so glad Joe was beside her, a solid presence.

The shadow took form as it moved into the orb of light. It was a manta ray, and it was absolutely huge.

It came straight up toward them. Blossom could not believe the size of what she was seeing! Knowing something weighed a thousand pounds, or more, and actually seeing that—sharing the water with that—were two entirely different things!

The old Blossom might have panicked. But the new Blossom drew in a deep breath through her snorkel, let go of the board for a minute, found Joe's hand and squeezed.

The ray, diamond-shaped, was easily twelve feet long, and its winglike fins were even larger. As it effortlessly closed the distance between them, its huge mouth was open, so they could see inside it to the marvel of its gills as it scooped up plankton.

A sense filled Blossom like nothing she had ever quite felt before.

To be this close to this magnificent creature of the sea left her feeling raw and awed.

The manta ray surged up in an impossibly graceful motion, until it was mere inches from Blossom and Joe. When it seemed it would collide with the board, or them, it arced leisurely backward, turned its large, spotted white belly up to the board, performed a slow-motion somersault that completed the circle that took it back into the depths, where it once again became invisible.

But then another manta ray, even larger than the first, appeared, soaring toward them. Up, up, up, belly turn, and back down.

And after that one, two manta rays came up together in an amazing ballet, white bellies nearly touching and then gently parting in opposite directions, each move perfectly choreographed, perfectly synchronized.

Another pair came from the bottom, rising toward Blossom and Joe. This time, as they came by her and Joe, Blossom felt the nudge of one of the huge fish.

That brief bump felt like a blessing.

Ray after ray after ray came, performing an impossibly delicate dance for creatures so gigantic. They were completely soundless. Sometimes they came as singles and sometimes in pairs. They would come out of the darkness, far, far below the board, rise to the light, parting, complete the circle and come again.

The cold seeped into her. Blossom had never had an experience like this. She was incredibly cold and her hands stretched out over her head holding the board ached unbearably. And yet she was nearly delirious with joy at the same time.

She had a sense of being extraordinarily privileged to witness these gentle giants doing their ancient dance.

Finally, Sara switched off the light. Blossom's limbs were so cold they felt heavy. Joe had to push her from behind to get her up the ladder and back onto the boat. Blossom was shaking uncontrollably. The wetsuit shirt must have offered some protection, but even with it she was cold to her core.

Joe was right behind her. Oblivious to his own discomfort, he helped her peel off the wetsuit shirt.

"I'm as frozen as I've ever been," she said through chattering teeth, "and I'm Canadian! We're supposed to be used to the cold."

"I should have asked them to get us in sooner," Joe said regretfully. He toweled her hair tenderly, then wrapped the towel around her and rubbed hard. He looked around, found his hoodie and dropped it over her head.

"No," she said, still shivering. "I wouldn't have wanted it to end sooner. I've never felt that way before—so cold I was thinking, *please be over*, and so enthralled I was thinking, *please never end*, at the same time. It was the best thing I've ever experienced, ever." She paused, looked at him deeply. "Second best."

"That was so awesome," Sara said. "I've never, in all the time I've been doing this, had so many manta rays show up so continuously."

She beamed at Blossom and Joe. "Remember I said they can feel your heartbeats? You two must have incredible energy. Love is in the air!"

Blossom shot Joe a look to see his reaction to that.

He still had his wetsuit shirt on. He didn't react at all, focused on a hot mug of tea the captain had waiting. He passed it to Blossom.

He made sure she was looked after before he looked after himself. Only after she was sipping her tea did he peel off his own wetsuit.

And that was love, wasn't it? This simple, selfless force that showed itself in the most mundane things.

Passing your beloved a cup of tea.

Beloved.

Looking at him, his skin pebbled, his hair dripping water down his skin, Blossom was filled with a sense of knowing as she mulled over that word.

Beloved.

A truth, startling and ancient, rose up out of the darkness toward the light, just as those manta rays had.

The manta rays who *knew.*

Who could tell from the beat of your heart.

Of course, Blossom realized, she had always known. From the moment she had first met Joe, from the moment his hand had closed around hers and they had danced to "Hunger," her eyes looking into his, she had known.

Meant to be.

That feeling of knowing him had only grown as the months of their courtship went by, when she had said an exuberant yes to Joe's proposal.

She loved this man. She had never stopped and she would never stop. She didn't love him because he had money and could make her feel safe and secure forever.

She loved him because he was a man who would get down in the gutter to rescue a cat. She loved him because he was rock-steady, innately stable, in a world that could be anything but.

It wasn't Hawaii that was making her feel more alive, more bold, on fire with curiosity and a sense of discovery, though of course Hawaii was the most amazing backdrop for what she was experiencing.

Love.

Love made more exquisite by the fact it had nearly been lost.

Even with the roof up on the four-wheel drive vehicle, it seemed it was not made to hold the warmth that blasted out of the heater. She was still wearing Joe's hoodie, but her bathing suit was clammy against her skin, and she could not get warm on the way home. Her teeth continued to chatter. From the cold? From the enormity of what was singing inside her?

Or from some combination of both?

I love him. I love him. I love him.

And so, when they arrived at Hale Alana, it seemed like the most natural thing in the world when he came around to her side of the vehicle and lifted her out. Her arms twined around his neck as he scooped her up, with easy strength, into his arms.

She snuggled into his warmth. How could he be so warm?

On fire, almost.

He walked to the front door, juggled her weight easily, put in the code and carried her across the threshold.

She drew in her breath.

This was how it was supposed to have been. This was how it would have been if they had arrived here on their honeymoon.

What kind of miracle was it that time had rewound, and

that they were being given a chance to do it right? To do it the way it had been meant to be all along?

Blossom reached up with her hand and explored the beautiful, familiar lines of Joe's face. For a moment, he looked as if he intended to resist her. But perhaps the cold had sapped some of his strength, too, because when she touched his lip with her finger, ever so gently, he growled, a low sound of surrender, deep in his throat.

Possibly the most beautiful sound Blossom had ever heard.

And then he nipped her finger, where it rested on his lip.

"Joe," she said, her voice hoarse with need, "I want you."

He drank her in, closed his eyes, and when he opened them again, a new light shone in them.

He went right through the house, slid open one of the back doors and carried her through it. With his elbow he turned on the pool lights and carried her across the stone deck to the hot tub. Only there did he set her down.

He had avoided this temptation once today. But things that were meant to be could be avoided, but not stopped.

Her focus felt oddly wide—taking in the lush greenery around them, the delicate bloom of a hibiscus, the blue of the water, the steam rising off the hot tub—and narrow at the same time. As if Joe—that look in his eyes, the cut of his jaw, the line of his lips, the sea scent of him—was all there was in the entire world.

They drank each other in, in complete wonder, as if this was the very first time. He touched her hair with his hands. Reverent.

She slid into him, pressed herself against the full length of him, felt the sinewy strength of his muscles, the sensual, velvety softness of his skin.

Her flesh still felt as cold as marble, but his heat seeped into her, and she felt like a cold vessel slowly filling with warm fluid.

"Blossom," he said hoarsely, "are you—"

She answered him by claiming his lips with her own.

She knew what his question was going to be. Are you sure?

She had never been more sure of anything in her entire life. She took his lips with everything that Hawaii, that this time together, had given her.

"Aloha, Joe," she whispered. She took his lips with boldness and curiosity and welcome. And with absolute certainty.

He reached down to the hem of his hoodie and tugged it over her head. She held her arms up willingly, to make it easier for him.

And then she stood before him in nothing but her bathing suit.

He reached behind her and, with a flick of his strong wrist, freed the top. It felt so good to be free of the cold, wet fabric, the tropical air touching her skin as if it was anointing it. She reached down and scraped the clingy wet bottom of the bathing suit down and then shinnied out of it.

And then she stood before him in nothing at all.

Eve before Adam, in their own private garden of Eden, at the dawn of time.

He shucked off his shorts and she shivered, but not from cold. Not this time. But from the raw, male beauty of him. And the recognition that it belonged to her.

Joe went into the hot tub and sat on the ledge that circled the interior of it. When she entered, he pulled her onto his lap, closing his arms around her.

His lips met hers, gently at first, inquisitive, welcoming.

"I've missed you so much," he murmured. "I thought we should try getting to know each other without this. I thought maybe it was making it so we didn't think clearly."

"And now?"

"I can't imagine knowing you without this. It's not a capitulation to give in to this energy that is between us. It's a celebration. Of every single part of who we are, of every single part of you. It feels as if our very cells are singing to each other in recognition."

And then there were no more words. His lips were less gentle now. Demanding. Commanding.

And she willingly gave him everything he demanded. Everything he commanded.

Coming home to him.

Awakening to him. It was as if Hale Alana had always held the promise that was about to be realized between them.

CHAPTER FIFTEEN

WHEN IT FELT as if the water around them would boil from the heat they were generating, Joe once again scooped Blossom up into his arms. He strode through the darkened house and into his bedroom.

He laid her on the crisp, white lines of the bed and looked at her, his gaze dark with hunger. With passion. With a look of such complete wanting that any woman would die to see it on the face of her lover.

And then with a sigh of complete surrender, he laid himself on top of her. Holding his weight off her with his elbows, so that his skin skimmed hers, he took her in.

Tenderly with his eyes, and his lips, and his hands, he explored every inch of her. He started by flicking her lip with his tongue. And then each of her ears. He made his way slowly, exploring the curve of neck and collarbone, the swell of breast, the hollow of her belly button. He went from the top of her head to the tips of her toes, anointing her with fire.

And then, vibrating with exquisite and torturous tension,

she turned the tables on him, scooted out from under him, pressed him into the deep softness of the bed.

She bent her head to explore every inch of him, reveling in his familiar lines, in the taste of him, in the feel of his silky skin beneath her tongue and her fingertips.

When they had teased and tantalized each other until their nerve endings were screaming with awareness and desire, they took it to the next level.

Somewhere, on this island, a volcano was erupting.

And they were, too, shooting fiery sparks up higher and higher, until the sparks seemed as if they would join the stars. But the sparks did not join the stars. They lost heat, cooled and fell back to the earth, where they dissolved.

Where they became hibiscus and manta ray, blue water, and black earth.

Where they became the beginning and the end.

Where they became nothing at all and everything there was.

Joe thought it was probably a good thing that he and Blossom had seen so much of the Big Island, and done so many things, before *this*.

Before they became lovers again.

Perhaps it was all that holding back that had made their surrender after the night with manta rays so exquisite.

Now they were like people who had crawled across the desert to find the oasis, which was each other. They could not drink enough to quench the thirst. They were like starving people presented with a banquet. They could not leave the table.

There was no room for anything else, no inclination toward distractions. There was no more sightseeing, no more snorkeling, no more boogie boarding at Hapuna.

Hadn't he suspected this element—this intensity between them, this passion—clouded everything about their relationship?

Their last days in Hawaii they never left Hale Alana. They lounged around the pool with books, and they made love, and they had something to eat, and they made love, and they drank wine in the hot tub, and they made love,

And for something that clouded everything, Joe had never felt quite so clear.

He simply could not live without Blossom. He could not imagine a life without her in it. Tomorrow, they were leaving.

And still, neither of them had mentioned the future.

It was as if they had put the honeymoon before the horse!

It was time to address the future. To figure out exactly where and why things had gone wrong, fix it and move on.

He was going to ask her to marry him. Again. It was obvious they were made to be together. He had the ring. Of course he had the ring! He'd kept it close to him since the day she'd given it back.

He found the bottle of champagne he had put in the fridge nine days ago.

"Hey," she said, coming into the kitchen. She was in bare feet and her hair was tousled. She was wearing a Hawaiian shirt that she had insisted on buying for him on one of their rare excursions, when hunger had forced them out of Hale Alana.

She was wearing nothing besides that shirt.

"I thought we weren't spending any money," he'd said when she had given it to him as a gift.

"No, you aren't spending any money. I can spend until my credit card is declined. Which I'm amazed hasn't happened already."

There was a new openness about her. The Blossom he'd been engaged to before would have never been so open about her financial difficulties. Not that she really had any financial difficulties. Bliss had texted him that it was all looked after.

He'd let her know tonight.

The shirt was neon green, covered in pink flowers.

It was the kind of thing he never wore. But he had worn it for her. Because it made her laugh.

"That shirt looks way better on you," he said.

"Thanks," she said, and gave him a smile that almost made him forget he was a man on a mission. "Those are my favorite shorts on you, too."

He glanced down at himself. Of course it was the pelican shorts. The ring felt as if it was burning a hole in his pocket.

"What's the occasion?" she said, nodding at the champagne.

"Our last night here," he said. "I thought we should celebrate."

"Oh." Her face fell, as if she thought he wanted to celebrate the fact it was their last night. This was exactly what had gotten them in trouble last time.

She was so sensitive. She was always looking for trouble.

Her sister had said she didn't believe good things could happen to her.

He frowned down at the champagne bottle. Would she think he was a good thing? He'd thought so last time.

But how quickly she had run away from it all.

He remembered the first time he'd proposed. He'd rented

a penthouse suite at the best hotel in Vancouver. He'd filled up the room with roses and scattered rose petals on the bed. He'd had a private dinner catered for them.

And then, he'd gotten down on one knee.

"Do you feel like some popcorn?" she asked, interrupting Joe's memories of the last proposal.

"Sure."

In what world did popcorn go with champagne and wedding proposals?

His world. His world with her in it. *Their world.*

"You can thank me that the cork didn't pop," he said, sliding it from the bottle.

"Isn't it supposed to pop? And the champagne go all over the place?"

"That's what happens if you don't chill the bottle. The champagne is too gassy if you try to open it warm. And if you serve it too cold, it loses some of its flavor."

"Rich people stuff," she said. And then she gave him a wink, came and took the bottle from him and took a drink straight from it She passed it back to him. "I wouldn't want you to become a snob," she said.

Joe took a drink straight from the bottle, too. Why not just go with it? It's not as if the formal proposal that he had so carefully orchestrated all those months ago had ended well.

A few minutes later, they sat in an egg-shaped, pillow-stuffed chair for two, at the pool. They watched the stars come out, took turns sipping from the bottle of champagne, and munched popcorn.

"You want to go for a swim?" Blossom asked him, her voice husky.

He knew what that meant. She'd shuck off that shirt and

swim in the pool nude, an enchantress who could not be resisted.

There *it* was, getting in the way, the ultimate distraction, that hum of electricity and awareness between them. Why did she make such a mockery of all his missions?

But he was determined it wasn't going to foil his plans tonight.

"Maybe later. Right now, I want to ask you—"

To marry me.

He hesitated. Maybe they *should* go for a swim. He was sweating, and it wasn't because of the gentle warmth of the evening, either.

"I figured we'd talk about *that* tonight," she said.

"What?" Had she guessed? He was trying to feel around in his pocket for the ring, without her noticing.

"That day in Essence that I gave you back the ring."

He didn't want to talk about that, at all. He wanted to be the one to give her back the ring this time. Under better circumstances, of course.

"It's just that all of a sudden," she said softly, "you seemed reluctant about the wedding. About me."

"I wasn't ever reluctant about you, Blossom, ever."

And he was about to prove it, if she'd just let him.

"I was feeling insecure anyway, because of something that had happened."

His fingers closed around the ring in his pocket.

"Remember when we had dinner at your parents'? It was the Sunday before we met for lunch."

"Barely," he said.

He should definitely get down on one knee.

"I probably wouldn't remember it, either, except something happened."

"Something happened," he repeated absently. "At my parents' house?"

In his mind he rehearsed, *Blossom, I'm crazy about you. I can't imagine life without—*

"Your dad was waiting for me when I came out of the bathroom. He said something to me."

His proposal rehearsal came to an abrupt end inside his own head. Joe felt dread crawling along his spine. "What did he say?"

"He said, *'I know what you're up to.'*"

Joe thought he should have known as soon as the champagne didn't go quite as planned, that maybe this proposal was going to go sideways.

"As if I was sneaking my way into the Blackwell family, and he could see right through me."

Joe drew in a sharp breath. "Why didn't you tell me?"

"I was shocked. And embarrassed. I wondered if I had heard him right."

He drew in a deep breath. It was time to tell her. Long past time, really.

"I think you heard him right," Joe said slowly. "I wish I'd known he said that to you. That's why I was putting out feelers about maybe changing the wedding. My mom had just told me they couldn't come. Wouldn't."

"To our wedding?"

He heard the distress in her voice. "Not because of you, Blossom. They adore you."

"Well, apparently not your dad," she said. "Your parents had decided not to come to our wedding? And you didn't tell me?"

"Blossom," he said more sharply than he intended. "It's not about you!"

"Why should it be different now? Both you and Bliss have let me know it was all about me ever since I started planning the wedding."

What was it about the damned wedding that got her going like this? He took his fingers off the ring. In fact, he took his hand out of his pocket.

"My dad's sick," he told her.

She blinked. The agitation fled her face. "What? What's wrong?"

"They're not exactly sure," Joe admitted. "There hasn't been an official diagnosis. But there are suspicions. My mom's been noticing he was *off* for quite a while. I mean, as soon as she told me, I could think of things, too. Odd things. Just like what you just mentioned. Hostility. An accusatory tone when it's not called for."

"Joe! What do they think it is?"

The words felt so painful. Did saying them make the thing he most wanted not to be real, real? Was that why he'd avoided telling her?

"His doctor thinks it's a form of dementia."

There. He'd said it out loud.

"Not the most typical form," he continued, realizing it felt good to talk about it, as if he'd been keeping a dirty secret. "Because his working memory is pretty good. Mom said they think it's a behavioral variant. So, a complete lack of filters. Inappropriate behavior. Outbursts."

"Joe, I'm so sorry," she said. "I don't understand why you didn't just tell me."

I didn't want it to be real.

"I had just heard," he said. "Minutes before I met you. Mom asked me not to tell anyone. Not just yet. She's trying to protect him. She thinks people will look at him differently once they know."

Blossom stared at him. "And I'm *anyone?*"

Joe didn't like that look on her face.

"Not trying to make it all about me," Blossom said, and there was no mistaking the edge to her voice, "but you and I were two weeks from getting married. I was two weeks away from being part of your family.

"Actually, want to hear something funny? I already thought of myself as part of your family. But I guess not. I couldn't be trusted with devastating family news. I couldn't be trusted to do the right thing. I was placed on the outside of the circle."

"That's not it." The relief he had felt confiding in her was fleeing. Fast.

"Joe, I would have changed our wedding plans in a heartbeat if I'd known any of this. You didn't have to start hinting about camping instead. One line from you, the truth, and all of this could have been avoided."

All of this could have been avoided?

Did she mean the last ten days? Okay, it hadn't been the honeymoon as planned.

He thought of snorkeling, and boogie boarding. He thought of lava forming a lake in a volcano, and the cool, dark depths of a lava tube.

He thought of wonder and laughter. In some ways it had been so much better than anything they could have ever planned. She regretted the last days, when they had been the best in his life?

"What if I have it?" he asked, aware, somehow, that was the real question, the real concern.

She stared at him. Tears sparked in her eyes. Already pitying him, just as he'd feared.

"You know what's sad?" she asked him tersely, no pity in her voice at all. "You think you're protecting me from the potential for something horrible happening in the future."

That was it exactly. So, why didn't she look pleased?

"But it's really about not trusting me. To be strong enough. To know the right things to do. To be there unfailingly through life's challenges. To trust love will give us what we need to live up to every single vow we would have taken if we had gone through with the wedding."

He was stunned by that perspective.

"Is there anything else you're keeping from me?" she said snootily.

How dare she treat him as if he was allergic to the truth because of one omission? But then he realized there was something else he *was* keeping from her.

"The reason your credit card hasn't been declined is because I paid for the wedding," he said.

She looked aghast, as if he had announced that he was involved in the illegal trade of drugs.

"I asked you not to!" she stormed.

"It's not a big deal."

"It's not a big deal *to you*. It's a big deal to me. It's about respect."

"You know what it's really about?" he asked her. "You're just spoiling for a fight. Because your life has been too good, and it's just like Bliss said. You cannot believe good things can happen to you."

"Bliss and you discussed me?"

"Not exactly," he said uncomfortably. "And don't act as if Bliss and you haven't discussed me."

"That is not the same thing, at all."

"And, Miss High and Mighty, while we're at it, don't act as if you trusted me with any of your family secrets, either."

"Miss High and Mighty?" she said.

"Yeah, and thank God it isn't Mrs." He was glad that ring was still in his pocket, because if he'd given it to her, he was pretty sure she would have thrown it back at him right about now.

The Mrs. crack hit. He wished as soon as it had left his mouth he could take it back.

She tossed her hair over her shoulder. Picked up her towel and stomped away. He could hear her crashing around in her bedroom.

And then the front door opened and slammed shut.

He heard the vehicle start. She was stealing his car. For a moment he felt worried. He should go after her, but how? He didn't have a vehicle.

Then he thought wearily, *let her go.*

Blossom barely drove out of the driveway. She hadn't had enough to drink that she needed to worry about that—only three or four sips of champagne—but she was shaking with emotion.

She found some shrubs and pulled over, turned off the vehicle. Her plane wasn't scheduled to leave until tomorrow. But thank goodness she still *had* a plane scheduled to leave tomorrow, even though they had planned to return to Vancouver on Joe's private jet.

Plans.

Her mother was fond of saying that was what you made if you wanted to make the gods laugh.

Blossom had allowed herself to get her hopes up one more time.

Didn't she ever learn?

CHAPTER SIXTEEN

IT WAS JUST exactly what Joe had thrown in her face, Blossom reflected. She could not believe good things could happen to her. And there was a good reason for that. Because they didn't!

It was a shock about his dad. She suddenly felt ashamed of herself. She *had* made it all about *her*. This news must be devastating for Joe.

On the other hand, he'd played it awfully close to his chest. She could understand at the restaurant the day she had cancelled the wedding, that Joe had just heard the news about his father, that he hadn't known what to do with it. But now? He'd had plenty of opportunities over the last days to tell her what was going on.

But, no, he had chosen not to trust her with it.

And Joe had said his dad's illness removed his filters. So did that mean James now said what he really thought all along, instead of hiding it? Did Mr. Blackwell now blurt out whatever was on his mind, unable to stop it with manners and decorum?

She had more immediate problems than what Joe's dad really thought of her. What was she going to do for tonight?

Her credit card was paid off. She could go get a hotel room.

But thinking about that credit card being paid off filled her with a fresh wave of fury. How dare Joe? She was going to have to pay him back. It was a point of pride now. So, she couldn't be wasting any money on a hotel room.

She crawled into the back seat.

"It's not as if living in a car is anything new to you," she told herself.

And at least she didn't have to worry about being cold.

That was the last time, for a long while, that Blossom didn't have to worry about cold. Back in Vancouver, the promise of that bright spring day when she had sashayed through Gastown to meet Joe at Essence had fizzled.

It was raining in the coastal city as if it never planned to stop. Cold winds drove the constant drizzle off the ocean. The skies were leaden and gray. The spring flowers were drooping and turned in on themselves. In contrast to Hawaii, it was all exceedingly depressing.

Though, admittedly, the dreariness matched her mood. For the first time in her memory, she and Bliss were standoffish with each other.

They weren't exactly fighting, though that might have been better.

No, they had argued about Joe paying for the wedding. Blossom had insisted they give him back his money, and Bliss had, maybe sensibly, refused.

"I'm not risking everything I—" *I, not we* "—have worked so hard for because you're making a point of pride.

If you want to pay him back, you do that, but you save your own money to do it. It's not coming out of the company."

Blossom didn't address her sister's betrayal—talking about her with Joe behind her back. Instead, they lived in this state of strained aloofness at home and at work, which left Blossom feeling as alone as she had ever felt in her life.

Still, she had an obligation, ironically, to plan happily-ever-afters for others.

And oddly, she still loved the work, and immersed herself in it as completely as she could.

Finally, one night when she was in bed, her door creaked open and Bliss peeked in.

"I can't stand it anymore," Bliss said, her voice breaking.

"Me, either." Blossom scooted over in the bed. As Bliss lay down beside her, Bartholomew, Blossom's constant companion, gave an annoyed mew of protest at being replaced and hopped off the bed.

Blossom and Bliss both sighed.

"You're not just mad at me about the money, are you?" Bliss asked.

"I'm mad at the whole world," Blossom admitted. "I have not singled you out."

Bliss laughed. It was so good to hear her sister's laughter.

"I'm not as mad about the money as you talking to Joe behind my back," Blossom said. "You told him I didn't believe good things can happen to me."

"Yes, I did," Bliss said, not in the least contrite. "I also told him you're afraid to hope. I guess I thought I could help him fix things between you. But now I've realized I made an error. No matter how much he loves you, Joe can't fix that, Blossom. He can't fix your suspicion of happiness, your fear of hope. Only you can do that."

No matter how much he loves you.

Blossom felt the absolute truth of that. He loved her. And she had run away from it, not once but twice.

Both times, she had run away on the flimsiest of excuses.

Not because she didn't believe in his love.

But somehow, because she believed she was not worthy of it. Somehow, she believed it would hurt less to give up on it now than if it all fell apart later. When she had allowed herself to love him even more.

Wasn't that part of what had happened in Hawaii?

She was falling in love with him even more. Leaving herself even more vulnerable to the pain of the inevitable.

"Things never worked out for us, Bliss. Every time we ever hoped for anything—whether it was a home that we could stay in, or a normal birthday party, or the promise of a fairy-tale senior prom—we never, ever got it."

Bliss was silent for a moment.

"We got something else instead," she finally said, quietly and firmly.

"What?" Blossom made no attempt to take the skeptical edge out of her voice.

"Creativity, resiliency, an ability to adapt quickly, to think on our feet when things don't go right. It's really why we're in this business."

"Creating the happily-ever-afters that we dreamed of and never got?"

"No, silly, believing in love. Don't you see? Whether we were living in a car or surviving the snubs of Mary-Beth—"

"It was Beth-Anne."

"Our love for each other got us through. I mean Mom was—is—flawed and wacky and eccentric and spontaneous. But have you ever once doubted she loved us?"

"No," Blossom said. "Not even once."

"That's why Blossoms and Bliss is such a success. Because that single message underlies every single thing we do. Because we've lived it, and so we know the absolute truth of it."

"And what is that message?" Blossom whispered.

"Love will get us through."

Try as he might to fill his days with activities, with business, with outings with Lance and his other pals, Joe could not stop thinking about Blossom. And Hawaii.

At least this time he wasn't trying to drown his sorrows. Somehow, he knew he needed absolute clarity.

And part of that clarity was that when he thought about Hawaii, it was not the many adventures—snorkeling, swimming with manta rays, exploring the mysteries of the volcano—that occupied his thoughts.

Nor was it the exquisite days after that night swim, where the chemistry between them had exploded and the world had become totally about their exquisite and joyous pleasure in each other.

Instead, Joe thought of the simplest of things, those quiet evenings at Waialea, just him and her, shoulders touching, the sun going down. Hot dogs. Spontaneous dancing. Talking. Connecting.

And he thought, often, of Blossom revealing her secrets to him.

Living in a car.

A jar of peanut butter making her feel safe.

That seventh birthday party with the ponies.

In those revelations was the secret to why she had run away from him, not just once, but twice.

Pride nursed his resentments and stoked his anger and his utter frustration with her. How could she be so unreasonable? Pride told him to let her go.

But love wouldn't let him.

Love insisted on revisiting Waialea, and remembering not so much what they had said and done, but how it had felt.

Love ached for the Blossom that didn't believe good things could happen to her—and then set out to make sure they didn't.

Love ached for the Blossom who was afraid to hope—and sabotaged all the things that could bring her happiness because of that.

Love told him that it required him to be a better man.

Love told him to ride in on his white charger and rescue her.

And in the act of rescuing her, somehow he would also rescue himself.

He realized the time for thinking—the endless loop it got him on—was over. The time was for action.

They could either have a life together or they couldn't, but he needed to satisfy that question in himself, once and for all.

No preparation this time. Just the ring in his pocket and a quick stop at the grocery store, a walk through the chilling rain.

He stood outside Blossoms and Bliss.

This building, he realized, represented her deepest self. The part of her that wanted to believe in dreams.

He rang the doorbell.

It was Bliss who answered. Her eyes widened when she saw him, and then she stood up on her tiptoes and kissed his cheek in welcome, as if he was her long-lost brother re-turned home.

Which gave him great hope.

"I was just stepping out," she said, grabbing her raincoat off a hanger beside the door and slipping into the night.

Joe went up the stairs to the apartment above the store-front.

Blossom was curled up on one end of the couch, a blanket over her legs, her feet tucked underneath her, so engrossed in a television program she didn't look up.

Bartholomew was enjoying her lap and ear rubs and gave Joe the baleful look of one who recognizes a competitor for affection.

Thanks, buddy. Remember who saved your life?

Unless he was mistaken, Blossom was wearing one of his T-shirts. That gave him as much hope as Bliss' peck on the cheek.

"They eliminated Nathan and Kim," she said. "Who was at the door?"

And then she looked up.

And the look on her face deepened his hope again.

"Joe. Oh! W-what? W-why?"

He took off his wet coat, as if she'd invited him to. He went and sat beside her on the couch. Bartholomew gave him a dirty look, jumped down and stalked off.

"How's your dad?" she asked softly.

The question made him realize why he was here. It made him see who she really was.

"It's a new reality for all of us," he said, quietly. "I'm getting through it."

"Love does that," she said quietly. "Gets people through. The impossible. The heartbreaking."

"That's what I've learned from you, Blossom."

"From me?"

"When I look at the challenges you had growing up, I can see so clearly what you can't always see. They didn't make you less. They made you more. More strong. More compassionate. More creative. More resilient."

"Bliss just said that," she whispered.

"And now I see my dad's illness is the same thing. It has to make us more. Not less. It has to.

"And I'm not sure if I can live without you showing me the way, Blossom. Showing me the way to turn lead into gold, darkness into light, tests into triumphs."

"Me?" she squeaked.

"Yes, you," he said. "The one who never sees herself clearly. I promise you this—I will always see you, even when you lose sight of yourself. I will always see your innate courage. Your innate hopefulness. Your ability to dream. Always."

She went absolutely still, but tears were shining in her eyes.

"I brought you something," he said. He handed her the paper bag, gone soft from the rain.

She looked at him.

And he saw it.

Just a flicker of what she didn't want him to see. The naked love for him that was making her so vulnerable. And so, so afraid.

And then she opened the bag. She stared at the contents. Her face crumpled. The tears that had been shining in her eyes slid free. And then she began to weep, noisily.

Peanut butter. His simple message to her.

"I want you to know," he said, "things will be okay."

She came gently into his arms, trustingly, like that soaked kitten of all those months ago. Even though she was sobbing against him, it was homecoming.

He lifted her chin and scanned her tearstained face.

And he saw everything there that he needed to see. Hope and fear of hope. Happiness and fear of happiness.

But also that innate courage he loved so much, the courage of being willing to give life—and love—more chances.

He didn't ask her this time. He stated his truth. "I need to marry you."

"Oh, Joe, I've been so—"

"Scared?"

"Yes."

"I don't want you to be scared anymore. I want us to get married, and I want to spend every day showing you things will be okay. Every. Single. Day. And every single day you can show me what pure bravery looks like and where it leads. What do you say?"

She gave him a smile and hugged that jar of peanut butter to herself.

In that smile was everything that Blossom was: valiant and flawed. And totally, totally in love with him. Enough in love with him to grab on to that hope he held out to her.

Even with the rain pounding outside her window, the sun came out in his world.

"Yes," she whispered. And then louder, "I say yes."

Joe laid his forehead against hers.

"Aloha, Blossom."

CHAPTER SEVENTEEN

THE SUN WAS going down over Waialea Beach. As always, everything stopped in Hawaii as people paid homage, with their quiet reverence, to another day in paradise.

Blossom DuPont and Joe Blackwell said *I do* just before that moment when the whole world went still.

It was not the wedding Blossom had imagined. It was, indeed, not like any wedding that Blossoms and Bliss had ever planned.

On rare occasions, she thought, her hand in Joe's as she leaned into the shoulder of *her husband*, things went better than you could possibly ever plan them.

And their wedding was one of those occasions.

There was a tropical storm brewing over the Pacific, but it had held off. It was predicted to be bad enough that they had considered canceling, but in the end, they had decided to take their chances.

Things will be okay.

And they had been. As the day gave way to night, the weather could not have been more perfect.

She was barefoot, in the simplest of white dresses—Wally Wiggles, twenty-nine dollars and ninety-nine cents—with a lei of frangipani in her hair that fell loose over her shoulders.

Joe was barefoot and in a crisp white shirt, paired with the wildest shorts they could find, turquoise and black with flowers all over them.

Bliss stood beside her, and his best friend, Lance, stood beside him. The only little glitch seemed to be some tension between Lance and Bliss.

Her mom was there, and Joe's mom and dad. The three parents stood as a unit.

Indeed, Sahara had stepped up to the plate in unexpected ways when she had heard about James's illness. She had seen that Celia was completely overwhelmed by the new reality of her husband, and quietly, and with certainty, she was just there.

Offering a hand. Showing James how to paint a picture. Watching a movie with him. Allowing Celia time away.

Her mother, unexpectedly, maybe because of her artistic soul, found ways to connect to James. Often, you could hear them laughing together.

"That's what family does," Sahara had said, surprised when Joe expressed his gratitude for her being there, for her finding remnants of his father that seemed to be lost.

But Joe himself was also there for his father, and watching his patience and strength in the face of such a devastating illness only made Blossom love this man, who was now her husband, more. On every level, Joe had shown how loyal he was, how able to be there when the going got tough, how family was already a vow—his deepest obligation—even if no words were spoken out loud.

Blossom glanced over at Joe's dad. He glared back at her.

"I know what you're up to," James yelled, as Celia and Sahara both tried to shush him.

Blossom gave her new husband's hand one last squeeze and went over to his father. She took James's hands and looked deeply into his eyes.

She looked at him with intuition. More and more, Blossom was aware of the gifts her mother had given her. And this was one of them.

Intuition. Seeing with your soul, instead of your thoughts.

Having the odd period when peanut butter was your mainstay seemed like a small price to pay for such an incredible gift.

As she looked at James, Blossom saw Joe there, in his father's eyes. She saw who Mr. Blackwell really was beneath this crushing illness. She saw the strength in him, the calm, the intelligence.

"I love you," she said to him quietly, from the bottom of her heart, this man who had been part of that incredible family unit that had made Joe everything he was.

James went very still. The angry look left his face. His eyes teared up.

Wasn't that just what everyone wanted, after all? To be seen?

She kissed both his cheeks, let go of his hands and hugged her mother-in-law.

She found herself in her mother's arms. Sahara kissed the top of her head, held her away from her and smiled through tears. Her pride and her love shone in her eyes.

"Most beautiful bride ever," her mom said. "Best wedding *ever.*"

That was true. Because what made a wedding the best

was being surrounded by the people you cared most deeply about. And these people here were the ones who had proved they would stand with them, no matter what.

What made a wedding the best was the love singing between her and Joe. Love that had been tested. Love that had walked through the fire and come out the other side, made stronger for the scorching, like wood that had been preserved with the Japanese burning technique *shou sugi ban*.

There was a picnic basket there, and now Joe took out a bottle of champagne, iced, so that the cork wouldn't pop, and Blossom handed out plastic glasses.

They toasted. The glory of the day. The sunset. Each other. And each member of the wedding party. Their families. And life. And the future.

Sahara, of course, had quite a lengthy speech she wanted to make, and as she made it, out of the corner of her eye, Blossom noticed Bliss slipping away. She set down her glass and went and followed her.

Bliss had found her way into the huge monkey pod trees that lined the upper area of Waialea. She looked gorgeous sitting there in the sand, looking out to sea in the fading light, her hair being lifted by the wind, like a girl in a painting.

She always had flair, and she had chosen a short, pink dress to stand beside her twin. Now her arms were wrapped around her naked knees, and her expression pensive.

The wind was coming up, seemingly out of nowhere, and Bliss shivered. Blossom came and sat down beside her, put her arm around her. In the distance, they could still see the wedding party.

"I'm just like a manta ray," she told Bliss. "I can feel the beating of your heart."

Bliss laid her head on her shoulder.

"Is something wrong?" Blossom asked her quietly.

"Of course not! Most perfect day ever!"

"You know, you can lie to other people, but not to me. Is something up between you and Lance? I sense a bit of tension."

"Oh, *him*," Bliss said, as if he were a bothersome fly. "No, that's not it."

"You can tell me."

Bliss slid her a look and then sighed. "You know, when you came here for your honeymoon that wasn't—and then was—it was the longest we'd ever been apart. I've never been without you in my life before. The constant. My family. I have no doubt of Mom's love for us—and I adore the kind of over-the-top extravagance of it—but constant she was not."

Blossom got exactly what Bliss was saying.

"I guess I'm scared, Blossom," her twin confided in her. "That everything between us will change now that you're married. That I won't be the most important person in your life anymore. And then, when you have kids..." Her voice drifted away.

Blossom tightened her hold around her sister's slender shoulders.

"Love isn't like that," Blossom said finally, measuring her words. "I don't have less of it to give you because I'm in love with Joe. It multiplies. It doesn't divide. I have more of it than ever."

"Love works in mysterious ways," Bliss said with a sigh. "According to Ed Sheeran."

Did her gaze drift to Lance for just a second when she said that?

"Who is that?"

"A singer. We play him at every wedding."

"That's why you're in charge of music."

"You're such a dork sometimes, Blossom."

"A dork is actually a whale's penis."

"The fact that you know that proves my point exactly."

"Just for the record," Blossom said, "I already know you'll be the best auntie ever."

"That's true," Bliss said, some of her old self back in the grin she gave Blossom. "I will be really good at that. Evil, though. The one slipping the kids chocolate before dinner and bringing them to movies they're not allowed to see."

The silence stretched between them, comfortable.

"How come you've never gotten married, Bliss?" Blossom asked. She could see her sister as a mom. The fun element aside, Bliss had so much love to give. "I mean you've had about a million men fall in love with you."

"Not that many. Nine hundred thousand."

They both chuckled.

"There's the rub," Bliss said thoughtfully. "I've had all those men fall in love with me, and I've never fallen in love back."

"Not even once?"

"No."

"Do you want to?"

"Yes."

The silence was long, again, and then Bliss said, "I'm scared now, though. I've broken so many hearts that when I fall in love, he's going to break mine. I just know it. Lance is the kind of guy who could show me what a bitch karma can be."

Blossom didn't say anything.

"He asked me out after the Lee wedding."

"He did?"

"You were so wrapped up in Joe you didn't notice him hanging around when we were cleaning up. What a jerk! He'd come with someone else. That's why when he said he'd like to see me, I said no. He's actually miffed about it. I don't think he's had women say no to him very often."

Blossom thought of Joe's tall, dark and handsome friend. She was pretty sure Bliss was right on that account.

"Anyway, he persisted. I threw a vase of flowers at him."

Blossom contemplated this overreaction with interest. It was not like Bliss. At all.

Blossom filed that away about Lance. "Karma," she said thoughtfully. "Now you sound like Mom."

"Sometimes I wonder if I'll turn into her." Bliss sighed pensively. "Flaky. Alone."

"You won't. I won't let you. You'll always have me."

"And you'll always have me," Bliss said. "Let's go back."

The sisters stood up together and walked back to the gathering on the beach, arm in arm.

Their mother was looking through the cooler. "What's in here?"

Joe saw Blossom coming. His expression was so tender, and so welcoming. He came toward her, and she slipped away from Bliss and toward him.

Toward every single thing she had ever hoped for her future.

He put his arms around her waist, looked deeply into her eyes and said, with the most wonderful smile tickling the beautiful line of his mouth, "You know what's in that cooler?"

"Peanut butter?" she heard her mother, the one who hated extravagance, exclaim, appalled. "Who serves peanut butter at a wedding?"

* * * * *

Pretend Honeymoon With The Best Man

Andrea Bolter

Andrea Bolter has always been fascinated by matters of the heart. In fact, she's the one her girlfriends turn to for advice with their love lives. A city mouse, she lives in Los Angeles with her husband and daughter. She loves travel, rock 'n' roll, sitting at cafés and watching romantic comedies she's already seen a hundred times. Say hi at andreabolter.com.

Books by Andrea Bolter

Billion-Dollar Matches collection

Caribbean Nights with the Tycoon

Her Las Vegas Wedding
The Italian's Runaway Princess
The Prince's Cinderella
His Convenient New York Bride
Captivated by Her Parisian Billionaire
Wedding Date with the Billionaire
Adventure with a Secret Prince

Visit the Author Profile page
at millsandboon.com.au for more titles.

Dear Reader,

Just as I might ask other authors, readers ask me what my inspiration might be for a particular book. For this one, it was my hero. I had a clear picture of Ian in my mind, how he looked, talked, moved, felt. A man loyal to his family and their livelihood but a romantic at heart, and who gets to live out some of his charming fantasies, like rowing a beautiful woman in a boat on a pond. (Of course, I interrupted the bliss with a surprise for him!) Throughout the story I agonized for him and made sure that, as long as he had Laney by his side, his ever after would be happy.

Another inspiration for this book was pink sand. Yes. Pink. Sand. I've yet to visit a place where the beaches were pink. But looking at some photos of Bermuda, I thought that was one of the most beautiful sights I'd ever seen, and wouldn't it be lovely to let Laney and Ian spend time there? That is, between Boston, where they start, and New York, where their relationship takes a major turn.

So, there we have it. Ian and pink sand, my sparks for this story. Enjoy!

Andrea x

For STAY

CHAPTER ONE

"THAT FLOWER ARRANGEMENT is blocking Melissa's face a little bit."

"It's fine."

"It's not. Help me move it," urged Laney Sullivan, the maid of honor that best man Ian Luss had just met yesterday.

They were watching the bride and groom prepare for rehearsal dinner photos to be taken next to a mammoth display of orange gladiolas.

"Come on, Ian."

Really not agreeing that they should be the ones to make any adjustment, he hesitated. "Wait for the photographer," he said, reiterating his opinion.

"You're not going to get your nice suit dirty, if that's what you're worried about." That wasn't his concern, although it was a valid one. They weren't in wedding attire, as the big event was tomorrow, but were dressed for the dinner and the photo shoot that had been scheduled. In his bespoke navy suit, he needed to stay preened and tucked into photogenic readiness. However, his true objection to Laney's request was that they were at the Fletcher Club, Boston's most austere and opulent private establishment. The premiere wedding destination in town no doubt had staff assigned for every task under the sun. He and the maid of honor did not need to be touching the flowers.

After a run-through of the ceremony on the twenty-seventh harbor-view floor where Melissa Kraft and Clayton Trescott would marry, they'd adjourned and traveled one floor down to the cocktail lounge, which offered a panoramic vista of downtown. At twilight the sky was a glinting blue, the city beginning to twinkle into evening. An area near the windows had been stanchioned off with velvet ropes for the photo session, where the Custom House Tower, Faneuil Hall and more city landmarks would serve as the backdrop.

Melissa wore a tight dress in emerald-green, the wedding party color, as she hung on Clayton's arm while they chatted with guests. Ian knew Clayton from university days and they'd stayed close over the years. His friend was clearly head-over-heels smitten with his bride, his sparkling eyes telling the tale. Ian had no wife or girlfriend but couldn't imagine being married to a woman like Melissa, who never walked past a mirror without looking in it. Who shortly after getting engaged to Clayton made a point of telling Ian, as well as posting on social media, the carat count of her diamond engagement ring.

Truthfully, Ian didn't know what type of woman he'd marry, other than one who understood the basic tenet that a Luss such as himself, of Luss Global Holdings, considered marriage as a strategic merger, just as his family's acquisitions of land were. Marriage was a big thing to the Lusses, although not in the way most people would think of it. Position and thorough breeding were everything. Love and passion were not factors. At thirty, he was expected to make one of those fortuitous marriages soon.

To the matter at hand, in addition to not moving the flowers Laney was worried about, another way Ian didn't think he should get involved with things would be in mentioning to the maid of honor that her hair was a mess and needed attention. It had probably been carefully styled earlier, and now, for whatever reason, several golden locks had escaped the twisty roll they'd been sculpted into. The errant strands looked less like they were well thought out to frame her face or give a sexy allure and were, instead, more like she was a kid who had been out playing in the yard wearing her fancy clothes after she was told not to. It was actually kind of cute, like she didn't really care about her appearance. Although it wouldn't do, and hopefully, a female member of the wedding party would take her aside and smooth everything back into place.

A couple of guests milling around took out their phones and began snapping candid shots of the bride and groom, the prephoto photos. Next, would some other group take photos of the group taking photos of the prephotos for the prewedding?

He knew that he'd be going through some wedding traditions himself before long. In fact, his grandfather Hugo had begun speaking with some of his old cronies, the wealthiest men in New England, to check on the marital status of their granddaughters. That's how the Luss family did things, nothing left to chance after a couple of slipups had almost brought their fortunes to the ground. He glanced over to Clayton and his big smile, admiring his happiness. Ian's own wedding surely wouldn't be the best day of his life like it might be for an enchanted groom. That was all right, he told himself. Everyone had their roles in life.

"Just help me for a minute."

Ian heard the words enter his ears while he stared at Clayton, wondering what this moment was like for him. Pure, unadulterated joy and certainty about his life ahead of him? What did expressions of love feel like, Ian wondered, as the groom kissed his bride's cheek? What really was romance? He'd seen examples of it, watched other couples in action, but he didn't know what it did to someone on the inside?

Ian's grandfather, and all the way back to his grandfather's grandfather, were probably right that emotional distractions could be costly, and an amicable business-type partnership was best. Love, but without the intensity of being *in love*. After all, it took steely determination to amass an empire such as theirs. Still, as Ian watched Clayton's hand slide around Melissa's waist, he mused on the trade-off, on what he might miss out on. What he'd always read about in books and seen in movies. Courtship! Heart song! Passion!

"Ian, Earth is calling. Just help me out for a minute," Laney repeated, snapping him out of his trance.

The maid of honor was still adamant that the flowers needed some sort of tweak, so she wrapped her fingers around his forearm and gave him a little tug toward the staging area. A strange shock ran through him at her touch, like an electrical current. It was a wholly unfamiliar sensation, and he eyed her disapprovingly for causing it.

She enlisted him to help her rotate the tall glass cylinder of flowers so that the offending bloom was no longer obscuring her cousin Melissa's face.

"Edge it that way," she gestured.

As they did so, the official photographer arrived with cameras around her neck. All of the amateur cell phone snappers respectfully took a step backward.

"Satisfied?" he asked Laney, regarding the flowers, although the difference was minuscule. The bride's larger-than-life orange-lipped grin faded the colors of everything else around them. Yet again, he watched the radiance that took over Clayton's face at his bride's every move. A lurch gripped Ian's stomach. Still, he wondered what love might feel like, literally how it might inhabit the cells of someone's body. How it could influence thought. Maybe even have an involuntary effect on breathing. All things he had never experienced and probably never would. Well, there was that one talk he had with his late grandmother Rosalie, but that was years ago. His friend's wedding was prompting a lot of questions Ian had never asked before.

"It seemed easier to do it than wait around," Laney said beside him.

"Fine. Whatever," Ian said. The photographer brought her meters to Melissa's face and then to Clayton's. "Are you due in makeup before the shoot?"

Whereas the bride and the bridesmaids who were filing into the room were wearing the world's current supply of makeup, they hadn't seemed to have left any for Laney, because she didn't appear to have a drop of it on. Her skin was pale and untouched, and her lips their given shade of dusty pink. Truth be told, she was absolutely lovely, natural and real, even with that messy hair. Yet he was curious if she'd forgotten that one of her duties as maid of honor was to tolerate what was sure to be a barrage of photos in various settings. She was on the shorter side and was dressed for tonight's festivities in a slinky silver dress that showed off major curves he attempted not to pay too much attention to.

"No, I don't wear makeup," Laney answered defiantly, as if she'd been accused of something. "I've tried it, and it's so itchy it makes my skin crawl."

She looked down to her fingernails and rubbed them as if she was making sure they were clean. She didn't have nail polish on either, another convention he was used to seeing on women wearing dressy clothes. Clayton had told him that Laney was moving back to Boston after a failed attempt at running a café in Pittsfield, in the scenic Berkshires region of Western Massachusetts. She surely had the look of someone who spent more time doing something with her hands than she did with them in a manicurist's shop. Clayton had also mentioned something about an ex.

In any case, based on her sharp response he might have insulted her in asking about the lack of makeup. "Forgive me," he said, bringing his palm flat to his chest, "it's just that... I think if you check yourself in the mirror, you'll find that your hair is...a little out of sorts."

She looked him straight in the eyes as her cheeks puffed out as round as they could go, and she exhaled in a slow, steady stream until they deflated. "Thanks for the tip," she said, then pivoted and walked away.

"I was only trying to be helpful," he called after her. "We're best man and maid of honor. Isn't it our job to try to make everything flawless?"

Argh! Saying that she was anything other than flawless was another wrong statement. He was strangely flustered around her, whereas generally, he was in steely control. Not that his words had any effect because Laney and her curves continued sashaying away from him, out of the bar area completely and blasting through the double doors that led to the wedding party's dressing rooms. His eyes stayed on her until a staff member wheeling a cart obstructed his view.

"Okay, fine." Laney surrendered to the makeup artist's third plea to allow a little lip gloss for the photos. She had not been the first choice for maid of honor, and it showed. As the bride's cousin, she was to be a bridesmaid until Melissa's best friend pulled out at the last minute because of a difficult pregnancy. Laney and Melissa could hardly be more unalike and didn't see a lot of each other as children. Laney grew up with a single mom on the wrong side of Boston, whereas Melissa hailed from the wealthy suburb of Wellesley. Laney's mother was never close with her brother, the father of the bride.

"Thank you for filling in," Melissa said as Laney allowed the makeup artist to glob the goop onto her lips.

Laney figured she'd only need to leave it on for the shoot, then they'd go right to dinner, and it would be perfectly legitimate for her to wipe it off. Likewise tomorrow, glop for the ceremony and more photos, slime wiped off for cocktails and hors d'oeuvres. She could manage this.

"You're welcome," said Laney.

The makeup artist finally moved on, and the two returned from the dressing room to the cocktail lounge.

"You were saying on the phone that you've had a hard time of it lately?" the bride asked.

"Yeah, it turned out I was unlucky in both love and business."

This modern fairy-tale wedding of lipstick and party salons high in the sky was what Laney thought she was heading toward when she met Enrique Sanz. He'd come into the

Cambridge café near Harvard University where she'd been working and changed her life. Handsome and cultured, he was in Boston after just finishing a master's degree in business. She thought they were in love. He even consented to buying the café in Pittsfield that they ran together. Although he was always reminding her that she was "not the type he could have on his arm forever." Apparently, owning a café was okay for a short time, but it wasn't a lofty enough goal for a man whose family supplied half of Spain with lumber.

"I hope things get better for you," Melissa muttered sympathetically. "Clayton says I could sell my shop, but I'm going to keep it, at least for now."

"Right."

In addition to being a glamazonian piece of eye candy and marrying a high-ranking bank executive, Melissa had a handbag shop in Beacon Hill that attracted the Boston elite. "Of course, we're hoping to get preggers as soon as possible!"

"I wish you the best."

"Hey, you know, there are some really great single men coming this weekend. Don't people say weddings are a great place to meet?"

Sure, as if any man in Melissa's social circle would be interested in her. A wave of irritation swept over Laney as she recalled her own misfortune. The café attempt was a disaster and Enrique broke her heart. Having wedding duties just as she'd returned to town wasn't ideal. However, it was time to put all of that aside and get through this weekend. Then she could start over. That first task might be easier without Ian Luss, the best man, who was now striding toward her. She'd only met him enough to say hello yesterday, but an hour or so ago, when she asked him for help moving the flowers, he seemed lost in space, and she could hardly get his attention.

Then he'd rubbed her the wrong way with telling her that she needed to fix her hair, just like some criticism Enrique might have had. As he approached, he looked straight to her lips, which were now no doubt so shiny he could see himself in their reflection. He was probably gloating about having asked her if she was due in the makeup chair and her defensively proclaiming that she didn't paint her face. Although he might be annoying, she had to admit that he was good-looking, with his big brown eyes and black hair that almost reached his shoulders. He stood tall in his finely tailored suit that fit slim along his broad shoulders and long legs. Not that she found him *attractive* attractive. She was just admiring him as one does a piece of art, for example. Attraction to men could only lead to more trouble. She needed a major life do-over and that would start with steering clear of the male species.

"All right, wedding party, let's gather," the photographer called out. "We'll start with the bride and groom, best man and maid of honor."

"That's us," Melissa bubbled as she left Laney's side to take Clayton's hand.

Ian gestured for Laney to go ahead of him toward the photo spot, which was now set with reflectors to produce the best possible lighting. The photographer had some fun poses, such as one where Clayton held out a single orange rose to Melissa as they stood above a seated maid of honor and best man, Ian gifting Laney a rose as well. Laney's heart thumped a beat at Ian's eyes locking onto hers during the motion, making it an unexpected exchange between them. The wedding party was then brought into the shots, followed by various configurations of family holding flowers of their own.

Afterward, the staging area was quickly dismantled, and waiters dressed in black with gold aprons passed Bellinis from silver trays. Laney made sure to grab a napkin with hers, as her lip goo time was officially over, and she happily wiped it off. Ian, talking to a couple of the groomsmen just a few feet away, caught the move, and the tip of his mouth curled up. She really wasn't sure whether he was cute or aggravating, although it really didn't matter, because she was off men. Plus, she'd never see him again after this wedding. Or until Melissa and Clayton's first baby had a birthday party, or something like that.

Appetizer stations were set out. At the mozzarella sampling bar, Laney was trying a burrata with roasted pistachio when Ian came up beside her. "Are you giving a speech?"

She finished chewing before answering, "I don't know if I'd call it a speech, but they asked me to say a few words tonight and leave the traditional speech to you tomorrow."

He grabbed his throat like he was being choked. "The pressure. The pressure."

"Just say something romantic. That's what brides like," Laney said.

He took in her words as if he'd never heard anything like them before.

He helped himself to a piece of the *fior di latte* cheese on a square of focaccia. "So, what, you don't want to paint your nails and gussy up, but you still want the princess tiara and the happily-ever-after thing? You'll make it tough for a guy to figure out, or are you already spoken for?"

"No one is speaking for me." She grabbed a hunk of that milky *fior* with her fingers and popped it in her mouth.

Ian reached over and flicked a speck of cheese from the front of her dress where it had landed.

She rolled her eyes. "Again? First it was my hair. Then my lack of makeup. Now you're cleaning food off me?"

"You're welcome."

"I'm sure a crumb has never dared touch a piece of your fine woolens, but could you just keep your business to yourself, and I'll do the same with mine?"

"I was only trying to help."

"Don't."

He lifted his palms up in surrender and walked away.

Laney fisted her hands in frustration. She knew he only meant well, but the criticism was hard for her to take. She'd had enough to last a lifetime. Of course, Ian and his comments didn't mean anything to her. He didn't have the ability to wound her as Enrique had with his constant disapproval. Whom she should have known from the beginning wasn't a gentleman, but she was fooled. He'd whispered things into her ear that made her think they were truly together. That he'd take her to live in Madrid with him. It was all so exciting. Until he started picking on her. Where she went, how she looked, what she wore. How drab it was that all she wanted was her own café. In retrospect, she didn't know what she saw in him, except that his European glamour was nothing like the small-minded sons born of the rough streets in Dorchester.

When it was speech time, Laney stood holding a mic in front of the guests seated for the rehearsal dinner. "I know people like to share a famous quote about marriage," she said, continuing her toast. A plate clinked at one table, then another as the waitstaff delivered the salads. Voices here and there were in conversation. She lifted her Bellini. "To

Melissa and Clayton. Writer H. L. Mencken said, 'Love is the triumph of imagination over intelligence.'"

What she'd meant as a funny bit of cynicism flopped royally. The room fell silent. The bride's big tangerine smile drooped like a sad clown. Laney looked to Ian at her table. He winced at her failure.

This is going to be a long weekend, Ian thought to himself as he finished the pasta flight that had been set in front of him and each guest at the rehearsal dinner. A wooden board with four carved out grooves had contained corn spaghetti carbonara, pesto potato gnocchi, rigatoni with Bolognese and fusilli with raw tomatoes and basil. He'd made short work of the presentation, as he was hungry, and concentration on his food meant less time blathering about nothing with the groomsman and his wife who sat to his right. They were the only ones to talk to because to his left, Clayton was continuously occupied with well-wishers who approached in an endless parade.

The groomsman and his wife beside Ian were from Albany, New York. She pulled out her phone to show Ian their three children, who hadn't come along to the wedding because they were at summer camp. The woman elaborated excitedly on every activity the kids would be involved in while there, from learning computer coding to performing in musical theater. Ian feigned interest.

Politely excusing himself from the table, he wandered from the dining salon back into the cocktail lounge. It wasn't that kids and summer camp were of no matter. After all, Ian planned on having his own offspring and hoped he'd take pride in their accomplishments. It was only that with the Luss methods for maintaining their fortune, which had already been mapped out for the next century, marriage and family were, first and foremost, matters of practicality and logic. Indeed, that's how his parents treated him and his sister, as coworkers, partners and friends. With regard but without warmth. So he wasn't sure how much exuberance there would be over cell phone photos of science experiments.

Ian never saw his parents engage in the gestures of romance that he noticed with other people and in the arts. He worried that having the sense there was a larger emotional life out there, one he couldn't do without, would prevent him from being able to fit into the box his family was saving for him. He strode to the bar and asked the bartender for a maple whiskey rocks. He took a tight sip and glanced around the mostly empty lounge, as the majority of rehearsal dinner guests were in the main room about to enjoy dessert.

"Was that the worst quote in the world?" Laney headed toward him, her satiny dress giving a little swish with every step. Once again, Ian tried not to get caught eyeing her from top to bottom. She surely filled that dress out nicely with her ample bosom and hips. He looked to her pretty face. "I thought it was going to get a laugh, but I think I bombed."

"You did." He had to chuckle. He didn't want to offend her once more, something he seemed to have a knack for, but he wasn't going to lie. Fortunately, she snickered a little bit herself. "Can I get you a drink?"

"What are you having?"

"Maple whiskey on the rocks."

"I'll have the same."

Ian gestured to the bartender.

"Thanks."

Drink delivered, they both gazed out at the skyline.

"Are you from Boston?"

"Dorchester, born and raised."

"Dorchester?"

"Don't sound so shocked. Melissa and I are related, but we didn't have the same kind of childhood."

"What kind of childhood was that?" So, Laney was a scrapper. Who had survived living in one of the most crime-infested parts of Boston, and it didn't seem to have swallowed her up.

"It was just me and my mom pooling our resources. Not these kinds of resources," she gestured around the posh Fletcher Club.

"Is your mom here?"

"No, she's living in Arizona now. She recently had an operation and couldn't make the journey."

"What about your dad?"

Laney took a sip of her drink. "I never knew him. They weren't really together. He took off once she got pregnant."

Ian gulped at that lack of duty. That was why he'd never do anything to defy his family and would fit whatever mold he had to. The Lusses were unflinchingly loyal. For better or for worse, they took care of each other, ran as a pack. Didn't impregnate women they weren't married to. "Clayton told me you'd left Boston for a while."

"I was in the Berkshires for two years. I only returned this week. I'm still adjusting back to city life."

"Where were you?"

"Pittsfield."

"What were you doing there?"

"Operating a café."

"Hmm." He sipped his drink. "How specific."

"Specific? You mean how small-time and limited."

Uh-oh. Had he replied wrong again? He'd only been trying to make chitchat. As people did when they were getting to know each other. "That's not what I meant."

"What did you mean, then?" She cast her eyes down to her drink and swirled the amber liquid in the glass.

"You were running a café. I'm sure the duties were very clear." He shrugged. "Whereas I have no idea what I actually do all day."

Her eyes shot up to meet his. "How do you figure that?"

"I work with my family. We consider purchases."

"Of what?"

"Land."

"That you buy and build on?"

"No. We buy it and hold it. Sometimes we sell it."

"Land?"

"Yes. Mountain ranges and private deserts, things like that."

"How many 'things like that' does your family own?"

"About three hundred worldwide."

"Hmm. That sounds like you're doing *a lot* of things in a day. What's your part?"

"I consult with appraisers."

"Weren't you named in some list of the city's most eligible bachelors?"

"Embarrassing."

"Mountain ranges," she repeated.

He took another pull on his whiskey. One of the city's eligible bachelors implied that he was some kind of prey. To be snatched up. As much as he nodded his head in acquiesce when his grandfather told him it was time to let him choose a bride for him, in reality, Ian didn't want him to. Sure, he might hit it off with one of the highbrow women chosen for her family's name and history. It was possible that would be the woman he was destined to be with. Although he doubted it.

He knew that marriage could be more than what his family outlined. That with the right person, there could be the state of being in love. And that could be what made life truly worthwhile. A union built when two minds, two hearts and two souls melded together and moved through the world as one. Worse still, he sometimes thought that without that, he might never be completely fulfilled and would die empty. He even had the notion that the someone he was meant to be with really was actually out there for him.

Nonsense. He tried to admonish himself. Everyone had their lot, and his was to continue family traditions that hundreds of Luss employees were counting on. Why fix something that wasn't broken? The Luss family didn't have time for romance. That could be left to others. And the more he let himself dwell on silly fantasies, such as one true love, the harder it was going to be to step into the role expected of him.

"Weddings bring up strange thoughts, don't they?" he asked aloud.

"That's for sure."

"So, why aren't you still running that café?"

"It burned down."

He let out a throat-clearing cough. "It what?"

"An electrical line toppled over and started a fire. By time it was extinguished, the damage was beyond repair."

"Oh, gosh. Was anyone hurt?"

"Thankfully, no. But the insurance wasn't enough to rebuild."

"And it left you out of a job. That's why you're back in Boston."

"Yes, and I was in partnership with someone, and that didn't work out, either."

"Oh, sorry to hear that. What are you planning to do now?"

"It's been a heck of a couple of years. I need to regroup. Restart."

"So, you'll get another job?" He sensed she wasn't telling him everything that was going on with her. That she was hurting. Not that it was any of his concern. "What is it that you really want?"

"I've always wanted my own café, so I had that for a minute. I'll have to start from the bottom again and build back up."

"I'm sure there are lots of stories of the humble barista who rises to the top of the café world."

"The humble barista?"

"I've offended you yet again." He shook his head. "I don't talk to many people outside of work. I'm terrible at small talk." Even if he was to marry solely for the family merger, he was going to have to learn to be pleasant company. Something he wasn't doing very well at with Laney so far.

"Oh, right. You have nothing to talk about with the humble barista."

She started to walk away. Without a thought, his hand reached for her arm. Her skin was so silky it startled him. "Laney, don't go. I'd like to hear about owning a café."

She shook off his hold. "It's late. See you tomorrow."

CHAPTER TWO

"BY THE POWERS vested in me by the state of Massachusetts, I now pronounce you husband and wife. You may kiss the bride."

As the officiant concluded the ceremony, Laney stood beside Melissa, holding her bouquet. Like they had rehearsed, Laney handed her own bouquet to the bridesmaid on her right, thereby freeing her hands to hold the bride's formidable array of both pale and vivid orange blooms. As Ian had fulfilled his role of taking care of the wedding rings, the maid of honor and best man executed their duties. They both watched, Ian from his side and Laney from hers, as Clayton took his wife in his arms and kissed her to the cheers of the two hundred in attendance.

The string quartet began the wedding recessional, and Melissa and Clayton turned to glide past the guests down the aisle. It struck Laney how profound the past twenty minutes had been. Melissa and Clayton had walked to the altar single and returned as a married couple, their lives forever changed and defined by what had happened there. With family and friends to witness the ceremony and help launch them forward. What was before was nevermore. They strode forward as one.

It was what Laney had thought she was going to have. What her mother never had but Laney wanted. And was expecting. What she had begun to plan for in her mind. A future where Enrique was solid and committed to her. Even though she'd been fooling herself, and the signs were there all along. Then, indeed, everything was taken from her. She felt the loss down into her bones.

Laney swallowed hard. This was not the time for self-pity. It was time to move her feet toward the head of the aisle, where she met up with the best man. She hoped they could get through the evening without grating on each other's nerves like they had yesterday. She liked how he looked born to wear his well-tailored tux, even with hair a little longer than was conventional. At last night's rehearsal and dinner, he didn't seem to have a date with him. So she assumed he was alone tonight as well. Did he have a girlfriend, though? Or a boyfriend? Someone stashed away in another city who didn't come to the wedding with him for whatever reason? She wasn't sure, but instinct told her no.

Linking her arm into his, her hand settled on the warmth of his sturdy muscle. He was so…formidable. Substantial. The kind of man a person could wade through the waters with. Her eyes blinked a couple of times as they took their first steps together while she tried not to feel defeated. Things had not gone her way.

"Ceremony went well," Ian whispered into her ear, which prickled from the sensation of his breath. "What did you think of the poem Clayton recited?"

"It rhymed. Need I say more?" She bit her lip to squelch

a laugh as the photographer snapped continuously during their march. "The flower girl was adorable."

"She was. Especially when she started picking up all the petals after she'd scattered them."

"A hard worker."

Like her. Laney would make it through this wedding weekend, get a job, and move off her friend Shanice's couch. It wasn't Madrid, where she'd concocted all sorts of scenarios about some perfect life she was going to have there. Boston wasn't the worst place to begin again. Although, the truth was that she was tired. She'd barely caught her breath dealing with the café burning down, then Enrique leaving her a week later. She wished she could get a break. Just for a little while. To rest, relax and plan. Although nothing like that was in her current budget, which was about zero, save for her old roommate Shanice's generosity.

At the end of the aisle, Laney let go of her link to the crook of Ian's arm. And missed the feel of it instantly. *Huh.*

"Best man and maid of honor, please hurry to the mezzanine for first toasts," an attendant called to them.

"Let's go." She gave him a tug and maneuvered them quickly through the crowded area where the guests were assembling. The wedding manager waved them into a side entrance, where they climbed a half flight of stairs onto a raised glass platform that jutted out above the cocktail lounge like a stage in the sky so that all the guests could see them. This was where Melissa and Clayton would make their first appearance.

"Now?" Ian asked, verifying with the manager who handed him a microphone. Melissa had wanted the best man's speech to be before dinner. Laney didn't really have anything to do, but she stood beside him with two flutes of champagne, urging him to take one with his free hand.

He hit all the proper notes. Thanking the guests who came from near and far. Saying how lovely and sweet Melissa was. Congratulating his old friend Clayton on finding his mate. Wishing them a long and happy life together. Whereas Laney had bombed last night with her quote that fell flat, Ian's toast was tasteful and reserved and, well, kind of dull. She'd wished he'd gone out on more of a limb. He ended with a quote by Mignon McLaughlin: "A successful marriage requires falling in love many times, always with the same person."

Laney swallowed hard at that. That was a much more romantic closer than she was expecting from him. Falling in love over and over again. Yes, that did indeed sound like a real marriage. Something Enrique wasn't capable of, or not with her anyway.

Then it was time for the *big wow*. The overheads in the room dimmed so that the fairy lights strung everywhere created a magical glow. Laney and Ian stepped down from the elevated platform, her wobbly on her high heels and grabbing his reliable arm for balance. A spotlight was poised, waiting for the stars of the evening. A voice boomed, "Without further ado, I introduce to you for the first time as husband and wife, Mr. and Mrs. Clayton Trescott."

Melissa and Clayton appeared from within the darkened area and stepped onto the platform and into the spotlight to cheers and applause. Melissa had changed into a mermaid-style gown that glistened like a mirror ball, and her face looked like it was going to crack open from smiling so wide.

Laney and Ian watched from the sideline. She tugged the side of her emerald-green maid of honor gown made of a silk shantung, which was actually scratchy and uncomfortable. They still had a long evening ahead of them.

Laney coached herself again. *Just make it through the weekend.*

The band's horn section jammed as the wedding party bounded through the doors into the reception hall in a gaggle just as the photographer had instructed them to. Then, like a blooming flower, the petals that made up the groomsmen and the bridesmaids opened away from the center. Next, the maid of honor and best man stepped away to reveal the bride and groom who, were met by guests clanging knives against water glasses. In response, they kissed. Melissa had changed into another wedding gown, a custom Ian didn't quite understand yet had witnessed at a few of the upscale weddings he'd been to lately.

He supposed it was simply that women loved to dress up, so why have one wedding dress when you could have six? Yes, six, as the bride at a wedding he'd been to a few months ago had worn. He hoped their marriage was going to last long enough to pay the bill on that wardrobe. Melissa's second dress was a tight-fitting number with a weird extra bottom part that swished like a fish's fin.

Once he and Laney circled the happy couple with the choreography that seemed to him like a square dance's do-si-do and he reunited with Laney, he asked her, "What is a dress that style called?"

They smiled for the photographer, now having mastered bringing their cheeks close to each other for the cute close-up. Ian was determined not to give heed to the delightful feeling of Laney's face near his or the empty sensation every time she pulled it away.

"Mermaid," she answered.

Aha! He was right in his marine reference.

"Do you like it?"

"No. The way it comes in tight over her...behind...and then flares out the size of a lace tablecloth."

A waiter presented a tray of purplish cocktails in stemmed tulip glasses. "This is the bride and groom's signature cocktail, the Mel-Clay. Lemon vodka, blueberry cordial and ginger ale."

They each took a purple potion from the waiter's tray. Bespoke cocktails were another part of the careful attention that went into grand weddings these days. Because his friends were around thirty like him, marrying age, Ian had attended a lot of weddings lately. If the wife he'd take someday wanted to look like a strange creature from the sea, what would he care?

"Have you ever been married?" Laney asked.

"Heavens, no," said Ian. "If I had, I'd still be. One and done. You?"

"Never. Like I was telling you, I co-owned that café with Mr. Almost. When it burned down, so did we."

"Why? The disappointment?"

"Something like that. He blamed me for the fire."

"How so?"

"You name it. Accusing me of not having it inspected thoroughly enough before he bought it. That I didn't have the professional know-how or education to run the operation. That I wasn't on top of the upkeep. In reality, he was ready to break up with me, so he used it as an excuse."

"What a jerk."

Between that and a father that skipped out, she hadn't had much of an example of what a decent man was.

"Do you picture having a big wedding?" Laney asked, moving on from the subject.

"I suppose. My family will want it to be as much a PR event as anything else. It's time for my grandfather to retire, but not until he sees me settled and ready to breed the next in succession for Luss Global Holdings."

"Sounds dreamy." She smirked.

"Anything but. That's kind of the point. The Luss family doesn't spend time or resources on emotions." Why did that sound so awful coming out of his mouth? It was true, but it was so cold-blooded. He'd had limited dealings with women thus far, his imagination far more active than he was. The young women who he'd dated during his Oxford years made it their business to find out about his family's wealth and tried to snare him. Their efforts were so insincere they fell into their own traps, making sure he was wary and distrustful of them. His grandfather's plan was at least safer, two families going into partnership for mutual benefit with both parties vetted.

So far, even dating casually, he'd never gotten close to a woman, so he hadn't had to worry about feelings being ignited. He couldn't take any chances at not keeping love at bay and then ruining everything generations of his family had worked so hard for. His great-great-uncle Phillip had almost destroyed the company in its formative years because of a woman. And when Ian was a child, his father's brother Harley had lost them tens of millions of dollars by acting on impulse. Ian's grandfather would see to it that nothing like that ever happened again.

"Did you just say your family doesn't waste resources on emotions?"

"Right. Marriages are trade alliances."

The music quieted and the band leader took the mic. "Ladies and gentlemen, let's welcome the bride and groom for their first dance."

As Ian watched the mermaid and her fisherman take to the center of the dance floor, he felt that little lurch in his stomach as he had earlier. Because it wasn't as cut and dry as he'd just explained to Laney. In his secret heart of hearts, he'd always wanted to experience a little bit of emotional love, just to know what it felt like. To let himself be seduced into a whirlwind romance with a woman, to know that. Even once. Sure, there'd be a risk that it could be like getting lost and not being able to find the way home. Yet, he was a level-headed grown man. He could see his way back from the journey. He was not going to fall into any snares and let his grandfather or the Luss Global employees down. Of course, he had no idea how he'd ever go about something like that. Women had their own ideas and would have no interest in playing his game. Therefore, he smiled wistfully at the man and the fish, and that was that.

"What, you're an anti-romantic?"

He looked around the reception hall and wondered, if maybe for the first time, what conceptions each and every person here had about love. Old and young, rich and poor, single, married, widowed or divorced. "Anti-romantic? I guess you could say that."

That was his official position and he was sticking to it, even if it wasn't what he really harbored inside. And Laney's sable eyes, the sparkling lights, the passionate purple cocktail and the bride's fish fin of a dress were making him question everything even more.

He watched Clayton again. Why was the expression on his face so difficult for Ian? He'd known his friend's face for a long time. Yet he looked changed tonight. Finished. Anchored. It rocked Ian to the core.

The band leader said, "May we be joined on the dance floor by the maid of honor and the best man?"

"By the way, I don't know how to dance." Laney put her drink down at a side table, and Ian followed.

"I don't know how to do anything elaborate. It's just that one-two-three, one-two-three bit."

"That you learned at cotillion?"

"Yup. From when I was twelve." More formalities from his youth. Step-two-three, with snobby rich girls, step-two-three. No sex or soul in it, even though his body told him that dancing could have been both a sensual and profound act.

"Heaven help you."

"What I want is right there." The band leader began to sing a popular love song. "We were meant as a pair."

For some unexplainable reason, Ian felt giddy as he and Laney took to the dance floor beside Melissa and Clayton, the eyes of all of the guests on them. Was there something so unusual about Laney that it threw his usual steady equilibrium off? Because when he put his arm at her waist, he felt that something he suspected was out there. Not nothing but something. A serious something.

"Ready?" he asked once they were in position. "And one, two, three, one…"

He continued counting, hoping Laney would find the beat and they could sync into a rhythm.

"I would walk without fear," the band leader crooned, "every moment we share."

"Ouch," he couldn't help but snap his foot back as she stepped hard on his toes.

"Sorry, yeah, yeah." She tried to follow his movements. It wasn't going well. "Stop pulling on me!"

"I'm not pulling on you. It's called leading. You're supposed to follow me."

"How am I supposed to know what you're doing so I can follow? I can't see your feet."

"You're supposed to move with me."

"Where?"

"Move with my movements. Ow."

Another stab to the top of his foot. He knew Laney didn't mean to be so bad at this, but he couldn't wait for it to be over. This wasn't how it went in the movies.

As she looked at herself in the Ladies Room mirror, Laney was coming unglued. The armpits of her dress had stretched out and were showing under-boob and sweat stains. The circles under her eyes were dark. Unglued mentally and emotionally, too. Everything about this wedding was harder than she had anticipated it was going to be. Being back in Boston. Knowing that the café in Pittsfield was gone. Enrique out of her life, but not without leaving a figurative scar on her psyche. Here in spirit to remind her that fairy tale weddings weren't for her.

Ian wasn't helping matters any. What a disaster dancing, or attempting to dance, with him had been. She didn't know how to dance with a partner and hadn't thought to learn, hadn't considered that would be one of her last-minute maid of honor responsibilities. Instead, she stumbled all over his feet, feeling like a klutz. Plus, he'd spoken of meeting the right sort of woman to marry and all of that, driving it home for the thousandth time that Laney would be no one at this party's consideration. Ian was just like Enrique.

Except he wasn't. She couldn't exactly put her finger on it yet, but there was something inside his eyes. A longing that was lingering under the surface, something caught and unable to make itself known yet. It was none of her concern, even though she kept thinking about it. That secret within him haunted her.

"Here. I think our drinks disappeared while we were dancing," Ian said, standing on the sidelines of the reception hall when Laney returned. He handed her a fresh purple Mel-Clay, the silly unimaginative cocktail name for the bride and groom's brew.

As Laney accepted the drink from him, their fingers brushed along the glass's stem during the handoff. An unexpected current sizzled up her finger. She took a grateful sip, thirsty from their dancing fiasco. "If we could call what we did dancing. I'm sorry I stepped on your foot that once."

"It was four times, but who's counting? I'm beginning to get some feeling back in my feet now." They stood watching older people boogie to an upbeat tune. "I take it you haven't done much dancing with a partner?"

"Yeah, that would be none."

"Crackled cauliflower with a sriracha glaze?" A server thrust her tray at them.

"Oh, yes," Laney said while grabbing a crunchy-looking morsel speared on a pick. "I don't know what 'crackled' means, but I'm starving."

Ian picked a spear also. "Me too."

"Yummy. The sauce is spicy, but it's cut with the sweetness in the glaze."

Another server approached. "Melon cubes wrapped in prosciutto?"

"You bet." Ian answered for them both as he grabbed two

and two napkins, which were the same emerald green as Laney's dress and Ian's tie and cummerbund.

The corner of the napkin was decorated with a heart that had *M&C* inside of it. Laney wondered what hors d'oeuvres she might have served at the L&E wedding that was never to happen.

"Nice," she said, voting on her bite. "A little balsamic on the melon to contrast the flavors."

"This isn't the city's most renowned wedding venue for no reason."

"Would you like to get married in a swanky place like this? Or are you more the orchard and barn type? Or the tropical island destination wedding?"

Ian laughed. "I haven't got the slightest idea. I don't even know who I'm marrying. She can choose what she wants, no matter to me."

Right after he said that, his eyes clicked to Clayton, who was dancing with Melissa. Laney wondered what Ian was thinking. That all this wedding folderol was nonsense?

"Melissa and Clayton are going to Bermuda tomorrow for their honeymoon. But just the two of them, no wedding party on the beach thing."

The bandleader announced, "Ladies and gentlemen, please return to the tables for dinner."

"We have to be host-y and make sure Melissa and Clayton have everything they need."

Laney rushed to help Melissa and that extra piece of dress, as Ian called it, get properly seated at the sweetheart table, which was placed in the center of the room so that all of the guests could see the bride and groom while they ate, an option Laney thought was a horrible fate. Guaranteeing that if a piece of bread went awkwardly into her mouth, the entire room would see it. But Melissa and Clayton chose to sit on an old-timey orange settee, surrounded by floral displays as if they were in the center of a Victorian garden.

After stepping back once the bride and groom were situated, she said to Ian, "It's sweet. Kind of."

"Clayton told me they were adding some special foods to their menu to make things extra unique. A private label wine. Some kind of elite oysters that come from a small-scale farm. They're supposed to be the finest in the world and cost something like a hundred dollars each."

"I hope they're worth it." They took places next to each other at the wedding party's table. With great formality, he pulled the chair out for her to sit.

She looked at him quizzically.

"What?" he asked.

"Nothing."

"Is there something wrong with pulling a chair out for a lady?"

"It's just so… I'm not used to it."

"Your ex didn't pull a chair out for you?"

"I'm surprised he didn't make me pull his out for him."

Ian frowned. "It sounds like you're better off without him." He made a big gesture of sweeping his hand across the chair. "Mademoiselle."

She giggled.

They ate beef tenderloin with chimichurri sauce and red new potatoes while Laney watched Melissa and Clayton feed each other the hundred-dollar oysters. Laney tried not to be sad. It was a challenge. She'd loved Enrique, or at least loved the idea of him. Why wouldn't she have wanted to move to Madrid with an exciting man and open a café there? They might have had a sweet life, might have had children.

She really didn't want to think about Enrique anymore tonight. So she asked Ian some trivial questions. Favorite food, things about Boston and so on. His mind seemed a million miles away, and he barely answered her questions out of the side of his mouth. She'd be glad when she was done being coupled off with him. He was too hard to read. She spent the rest of the meal listening to the bridesmaid seated on her other side blather about her own recent breakup. Laney couldn't wait to get out of her dress, into a pair of jeans and on with her life.

By the time the grapefruit sorbet course arrived, she needed to get some fresh air, so excused herself and made her way through the cocktail lounge to the outdoor terrace. Slipping through the doors, she took a breath of the warm evening air. She sighed at the night-lights, contemplating what was to be her fate. Would she end up alone, like her mother? Then, surely, being a single parent would be her only option for motherhood. With maybe an accidental pregnancy, or adoption or by using a sperm donor. Maybe that would be okay, like it was for her and her mom. *Relax*, she told herself. Everything didn't have to be figured out this weekend. She'd fall back into her place in the city.

On her fifth deep breath, she heard the terrace door open behind her.

It was Ian. "Oh, you're here, too," he said.

She shook her head. There was no getting away from him.

CHAPTER THREE

"Hi."

One of the bridesmaids sidled up to Ian at the bar, where he was having a quiet cordial. Carolyn, Caroline, Carolina... What was her name?

"Hi," he managed to say.

"Do you live in Boston, Ian?"

"Yes. In Back Bay."

"Oh, that's nice." Back Bay was one of the city's most expensive and desirable neighborhoods, with its European flair and great shopping and restaurants. "I'm thinking of moving to town. I'm in West Roxbury with my parents."

"What would be prompting the move?" he asked to continue the conversation. That's what people did, right? Asked questions. Looked for connection points. He needed to start practicing so that he could discern if he liked one woman more than the other. In order for him to choose one, or that they could choose each other and settle down into couple-dom. That sounded so bloodless he wanted to scream, but it was his truth. No point fighting it.

The bridesmaid used her pinkie finger to touch one corner of her mouth and then the other. Presumably, she was concerned about her lipstick. "I read you were named one of the city's most eligible bachelors." Based on his family's prominence. "Are you really single, Ian, or are you secretly with someone?" Hmm, that was straightforward. There was certainly nothing immediately apparent that was wrong with Carolyn/Caroline/Carolina. Other than that it felt like pulling teeth to prolong the chitchat. He knew he wasn't out for fireworks, but he at least wanted easy companionship, someone he could be authentic with. That wasn't too outlandish to hope for, was it?

He thought about Laney and a smile came to his face. She was so honest and forthcoming. The way her hair was an utter disaster at the photo shoot before the rehearsal dinner. The way she defiantly didn't want to wear makeup even with the stylist chasing after her. There was something funny and charming about that. Although an impeccable appearance would be required for whoever someone of Ian's standing married. The Luss women managed brains and beauty. His mother was a tall, cool blonde who never stepped out of the house unless she was flawless from head to toe.

"You guessed it. I actually am spoken for," he lied. There was no reason to hurt her feelings, especially after she'd made herself vulnerable. "She is...out of town this weekend."

Carolyn/Caroline/Carolina was a stunning woman, polished and primped. She didn't smack of desperation, just practicality, asking if he was truly single. Then he thought of Laney again, bombing in her wedding speech. She kept popping into his mind. Where was she now? After they'd accidentally both tried unsuccessfully to find solitude on the terrace, he'd come back inside. Had she?

He supposed it was about time to cut the cake, and he'd probably be expected to pose for yet more photos. "I think we're due back inside."

"I'll be there in a minute," Carolyn/Caroline/Carolina said. She'd noticed a couple of men leaning on the far side of the bar sipping drinks, so she sauntered over.

Inside the reception hall, the party was still in full swing. Half the guests were on the dance floor, and others huddled at the tables attempting to talk over the volume of the music. Melissa and Clayton stood in the center of it all receiving well wishes, their smiles maybe a little strained as the event wore on.

He moved farther into the room and watched an older lady dancing with a teenage boy who looked miserable. Every time he stepped away, the elderly lady yanked him back. When they swung apart again, Ian spotted Laney. She was dancing with a short dark-haired man. Ian had no idea who he was. They weren't touching, however they did seem to be looking into each other's eyes. He couldn't think of a reason to, but he felt jealous. Ian and Laney meant nothing to each other. He had no plans to see her after the wedding. They hadn't even established a cordial best man and maid of honor rapport; it had been prickly. Yet he wanted that man away from Laney—immediately. Which was crazy.

As if possessed by a spirit outside of himself, he moved into the thick of the dance floor to find them. He shimmied his shoulders a little bit as if he were into the groove.

"May I cut in?" he asked when he got close enough.

That was how it was done, wasn't it? It was an accepted social convention to ask her to excuse herself from dancing with the man and switch to dancing with him.

Maybe it should have been, except that Laney furrowed

her brows and said, "Uh, no. I'm dancing with…what was your name?"

"Quincy," the man answered, squirming left and right in his too-tight pants.

"Quincy," Laney repeated to Ian as if he hadn't just heard it.

It was ridiculous that any of this bothered him. Why did he want to swoop Laney into his arms and waltz with her like a prince at a ball? They'd already proven they couldn't dance like that together. Plus, that was the lovey-dovey stuff he was supposedly having no part of. Jealousy and sweeping a woman into his embrace! She'd declined his request to whisk her away, so he had to respect that. Which meant he stood on the dance floor alone, not knowing what to do with himself.

He caught sight of the flower girl, probably all of six-years-old in her matching emerald-green dress. He got her attention and followed the butterfly wing arms she was swirling around with. Ian enjoyed the pure impulsiveness and had a genuinely carefree few minutes sharing a giggle with the little girl but he did notice Laney studying him from the corner of her eye.

It was the wee hours before the last of the guests left. Some of the relatives who had traveled great distances were departing in the morning, so Melissa and Clayton pressed on, devoting time to each of them.

"Help me get the gifts onto these carts, and we'll bring them to the bridal suite for the night," Laney said, still ready to pitch in.

Too tired to argue that the wedding manager could call in some staff to do the task, Ian set to it. They stacked the gifts on the cart, larger ones on the bottom. Many were wrapped by the upscale store where Melissa and Clayton had done their registry, so he knew he was attending to thousands upon thousands of dollars' worth of merchandise.

"Home and kitchen goods, of course," Ian said. "That's what couples are given as gifts."

"It makes sense," Laney said. "In older times, when a bride and groom would be moving in together and had never lived alone out of their parents' house, they would need these things."

Ian had been mentally reviewing wedding customs all night. Making notes for his own. His apartment had a kitchen full of barely used state-of-the-art equipment and appliances. Would he need all new things when he married?

Clayton chatted with some relatives. He'd now switched from ecstatic to something else. Perspiration was beading on his upper lip; in fact, sweat from his brow was running down his face. He must have been exhausted after hours and hours of being *onstage*, as it were. Ian hoped that when he and Melissa got on the plane to Bermuda, they could let their hair down and soak in some much-needed relaxation.

"So, what, you liked dancing with that Quincy guy?" he asked Laney behind the pyramid of gifts.

"What does it matter to you?"

"Not a stitch. Just curious. I thought you were off men."

"I am. It was just something to do. Especially since I was a disaster at dancing with you, the evening got long."

"You just don't know how to dance. You could learn." That image of whirling her around the dance floor popped into his head again.

"Look at Melissa over there." Laney pointed at the bride, who was pale as a ghost as she bid someone farewell. "Her coloring is kind of gray at this point."

"Green, actually," said Ian.

They stood bearing witness as Melissa suddenly put her hand over her stomach.

"Yeah, she doesn't seem right."

"Neither does Clayton." Clayton's face had become red, and sweat had soaked the front of his tuxedo shirt. They turned back to Melissa, whose head rotated in a circle like she was in a daze.

"They can't take much more of this. Should we do something?" said Laney.

Ian and Laney watched Melissa mouth *Excuse me* to her guests and then dash across the reception hall toward the Ladies Room.

"Food poisoning. And judging from the fact that they both have fevers, a bad case of it." The club's on-duty physician was quickly able to piece together a diagnosis.

As the last of the out-of-town relatives had said their goodbyes long after the clock had struck midnight, Melissa and Clayton simultaneously began vomiting in the deserted bathrooms.

"The oysters," Ian said to Laney.

"In August. A month that doesn't have an R in it." The age-old advice not to eat oysters in warm weather should have been heeded.

"The special menu that only the bride and groom ate."

"Clayton told me they were some kind of rare breed of oysters and cost a hundred dollars each!"

"Money well spent. Not."

"Can we sue the caterer?"

The service lamps were on. No longer were the party lights casting a flattering glow on the guests. The staff had cleared away everything from the last plate to spoon to linen, uncovering the tabletops made from plastic and metal. Ian and Laney sat side by side at one of the long-vacated tables. One of the waiters had been kind enough to provide them with a carafe of coffee and a couple of cups. The doctor promised to check back in a little while.

The bride and groom were now slumped on the settee of their long-planned sweetheart table where they had eaten the offending oysters. Melissa's third dress of the evening, a slinky retro movie-star-type gown that clung to her body, was wet and off-kilter from its many trips to the Ladies Room. Clayton didn't look much better in his untucked and soiled shirt, the tie and jacket long since tossed off. They dabbed their faces with cold washcloths. The sequence that had now repeated itself several times began with one of them making a groaning sound. That was followed with a stomach cramp, quickly followed by a mad dash to the bathroom. After a few minutes, one or the other would return with less of a cry than a whimper as they staggered back to the settee. Then a plop down next to the other.

"I love you Mel," Clayton would manage.

"I love you, too, Clay." Then a groan would come and the steps would be repeated.

"We're supposed to be on the way to our honeymoon in a couple of hours," Melissa said in a labored, scratchy voice.

"The resort in Bermuda is expecting us."

"I can't get on a plane."

"I guess we'll have to postpone." Clayton scrunched his face in distress at the realization.

"The doctor said we probably wouldn't be eating normally again for a week."

"Don't mention food."

"I don't think I've ever felt sicker."

"Ian," Clayton called over to him in a feeble voice. "Can you look up the cancellation procedure for the resort?"

"Of course." He reached for his phone in his tuxedo pants pocket and began.

Laney felt so bad for them. Any bride and groom were probably so looking forward to their honeymoon. To recuperate from all the planning and decisions and details that had gone into their wedding day. Even though it was for different reasons, Laney could relate. How much she'd love to be heading to a resort in Bermuda with its pink sand beaches, clear waters and a luxury resort.

It would surely be nice. Oh, to walk with her toes in the water, taking in the ocean breezes and allowing her mind to clear. She could let go of the past, and physically, mentally and spiritually prepare to start over. Of course, she didn't have the money for an exotic island destination. Nothing like that was in her future. Maybe a walk along the city's Charles River next week.

"Not great news," Ian announced, reading from his phone. "There are no cancellations within forty-eight hours of scheduled arrival. I texted the concierge on twenty-four-hour call, and she apologized but restated their policy."

"Oh, great," Melissa said, sulking. "Not only are we not able to go, we'll lose all of the money we spent. We'd booked a first-class flight, the resort's most lavish villa, private beach, private garden, the whole thing."

Laney figured they could afford to rebook sometime later, but still, it was a terrible shame that such a glorious escapade would go unclaimed.

"Private golf cart," Clayton added.

"Gourmet meals," Melissa threw in.

At the word *gourmet*, Clayton lurched and then made his next dash to the Men's Room.

"Unless anybody needs anything," Ian announced after finishing his coffee, "I'm going to check on Clayton and then head to my room."

Some of the wedding party were staying in the exclusive hotel that occupied the lower five floors of the Fletcher Club, compliments of the groom.

Melissa pouted, "Thank you for everything, Ian. It was a beautiful wedding until...it wasn't."

Laney piped up, trying to be helpful. "It will all make for a memory you'll laugh over with your grandchildren someday."

Ian tilted his head and looked at Laney with a wry smile that somehow shot right into her heart. He lifted his shoulders. "Grandchildren. There's a thought. Goodnight. Or should I say, good morning."

"See you in a few hours," said Laney.

They'd agreed to reconvene and help the newlyweds get packed up and get everything out of the club.

Melissa's head lolled back, so she didn't witness Laney eyeing Ian walk across the reception hall as he left. He confused her. Why did his stare pierce through her at the mention of grandkids? As he'd explained, marriage and breeding for him was just part of an overall corporate strategy. In turn, grandchildren extended the family's master scheme for another generation. The Lusses were a strange breed from what he had told her.

Although, perhaps they had a mentality shared with the uber-rich of the world. Mate with your head, not with your heart. Sound thinking, really. That wasn't her, though. She was all or nothing. Madly in love or totally alone, thank you very much. Yet, there was something so adorable about the way Ian had fluttered butterfly arms with the flower girl while Laney was dancing with Quincy. She couldn't imagine him as a dry and distant father.

Laney had found things complicated when he had tried to cut in on her with Quincy. On principle, she wasn't going to let him decide who she was and wasn't going to dance with. Enrique would have objected, which he did most unsubtly, if he didn't like her interactions with other men. Ian had no right and no cause.

Yet, Laney had to admit how much she liked it when he had tried to take her from Quincy. She'd never let him know, but that made her feel coveted. It wasn't something she'd felt very often, and it tickled her from the roots of her hair to the tippy tops of her toes. She was glad she said no, but she thought she might remember the interaction forever.

And what Ian didn't see later was that Quincy kept trying to hold her by the hips even though they weren't partner dancing. She ended up slipping out of his clutches at the earliest opportunity.

"Laney." Melissa bobbled her head up and spoke in a drunken-sounding voice, no doubt loopy from being sick and awake all night. "I have an idea. Why don't you go to Bermuda and enjoy my honeymoon?" The bride giggled at herself.

"What?" Laney sat down near her.

"The nonrefundable villa in Bermuda. The first-class plane tickets. You should go instead."

"Like I'd just go by myself? To your private villa."

"Yeah, why not? I know that you've been through a lot lately. Couldn't you use the vacation and relaxation?"

Melissa had no idea! She was offering a place where

Laney could walk on the beach? To think and sort herself out. To send the hurts of the past ebbing away with the tide. To let sunrises fill her with energy and enthusiasm for starting anew. What an extraordinary offer.

"Are you sure?"

"Why not? What's the point of letting my beautiful honeymoon go to waste?" She frowned.

"You'll reschedule when you're better. You have your whole lives together."

"I know, right? I'm a married lady now."

"You sure are."

"You'll meet your man soon, too. I'm certain of it."

Laney doubted that. "Sure."

"Hey, what time is it?" the disheveled bride asked. "We had an early flight. You'd better hurry. We have a car booked to take us—uh, you, to the airport."

"Are you sure about this?"

"Yeah. It's not like we're going to be able to go."

With the snap of a finger, Laney was headed to a vacation in paradise. She couldn't think of a reason in the world not to say yes to the lovely offer. Well, maybe one. She and Ian were supposed to help Melissa and Clayton get packed up this morning. If she had a plane to catch, she wouldn't be able to complete her maid of honor duties. Obviously, Melissa wouldn't mind. Although it did bother Laney that she wouldn't be seeing Ian again this weekend. Which was absurd and didn't matter in the slightest. Not a bit.

"Again?"

"I can't believe..."

"Yup." Ian scratched his chin as he watched Clayton make another beeline to the bathroom, this time in the honeymoon suite. When Ian had found him lying on towels in the Men's Room in the reception hall, he helped him to the suite and texted Melissa that he'd done so. The groom plunked down on the gold satin linens of the king-size bed where wedding nights continued. Long after the band had finished, the ballroom lights had been dimmed and the aunties had gone home, private celebrations would start. Where a bride and groom, whether it was for the first time or whether they'd been sharing a bed for years, would lay down together as husband and wife. Ian found something ancient and sacred in that, the couple commemorating their legal union with a physical act.

"Some wedding night," Clayton lifted his head. "I'm dizzy, but not in a favorable way. Where's my bride?"

"Last I saw her, she was availing herself of the bathroom in the reception hall. Laney was with her."

Ambling around the suite, Ian stopped to finger the petals of a white long-stemmed rose that stood with eleven others in a beveled vase. The petal felt like velvet, an amazing achievement by Mother Nature. Along with, for example, Laney's luminous light brown eyes. *Wait, what?* He was comparing the wonders of a rose to the eyes of a woman he barely knew and who was no part of his life. He was definitely going cuckoo. He needed a vacation.

"Oh, my wife," Clayton blubbered dramatically into the air, knowing she couldn't hear him, then wiped his face with a wet towel.

Still fingering the flower, Ian asked, "How did you know Melissa was the right woman for you?"

Ian and Clayton had met at Oxford University and found they both hailed from Boston. They were sons and grandsons of giants, the American elite of the elite. They never heard the word *no*. Even so, they were taught to be honorable people, and they didn't lord their power over women. They didn't have to. Women flocked to them. They posed and paraded around them like display items for sale. That was when Ian realized that finding someone to trust, someone who liked him for him and not only for his family name, wasn't going to be easy. And on the other hand, the life of a Luss wife was what he had to offer, and he did want someone who understood what would and wouldn't be the arrangement.

"I knew Melissa was the one because when I wasn't around her, I wanted to be." Clayton let out a growl at his predicament. "My stomach is killing me!"

"Do you want some water?"

"Definitely not," he answered with a small heave.

"Anyway..." Perhaps it would help to keep Clayton distracted from his discomfort.

"Anyway, when I'm with her, I feel I'm at my best. Like our hearts are connected. Hopeful. Safe. And what makes it even better is to know I make her feel those things, too."

"When you know, you know?"

"Yeah."

Clayton's family didn't have quite the hard and fast rules about mating that Ian's did. That was okay. Family was family. He was proud that Luss Global Holdings employed hundreds of people who counted on the company's leadership to make smart decisions. "I'm very happy for you, Clayton. Other than the vomiting and all."

At that, he got a comic sneer from his friend. "I know Melissa is going to be disappointed—tomorrow, this morning or whatever the heck time it is—that we're not going to Bermuda."

"You'll reschedule."

"Hey, do you want to go?"

"To Bermuda?"

"Yeah. Use the reservation. Might as well. Otherwise, I'll lose the money."

"Go to the resort?"

"For that matter, you could invite someone if you wanted to. Any female prospects you've encountered lately?"

"No." Ian snickered.

Nothing could be further from the truth. His grandfather Hugo had been pressuring him to find someone. He wouldn't retire until Ian was settled so that the succession was secured. His son, Rupert, Ian's father, was in Zurich running the international arm of the company. And since Ian's uncle Harley proved himself unable to take over the domestic arm from Hugo, Ian would do it, stepping up from his current position directing appraisals and risk management. Ian would produce children and Luss Global Holdings would continue to grow. All of it outlined and scheduled. In fact, Hugo had already set Ian up on a couple of dates with appropriate women, none to his liking.

Ingrid was a chilly neuroscience researcher at Massachusetts General Hospital. During the two dates they went on, she spoke of nothing but her work, using terms like *basolateral amygdala* and *temporal lobe structure*. He was impressed with her distinguished career, but he thought she'd be better suited with someone in a similar field. He had to have *something* he could talk about with his mate.

Thea was part of a family like Ian's, whose domination in their field, of manufacturing plastic goods, made them a massive fortune. With dark hair and thick, busy eyebrows, she was a numbers cruncher, and there were three guests at their dinner together. Ian, Thea and her the calculator app on her phone. She showed Ian one financial scenario after the next, if they were to expand into India. This set of numbers if they forged into Africa. By the time dessert arrived, Ian's eyes were rolling back in his head. He didn't need a wife who exhausted him. The search wasn't going to be easy.

"So go on your own," Clayton suggested. "You could probably use a vacation. When was the last time you traveled when it wasn't for work?"

Clayton had him there. Why shouldn't he take a little time off and just walk on a beach alone? He could think about how he was going to know what woman was right for him. Someone who could really go the distance under their family's rules but who he could live contentedly with.

Ian's mother and father did. Vera was involved in her charities, in her case raising money for women's groups in war-torn areas of the world. His mother also had her female friends who met for lunch and cocktails and shopping all over Europe. She and Ian's dad had that cordial, serviceable and supportive relationship that the Luss family required. Everyone understood what was expected of them, and it all fit together like a puzzle.

His grandmother told him something else, words that spoke to him in the dark of night, but that was beside the point.

Warm sand under his feet and the notifications on his phone set to Off sounded pretty nice.

"Okay," he tilted his head so it was in line with Clayton's. "Thanks. I'll go."

"Great. We booked an early flight, so you'll need to head out soon."

"You know, the maid of honor and I were supposed to supervise getting your gifts and clothes and whatnot rounded up and out. I'll be leaving that all to Laney." That stuck in his craw. He'd not only renege on his duty but miss the chance to spend a little more time with her. She somehow exasperated and intrigued him at the same time with her sincerity and frankness. *Oh, well.* It couldn't be helped.

"Don't worry about it. My mom or Melissa's mom will deal with it. They live for that sort of thing."

"Well then, I guess I'm on my way to your honeymoon."

CHAPTER FOUR

IT WAS ALL happening so fast. A chauffer in full uniform held open the door of a shiny black stretch limo in front of the Fletcher Club. Laney had never been in a limo and slid into the soft leather of the back seat, swinging her legs in after her as glamorous as a movie star. After making sure she was comfortably situated, the driver gently closed the door.

Take that, Enrique. As she had told Ian, Enrique never held a door open for her, always leaving her standing in the cold as he first let himself into a car, sometimes putting on sunglasses or taking off a scarf before he bothered to click the button that opened the passenger door. She never knew whether he was like that with all women, himself the golden child whose mother thought he walked on water, or whether he didn't deem Laney worthy of the chivalrous treatment. He thought he was *slumming it* with her; he made that clear. Why she was dumb enough to think he'd fall in love with her and none of that would matter, she had no idea. Wishful thinking. Lesson learned.

As the limo pulled away, the driver informed her, "Ma'am,

in the tray in front of you, you'll find coffee, freshly squeezed orange juice and a bucket of champagne on ice. There's also fruit and warm croissants. Is there anything else you'll need?"

"No," she choked out, trying to keep from laughing. "That ought to do it, thank you."

Of course, she didn't need more than that just to make it the short distance to the airport. She'd had coffee to keep herself awake while she hastily gathered up her belongings in order to catch the flight. She left the formal bridal party clothes behind. Melissa assured her that the resort in Bermuda had shops where she could pick up beach and casual clothes and whatever she needed. In fact, the honeymoon reservation included a generous shopping allowance.

At the airport, the driver pointed out to her where to go in the terminal, and from there, she was ushered straight into the first-class lounge, where a pink-suited attendant welcomed her. Melissa had been able to text her travel agent and get the name changed on the reservation. "I'm Serena from Pink Shores Resort. Will your significant other be joining you shortly?" Laney's mouth opened wide as if to answer, but no words came out. Significant other? She didn't know what this woman was talking about. "While you're waiting, perhaps you'd like a light breakfast. Coffee, freshly squeezed orange juice, champagne, fruit and warm croissants."

"Thank you."

The exact same menu the limo driver had offered. Hmm, that wasn't a half bad way to live! After all, there could never be too many buttery pastries in the world. Although she politely declined, having already gobbled two in the limo. Her rest and reset was getting off to a delicious start.

Boarding began. The first-class cabin was appointed with huge reclining chairs. Laney's was by the window, the one beside it vacant, no doubt the two seats that had been assigned to Melissa and Clayton. Laney began exploring the amenities for the two-hour flight. The headrest behind her was so plush she could sink right into it. A partition offered privacy. She had her own extra-large touch screen to watch whatever she wanted on the personal entertainment center. She flipped through the channels, ranging from first-run movies to hit television shows to live sporting events to dozens of types of music. Padded headphones were provided as well as the latest technology in earbuds. There was an e-reader loaded with hundreds of books. A pull-out tray was positioned for comfortable laptop use or for eating. There was a lighting panel with many options. The flight attendant offered never-used blankets and pillows for her comfort.

"We'll be departing shortly," Serena popped her head in. "Has your companion encountered a delay?"

Laney didn't know what to say or do. Since Melissa hadn't brought it up, she figured she'd just board the plane without any questions. She noticed that Serena was careful to use the words *companion* and *significant other*, not saying any names out loud for privacy and not making any gender assumptions.

"I'll try to reach him, but he'll take another flight if need be," she said, quickly fudging.

"As you know, Pink Shores Resort is a couples-only retreat."

Wait, what?

"We maintain our reputation as a five-star, world-renowned romantic destination by enforcing our protocol. We ask our couples to arrive and depart together."

"I'll call him right now." After Serena moved on, Laney called Melissa in a panic.

"Oh no!" Melissa shrieked in a still-woozy voice. "I didn't know the resort had that exclusivity."

"What should I do now? I lied and said my significant other was on his way. And then I said he was taking another flight."

"I'm so sorry. Maybe if you can just get to Bermuda, I'll call them and explain."

"Didn't Ian do that last night?" He'd relayed to the group the inflexibility of the booking restrictions.

"I'm sorry, Ms. Sullivan," Serena poked around the partition again. "The captain would like to prepare for takeoff. As I mentioned, we only allow our resort's couples on the flights. We'll have to ask you to deplane along with me, and then we'll gladly get you onto the next flight once your significant other has arrived. Perhaps you'd enjoy a croissant while you wait. Kindly follow me."

There went her ritzy vacation. That was Laney's luck. Nothing had gone right for her. Not Enrique. Not the café. Not even her interactions with the best man, Ian, this weekend. Now this.

With a resigned exhale, Laney rose. Embarrassed, she looked around at her fellow passengers in the first-class section, which seemed to be filled with Pink Shores Resort guests, based on an identifying tag clipped on the side of their seats. They were, indeed, all couples. Newlyweds and those who looked like they were commemorating milestone anniversaries. Maybe a twenty-fifth. Maybe even a fiftieth. Couples of mixed races, same-sex pairs, all whispering to each other or holding hands or leaning over to give one another a kiss. United in one solitary purpose. Excitedly on their way to celebrate their love. Laney felt horribly out of place.

As she reached down to grab her bag and then get off the plane, she heard a familiar male voice. "There was an accident on the highway that delayed my arrival to the airport."

Where did she know that voice from? She'd heard it recently. Whose was it?

"We're glad you made it," came Serena's voice. "Have a pleasant flight."

Bag in hand, Laney stood and turned to see who was rushing down the aisle.

No, no, no, no!

It was Ian! She sat back down.

The pilot announced over the sound system, "Flight crew, lock the doors for departure."

Ian slipped into the seat that the flight attendant had gestured to and swiveled his chair to face front. He observed that the occupant of the seat next to him had a shapely pair of legs. When he followed the legs up, he did a double take. It couldn't be.

"Laney?"

"What are *you* doing here?" she retorted.

"What are *you* doing here?"

"Melissa invited me."

"Clayton insisted I use the vacation so it didn't go to waste. Everything was prepaid and nonrefundable."

"Please fasten your seat belts for takeoff," a flight attendant instructed Ian, who pulled the strap to comply.

"I know, I was in the room when you called to try to explain the situation. Melissa wanted *me* to use the reservation."

"Without telling Clayton?"

"When you're lying down on the bathroom floor, perhaps you don't do your best thinking."

"Clayton was in about the same shape."

"Apparently, they didn't tell either of us that Pink Shores Resort is for couples only. The resort's representative was about to make me leave because I was onboard without my significant other."

Ian quickly called Clayton before he needed to turn off his cell phone. "Hey, thanks for the invite, but did you know that the resort is couples only? And did you know that Laney is on the plane? That Melissa told her to use the reservation."

"What? No. Melissa, did you...? Let me put you on speakerphone, she's right here."

"Melissa?" Laney brought her mouth close to the phone.

"Yeah." Ian switched the speaker on, and Melissa's voice came through. "Clay and I are lying in bed together, still in half of our wedding clothes. Honey, you texted the travel agent and put Ian on the reservation?"

"I forgot to tell you."

"Can we make some other arrangement with the resort?" Laney piped in. "The rep here told me we have the honeymooners' villa."

Ian asked, "Do you think we could swap it for two smaller rooms?"

"Just go and have a nice time," Clayton said. "I'm sure the villa is big enough that you won't even see each other."

There was nothing to be done. Ian knew he had about one minute to make his objection known, disrupt the flight and force his way off the plane. If he didn't, he'd be spending the week with Laney. She of the café au lait eyes and the bum luck of late.

"I guess we're on our way, then."

"I guess so." She pursed her lips, maybe as unsure about this as he was.

"I've got to get in one more call before the captain insists we shut our electronics down." He tapped his speed dial for a number he used frequently, although he turned off the speaker. "Grandfather."

"Where are you, Ian? It sounds like you're on an airplane."

"Yes, I'm on a commercial flight." Luss Global had its own jet and, if it was occupied, Ian would generally hire a private plane. "I just wanted to let you know that I'm taking a quick holiday to Bermuda."

"All right. But I want you to know that I've been speaking with colleagues, and I'm going to be gathering the names of some more women I want you to have dinner with as soon as you get back. And I need you to give each your serious consideration."

Ian glanced over to Laney, who was thumbing through a magazine. He was glad she wasn't hearing Hugo. The matchmaking was so old-school, it was a little humiliating, if efficient. He didn't like the frailty he heard in his grandfather's voice. After a long and prosperous career, and having lost his wife a couple of years ago, it really was time for him to step down. Ian knew he would stick to his word and not do so until his grandson found a bride. It was all on him.

"I will, grandfather."

The Luss marriage rulebook dated back to Hugo's grandfather, Frederick. He would be Ian's great-great-grandfather. Frederick was to partner with his brother Phillip to buy land using the inheritance that their father had left them, plus money they'd earned. Then Phillip met a wily woman who he fell madly in love with. He worshipped the ground she walked on. She told him that her family had forged south to Georgia, and that was where he should purchase the land. Phillip was too blinded by his love for the persuasive woman to cross his t's and dot his i's, and before he knew it, the land had been bought in the woman's name only, a result of her dishonest relatives brokering the sale. Phillip's half of the investment in the new venture with his brother was gone, and the woman disappeared.

After that, Frederick decided that unions between men and women would become trade agreements, mutually beneficial to all parties, with both families thoroughly scrutinized. The process worked well for several generations until Ian's Uncle Harley fell for a party girl, Nicole, a baroness of all things, who should have fit the bill. That was a disaster, and Harley's globe-trotting and reckless spending cost the company tens of millions of dollars. He knew his grandfather wouldn't loosen the reins after that.

"Ladies and gentlemen," the pilot instructed, "we're pulling out of the gate. Please turn off all of your devices or set them to Airplane Mode."

As Ian did, he gazed over at Laney again. He'd spent more time with her at the wedding than he probably had with any woman in ages, if ever. Now he'd be at a faraway resort with her.

"So, what, we have to pretend to be a couple?"

"Not only that, but because we have the honeymoon villa, we have to pretend to be newlyweds. In public, that is."

He'd never been part of a couple. Even with a cold contract sort of marriage, he'd still have to have some husbandly skills that a woman would want. This could be practice for him. Sure, Laney wasn't the pedigreed type he was ex-

pected to marry, but that didn't mean he couldn't masquerade at it with her.

"Is that okay with you? We'll act like we're together when
we're out and about at the resort?"

"It sounds kind of wacky, but sure. It seems to mean a lot
to Clayton and Melissa that the trip doesn't go to waste."

"Maybe if they feel better, they'll actually decide to come
in a few days. And then we'll leave."

They were not going to become fixtures in each other's
lives. It was only for a week at most. There was no reason
for this not to work out. Perhaps it was fortuitous. It was a
chance for Ian to prepare for the next phase of his life. When
he accepted Clayton's offer to use the reservation, one of
his first thoughts had been that in leaving, he wouldn't get
to say goodbye to Laney. In a way, a best man and maid of
honor are almost thrown together as a couple. There had already been cheek-to-cheek photos, pulling out chairs, com-
miserating about speeches and calamitous dancing.

Once the plane was in the air and had reached cruising
altitude, the flight attendant approached with a tray. "Can
I offer you a cup of fish chowder, a Bermudian favorite, or
perhaps you'd like an omelet?"

"I'd love to try the chowder," said Laney. "I love eating
like a local."

Ian smiled. "I'll have the same."

He liked that Laney was open to trying interesting food.
That was something they could do together on this trip. Plus,
as Clayton said, the honeymoon villa was likely to be large.
They could each claim their own space and spend the whole
week apart if they wanted to. Which he didn't. He wanted
to act like he was on his honeymoon. Still, that there were
options was a comfort.

The attendant laid cream-colored linen place mats onto their dining trays. She then added a matching napkin and silver utensils. Placing the soup tureens carefully, she presented them with a bread basket filled with warm rolls and a pot of butter.

"What else can I get you to drink?" she asked after also serving glasses of water with ice.

"I'll have a coke," Laney ordered.

"Sparkling water with lime," said Ian.

After a sip, Ian peered across the aisle to study an older couple. They were both holding stemmed glasses that looked to contain red wine. First, they clinked glasses as in a basic toast. Then, without either of them saying anything, they intertwined their arms to feed each other a sip from their own glass. That was followed by a knowing smile, and then the woman leaned closely toward the man and affectionately rubbed her cheek on his shoulder. Ian would bet that they had been together a long time, that there was so much between them that didn't need saying aloud.

"Mrs. Luss."

"What?" Laney looked up from her soup.

"Excellent. I was practicing to see if you'd answer to your new name."

"I don't have to take your name just because we're 'married.'" She made air quotes with her fingers.

"Why don't we just keep it simple and traditional? Less explaining."

"Okay, Mr. Luss. Have you tried the soup, husband? It's delicious."

She helped herself to another spoonful of the chowder, chunky with fish and aromatic vegetables. Then she broke off a piece of the warm roll and swirled it into the soup. Ian

expected her to eat it. Instead, she surprised him by popping the bite into his mouth. He fumbled in surprise and
then had to lick his lips to make sure all of it made it in.

"That's something couples would do, don't you think?"
she said.

A shiver ran down his spine, which was a surprise, ignited by her supple fingers touching his lips with the food
morsel. He bunched his forehead, almost annoyed that a
couple of fingertips could have such an effect on him. And
that wasn't the first time her touch had aroused him. That
was the only hitch about spending a week with Laney. She
stirred him up. Magic fingers creating involuntary muscle
tingles was precisely what he wasn't going to marry, so he
surely didn't need to train at it. Or maybe it was that he did
need to. To get those longings out of his system, once and
for all, so that he could turn his back on them and get on
with the future he'd planned.

Hmm. "We should agree on a common story about how
we met. Things people might ask."

"Three years ago at a wedding. How about that?"

"You were a bridesmaid and I asked everyone if they
knew you. And whether you were seeing anyone."

"Aw, that's cute."

It was at that. He continued, "I noticed you up at the
altar in a godawful yellow poofy dress. During the ceremony, you sensed me looking at you, and our eyes met. It
wasn't just your beauty, it was your essence, the way you
had about you."

"I wanted to stare into your eyes until eternity."

"You hit me like a thunderbolt. I knew you were the one
for me. That you'd be the woman I'd marry."

Was he reciting lines from a movie he'd seen or a book

he'd read? How else would all of that have come spilling out? Truthfully, he liked the story, liked the notion of love at first sight. Of souls igniting. Knowing in an instant that two people had been put on Earth for each other.

He glanced over to the older couple again. The man brought his wife's hand to his lips so that he could kiss the top of it. His blue eyes crinkled with gratitude.

A lump formed in Ian's throat.

"Welcome, honeymooners." A concierge in a pink jacket met Laney and Ian as soon as they arrived to the Pink Shores Resort. "I am Adalson, and the staff and I are at your service. On behalf of all of us, may we say congratulations on your nuptials, and we wish you a long and happy life together."

Very nice well-wishes after such a momentous milestone of getting married. Had she actually gotten married, that was. In fact, she was never going to get married. At twenty-eight and after Enrique, that was settled. And certainly not to the devastatingly handsome man next to her, who she barely knew.

"Yes, I'm a lucky man," Ian fake-boasted as he tried to lope his long arm around her so they could co-acknowledge Adalson's words. Except that Laney spontaneously jumped back and away from the swerve of his reach. Which left him hugging air. He stuttered, out of context, "We're the Lusses."

Adalson gave them both a confused look. "Perhaps it was a trying flight? Please look forward to relaxing Bermy style."

"Oh yeah, right," she mumbled and corrected herself by stepping into Ian's wingspan.

He gripped her by the shoulder and pulled her in. She

managed an inane grin, like her man was just so cute. Then she immediately had to *not* concentrate on how firm his hand on her was. She also had to *not* concentrate on the sturdy side of his body that was meeting hers. *Not* concentrate on how amazing he felt, holding her warm and tight, and how she melted against him. *Not* replay in her mind bringing that bite of chowder-soaked bread to his mouth when they were on the plane. She shouldn't have made such an intimate move in the first place, but he didn't have to turn it into something so sensual. Then the way she could only gawk as he licked his lips. This masquerade was already a challenge. And they'd just arrived.

"We'll bring your bags to your villa. Would you like to walk there on the beach or take a golf cart?"

"Beach," Laney answered.

"Golf cart," Ian blurted in unison, his voice on top of hers.

"I'm sorry, I meant golf cart," she said, trying again.

Right as Ian corrected with "Beach."

They looked at each other and fake-laughed. "Ha ha, ha ha."

Adalson again averted his eyes for discretion, clearly not knowing what to make of them.

Neither did Laney, other than that her head was starting to spin. Maybe this trip wasn't going to be as easy as it seemed.

"I think you may be a bit tired," Adalson interjected. "Why don't I take you in the cart, and you'll have plenty of occasions to walk on the beach later? That is, if you choose to leave the villa at all."

All three of them knew what he meant. If Laney was the blushing bride type, now would be the time. She wasn't, so she looked lovingly up to her husband, as any happy new wife would.

Adalson drove them along a path that cut through the vibrant green lawn.

"Oh my gosh!" Laney exclaimed when they rounded the corner that allowed them to face the shoreline.

"What?" Ian asked.

"The water is truly turquoise." Exactly like it was in the photos she researched online before she boarded the flight. She didn't know anything about Bermuda, and suddenly she was here. "And the sand. It really is pink."

It seemed like a minute ago that she could only stand idly by while firefighters tried in vain to salvage the café that was blazing away right before her very eyes. Now she was on an island in the middle of the Atlantic Ocean trying to fathom how sand could actually be pink.

"I'm amazed by it every time I come."

Oh, of course the rich guy had been here before. His family probably owned the island. Which didn't stop her jaw from hanging open at the stunning colors of the water and sand. She'd never seen anything like it in her life. It was incredible. She couldn't wait to take her first walk. She'd bet the sand was soft and would feel magical between her toes. And unlike what Adalson was insinuating, it wasn't as if she was going to be inside the whole time with her groom. She was going to be out on the beach and in the water.

"We're getting farther and farther away from the central buildings of the resort," she said to Ian as they rode through a grove of trees and into a secluded area.

"We've entered your private grounds. You have this entire beach to yourself. There's no access other than for you and staff," Adalson explained, "who will text you before entering your villa compound. So please consider this clothing optional."

"Uh-uh," Ian made a noise she couldn't interpret.

What she did understand, however, is the way the low timbre of his voice sent a hum right through her body. Clothing was going to be mandatory, not optional, around him. This little charade could become dangerous if she didn't protect herself. She couldn't withstand any more hurt. That wasn't what happened on *fake* honeymoons, anyway.

"This is your personal patio and garden." Adalson gestured.

A wooden deck with a white table and chairs, as well as two loungers, were positioned to enjoy a garden. Trees both short and tall swayed in the gentle breeze. A rainbow of flowers grew along a path. Which gave way to the entrance to the villa.

"Our finest and most luxurious accommodations at the resort."

"Wow," said Laney.

It was a house on a beach right at the shore, elevated from the water. The one-story building was painted pastel pink with white trim and a white roof, as was typical Bermudian style. Once Laney and Ian got out of the cart and approached the entrance, she could see that there was a wraparound balcony with a railing made of wooden slats.

"Three hundred and sixty degrees of balcony," Adalson confirmed. "Is that to your liking, ma'am?"

"It certainly is."

"So that you can take in sunrises and sunsets from whatever angle you choose." Ah, as if she might have to settle for only one panoramic view of the sea and sky. "May I show you inside?"

Ian thought quickly to grab her hand as people romantically involved might do. She liked his big palm with its thick fingers. Enrique had slender hands that, to be honest, she never enjoyed holding. He went for frequent manicures, and his hands were always powdery. She liked Ian's; they were strong and manly.

The kind of hand she might like to hold for the rest of her life.

Not Ian's, specifically. Of course.

She'd hold no man's hand until eternity.

Anyway, she was getting flustered in her own thoughts.

The point being that his hand felt good.

"Melissa and Clayton pulled out all the stops for this."

Ian squeezed her palm as a reminder. "I mean, our travel agents did well for us, honey. Didn't they?"

"They did, my beloved."

The beach-facing section of the balcony was a stunner. From French doors that opened into the house, there was a wide white staircase with white bannisters that led straight down into the water. A staircase into the ocean! All they had to do was descend the steps.

"This will do," Ian declared. Then he winked at Laney.

How could a wink feel like a kiss?

CHAPTER FIVE

ENTERING THE VILLA, Ian first thought the aisle of bright red on the floor between the two white sofas was an odd strip of carpeting. Once he got closer, he saw that it was rose petals. Thousands upon thousands of red rose petals created a pathway across the spacious living room.

"There are so many." Laney bent down and scooped up a handful. Bringing them to her nose, she took an exaggerated inhale and exhale. "Mmm."

"If you'll follow the roses—" Adalson gestured "—they'll take you to the newlywed master suite."

Ian managed a close-lipped smile while his stomach hopped. He hadn't had a chance to figure out what they were going to do for sleeping arrangements. Not knowing the other had invited a replacement, neither Melissa nor Clayton had any suggestions. Ian would work something out on how to split up the use of the villa later.

He followed Laney along the rose-petal trail through the next set of French doors, which were symmetrically in line with the set that led to the balcony and staircase into the ocean, all in a row to create a private aisle to the water. His eyes beheld the end of the rose petal trail at the foot of the king-size bed with its four-poster frame and gauzy curtains strung from every side. On top of the bed, many more thousands of red petals formed a gigantic heart atop the lavender-colored bedding. He looked at Laney. She looked at him. In each other's eyes, they almost panicked at the prospect of this giant bed.

Laney covered nicely with a phony yawn. "It's been a long day. I think I'd like to take a little nap before exploring the resort."

Adalson responded, "Ah, yes. Of course. Let me bring in your bags. A member of the housekeeping staff will be by to go over your needs. All of the concierges are available to help you plan activities or sightseeing."

He took his leave and returned with each of their small suitcases, as they'd come with only what they'd brought to the wedding. There hadn't been time for either of them to go home to pack additional bags.

Adalson put the two cases down. "Mr. Luss, I'm so sorry, there must have been a mix up. I will track down the rest of your luggage and have it brought to you immediately. I'm so terribly sorry."

"No, that's okay. That's all we brought."

Adalson tried to hide his surprise.

"We pack light. Like you said, Adalson," Laney said, jumping in. "We won't need many clothes. It's our honeymoon, after all!"

Ian's eyes popped wide and he mashed his lips together.

"Ah," Adalson nodded his head knowingly, although still doing a double-take at the two small wheelies he'd delivered. "I'll… Congratulations again."

He finally departed, and both Ian and Laney stuck out their tongues in relief.

The layout of the villa was clear. There was one enormous master bedroom with en suite showers, bathtubs and every amenity. There was a living room, sun room, dining room and kitchen, everything done in the finest materials with great detail. There were all of the private outdoor areas. What there wasn't was a second bed of any kind. Of course not. This was a honeymoon villa.

This wasn't a problem. All Ian wanted was to enjoy some time away to become mentally prepared to find a wife. So he could sleep on the floor, on the sofa, out on the balcony— it didn't matter. He and Laney would masquerade as husband and wife in front of other people. Which he still didn't mind the idea of, because it would give him some rehearsal at being a couple, the way he would present himself to the world as a married man.

Although when he saw Laney kicking off her shoes and floating from one open window to the next to take in the views, a longing washed through him. Maybe he wanted more than to playact at love for a week on an island far from his family. Maybe he wanted that connection that true lovers had. That way the older man on the plane cherished his white-haired love. They had something bottomless and profound between them. Something that would last forever, even into eternity. Maybe he wanted to experience those feelings, just once. Despite all of his party-line speak.

"Come see this bathroom," Laney called out, having made her way into the en suite. "I mean, look at this. The glassed-in shower is big enough for two elephants!"

"Interesting image."

"It has not one, not two, but eight water jets. Imagine how that would feel spraying onto your body."

No sirree, eight water jets spraying him was not going to be a smart thing for him to imagine. That sounded far too sensual. And he was definitely not going to imagine being in the shower with *her*, seeing what those curves he hadn't stopped admiring would look like wearing nothing but eight sprays of water. Much safer to picture two elephants getting extremely clean.

"What do you want to do?" Laney asked as she sauntered around the villa.

"Do?" Ian raised an eyebrow.

"Yeah, do you want to go into the ocean or check out some of the activities in the main buildings? There are lots of ways we could spend our time."

"I think newlyweds usually find something to do on their honeymoon, don't you?"

"Okay. Let's go in the water." She could cool off from the overheated feeling she got thinking about things she wasn't going to do with him.

"That sounds marvelous."

"Except I don't have a bathing suit," said Laney.

There was obviously not any swimming intended during Melissa and Clayton's city wedding weekend, so she'd had no reason to pack one.

"I don't, either."

Laney wasn't going to repeat what Adalson had said about the privacy of their lodgings making clothing optional. She was already sensing the weirdness of being in this villa with him separated from Boston by a lot of ocean. Pretending to be a couple. Clothes were staying on. She'd bet Ian would look incredible with optional clothing off, but nothing like that was going to be happening.

"Let's walk up to the resort shops to buy some, and we can check out the property while we're at it," Ian said.

"I could use some casual clothes, too," Laney said. She didn't have shorts or sandals or a cover-up.

"We'll have to make it a little bit of a spree then."

Shopping spree with Ian Luss. *Hmm.* That was a turn of events she would have never expected. Why not, though? They both knew the real score.

"Melissa said there was some kind of shopping allowance."

"Or I can buy you a bikini, for heaven's sake."

Suddenly, it occurred to her how self-conscious she'd be in a bathing suit around Ian. At the wedding, he'd commented on her hair, her lack of makeup, a spot on her dress. Although she could tell he'd only meant well, that was a trigger for her, made her feel like it was Enrique all over again, her short curvy body being measured against the tall skinny goddesses of the world. Maybe Ian would have the class to only think insulting thoughts about her body, not need to say them out loud like Enrique did.

She could still hear his voice. *That dress does nothing for your lumps.* Lumps. Not curves. Unattractive lumps.

The center of the resort was comprised of five buildings painted the signature pink and white, and grouped around a mosaic fountain. Guests, indeed in couples, not a single person alone or with children, passed to and fro. The shopping plaza had a row of establishments. One with mannequins in the window modeling several types of swimsuits from practical styles for water sports to high-fashion bikinis.

Laney decided she would love one of those suits that had

a matching cover-up. That would make her feel like a chic bride indeed. Oh, wait, she wasn't that. But, hey, she could have some fun.

As they browsed the store, Ian quickly grabbed a couple of selections, the men's swimsuits much more basic than the women's. Laney picked out a couple of the ensembles like she had in mind and proceeded to the fitting room to try them on. The first one was a modest top and bottom with plenty of coverage, the fabric a sort of ocean motif that had a dark blue, a lighter blue and a white pattern. The cover-up that went with it was styled akin to a man's shirt, buttons all the way down to the hem below knee length. She wasn't sure if she liked it or not. Ian was going to have to see her in these bathing suits at one point or another, so she decided to bite the bullet and poked out of the fitting room to summon his opinion.

"That's…" he stopped himself and she watched his Adam's apple bob as he looked her over from head to toe "…very nice."

She loved that he stumbled over his words. She could tell from his hooded eyelids and the lift to the corners of his mouth that he liked what he saw, that she wasn't getting the Enrique disapproval. She prickled under his observation, shoulders arching closer together. It was a strange turn-on the way he eyed her with a sort of appreciation, as if he were enjoying a leisurely and satisfying scrutiny.

"I don't need to put on makeup or have my hair done?" Her retort was snappy and defensive, harkening back to his comments at the wedding. Here, he didn't have any idea what she was referring to. Flustered, she covered with, "What do you think?"

"You look gorgeous. But shall we compare it to something else before you decide?"

Gorgeous. "Sure."

The next ensemble was far bolder. Solid black, the cut of the top covered much less skin than the first one. The bottoms were certainly more revealing than any she'd ever worn before, basically two triangles tied together on the sides. The sheer crepe kimono that flowed over it made her feel womanly and, well, just plain sexy. She strode toward Ian, whose face froze except for his mouth, which literally dropped open.

She would remember the moment until her dying day. Here she was with Ian Luss, who could have any woman in the world, and he was beaming at her like she was the most enticing creature he'd ever seen. In his gaze she, indeed, felt gorgeous.

It had been cumulative, the way Enrique made her feel not up to par, not attractive enough to keep him from ogling other women. Ian made her feel desirable, which had been hurtful to go so long without. She knew he'd go on to choose one of those classic beauties that billionaires married. But she'd always have today.

Unless...maybe he was just pretending at this, too. Playing the role of the lovestruck husband. He'd be too polite to let her know.

"Please get that," he said, stuttering in a way that made her giggle. He did, too.

Suddenly insecure, she wrapped the kimono tightly around her and cinched the belt. "I'll just buy a couple of these athletic suits," she said and pointed to a rack of high-neck one-piece suits in black and navy. "Maybe I'll be doing some water sports this week."

"Oh, okay, but you're buying the two you just tried on, as well."

"Why?"

He gave her another one of those crooked half-smiles that might make her faint if he kept them up. "Why, wifey, because you look so hot in them."

Now it was her turn to swallow hard. She wasn't sure if he'd just called her wifey because he wanted to remind her that this was phony talk. Since *Ian* should not say things to *Laney* like Mr. Luss would say to Mrs. Luss. In any case, he could have gotten away with not saying anything. He chose to, making her think that he wasn't just playacting. Picking out expensive items at a resort shop and having a handsome, refined man pay her compliments. Yes, this could be an excellent bridge from where she came from to where she was going. It was also the most fun shopping she'd ever had.

After they bought a few more things, Ian had the bags sent to the villa, and they walked past the shopping gallery to a glass atrium filled with tropical plants. In an open area at the center, couples were dancing to a quartet that played a classic love song.

"They're doing lessons," Laney said, observing an older man walking around the couples making corrections.

He lifted a man's arm just so, adjusted the distance another couple were standing from each other. Laney reflected on the awkward and uncomfortable dancing the two of them did as best man and maid of honor.

"That's what I could have used before the wedding."

The teacher spotted them spying on the ten or so couples who were involved in the class. He approached. "Don't tell me. Your first dance as husband and wife wasn't all you had hoped?"

Close enough to the truth, they both nodded.

"I am Hans. Please join us. This class is for couples who want to know the pleasures of partner dancing."

Ian and Laney looked at each other. She shrugged, "I know you already know how."

"But not with my wife." He held out his arm for her to take it. "May I have this dance?"

"Remember, partners," Hans called out, "in ballroom dancing, one of you is the leader."

"That didn't go well for me last time," Laney said to Ian as the dance instructor guided them into the center of the atrium.

"Here's your chance to learn."

"Leaders," Hans addressed the couples, "hold your partner at the waist. You do not push or pull. When the leader moves, the partner will naturally respond so that you keep your hold. One hand on the leader's shoulder. Join your other hands. And it's one, two, three…one, two, three…one, two, three…" Hans demonstrated with an invisible partner.

How nimble the elder gentleman was. Ian imagined he'd had a lifetime of dancing, and it was what kept him healthy and young at heart. Hans waltzed himself around to check on the other students. One younger couple were already sashaying all over the dance floor. Two middle-aged men were not so lucky, as they kept looking at their feet and couldn't get a rhythm going.

Ian and Laney made an attempt to get started.

"You're not supposed to come that close," she said, objecting when Ian put his arm around her waist and brought her toward him.

"You're right. We're supposed to keep the frame."

He backed away and tried again. He knew the basics of ballroom dancing, as his parents did, in fact, enroll him in lessons. Right now, though, he was having trouble maintaining his distance for this formal style. He wanted to bring Laney close, to feel her silky hair against his cheek, which he'd had a hint of in between her stepping on his toes at the wedding. To feel her luscious curves against his body again. The hills and valleys that had just been on glorious display when she was trying on those bathing suits.

The mere thought of that gave his body a jolt and he fumbled over his own feet. *Goodness!* That was taking the charade a little too far. All of this with Laney didn't feel completely fake, and that was terrifying. She brought up something from the very depths of him. Something lethal because of its power.

As she began to find it easier to follow his steps, an almost visible energy passed back and forth between them. A spark. His pulse sped up as he worried it was the very force that he needed to avoid. He imagined all sorts of green lights when he knew there were only red flags.

Like if Laney was really his bride, the first thing he would have done upon arrival to the villa would have been to pick her up in his arms and lay her down on that heart full of rose petals atop the bed. He'd brush his lips against hers, ever so lightly, leaving the tiniest space for air to pass between them. At first.

Then he'd caress the side of her face with his palms, learning the creaminess of her skin. He'd probably dot more wispy kisses all over her face. Until his lips returned to hers. This time his kisses would be more urgent. He'd let them tell her what was brewing inside of him. The passion that was going to erupt, that would blow those rose petals off the bed and leave them scattered all over the room. Because once he got his tongue...

He chuckled at himself in disbelief of where his mind and, judging from the sudden change in comfort of his trousers, lower down on his body had traveled to.

Get ahold of yourself, Mr. Luss!

He concentrated only on dancing. As he and Laney got more and more comfortable, he was swept into it, as if together they transcended space and time. As if they glided until their feet didn't even touch ground anymore. He loved the possibility. There was something so beautiful and timeless about it, two people's movements becoming a dance as one. The melding of bodies with music was such a lovely manifestation of their union. He was on cloud nine as he waltzed Laney all around the dance floor. Like another scene from a movie. Dancing around the room as if the two of them were the only people there.

Romance.

There it was. That forbidden word. The word his family thought was silly nonsense at best and a destructive force at worst. Yet something he'd always dreamed of feeling with every cell in his body. Was that something he could safely encounter this week, too?

Not safe at all, a fact not to be forgotten. Laney was what was firing him up in the first place, making him think about things like soulmates and joy and passion. There were a list of reasons Laney could never be the woman for him. He couldn't call his grandfather to tell him the search was over.

First of all, she'd made a vow to remain single, so she

wasn't even available. Second, he knew that his family expected him to partner with someone from their exclusive and privileged world. Not with a woman from Dorchester raised by a single mom. The Lusses didn't even divorce, let alone give birth out of wedlock. It had simply never happened and never would. Most importantly, most dangerously, was that he could never have a calculated and loveless agreement with her. No, around her, his blood ran hot. Boiling hot. The only possibility with her was an impossibility. The real deal.

By the second song, Hans commended them. "That's right. Now pivot just enough for her to sense you turning her a little bit. You don't want to make her dizzy, but you can add movement."

"We're getting better," Laney said with a melting smile.

"Next," Hans addressed the room, "should you want to dance more intimately, the same rules apply. You create a frame and stay locked in it. Partners, you will feel where the leader is moving. From that, you can dance closely, you can tango, you can do any dance."

After the lesson, they decided to take the long way back to their villa. There was a dirt trail through groves of trees that provided a breezy shade from the midday sun. They exchanged hellos with another couple who crossed their path, the woman wearing a wedding veil on her wet hair, though she was in a wetsuit, as was her groom, as if they'd just engaged in a water sport. While they walked, they talked animatedly about something.

Laney smiled at the sight. "How did she keep the veil on if they went scuba diving or something like that?"

But Ian's mood had changed. A tone of cynicism flew out of his mouth. "Love conquers all."

She wasn't fazed by his sarcasm. "You really don't believe in love?"

"It's not what my family concerns itself with."

"As you've explained. You're supposed to marry for a business merger, and that's that?"

"It sounds cut and dry but it's what we've been doing for generations."

"Your parents, too?"

"Yes, I grew up in town in a house that was run like a corporation. My mother and father kept mainly separate lives. They had morning and evening check-in meetings with agendas their assistants prepared. Even spending time with my sister and me as children was scheduled."

"That sure sounds cold."

"And on Sunday afternoon, there was family time—a contrived picnic or movie date followed by dinner at my grandfather's, where he and my grandmother lived the same routine."

"Did you feel loved?"

Hmm. He'd never really thought of it like that. "I can't say I didn't. My family cares for each other. Looks out for each other. One would take a bullet for the other. I think my parents love each other, rooted in friendship and loyalty. There's just no room in our family for grand expressions and gratuitous emotions. Their position is that there's no logical purpose for romance."

"That's a strange way to grow up."

"It was. But you see, my family has only one agenda. What best serves Luss Global Holdings and protects our employees. My grandfather said it time and time again that success takes total dedication without distraction."

There was never a reason for waltzing around in the afternoon just for the heck of it. From when he was a young boy, Ian knew he was different. He observed other people, couples, and devoured dramatic books and movies. There was something that fascinated him about *feelings* even though they were frowned upon, in fact, maybe because they were frowned upon. They were what made people know they were alive, a vital nutrient. They didn't scare him or hold him back or derail him. But he had to learn to hide them. Although, as his grandfather began to push him into finding a mate, he was no longer sure he could keep everything under the lid forever.

They strolled through a particularly dense grove of low-lying plants that created a wonderful mist. It was almost like they were in another mythical world. The sun streaming in thin rays between the palm trees above made Laney's golden hair absolutely glisten. He so wanted to touch it. Run his fingers through it. Just because. On a whim. Something they might both enjoy the sensation of. If he were another person. And if they were a real couple, of course.

She mused as if she were trying to fathom him. "No one else in your family feels like they're missing out?"

His grandmother found her private way. But his sister was already carrying on the Luss tradition. She married an investment banker, and they settled outside of Boston in exclusive Weston, where they had three young children. They came into the city to have ice cream with Grandfather on Sundays. No deviation from the program.

"How well has love worked out for you?" Oh, he didn't like how that sounded coming out of his mouth. He didn't intend to lack compassion or criticize the love for Enrique that Laney spoke of, but it sounded like it ended poorly.

Nonetheless, her face fell.

"I'm sorry, that didn't come out the way I meant it."

She looked down as they continued on their path. "No. You're right. Perhaps if I hadn't fallen for someone who didn't love me back, I wouldn't be in the situation I am now. Maybe you and your family's singleness of purpose is the better way to live."

Which couldn't be less appropriate given their surroundings. The elderly couple that Ian had seen being lovey-dovey on the plane to Bermuda were ahead. They held hands and shot bright smiles to Ian and Laney as they passed by, the woman saying, "We're celebrating our sixtieth wedding anniversary."

"How lovely," Laney said enthusiastically.

"You keep falling in love with each other, as we have."

Sixty years of falling in love.

Ian wanted to cry.

CHAPTER SIX

WHEN THEY GOT back to the villa, Ian emptied the bag of newly purchased items onto one of the big white sofas in the living room. Laney hadn't forgotten that comment he'd made about how love hadn't been working out that well for her and was still smarting a bit from it. It was true, but it really wasn't his place to say it. Fortunately, the rest of the walk through the peaceful grove and interacting with that charming elderly couple had diffused the situation.

Grabbing a pair of trunks and veering toward the small second bathroom off the living room, he said, "I'm going to change into a swimsuit, and then let's get in the water."

"Right. Sounds perfect." She took her suit into the master en suite.

She emerged a few minutes later with a tube of sunscreen. "Can you get my back?"

He cleared his throat. "Oh, yes, of course."

He seemed distant and she wondered what was on his mind. Perhaps he hadn't told a lot of people in detail about his family like he'd shared with her. Gift cards for his birthday instead of presents, regimented family togetherness times. Laney's mom had to scrimp and save to care for her daughter. Still, she always managed a little bit of spontaneity here and there, even if it was just to go out for a walk on a summer night. A life of ice cream on the third Sunday of the month from two o'clock until two thirty didn't sound healthy.

Still it was quite something that after being thrown together, Laney and Ian told each other a lot about their lives. Far beyond what she'd have figured as a maid of honor with her best man. More than she'd expect with anyone, really. Despite his fortune-focused upbringing, his family couldn't have been too terrible. He was raised to be an honorable man who had sympathy and who listened. Somehow an openness had formed between them. Like nothing she'd ever felt before.

"No one can ever get their own back, can they?" said Ian.

They walked toward each other, and she handed him the tube, then turned around.

"I wonder how people do it if they're alone." Might that be her someday?

Her vow to not put her heart on the line was unlike Ian's. For her, it was the issue of loving too much having done her in as opposed to not loving. What would being alone really be like, especially as the years rolled on? What if she was on a solo vacation and had no one to protect her middle back from harmful overexposure to the rays of the sun? Life was to be lived with others.

However, all musings were halted and siphoned out of her mind and body as soon as Ian's palm laid flat on her back. She was only human, after all, and his hand felt so lovely. She froze and was a little bit embarrassed at her automatic reaction to his touch.

"Is the cream too cold?" he asked, alarmed by her body's sudden stiffness.

"Oh, no, it's fine. Carry on." She couldn't tell him to stop.

No, she needed his ministrations. There was nothing to worry about. By the next time they did this, she'd be immune to the feel of his wide hand that pressed flat between her shoulder blades. He began swirling his hand outward in a slow spiral. That made her eyelids blink rapidly. She shouldn't let him provoke so much physical response. This was billionaire Ian Luss, who she was thrown onto this trip with by no choice of her own and who she would have no future relationship with regardless of what transpired between them. Yet, his hand on her back was intoxicating. Worse still, he seemed to be enjoying it, too, as he circled slowly over and over and over, making sure to rub in the cream, using his fingertips as needed to be sure it penetrated every inch.

A swirl with his palm, swirl with his palm, a rub in with the heel of his hand, rub in with the heel of his hand, finger in the contours, finger in the contours! The rhythm he established was completely unfair. Rendering her defenseless. Her eyes decided to fully close when his movements became overwhelming, dizzying. Fortunately, with her back to him, he didn't know that she could no longer keep her eyes open. Besides, she wanted him to finish soon. And she wanted more than anything in the world for him to not finish anytime soon.

She was sure she could feel the stream of his every exhale causing goose bumps to break out all over her skin. Was it necessary for him to stand so close that she could feel his lungs function? His hands slid down beyond the strap of her bikini top in order to apply the cream to her lower back. She made an involuntary *whoop* sound and her eyes popped open.

"Am I getting everywhere you want me to?"

Somehow those words poured out of him in a slow ooze like honey from a jar. *Am I getting everywhere you want me to?* It was an innocent question but sounded like sin with his cadence. Delectable sin that probably tasted like honey. She was glad she'd at least chosen the slightly more modest blue patterned bathing suit as opposed to the tiny triangles that comprised the black one. Still, she started imagining his hand traveling farther south than the small of her back, perhaps slipping under the fabric and squeezing and lifting and...

"Okay, I think we're good."

She inhaled and although it took all she had, she managed to take one step forward away from those hands that seemed like they were chasing her. And in fact, his hands did catch her to grab her by the sides and smooth the remaining sunscreen in his hands there.

"Wait, you don't want to burn anywhere, do you?"

She was glad that she'd put enough sunscreen on the front of her body while changing that he'd have absolutely no work there. Which isn't to say that her breasts didn't perk up at the idea of his hands getting near them. What if they had taken advantage of the beach being clothing optional and she wasn't wearing anything at all? Maybe he'd want to handle her sunscreen duties from head to toe.

Perhaps one of his hands might slip between her legs. At the thought, that very area contracted. Then released. Then contracted again. *Wow.* She ordered her body and mind to stop all of this. This had no place in the fake newlywed game.

Finally, after all of that, she turned around. He looked shocked. Blood had drained from his cheeks and his jaw was ticking. His discomfort was obvious.

"Ian, what's wrong?"

Ian wasn't doing a sufficient job at hiding his reaction after applying lucky glugs of sunscreen to Laney's supple skin. He realized the look on his face was probably a combination of unbridled arousal and utter horror. He couldn't even begin to contend with the response inside his bathing trunks. How dare she have skin like that all over! How dare her curves make a man want to keep exploring the swerves and planes until the sun went down and then rose again in the morning!

It had not occurred to him that sharing space with her was going to present this sort of a challenge. He hadn't imagined her modeling sexy bikinis in a resort shop. Or gliding around a dance floor like they were waltzing on clouds. Not to mention that he'd shared with her all sorts of personal things about himself. With a frankness he'd never spoken out loud. Her thoughts did bring him further confusion about the way his family was at odds with his soul's desire. Making him fear he might not be able to keep stuffing down his truth, which left him feeling not only exposed but like a bit of a freak.

To the matter at hand, literally, he'd have to get through this week alongside Laney's luscious flesh. Because his blood vessels told him that his reaction to her wasn't just about her alluring beauty but that she was knocking on what was buried down low. In fact, the very thing he wanted to play at here in Bermuda, like an itch he could scratch. Though he was beginning to doubt that was possible, if he'd ever be able to purge the yearning out of his system. This week could become a disaster he'd carry for life if he wasn't careful.

He lotioned himself. He'd take a chance on his back being burned sooner than he'd let her hands glide all over him the way his just had on her. He willed the inside of his trunks to settle down. The cool Atlantic would help.

"Let's go."

He threw wide the doors that opened to the balcony with its staircase leading down into the ocean. The water glistened as the sun was cresting over into late afternoon. The trade winds created a sultry breeze. Laney took the railing and descended like a Venus born of a pearl in the sea she was returning to. He quickly ran down a few stairs to get ahead of her in case she needed a hand to help her down. Husband behavior, check.

"You're so beautiful." Those words fell out of his mouth. Okay, that wasn't too much, was it? Even a woman he wouldn't be in love with but would marry might still like to hear flattery. Like flowers and chocolates, all the contrived things still had their place.

"Not if you'd heard Enrique's opinions," Laney said. "Which he had a lot of."

"About your beauty."

"About my imperfections."

"Laney, believe me, you have no imperfections."

She tilted her head in contemplation.

"What were these supposed imperfections?"

"He told me I was too lumpy."

"Aren't women supposed to be lumpy?"

"Well, my lumps weren't *elegant*—I think that was his word."

Ian's breath caught. "That's disgusting. Your lumps are everything they should be. You fell for the wrong man." No question, her lumps were quite right just as they were. Every cell in his body was in agreement with that.

"The wrong man. I thought you didn't believe in the *meant to be* mate."

"Not for me. I have hopes for you." He chuckled.

"No way."

With that, they stepped off the last stair and into the ocean, which at that point was only ankle deep. They proceeded to walk farther and farther straight into the water as if they were promenading down the wedding aisle to be married. He wanted to take her arm in his, but of course, didn't, as a weird underwater wedding ceremony was probably the last thing on her mind.

When the water reached their waists, they both dove in, immersing themselves in the cool, clear water. After a few swim strokes, they bobbed their heads up. The water brushed back all of Laney's hair, leaving her shining face exposed, so exquisite it stole Ian's breath.

By the end of the day, Laney and Ian were tired. They decided to make do with the many gourmet snacks and big bowl of fresh fruit that had been left for them in the villa and to call for a proper dinner the next day. A countertop held raised platters with a variety of nuts, cheeses, salads, breads and the gooiest chocolate brownies ever made. There was more than enough to munch on, and they washed it all down with refreshing fruit drinks. Neither cared to open the champagne on ice.

They sat outside on lounge chairs facing the ocean's horizon as the sun set, watching the sky turn almost every color of the rainbow from red to orange to pink to the dark of night. They spoke of trivial matters, childhood things that weren't heavy like they had before—about Laney's poverty and lack of a father and Ian's family with their strange customs. They counted the stars in the sky.

When they decided to go inside, there *it* was, just as they'd left it before they went out. The master bedroom. Still easy to locate by the trail of rose petals that remained on the rich wooden floorboards. And the bed decorated with the gigantic rose petal heart. Where couples immersed in passion, the enticing scent of the flowers reminding them with every breath that tonight was one of the most significant nights of their lives.

Laney thought she might have had a honeymoon night like this with the man she thought loved her. A night to remember with every tiny detail as special as it could be. One she'd treasure not only through photos and videos but in her soul and heart as a commemoration of the beginning of the rest of their lives.

Instead, she was acting in this strange and almost tragic play, one that to Ian was emancipating. Whereas he was clearly fantasizing about a romantic love he wouldn't have, it could turn painful for her if she let herself get sucked into any of it. She was here to recreate, and there was nothing wrong with doing so in the company of a soulful man as long as she kept reality front and center in her mind.

Ian said it first. "We haven't discussed the sleeping arrangements."

Right. Exactly.

"It's kind of funny, all of this elaborate honeymoon stuff just for us. No one knowing that we're just bunking together."

"I'll have to remember to definitely *not* book a place like this for my own honeymoon when the time comes."

"What do you mean?"

He leaned over to the bed to run his hand through the velvety rose petals. "This. Champagne and petals. The romance checklist."

"You don't even want that on your honeymoon?"

"I suppose if my bride wanted it. As long as she understood that it's just for show. That our purpose is to produce the heir and the spare."

"Do you have that etched on a plaque in the office conference room?"

His face shot sharply toward hers, and for a moment, she was worried she had insulted him. His family was clearly suffocating, but she had no right to pass judgment on it.

"I do know one thing," he said after whatever bothered him had passed. "One of us could surely sleep on a sofa or one of the loungers on the balcony."

Sleeping outside alone. That didn't sound too good. "What if creatures from the sea with gigantic tentacles swept up to the mainland, encircled me and pulled me into the ocean? I wouldn't want that to be your fate, either."

"Glad to hear, thank you."

She glanced into the living room at the two sofas as if they would have gone anywhere since she last looked at them. And then she eyed the ginormous bed again.

"That's not a standard size, is it? It has to be custom-made. It's so big." There was fear in her voice.

Surely she wasn't worried that Ian was going to morph into one of those woman-eating invertebrates with tentacles and capture her, turning her into a sea creature who existed only for his pleasure.

Oh, Lordy. What was she thinking, and why did that sound not half bad? A crazy little wave splashed through her insides. Him capturing her with his tentacles.

"Yes, that bed looks as if it were custom-made." His jaw jutted forward. He was having some thoughts of his own.

"I'd imagine we can put a row of pillows down the center as a barrier and do okay."

"A barrier to what?" His eyebrows rose.

"I just… I just…maybe seems a little inappropriate to be sharing a bed with…"

"Don't worry, I think I'll be able to make it through the evening without throwing myself on you." It might not have been him that she was worried about. Reminiscing about his hand thoroughly rubbing that sunscreen into her back was enough to make her grow a couple of tentacles herself.

"I'm sorry, I didn't mean to imply anything. It's only— well, come on, this is unusual, isn't it?"

He turned his head away from her, but she followed it until she could get him to look into her eyes again. She hadn't meant to accuse him of anything untoward. And she was probably silly to think for even a minute that he might have been contemplating the activities that could transpire in that bed meant for lovers. He certainly wasn't thinking of said activities with *her.* Even though he professed to like her lumps, they both knew what he was after in a woman. And what she wasn't.

Although he was hard to second-guess. His eyes were so mesmerizing, dark and big. Like someone could just jump into them and be immersed, whole and surrounded. They locked stares for far too long. With all the strength she had, she was the one to finally pull away. His face twitched a little bit. She didn't dare imagine it was disappointment.

Finally, he said, "I do tend to toss around in my sleep, so let's use many pillows for your barricade."

He gestured at the dozen or so along the headboard. Turquoise, silver and blue cases covered pillows of varying sizes. Together, they built a sort of fortress going down a straight line from top to bottom, quite evenly dividing the bed in half, scattering some of the rose petals in the process. They backed off at the foot and checked their handiwork.

"This is like summer camp," she remarked.

"I didn't go to summer camp."

"Neither did I." She shrugged.

"In any case, it'll do."

He dug into his bag for a T-shirt, and headed over to the extra bathroom. While he was away, she slipped into the master bath to wash up and change as well. A peach-colored tank top with matching pajama shorts was what she'd brought to sleep in after the wedding. She claimed one side of the bed as hers and brought a bottle of water, a tablet and a book to the nightstand. She couldn't think of anything else she'd need for the night.

It was no big deal, she told herself. She was just going to spend the night—oh, wait, the week—with Ian, sharing the same bed. Once they stepped out the villa doors, they were Mr. and Mrs. Luss, but in here, they were just acquaintances taking advantage of an unused ritzy vacation.

It's no big deal, she chanted to herself. They should be able to just kick back and relax. No big deal. Her heart was beating faster than normal, but it was no big deal...

She climbed into bed and watched Ian reenter the room. He tucked himself into his side, and when both of them were lying on their backs, they couldn't see each other over the pillow wall they'd built.

"Goodnight then," he said, somewhat abruptly.

"The fragrance of these rose petals is really strong."

"G'night." He was done talking.

Hours later, she was still awake, willing morning to come. She listened to Ian breathing in rhythmic slumber. A thought circled around her, indeed like a tentacled beast, except this one was yelling at her to hold on and brace herself. Because the tide was rising.

CHAPTER SEVEN

IAN WONDERED WHAT a honeymoon night for a regular couple was supposed to be like as he tried not to toss and turn too much in the bed. He supposed it would surround the betrothed in a celestial cocoon. Whether it was filled with tender affection or driving passion, it would be the couple's own. It was a snapshot of their marriage they'd hold forever. He guessed that's what it would have been like if Melissa and Clayton were in this bed as intended. They'd have already had a wedding night in the presidential suite of the Fletcher Club, probably been excited and elated and punch-drunk from the wedding and reception. Plus, they already lived together, so it wasn't like in older times when the wedding night was the first time they'd have sex.

By tonight, here at the villa, they would have been able to finally exhale into the hope and calm that they believed matrimony was to bring them. Ian figured that even sick and gray in Boston from the food poisoning, they were managing moments of both positive memories and plans for the future. He was sure their good humor would incorporate the offending oysters into their personal folklore.

As for Ian, he was as restless as a slippery eel. He couldn't see over the pillow wall to gauge whether or not Laney was sleeping. The bed was so big that her movements didn't even register on his side. All he knew was that he was sleepy but wide awake at the same time, and this was turning into a nightmare of a honeymoon night.

He was ruminating over and over again on two points. One was what a genuine night on a honeymoon would be like for him. The other was on the pretend bride he found himself in bed with. He couldn't get off the idea that a lot of realness had actually passed between them and that, in her company, he experienced himself in a way he never had before. Which was absurd, because in reality, it was just the situation that was getting to him.

Still, that authenticity with her nagged at him. It was so unexpected. He thought about that creep Enrique making her feel unwanted and how he'd like to give him a piece of his mind. Not treating her right in the first place and then leaving when her café burned down. Unconscionable. Not that there was anything to be done about it.

He tried to clear his head and meditate until the morning finally broke.

He finally heard Laney's voice after he'd watched the slow turn of sunrise over the ocean through the master bedroom windows. Feeling it was okay to do so, he yanked a few of the pillows separating them and tossed them to the floor.

"How did you sleep?" Laney asked.

"Great," he lied. "How about you?"

She rolled over onto her side toward him, and he followed suit to face her, but he was careful not to get too close physically. "Slept like a baby."

"Where does that expression come from? Babies wake up all night screaming for bottles or to be held, don't they?"

"Yeah, I guess so. How about I slept like a rock?"

"That makes more sense." Now he was engaging in pillow talk while Laney's hair splayed across the sheets, absolutely shimmering in the glow of morning. It was like every moment shared with her was a special one. As if he wasn't waking to the world alone. Just like a couple in love.

He needed to put a stop to all of those thoughts. It was one thing to go through all the actions and even feelings a newly married man might have. But it was another entirely to start thinking of Laney as his real wife. He needed to figure out a way to balance immersing himself in the encounter while not forgetting what it wasn't. That would have to be enough. They should get out of bed immediately. As a matter of fact, out of the villa.

"Shall we get some breakfast? Let's go to one of the restaurants."

"Good morning, and congratulations." The restaurant hostess identified them as honeymooners as soon as Ian mentioned which villa they were in.

With him in a pair of khakis and an untucked white shirt plus a pair of sneakers and Laney in a pretty white dress with orange-and-green-flower detail that she must have brought to wear to one of the wedding events, they appeared as a newly married couple enjoying the paradise they were surrounded by. The outdoor restaurant was under a canopy of shade plants. Every table set a bit apart from the next, with foliage hedges to make each one private.

"Look around," Laney half whispered, "there are only tables for two."

"Yes, remember, this is a couples-only resort."

"What if we made friends while we were here?"

"Let's don't. We already have enough to do convincing the staff that we're a couple."

A waiter arrived with two odd white mugs filled with coffee. Each was shaped into a curvy heart. Ian wasn't exactly sure where he was supposed to sip from, so he took an awkward slurp.

The waiter asked, "Lovers' breakfast for two?"

Ian didn't have a clue as to what lovers ate for breakfast that was different than what ordinary mortals did, but he wanted to find out.

"Well, that's a...presentation." Laney chose her words carefully when the meal was served.

A carafe of mimosas was brought to the table in an ice bucket shaped and painted like a top hat. The waiter poured the drink into two champagne flutes, which were made of glass but also curiously heart-shaped.

Once he left Laney asked, "How do they manufacture mugs and champagne glasses shaped into hearts?"

"I've never seen them before. I'd guess it's just a question of making the molds."

All the tables that Ian could see had the same setup. A couple of women laughed heartily. A young couple sat in silence. Perhaps something had gone wrong the night before in the lovemaking department. Or there had been an argument about something petty. A couples' resort could be fraught with potential peril, there was so much expecatation. Once again, keeping emotions out of partnering made so much sense. The right woman for Ian would be the one who didn't make him feel.

Ian wouldn't put his Luss wife, when he found her,

through having to deal with things like heart-shaped mugs and big smiles if she didn't want them. That was a relief.

Laney brought her mug close to his. "See, they fit together."

She slid the open curve side of her mug into the rounded side of his until they formed a whole. Like the yin and yang symbol. Representing togetherness. One bending to accommodate the other. In flow, in fullness.

As she locked her mug into place, her finger ran along his, which gave his body another one of those tingles. This was the spell lovers cast over each other. A mere touch could change the other's physiology. He was sure that if he and Laney had a legitimate honeymoon night, nothing would have gone wrong in their lovemaking. In fact, he would have seen to it that what transpired in their bed would have been something to remember for the rest of their lives.

Next, a tray was brought to the table. On top of it was a dome formed of white lace.

"It's a wedding veil!" Laney exclaimed, showing Ian the way the fabric gathered to a point that was attached to a clear plastic comb. "See, that's what goes in your hair."

"My hair?"

She laughed. "It could. Traditionally, it would be for my hair. You know, Melissa wore one."

"Yes, I know what a wedding veil is, I just don't know why it's on top of my eggs."

"Romance." They both sniggered.

"Well, thank you for clearing that up. I had no idea how unromantic my breakfasts had been in the past."

They dug into their eggs, breakfast meats and the basket of hot toast.

"Yes, the toast is heart-shaped," Laney said.

"Couldn't they think of some other shape to make the toast?"

"Like what?"

"What about round with a little protruding triangle like a diamond ring?"

"I love it! I'm going to suggest that to the chef."

"No, let's keep it a secret, and you can use it for your café when you open one."

Laney's head dropped sideways, looking both at him and past him. "You're so sure I'm going to?"

"Well, of course. Why not?"

"Nothing. I just appreciate the vote of confidence."

"Right. What that idiot you were with didn't give you."

She studied him in a silence that said more than a thousand words could. This funny, smart, lovely woman had not been valued. In a parallel world, he might like to spend the rest of his life showing Laney just how wonderful and appreciated she was.

"We should go before they give us a cake shaped like a wedding dress," she joked with a childlike enthusiasm.

"Do you think they might?"

As they strolled back to the villa, an idea hit Ian. "Unless you had something in mind for today, I'd like to take you somewhere."

"Okay."

He punched numbers into his phone.

Seemingly minutes after his call, he heard a car pull up alongside the villa. Adalson from the staff exited the high-end sports car convertible as Ian opened the front door. "For your leisure, Mr. Luss."

Laney, apparently hearing that they had a visitor, came to the door as well.

"How are you this morning, Mrs. Luss?"

"Great, thanks."

They were becoming less and less shocked every time they heard themselves referred to as husband and wife. In fact, it was becoming natural. That was the plan. Ian continued the conversation with himself as they sped up the highway. He wanted all of these married couple situations. For example, it would be okay if he thought his wife was pretty and intelligent and interesting, wouldn't it? As long as he didn't fall in love with her. Okay, that was tricky. In the meantime, Laney would have achieved her goal of relaxing and gearing up to start again in Boston. Then they would go their separate ways.

Of course, as much as he told himself all of that, his mind was a confused jumble, and his heart was sending messages that were becoming impossible to ignore.

"Where are we going?" Laney asked as Ian took the turns of the highway, wind blowing their hair.

"We'll be there in a few minutes," he answered and reached across the car's center console to squeeze to her forearm.

He didn't mean to do that. Which made him again question attraction and desire and how he was going to keep that all straight. Because the minute his fingers made contact with Laney's lithe arm, he wanted to leave it there and cursed the road for needing both of his hands on the steering wheel to navigate the twists as he steered inland from the coastal highway. They reached the saltwater pond surrounded by marshland that he'd read about.

"I thought it might be nice to be in still water today before we go back into the ocean."

As can only happen when one is staying at a top-notch resort where the answer is never *no*, the rowboat he requested was at shore. Alongside it were blankets and a basket no doubt filled with goodies.

"We're rowing?"

"I'm rowing. Your job is to take in the atmosphere." A charge ran through him at his own words. He was about to embark on something scary to him. And it wasn't using oars.

He helped her into the boat, where she sat on one of the two benches. With feet still on dry ground, he pushed the boat into the water and then quickly climbed in. He sat on the opposite bench facing her. He took the oars and began rowing away from shore.

It was happening. They were in a rowboat, the only ones in the pond. The sky was blue. There was enough breeze in the air to keep it from being hot. The overgrowth of the marshes swayed gently. He was reenacting a scene from a movie he remembered first seeing when he was a young teen, just at puberty.

In the movie he'd since watched many times, an impossibly handsome strapping man in a white shirt with the sleeves rolled up was rowing a boat like this. Across from him sat a beautiful redheaded woman with pale skin and freckles. She wore a wide-brimmed straw hat with a black ribbon. All of which made them appear like they were in a period piece, although, actually, it was present day when the film was made.

The sort of classicism of the way the couple looked made an impression on young hormonal Ian. Like a painting come to life. The woman was ethereal in her beauty and pure in her grace. As the man rowed, he was solely responsible for her safety, and reveling in that honor and responsibility, their eyes told each other how in love they were.

Ian was so moved by the gesture of manhood in his rowing, something he'd never felt so distinctly before. It wasn't a question of the woman being dependent or fragile. It was simply that in taking charge of the rowboat, he was able to directly display his own masculinity and chivalry in a way that felt so natural, not confusing like the rest of puberty was.

Someday, he told himself back then, someday he would take a woman rowing, and she'd smile a pretty smile, and the thing that passed between couples would pass between them, giving him stature, giving him pride, giving him his place.

Of course, that was all before he understood about family codes and the Luss way of doing things. Secretly, though, he always hoped he'd get a once-in-a-lifetime chance to live out that scene from the movie that meant so much to him.

With his pulse jumping, lower parts in total chaos and all of his will, he embarked on the next part of the scene, when the man stands up in the boat and sings to his beloved. When he was teen, Ian had rehearsed it in front of the mirror using a variety of popular love songs. This time, he was going to sing the song that he and Laney had danced disastrously to at the wedding: "Meant as a Pair." That was going to be *their* song.

He took a wide stance to balance himself in the boat. "What I want is right there. We were meant as a pair. I would walk without fear," he crooned at the top of his lungs, a smiling Laney looking up at him with sparkling eyes. "Every moment we share."

Almost in disbelief that this moment was finally coming true, Ian stretched his arms out as wide as they would open, feeling the freest he'd ever been...

And with that the rowboat toppled over, submerging him and Laney down into the pond.

Oh, cripes! That wasn't part of the scene. He quickly brought his head above water and saw Laney's bobbing as well. "Are you okay?"

"Yes," she called out.

He swam the few strokes to her. The water wasn't deep, and they were able to get their footing. Holding her, he brushed her now wet and weedy hair back from her face.

"I'm so sorry."

"I'll bet," she said with a grin.

Without remembering not to, or deciding to ignore remembering not to, he took her face in his hands and brought his lips to hers. At first, he just brushed his against hers, taking in their pillowy coolness. But the second—yes, second—kiss lasted longer.

Ian didn't pull away. Didn't want to. He pressed his lips into hers with urgency. Which she met. And then he did it again. And again. The more he kissed her, the more he wanted to. His hands caressed her cheeks, finding her bones, getting to know them with his fingers while his lips still pressed into her plush mouth.

His lips parted so that his tongue could meet hers. Warm, almost hot, his throat let out a little moan he couldn't prevent. His hands moved to the back of her head so that he could bring her closer. Her hair was soaked and heavy. His mouth roamed from her forehead to her nose to her chin to her jaw.

This wasn't how the scene ended in that movie from his

childhood. It simply cut to the next where the couple continued to flirt. The reenacting was over. This was real life.

Laney picked some leaves from his hair.

"Do you know anything about the Bermuda Triangle?" he asked in between kisses after it popped into his mind. "Why does this place have that name and reputation?"

"I read about it on the plane. It's also called the Devil's Triangle. A geographical region of the Atlantic Ocean where strange disappearances have supposedly taken place."

Disappear with me, Laney.

He kissed her again. "Strange how?"

"People say there's some kind of supernatural vortex."

"What has disappeared?"

"Supposedly, aircraft and ships, although there's no scientific proof. Mostly around the mid-twentieth century. There was a famous case of five navy torpedo bombers that went missing. But when the investigations were complete, they had just run out of fuel."

He kissed her yet again. Maybe there *was* something supernatural about Bermuda. He was definitely being absorbed into a vortex. The Laney Triangle.

Lifeguard! Rescue ship! SOS! Someone please pull Laney away from Ian's insistent lips! Talk about the Bermuda Triangle.

She had those thoughts, yet it was like a dream in which somebody was mouthing words but no sounds were coming out. Maybe because her mouth was completely preoccupied. Her hair was sopping wet, she was mucky, her clothed body still immersed in water, yet none of that mattered. Not when Ian's seductive lips mashed against her mouth, hungry and demanding. She'd never been kissed like this and knew immediately that every kiss she'd receive for the rest of her life, if there were any, would be dull in comparison.

He tilted his head one way and then the other as he took from her with his mouth. In return, he tasted like the sweet and tart lemonade they had sipped in the boat before it capsized. Nothing had ever tasted so good. His kisses were telling her something. A mystery about him. Or a piece of wisdom about what two people could share. For someone who professed to have no future that included romance, his lips told another story. One of passion. One of bond. One of naked truth.

"What are you doing to me, Laney?" he whispered against her mouth, unwilling to pull himself away to even ask the question. The vibration of his lips as he spoke each word confirmed she was in the earthly world and not hallucinating. "I can't get enough of kissing you."

"This isn't supposed to be happening." There. As if saying that out loud excused the predicament. Yet they kept kissing. "There's no one around. We don't have to pretend to be a couple."

"I don't know what's come over me."

"We should stop."

They should have. They didn't. She wrapped her arms around his neck, feeling the wetness of his shirt collar under his hair.

"Laney."

Ian's loveless mission made no sense. Enrique's rejection of her—and he never kissed her like that anyway—made no sense. The only thing that made sense was Ian and Laney in the middle of a mucky pond in the middle of an island in the middle of an ocean. That was all there was and all that mattered.

Wait a minute! "Ian, stop. Stop."

He respected her sudden exclamation and pulled back.

"We can't do this. We're not together. Nor will we ever be."

He raked his fingers back through his long hair that, while wet, almost brushed his shoulders. Impossibly sexy. "Of course, you're right. It must have been those stupid heart-shaped mugs at breakfast that made my mental circuits cross-fire. Or your devastatingly beautiful face."

"It's weird when you call me beautiful." Weird and sort of painful, like a wound reopening.

"But you are."

She smiled with a nod, "Enrique wanted me to have cosmetic surgery on my nose."

Ian stretched out his middle finger, which he used to stroke from the top of her nose all the way down to where it met her lips. "What on earth is wrong with your nose?"

"He thought it would look better if it tipped up at the end."

Ian gritted his teeth in disapproval. "That's repulsive, don't you think? I mean, I don't begrudge someone wanting to correct something they don't like about their appearance. But to have that come from someone else? That's just sick."

"Thank you for saying that, Ian," she sighed with a slow exhale. "I didn't think I would ever get close to a man after everything with him. But spending this time with you is making me realize that maybe I could someday, far in the future. With a better man. When everything doesn't conjure up bad memories anymore."

"If you were mine... I'm sure you'll meet the right person someday."

If you were mine.

He stopped himself after that, knowing she could never be his, and it seemed like he sensed it was best not to finish his thought and have it in the atmosphere. She, too, knew that outcome wasn't possible so there had to be a limit on how far this fantasy enactment that they were together went.

"What about you? Ian, those kisses just then didn't feel like they came from a man who has no interest in passion."

"It's your fault. You bring it out in me."

"My fault? Nah, you don't get to tag me with that one," she said with a nervous giggle.

"The secluded pond, your pretty dress, the rowboat, the song. I…lost my reserve."

"Probably something that doesn't happen to you much."

"Never again, if I can help it. You're dangerous, miss."

They smiled at each other for a bit too long. Okay, a lot too long. She had a responsibility here. He could potentially become out of control with this pretend honeymoon, and for her own safety, she needed to make sure that didn't happen. His effusive compliments. That passion directed at her. He was living out the person he truly was inside, maybe for the first and last time. It was like a dream. Too much to ask for her to play along without forgetting the temporary nature of it all.

She was only human, and being treated so nicely was something she was unfortunately not accustomed to. She wasn't immune to romance, either. It was all on her to keep it from going too far, as much fun as it was. To remember that she was on a magical adventure where the sand was pink, the man kissed like his life depended on it, and in a week's time, she'd be in Boston looking for a job and a place to live. Ian would return to buying mountain ranges, and they'd have some unforgettable memories to file away in a locked mental shoebox.

"We should get out of the water."

When they returned to the villa, after they finished picking marsh weeds from each other's hair and clothes, they retreated to separate showers.

His cheeks were flushed as he entered the bedroom afterward, dressed in a thick white robe and drying his hair with a towel. He regarded the bed, which had been cleaned and made up by the resort staff. Tonight's extra touch after the cascade of rose petals from the night before was a single chocolate rose and a scattering of individually wrapped other chocolates on the pillows.

Laney brushed the chocolates into her hand and put them on the nightstand. "We'll have to rebuild our pillow fort. I wonder what the housekeeper thought."

"On second thought, why don't I just grab a few pillows, and I'll sleep on one of the sofas," he said and gestured into the living room.

"Oh." She felt a sting of rejection. "Okay. Or I could."

"No, no, I insist. You enjoy the bed."

She didn't want to ask the reason for his decision. Although she knew fully well what it was. After those kisses that shouldn't have happened, he didn't want to share a bed with her. She could understand. The attraction to each other at the pond was not diminished now that they were back at the resort. Quite the opposite.

The villa was Mr. and Mrs. Luss's home away from home and felt as such. It was only too easy to imagine the next logical course of action. After a day together that included a lengthy interlude of kissing, they would fall into bed to continue. In fact, it might take making love all night long to satisfy the fervor for each other that had built up under the warm sunny skies. It was hard to even think of anything else.

She managed to say, "I'll order dinner."

CHAPTER EIGHT

WHEN SUNLIGHT STREAMED into the villa's living room, Ian was glad he was lying on his back on the sofa. He looked up to the whirl of the ceiling fan that had kept him cool all night. And cooling off was what he had needed following the events of yesterday. He was supposed to be practicing so that he'd have advanced knowledge of how to behave when he met the woman he was to marry. Husband training. The island, the resort, eggs under a wedding veil.

If only he'd stopped there. He'd had that adolescent memory of the movie where the man was rowing a boat with a pretty redhead on a tranquil pond. And he got to live that out. It really did fill his heart to indulge in the romantic notions he'd thought so much about. Even if he had to leave it at that, at just the once. Then, like an idiot, he accidentally tipped the boat over, which led to wet hair and a whole bunch of kisses. A whole bunch. An amount and quality he would not easily forget.

So the lesson learned was that he should not marry someone he wanted to kiss that much.

"Good morning." Laney made her way into the living

room from the master suite, rubbing her eyes to get the sleep dust out of them. "I'm hungry. Are we ready for eggs under the wedding veil again?"

"I was reading that a Bermuda breakfast is a *thing*. Let's skip the bridal brekkie ball and go into town. I found a place that's well rated for serving an authentic Sunday codfish breakfast."

"It's not Sunday."

"That's what it's called, and the restaurant prefers to make money every day."

"Ha ha. Okay, I'll throw some clothes on."

She retreated to get dressed.

He tried to shut down the vision, but failed, that she'd be removing clothes in order to put others on.

As they tooled off the resort grounds in the sports car that now had become theirs for use, Laney adjusted herself in the car seat. She'd put on a white blouse that had a little ruffling at the V neckline, a tan skirt and a pair of beige sandals, all of which she'd picked up at the resort shops. He glanced over to her bare legs. She caught him doing so and adjusted her skirt again. He sensed she was feeling awkward about the kiss fest. He wasn't sure whether there was any-thing left to discuss about it, though. They'd agreed quite matter-of-factly on the drive back that it was a mistake and wouldn't happen again.

His body had told him otherwise in the shower when they'd returned to the villa. While she went to the en suite rainforest shower that had become hers, he again took the smaller bathroom. It was a more than adequate shower, and once in, he soaped up to wash off the pond water that had saturated through his clothes. Using the thick bar of sea-breeze-scented soap directly against his tight skin, he circled everywhere, hoping the suds would relax all of the tension that had built by his and Laney's torrent of kisses.

Unfortunately, all the ocean fragrance and running water served to do was arouse him further, making his groin surge for relief. He pulsed at the thought of her soaping herself up in the other shower. Then he indulged in an even more dangerous thought. If he was the one lathering her. Wasn't he supposed to be picturing elephants in the shower to keep those thoughts at bay? It wasn't working.

Then he was throbbing and turned the shower faucet to a cooler temperature in hopes that would calm his inflamed body. Yet, all he could concentrate on was running his palms down her arms in the pond, skimming along the swell of her breasts, noting in that instant how firm yet pliable they were. As the water cascaded down on him, he succumbed to a mental replay of the swirl of their tongues. He stroked his erection. At first, slowly, like the kisses. Until his whole body began to rollick and he became desperate for release. With long pulls he massaged into his need, bringing himself powerfully closer, closer, closer and then finally into an explosion that left him shaking under the water tap until his heart rate returned to normal. Once he recovered, he toweled off.

"There it is." When they got into the capital city of Hamilton, Ian pointed to the homey-looking shack.

Now that he'd spent most of the car ride reliving his urgent needs from last night, he implored himself to at least be present and enjoy breakfast with Laney, who should *not* be in his shower in any form and with whom he would *not* engage in any further activity that would make it appear otherwise. What he could do was quell his ravenous hunger with a huge breakfast.

He'd found the restaurant online, and they chose a table under the shade awning. About half of the tables were taken.

A tall slim man in a floral printed shirt greeted them. "Welcome. You ready for a big greeze?"

"We're tourists, what does that mean?" Laney asked.

"A great big meal. You're gonna let this old onion feed you a Bermy breakfast?"

"Yes, thanks. Onion?"

"Born and bred. We get that nickname because Bermuda onions are known all over the world. Call me Dack."

"Yes, feed us, please."

"You're staying at Pink Shores."

"How could you tell?"

"The glow of love. You can spot it a mile away."

Although what had passed between Ian and Laney was *not* love, he liked that it showed.

Dack quickly brought glasses of icy water, and they both took sips. "The codfish breakfast, right?"

"Yeah, we're here to try it."

As their food was being prepared, Ian asked, "So tell me about this café you want to open. Why a café in the first place?"

"I like café culture. I like to read and look out a window and sip something warm in the winter and cold in the summer. Of course, coffee and tea cost more than they used to, but you don't have to be a millionaire to buy a place to sit and unwind and daydream for an hour."

"Did you go to a lot of cafés when you were younger?"

"Oh yeah. There weren't many in Dorchester, but when I was a teenager, on the weekend, I'd take the T and find them all over the city."

"Because you liked looking out the window with a cup of coffee?"

"My mom worked all the time. So sure, it was nice to be around other people and just hang out. I didn't really like school."

A teenager with a working mom and a dad who'd skipped out. What lousy examples of men she'd had in her life. That knotted in Ian's gut. His family took care of their own.

"With all the brand-name coffee houses, is running your own café a viable business?" He couldn't help but put his professional hat on. Maybe he could help her.

"Well, I doubt anyone is going to get rich that way, but my business plan shows me making a living for myself after the first year when the expenses of opening are paid off."

"The codfish breakfast." Dack returned, each hand holding both an enormous plate and a smaller one. Once he laid everything down, he said, "Eat well."

"Oh my," Laney said as she surveyed what looked like enough food for a party. "What do we have here?"

"That's salted codfish." Dack pointed to the piles of shredded white fish. "Then boiled potatoes. Boiled eggs. Bananas. Avocado. Those are the traditional foods."

She gestured to the smaller plate that contained pancakes. "Corn cakes?"

"We call them johnny cakes. All right now, you dig in."

Ian forked up one of the potato slices and piled a bit of the codfish on top. The salt of the fish was nicely cut by the bland potato.

"Oh, I like the banana with the fish." Laney chimed in as they tried various combinations from their plate. "Such simple foods but so delicious together."

"I want to hear more about the café." Ian loved that Laney

had something so well thought out that she wanted for herself and that even though the Pittsfield place burned down, she was planning to start again.

"I'd like it to have a cozy feel. A small library on bookshelves where people could either donate a book or take one they wanted to read. Big comfortable furniture. Although, of course, all new and gleaming equipment behind the counter."

"That sounds like Café Emilia in New York. Have you ever been there?"

"No. That's the most famous Greenwich Village café. It's been there for, what, a hundred years?"

"You have to see it. It sounds like what you have in mind."

"I'm not glad Melissa and Clayton got sick, but I have to admit, it's nice being on this unexpected trip. It's getting my mind going about the future."

Ian was worried that his mind was going in a direction he couldn't let it. He dug into his food again.

While they were taking a walk afterward, his phone buzzed. The sound of crashing waves made it a challenge to hear.

"Grandfather, I'm at the beach."

"That's all right, Ian, I won't keep you. I'm just calling to let you know that I have the contact information for some women I'd like you to have dinner with."

Ian looked over at Laney beside him as they strolled barefoot in the sand, shoes in hand, the wind tousling her hair, a fun retro-type pair of sunglasses on her face. He didn't want to meet the women his grandfather had selected.

No one was going to compare to the woman he was with. The lines between practicing at being a husband and real feelings for Laney had become thoroughly blurred.

* * *

After exploring Hamilton, they toured the Crystal Cave and its magnificent mineral formations, thousands of powdery stalactites growing downward from the roof. Then it was back into the convertible, and Ian drove them toward the villa.

"If we can ever eat again after that breakfast, we have a booking for dinner at the resort's formal dining room," Ian said.

"Oh. I didn't notice that on the reservations. Melissa and Clayton booked it?" Laney asked.

"If you'd like to go, that is. Otherwise, I can cancel it."

"What would we do instead?" Laney turned her head toward Ian, whose eyes faced forward on the road ahead.

"Huh" escaped his lips.

What would we do instead? She was crazy to ask that aloud.

Surely what they should not do is be alone together. Not when memories of his kisses played over and over again on the sense memory of her skin. When her soul ached for more and her body tingled at the thought.

And if all of that wasn't bad enough, he had to go and say supportive things about her aspirations. As if her goal wasn't totally *basic*, as Enrique had criticized when he begrudgingly bought the café in Pittsfield. Ian heard her ideas as valid and interesting.

"Well, I've got a problem," she said.

"I'll try to have a solution."

That's how he thought. In solutions. She loved that about him. *Oops.* She *liked* that about him. She would never have any reason to *love* anything about Ian Luss. Enrique had all the right answers in the beginning, and look how that turned out.

"I don't have anything to wear. Everything I have with me is too casual," said Laney.

"I have a couple of suits with me, so I'm set. Book a personal shopper at the formal wear boutique at the resort. We'll buy you something as soon as we get back."

Again, Ian Luss was living on another planet than she was. Just book a shopper, buy a dress—that seemed obvious to him.

"If we've used up the shopping allowance, I'm paying for it, so there's no discussion about that."

Another matter of fact for him. Money, or lack thereof, was never an obstacle. Her life had been totally different on that score. Always budgeting, always compromising. Adding to the surrealness of this week were sports cars and rowboats and now, apparently, clothes.

When they got back to the central compound of the resort, Hans was leading one of his ballroom dancing lessons. Since they were trying to get to the shop, they didn't have time for a full lesson, but Ian waltzed Laney across the atrium to get to the other end.

"Well done," Hans yelled out to them. "You have the basics."

Laney was pleased by his comment.

They exchanged hellos with the older couple who had wished them the same sixty years of happiness they had shared. Laney adored how they took turns sipping from a paper cup of coffee while sitting on a bench by the fountain.

"Mr. and Mrs. Luss, I'm Solene." The austere, stiff-backed personal shopper introduced herself when they arrived at the dress shop.

Mannequins here and there were draped in high-fashion clothes, from a beaded gown to a little black dress worn with a strand of pearls to an architectural dress sculpted with a diagonal sash of fabric flowers. Laney was sure they'd be able to find something suitable for the evening.

Ian explained that they were dining in the formal room.

Solene asked, "What type of dress do you prefer?"

Laney didn't know. She thought of a time she had gotten dressed for a family function of Enrique's, and he didn't like what she was wearing. She understood *change into something else* in an entirely new way that night. That was the night she realized she'd never be who he wanted her to be. In fact, if she was honest with herself, that was the night she knew he would leave her. Her biggest regret was that she didn't leave him first.

She blurted, "Something simple."

"You looked great in green at the wedding," Ian explained to Solene, "She was the maid of honor."

Oops.

"At the wedding of some friends of ours last month," Laney said, jumping in, covering for Ian's foible.

He bit his lip in the most adorable way, like a five-year-old with his hand caught in the cookie jar.

"I like blue, too."

"I think you'd look best in a belted dress with a full skirt," Solene suggested. "That would flatter your figure."

Why did she make *flatter* sound like an insult? Thank heavens Laney had been able to shop on her own for those swimsuits in the casual shop the other day. Otherwise, the saleswomen there would have had a field day!

Ian must have seen the reaction in her face, because he

chimed in. "Solene, you don't have to worry about that. Laney looks fantastic in everything."

A grin broke out on Laney's face that she couldn't contain. He was a special man, even if his future entailed squelching the best of himself. The pride and old-fashioned charm he had while rowing them on that boat, serenading her—wow. Before the tip-over, of course.

"Would you like to follow me to the dressing room?" Solene asked.

Laney couldn't lie. The shimmery navy-colored dress with a belt made of the same fabric did look great on her. The scooped neckline revealed plenty of cleavage but remained utterly tasteful. The full skirt wasn't too much, and it fell to midcalf. Laney thought that was called tea length.

"I like it."

"Would you like to show your husband?"

Husband lingered in the air for a few seconds, sounding like far too lovely a word. As for the dress, she knew she didn't need his approval, but she wanted it nonetheless. So she nodded and came out from the dressing room.

He raised his eyebrows at her. "My wife, you look stunning as usual."

"You like it, husband?"

"I do."

"*I do.* You've been saying those two words a lot lately, haven't you?"

"They will never get old."

Solene ducked into a storage area and reappeared with boxes. She opened them and removed two pairs of shoes. One pair were the highest, thinnest, heels Laney had ever seen, the vamp crusted in jewels that would go with the color of the dress. The second pair also had sky-high heels and a bunch of ribbons she didn't understand.

"Do you have any flats?" It was her honeymoon, after all. She deserved to be comfortable.

"Of course. But I think you'll find that a high heel gives a long and lean look that won't be achieved with flats."

There we go again. There was always something not perfect about her. She wasn't *long* enough. She wasn't *lean* enough.

"Let's see." Solene came up behind her. She lifted Laney's hair into a twist atop her head. "Perhaps an updo. You can visit the resort's salon, or I can have hair, makeup and nail services sent to your villa."

"I'll wear my hair down, thank you."

"She doesn't wear makeup," Ian interjected, like this was a tedious conversation they'd had a hundred times.

Solene's eyes sprang wide. "Certainly, Mr. Luss. I was only concerned that Mrs. Luss might feel uncomfortable if she was underdressed in comparison to the other ladies who will be guests in the dining room tonight."

"Why don't we let my wife decide for herself? She isn't concerned with comparing herself to others." It wasn't a question. "Darling, would you like to change out of that dress for now? I'm sure Solene will have it sent to the villa."

Gussied up for dinner, Ian and Laney entered the resort's fine-dining restaurant. Located on the second story of one of the buildings, three of its walls were made of glass, so there was an unobstructed view of the waves under the setting sun.

Ian gestured to the bar, "Let's have a drink."

"Good evening. What can I get you?" The bartender welcomed them, wearing a white shirt with a colorful print bow tie.

"Shall we try something local?" Ian asked Laney.

She nodded.

The bartender said, "One of Bermuda's signature cocktails is the Rum Swizzle. May I prepare two of them for you?"

"Sounds yummy."

"Here at Pink Shores, we use two kinds of rum, light and dark, for the subtle difference in taste and depth." The bartender narrated as he made the drinks, beginning by adding ice to a stainless-steel mixing pitcher. "Orange juice and pineapple juice. Grenadine. A few dashes of bitters. You can imagine how the bitters will contrast the sweet juices and grenadine in a most refreshing way."

"I can't wait to try it," Laney said excitedly.

"The most important thing," the bartender said, "is the tradition of churning the drink. This makes it airy and frosty. We use a mixing spoon, but traditionally swizzles were used, which are thin stems from a tree grown in the Caribbean." He poured the drinks into tall glasses, garnishing each with a slice of pineapple, a slice of orange and a cherry.

"Ooh, it is frosty to the touch," Laney said as she took hers. After a small tasting sip, she smiled at the bartender. "This is delicious."

"I'm so glad you like it. I'd recommend having a seat." He pointed to groupings of tables that lined the front-facing glass wall. "We should have a beautiful sunset in about twenty minutes. Very romantic."

"Great," Ian said. "After all, that's what we're here for."

He put his arm around Laney's shoulder, as a beau might

do, and in turn, she put hers around his waist. They were very easygoing by now. He moved, then she moved in response, just like dancing with a partner. He led her to a prime table with a 180-degree view of the water. He pulled out a chair for her and slid it closer to the table as she sat. So much like a dance that he didn't want the music to stop. He felt almost drunk before even taking a sip of his Rum Swizzle. Everything with Laney felt not only authentic but enthusiastic and alive and thrilling.

"This is truly paradise," Laney said as she took it all in.

Indeed.

She sipped her Rum Swizzle. "Where did you vacation as a child?"

"Oh, you know, rich people places. Summer on a yacht in the Greek islands, winter on the slopes of Aspen or the Alps. Made for great photos for the media."

"You didn't have a nice time?"

"It was fine. But I would sometimes look at other families who were being affectionate with each other and laughing all the time, sharing food from each other's forks in restaurants, and—I don't know, there's just a closeness between people that I've never felt."

Until her.

"You don't feel close to any of your family?"

"I love them dearly. I was closest to my grandmother. But we're like a monarchy—formal. There weren't private moments that were just ours away from our image. No being curled around each other in front of the fireplace at Christmas, that sort of thing."

"That could be lonely."

Although no one in his family would have left a woman

they'd impregnated to her own devices. "Were you happy as a child, Laney? It must have been difficult without a father."

"It was fine. I love my mom. That was what I knew. I didn't do well in school, although I think that was more the fault of the school than it was mine."

"What did your mother do for work?"

"She was a packer at a factory. It was hard on her back. Our world was small. That was why there was something for me about hanging out in cafés. They were places to stare into the middle distance. I would like sitting there imagining the lives of poets and astronauts and shipbuilders and grocery clerks, too. Thinking of the world as big."

They both reached for their drink at the same time, so Ian clinked her glass. Laney was endlessly interesting. He was used to the practicality of landowners and financiers in his orbit, not someone who talked of poets and daydreams.

Drink in one hand and fingers interlocking with the other, they looked out to one more of Bermuda's spectacular sunsets, just as the bartender had predicted it would be. The colors layered over the waves were truly awe-inspiring.

Finally, Ian said, "Too bad Melissa and Clayton missed out on this. It's a bang-up place for a honeymoon."

"Hey, we should call them, see how they're doing."

"Great idea."

Laney made a video call with her phone. Conveniently, both Melissa and Clayton were together. They were recuperating, and had managed to progress from their fare of plain toast and tea to applesauce and eggs. They'd decided not to come to Bermuda for the few days left on the trip, and would reschedule their honeymoon another time.

Laney tapped her phone, switching the camera lens to

facing outward at the dazzling view. "Bermuda sure is nice!"

"Are you kidding me?" Melissa called out. "Showing me that is mean." But she giggled.

"We hate you," Clayton said, chiming in.

"Don't worry, it only looks like this when the sun goes down," Ian teased.

"In the morning," Laney added, "when the sun is coming up and the sky turns from a pale pink to white to the milkiest of blue, it's no big thing."

"You two are evil!" Clayton said.

"We have to go now. We're having dinner in the formal dining room where the walls are made of glass overlooking the ocean."

"Enjoy your applesauce," Laney said mischievously before ending the call.

"Your table is ready." The maître d' came to summon them as Laney was putting her phone in her purse.

"Ian Luss?" A booming voice from behind called his name.

"If you'll follow me." The maître d' gestured.

"Ian Luss!" The sound was so thunderous it echoed through the dining room. "What are you doing here?"

"Oh no," he whispered to Laney as he turned and recognized the barrel of a man as big as his voice, his jacket button straining to contain the whole of him. "Connery Whitaker."

"Who's that?" Laney hissed back as the man approached with a snaky slip of a woman next to him.

"He's a fat-cat landowner from Maine," Ian said of the older man. "Luss Global has done business with him. A real blowhard."

"Ian Luss, Ian Luss." Connery stuck out his hand for a shake three feet ahead of reaching them. "Fancy meeting you here."

Ian met his hand with its corpulent pink fingers and accepted a comically robust handshake. "A surprise indeed."

"What are you doing at a couple's resort? I figured you for sewing wild oats in Beantown, taking all the hot young moneymakers in Boston for a ride."

He guided Laney closer to the conversation. "This is my...wife, Laney."

"Your wife, huh?" Connery regarded Laney with a leer from her cleavage to her toes. Then he spoke into Ian's ear but did a terrible job if he was intending for her not to hear. "You'll want to keep your options open with all the good-looking females at this resort. Nothing like a little honeymoon fling with another adventurous newlywed you get to say goodbye to afterward, if you know what I mean."

Ian mashed his lips, speechless.

Only then did Connery yank his companion into the fold. She was decades younger than him. Adorned with jewelry that looked like it could topple her over, she stuck out a hand as if for a shake and then decided not to bother and put her arm down.

"This is my new wife, Christie."

New wife? That sounded so off. Clearly the one that replaces the *old* wife. He wondered how many new models Connery had gone through.

"Nice to meet you." Ian forced a smile. He wasn't masking his discomfort with this chance encounter. He didn't need word getting back to the Boston finance community, or to anyone in his family, that he was spotted at a couples' resort in Bermuda.

Ian's eye caught the maître d', and he silently pleaded for help. Fortunately, he got the message. "Are you ready to be seated now, Mr. Luss?"

"Let's sit together," Connery announced rather than asked.

Ian whispered to the maître d', "Mr. Whitaker seems to be a bit tipsy."

"Understood, sir. Would you and Mrs. Luss like to follow me to your table? I'm sorry, Mr. Whitaker, but we only have tables for two available tonight."

"It was nice to run into you, Connery," Ian said as he took Laney's hand and quickly pulled her away.

Connery husked to Ian again, not quietly enough to miss being heard. "Funny, Luss. I would have figured you for a beauty queen wife. Must be love?" He guffawed and shrugged his shoulders, which made the jacket button at his belly lift up as if it was ready to pop. "Ya just never know, huh?" His shrill laugh swirled in a circle.

Ian shut his eyes for a moment, as he knew how insulting and obnoxious that intrusion was.

They were seated at a window table near one of the modern chandeliers made of glass blown into the shape of a wave, which fit perfectly with the ocean-blue upholstery of the high-back dining chairs and island wood tables. He could tell Laney was still reeling from that awful Connery. The fun of teasing Melissa and Clayton over the phone seemed like it happened hours ago.

Nonetheless, Ian ordered a bottle of the best champagne, the sommelier poured a small taste for his approval, glasses were filled, and Ian proposed a toast. "To the loveliest woman in the room." He tipped his glass toward her for a clink.

"As long as you don't care what work colleagues and personal shoppers think." She sniggered as she tapped her glass to his.

"I still say to the loveliest woman in the room."

She sighed at Ian's toast. "Can I order for us?"

"By all means. I eat everything under the sun."

"We'll start with the lobster and mango salad," Laney said when the waiter came. "Then we'll have the grilled wahoo. With that, we'll have jasmine rice and asparagus. And for dessert the Grand Mariner and dark chocolate soufflé."

"You don't fool around," Ian said.

She smiled.

As the first course of lobster was served, Ian asked, "At that café you're going to open, are you going to serve hearty food, or are you thinking of just the typical pastries and breakfast items?"

"I hope nothing I serve will be *typical*."

"Touché."

"I had the idea that I'd like to serve sandwiches and toasts with an international flavor. Most cultures put something yummy on top of bread. For example, an open-faced tartine or a pressed sandwich with appetizing grill marks on the bread. Yet uncomplicated. I wouldn't have a restaurant kitchen."

"I was telling you about Café Emilia in New York. They made clever use of their limited space by transforming an old wraparound bar in the back of the room for their food stations. Same idea as what you're talking about, just soups and pastries."

"I'll have to go see that someday."

"How about tonight?"

"What?"

"When we finish dinner. It will still be early."

"It's in New York."

"It is." Ian pulled his phone out from his pants pocket. After a few swipes and taps, he announced, "A private plane will meet us in an hour. We'll spend the night at the Hotel Le Luxe. I booked a penthouse suite."

"Just like that?"

"Yes, just like that. Although perhaps we'll cancel the soufflé and have dessert there."

CHAPTER NINE

"WELCOME TO NEW YORK," an attendant met Ian and Laney as they made their way down the boarding stairs after their small plane landed.

On cue, a limousine pulled right up on the tarmac, and a driver in a black suit and chauffeur's cap opened the passenger door for them to slide into the black butter-soft leather seat.

"I've taken the liberty of pouring some champagne," the driver said.

"Exactly where we left off in Bermuda." Ian noted that, per his instruction, the same champagne they were having with dinner was served to them in the limo.

"I still can't comprehend this," Laney said as she took the flute he offered. "The flight was like a blink, and now we're in New York. I didn't even change my clothes."

She was still in that attractive navy dress they'd bought earlier from the resort shop. Before they left for the flight, Ian suggested they quickly throw some things in a bag for the evening and morning, and then they'd take a flight to arrive back in Bermuda by lunch tomorrow. After all, they'd be eager to get back to their honeymoon.

He sensed Laney's breathlessness over the impromptu plans and was glad for it. Between that snooty saleswoman at the boutique and that awful Connery Whitaker they'd run into, he wanted her to have nothing but pleasure for the rest of the night. He really disliked that windbag, who was probably on his umpteenth wife and didn't have a clue how to treat a woman. That creature draped on his arm seemed uninterested in anything.

After just a bit of driving, Manhattan came into view, the glittering skyline with its skyscrapers and landmark buildings.

"The city never disappoints with its wow factor, does it?" said Ian.

"I've only ever approached it from a train, so I've never even seen it like this," said Laney.

When the driver parked in front of Café Emilia, he came around to open the door. "Here we are, sir."

"Just as I remembered it," Ian said and helped Laney out of the car.

She read the white cursive on the blue awning, "Café Emilia, Est. 1924." Then she looked up at the narrow red brick building, the second and third floors part of the café, window boxes displaying multicolored flowers.

"So here you are."

In between the two small outdoor patios was a heavy wood door, which he opened for Laney. They stepped inside.

She took a brisk inhale. "Smells so good. They roast their own coffee here."

"Freshly ground coffee, so aromatic."

The walls were covered with historic photographs in mismatched frames, the owner's family, celebrities and politicians, patrons over the years.

Laney moved toward some of the photos to get a better look. "I love it. Café life. Same as now." She swept her arm to gesture around at the room.

People sat on black metal parlor chairs around creaky wood tables, drinking, eating and talking. Larger groups sat on timeworn benches at long tables. The main room was huge and was divided into three seating sections.

"Between the din and the smell, it's like stepping into history," said Laney. "What a scale this is on. So much management."

"I think later generations of the original family still run it."

"Let's see those." She moved toward a wood case that housed antique espresso machines and other equipment, some chrome and some bronze. "Look at the detailed metal work that went into making those urns. Some have the café's name on them."

"And this collection of coffee cups and saucers spanning the years."

"It's so loud and alive in here."

"How would you like to work in a place like this every day?"

"Nothing wrong with that! But I'd imagined my own place to be a wee bit smaller," she said jokingly.

"Here's what I wanted to show you." Ian cupped her elbow to lead her into the back of the crowded room.

A curved bar top, the counter made of marble with brass fittings on top of a solid wood foundation was probably where customers in the early days would be served a quick espresso.

"See how they use this as their sandwich bar," Ian said.

Laney pulled him backward so as not to be in the way of the staff, who were filling orders at breakneck speed.

"Yes, I see." She pointed to one area where a few cooks in chef's jackets were preparing deli sandwiches. "They have everything well laid out to make the assembly as efficient as possible."

"And over there."

"Old panini presses. Ooey gooey sandwiches with a nice crisp on the outside, lovely with a hot cup of coffee."

"And over there—" he pointed to another station with cooks hard at work "—they're making toast."

"It's all perfect." Along another area was a pastry case filled with selections. "This is great. I've always wanted to come here."

Laney smiled so genuinely it turned Ian's belly to mush. Elation sparkled over him like glitter. Making her happy was profoundly satisfying. Wasn't that what made life worth living? Creating and sharing joyous and meaningful moments, and recognizing them as such.

Ian wondered if his parents had those small flashes of light that added up to a profound contentment. If they did, it didn't show. He never saw enthusiasm or exuberance. Nothing unpleasant, either, only that the day-to-day was all they made room for. They didn't seem *un*happy. Perhaps they had everything they needed. They were able to play by the rules and live within the lines. Still, Ian couldn't help thinking that they only lived half-lives without knowing passionate love.

After Laney had her fill of looking around, he said, "Let's go upstairs."

He followed her as she climbed up the wrought iron spiral staircase.

"Oh, just as it looks in all of the photos I've seen!" she exclaimed when they reached the second floor. "Like someone's living room. Someone who collects old books, that is."

"Yes."

Wall-to-wall bookshelves held thousands of volumes. Dusty hardcovers and paperbacks with cracked spines. More books than the shelves could handle. They were crammed in vertically, horizontally and even diagonally as needed. Some of the shelves buckled from the weight. Stacks of more books with heavy glass slabs atop them created makeshift tables, surrounded by a hodgepodge of chairs and sofas, leather, wood, metal.

Most of the tables were filled with small groupings of patrons involved in conversations as they bit into delectables from small plates and drank coffee. Cups with saucers and tiny espresso demitasse bore the current iteration of the café's name and logo, and tall glasses held milky recipes and frozen drinks.

"The vibe here is so excellent," Laney said, marveling. "Exactly how I thought it would be."

"Photos can only tell you so much. There's nothing quite like being here in person."

"I want to see the top floor."

Another go-round on the spiral staircase led them to a much smaller third-floor room furnished with larger tables and straight-backed chairs. This was the student haven.

In a sotto voice, she said, "I think customers respect that if you sit up here, it's meant as a quieter space."

"For people to read and write and study. It's lower key

up here, but you can still hear all the city sounds coming in from the open windows."

"Well, we *are* in New York, after all."

Laney went to one of the open windows and peered down to the Greenwich Village streets. People of every kind bustled to and fro, young and old, local and tourist, student, career person, downtrodden, everyone.

"After this, can we go for a walk?" Laney asked.

"Your wish is my command." Ian Luss didn't generally talk like a lord from the Regency era. Laney had the oddest effect on him.

He was ready to break into a poem but managed to hold himself back. Crooning from the rowboat was enough. The point of this week was to get his longings out of his system. Instead, he was letting them *in*, and *out* was not going to happen without a fight. He'd better start now. He'd better start fighting right now...

He really was having that thought, to gain control and put the week in perspective, but once they stepped out of the café to the breezy, leafy evening, he kissed her. Another unscheduled kiss! That he promised both her and himself they weren't going to have more of. Yet he kissed her, a long passionate press that could not be misunderstood. And there was no denying that she kissed him back with equal zeal.

"Oh, no, again? We're supposed to stay away from each other." She giggled as she backed away from his mouth, making him lunge forward when she moved her head to the side to avoid the contact.

They both laughed.

"Walk, we were going to walk," Ian said.

They did, about twenty steps to a traffic intersection,

where they had to wait for a green crossing light. And kiss. They had to kiss. As if it were the law.

"I have an idea," said Ian.

"What's that?" She slid her fingertips up and down along his arm, a sensation that was sent from heaven.

"I'll show you at the hotel." He tapped into his phone for the limo that came so quickly it was as if the driver was just around the corner.

They whirled uptown to reach the Hotel Le Luxe. With access activated from his phone, they rode a private elevator to the penthouse. The view from the suite of Central Park, its ground-level greenery and the tall buildings that bordered it was spectacular. The lavish layout, far more than they could utilize in one night, was furnished with fine black-and-white furniture, sage green accents and several fresh flower arrangements.

As soon as the door clicked shut, she toed off one shoe and then the other. Then she wrapped her arms around him and initiated another kiss, another five. She hushed into his ear, her mere tone making him twitch.

"What's your idea?"

"I was thinking," he answered in an otherworldly singsong, "and you don't have to agree. I was thinking that maybe the only hope for us is to take this honeymoon charade to its logical conclusion. We'll make love. Once and just once. That will put to rest the curiosity and temptation that we obviously feel. And then we'll have seen the fake honeymoon all the way through and be done with it. What do you think?"

It was as ludicrous as it sounded once he said it out loud. But she slid her hands down to his waist and brought him closer to her. So close, in fact, that there was no space between them.

"Excellent idea."

What was Laney doing on the plushest mattress ever made in a penthouse suite at the Hotel Le Luxe in New York? She wasn't going to be able to reason out an answer to that. Because a gorgeous six-foot-plus Ian Luss, with lips that ought to be illegal, was laying on top of her, planting his mouth into the crook of her neck and making mental capabilities impossible.

"Ian," she managed to say.

"Yes?" His breath was hot against her skin.

"Don't stop doing what you're doing."

"I can't promise that."

"Why?"

"Because I might need to do this instead." He threaded his fingers into her hair and with his thumb lifted up her chin so that he could focus his slow kisses down the front of her throat, making her moan repeatedly.

"Ian," she cried, all but begging.

"I'm still here."

"It's that I don't want you to stop doing."

"This?" he teased with the tiniest bite at the base of her throat. And then he returned to the swerve of her neck, where his bite was bigger and more forceful. "Or that?"

"Yes."

"Yes, which?"

"Yes."

"Yes?"

"Yes."

And with that, he silenced the conversation, at least for

the moment, by covering her lips with his, enveloping her with his arms and legs. His hands traveled from her face to her hips. Tugging up the skirt of the evening dress she still wore so that he could slide one hand between her bare legs, eliciting another desperate moan from somewhere far inside of her.

Meanwhile, her own hands wound around him on top of her to pull his shirt out from being tucked in his pants, needing similarly to feel his taut flesh in her palms.

"I think it's about time we get these clothes off. This is their second country in one day. They're tired."

He climbed off her, her whole being screaming at the loss, but knowing it was necessary. He unfastened the belt of her dress, satisfied to separate the two ends. Sliding his hands under her, he unzipped the back. From there, he was able to slip the dress over her shoulders and pull it down to reveal the silvery blue bra she'd worn underneath. Continuing his effort, he pulled the dress all the way down past the gray undies, along her legs and then off, tossing it to the bench beside the bed.

He cupped her breasts atop the smooth fabric covering them and deftly found the front clasp, which he was easily able to click open. He let out a gasp of pleasure that thrilled her to the bone as he held her bare breasts in his hands. He circled their contours, learning them, squeezing, buoying, pressing them together. He buried his face between them, tantalizing her with the slight scratch of stubble from his end-of-the-night facial hair. When his tongue flicked across one tight nipple, her head threw back on its own volition as current after current of yearning ran through her body.

"Oh," she piped, "I need to slow down."

"Of course."

"I want to savor every minute. Because we're only going to do this once."

"Yes. We want to get it right."

"Right," she repeated as she rolled on top of him, straddling his hips with one knee on either side of him and enjoying a slow unbuttoning of his shirt. Delighting in palming a few more inches of his solid chest with each button's release. Reveling in his arousal between her legs. She finally glided the shirt off him.

His hands went to her shoulders, and he flipped them so that he was on top of her again, where she was grateful that more of their naked flesh touched each other than before. Back to that path he was forging down the column of her throat, and this time going farther, between her breasts, down her ribcage to the elastic band of her undies. Where he stopped to deliver a million and a half tiny kisses, making her desperate for his mouth to go farther, to know more. At long last his tongue slid under the fabric, where he kissed across one hipbone and then to the other, intoxicating her with his patterns, sending her into an elated state she'd never been in before.

Just when she thought she couldn't stay still a moment longer, he bit into the gray silk of the underwear and used his teeth to drag them off her. With her sex uncovered for him to see, he used both of his hands to part her legs and then began another of his trails of kisses up the inside of one leg to her very center. Using the tip of his tongue to coax her open, she relaxed her legs and welcomed his attention. He made her bloom, opening and welcoming him more with his slow circles up one side and down the other. He varied the pressure of his tongue from barely making contact to long deliberate licks, occasionally rearing his head back to monitor the pleasure on her face as her eyelashes fluttered.

Her core clenched, contracting and releasing, contracting and releasing as his able tongue measured her responses. When the squeezing became more frequent, he slowed down, helping her prolong the inevitable. Finally, she couldn't hold on and went over the edge, free-falling as her body trembled and quaked while he kept his tongue in her. Then he held her and patiently waited until she stilled.

When she did, her hands appreciatively slid down his sides and then inward to the fly of his pants, where she quivered at the hardness inside. She unhooked the tab, released the zipper and, a bit to one side and then the other, inched them off him, along with the boxer briefs he wore underneath. His hips thrust forward, begging her hands to explore, and they eagerly obliged. His sex throbbed, and she knew the next thing she needed was to have him inside of her. He leaned away long enough to grab a condom from his bag, and she watched as he fit it onto himself.

He crawled back on top of her. His mouth took hers greedily. "I have to have you."

"Be inside me," she said, concurring.

She'd been through so much with him already. The kinship they'd developed. The open conversation, the confiding in each other, the frankness about their lives and their positions and their goals. This was the obvious next step, to learn each other this way, to know each other from the inside. She wanted this, too. Once.

Years from now, tonight would remain one of the defining moments of her life. This gorgeous, brilliant, distinguished man had shared this interlude with her, the week in

Bermuda, the pretend honeymoon, this spontaneous overnight to New York, and now this carnal joining. He wasn't Ian Luss of Luss Global Holdings and the constrictions that implied. And she wasn't Lumpy Laney from Dorchester. They were something much higher, much more elemental. They were man and woman. Light and dark. Hot and cold. Heart and soul. Sun and moon. Husband and wife.

It wasn't her fate to have him forevermore even if she was able to. He was only a moment in space and time that she hadn't known she needed. To make her feel hungered for, to put distance between her and the past. Most unexpectedly, they were thrown together to help each other get to where they were going next. Sent from providence for that purpose alone. And that was okay.

He needed to process his genuine torment about romantic love that he wasn't going to carry with him into his family-approved future. For her, he was a gift from the heavens, the recharge that came in a surprise package and would only stay a short while. Although a hunch within her knew it wasn't going to be so easy to say goodbye.

With an even greater level of need, he positioned his body on top of her. In one thrust he entered her sex, which was wet and waiting for him. It didn't surprise her body that he was a perfect fit, shifting into place, to where he belonged.

They rocked together as one being, coming almost apart but then pushing back together, as if their bodies couldn't withstand a full separation. With hips swirling and undulating, they danced a waltz they needed no lesson for, as their bodies somehow knew it already. The music their ears heard intuited how to dance toward the crescendo, the full articulation, the culmination, as the cymbals crashed together into ecstasy.

* * *

It was still the deepest black of the New York sky that reflected from the tall buildings when Ian looked out the windows. He'd already sat up, swiped open his phone and was putting the plan he'd devised during the night into play. Once done, he studied Laney beside him on the bed, asleep, resting her head on the palatial hotel pillows. A tug pulled at him from the sight of her like that, almost child-like in her peace, each breath filling her with slumber. She was almost too captivating to wake up. However, he had somewhere to take her.

Leaning over, his fingers couldn't resist threading through her hair and smoothing back the strands that had fallen forward. Her eyelashes flickered a bit. The back of his hand caressed her cheek until she woke enough to smile in acknowledgement of his contact.

"Why are you awake?" she cooed.

"We're going out."

"Wonderful idea. In a couple of hours."

She started to roll as if she were going to turn her back to him. Kisses to the top of her shoulder stopped her.

"No. Now."

"No." She laughed. "Later."

"It's urgent."

"Nothing could be that urgent."

"Okay." He buried his face into her hair and could see her point in refusing to leave the comfort of the bed. "You're going to miss the big surprise."

"Surprises are appreciated during daylight, too." He began administering little suction kisses up and down her neck that he knew would be annoying. He was successful.

She giggled and said, "Stop that!"

"Only if you get up." He pushed the blankets to the side, revealing her glorious nudity.

"Grar!" She made a funny grunt that sounded like it was coming from an old man, but she did get out of bed. "How am I supposed to dress for this surprise?"

"What you're wearing is fine."

All she had on was a little bit of perfume lingering from the night before. Which she didn't even need, because he adored the fragrance of her skin. Of her hair. The taste of her mouth. And of every part of her. Which he'd explored thoroughly and could have been ready to start again from the top and work his way down.

"Very funny."

"We brought jeans and jackets. It might be cold out right now."

"Where are we going before dawn, anyway?"

"You'll find out soon enough."

They rode the private elevator down to the hotel lobby, which was almost empty except for a couple of groups with luggage beside them, perhaps leaving for an early flight. The driver he'd booked was waiting outside as arranged, and Ian and Laney got into the back seat of the town car.

After a quick ride to the border of Central Park, the driver pulled over, and they exited.

"We're going to the park?"

"In a way." He held out the crook of his arm for her to take as he walked her away from the sidewalk and into the grassy dampness.

"What's happening?"

"Over there."

Illuminated by the milky glow of an old-fashioned lantern as morning mist began to lighten the sky, a man dressed in a top hat, black tailcoat and a plaid scarf sat in an open-air carriage led by a white horse. Ian couldn't manage any internal cool at all as they approached. A horse-drawn carriage at dawn was such a silly and cliché symbolism of romance. He was already loving every damn minute and was so glad he'd thought of it.

"What is this?" Laney tilted her head quizzically as he led her toward the carriage, the horse in its magnificence draped with a red satin cloth.

"Milady." The driver hopped down from his seat, crossed his hand around his midsection to bow forward at the waist, extending one foot into a pointed toe that would have been at home on a Broadway stage. "I am Farrell, and my horse's name is Sonny. We are at your service."

"We're going on a carriage ride?" Laney was flabbergasted, which brought a satisfied smile to Ian's lips. He wanted to dazzle her, and he seemed to have succeeded.

"Milady, would you like to get to know Sonny? Perhaps give him a snack?" Farrell pulled a carrot out of a sack and handed it to her.

She didn't hesitate and went right to the horse, with his pristine white coat, and fed him the carrot. Giving a gentle pet down the length of his face, she said, "Hello, Sonny. It's nice to meet you."

After a few minutes with him, Farrell suggested they get going. He brought Laney to the side of the carriage and saw to it that she hoisted herself safely up the step and into the carriage seat. Then Ian joined her. He made a fuss of unfolding a plaid flannel blanket over their laps. Farrell pointed to a picnic hamper on the floor beneath them. "Everything you ordered, sir."

Then they were on their way, *clippetty-clopping* into the

almost-silence of the park. Ian opened the hamper to find a large thermos, which he opened. He poured steaming liquid into the two heavy black ceramic mugs, which bore drawings of the carriage on them.

"Hot chocolate." He handed her one.

Off they went through the paths between trees, the sky opening more with every trot the horse took. Daylight was starting to grace the sky with a pale blue glow. The air smelled fresh and woodsy.

"Ian, I can't believe you thought of doing this."

"Honestly, I can't, either."

He reached into the hamper to pull out a crystal bowl filled with bright red strawberries. He wasted no time in feeding her a berry, enjoying in great detail her comely lips opening to accommodate the fruit.

"My turn," she teased and dipped her finger into the bowl to take one.

As she brought it to his lips, the veins in his body coursed with awareness. She put him through an exquisite pace by running the end of the strawberry slowly across his top lip and then around to his lower, making a full circle before feeding it to him. He bit in. It was as sweet and juicy as he knew it would be.

"This is fun."

"I'm glad you think so."

As the carriage passed the park's carousel, wordless without children in the sunlight of day, he dug into the hamper again to pull out a box of the tiny cupcakes he'd ordered. He chose a lemon one and brought it to her mouth, letting her think he was going to feed her the bite-size confection. But instead, he swiped his finger to get the frosting, which he painted across her lips, just as she'd done with the strawberry. Only he took it further and licked the sugary cream straight from her, thinking that was possibly the most delicious thing he had ever tasted. A little sigh of approval escaped her lips. He could imagine listening to both her laughter and her sounds of pleasure for the rest of his life.

Which brought up an interesting point, he thought to himself. The more he lived out these acts of romance, the more he wanted them. Her. It wasn't simply the idea of romance he was enchanted with. It was Laney. He didn't know why or how, but he knew he wanted her beside him and to be beside her. He didn't know how he was going to keep to their nonsensical pact to make love only once to rid themselves of the curiosity and then be done with it. This whole getaway had been so magical, so divine, he knew something absolute had happened. That he wanted to be only with her and for the rest of his life. It wasn't going to be merely hard to part when the honeymoon was over. It was going to be next to impossible, like having to leave his soul behind.

While his arm wrapped around Laney's shoulder, Farrell guided the carriage toward the Sheep Meadow section of the park, so named because actual sheep roamed the vast lawn a century ago. Sonny trotted through the paths that were populated only by a few early morning joggers. Ian felt as if they were galloping away from something and toward something new. As Sonny brought them closer to the Bethesda Terrace and Fountain, Ian heard the sound he was expecting as it seeped through the thick of the sunrise.

Laney turned her head for her ears to chase the sound she couldn't exactly make out. She asked, "What am I hearing?" When they got a little closer the sound came into focus. "Is that a violin?"

"Can you make out the song?"

She sang out the notes as she put it together. "What I want is right there. We were meant as a pair. Oh, it's 'Meant as a Pair.' From the wedding. And you sang it on the rowboat. How can that be?"

When they got to the terrace, she could see that a violinist stood in the shadows of dawn wearing a coat and tie, coaxing the melody from his strings.

"How could he be playing that song?"

"You mean *our* song?" He sang, "I would walk without fear. Every moment we share."

"Did you arrange this?"

"Of course."

"Oh, Ian." She brought her hand over her mouth. Tears welled in her eyes.

Farrell slowed the carriage to a stop.

Ian hopped out and then helped Laney down. He brought her closer to the music, each note resonant, almost weeping from the lone instrument. Then he placed his arm around her waist and began to lead them in a dance.

The violinist played on, accompanied by the morning hush.

"We know how to do this now," he murmured into her ear. "All of it."

Indeed they did, had learned how each other's bodies moved and reacted. In the penthouse bed as well as now. Inside the intimacy of the moment. In New York at dawn. They danced. Just them.

"Ian, for an anti-romantic, you sure know how to woo a girl."

CHAPTER TEN

"THAT WAS THE most incredible experience of my life." Laney gushed from her plane seat. She was holding the bouquet of purple asters that the carriage driver Farrell presented to her when the ride was over. That, of course, Ian had arranged.

He pointed out the window as the plane ascended into the skies. "The Empire State Building."

She watched until the landmark building was obscured from view by the clouds. Ian squeezed her hand in a gesture she could only interpret as togetherness.

"Really, Ian, I want to acknowledge everything you did to make this overnight to New York so special. It's the nicest thing anyone has ever done for me."

A wide smile cracked across his mouth. His grin, coupled with the sparkle in his eyes, made her gulp.

"I'm glad you enjoyed it so much. It was fun for me, too. Really. Really fun."

Although, plane rides and horse-drawn carriages and throwing money on wild things wasn't going to solve his real problem, which was how he was going to live day after day, year after year, without being true to himself. To who he was.

"You know, I think you're going to have to work a little romance into that *strictly business* marriage you keep talking about. It's in your makeup, you can't deny it."

His eyes shot to the middle distance, a bit of a sad pallor taking over his face.

She hated that she'd broken his smile. "I'm sorry, did I say the wrong thing?"

"No, no, it's fine," he said distractedly. "I'm just glad we have a couple of days more in Bermuda before the week is out."

"Yeah." Laney chewed her lip.

The mood in the private plane's small cabin had turned melancholy. Could he have been thinking what she was? That maybe making love was a mistake. Making heart-pounding, all-encompassing, heavenly love put them in jeopardy. Because in Bermuda at the resort, they were pretending to be a couple. Alone at the pond, they'd had no such obligation. Or in New York at the café. Or at the penthouse. Where they were merely Laney and Ian. They didn't have to convince anyone they were together. There was no reason what happened had to happen. Except that it had.

"What would you like to do when we get back to the island?"

She could tell he was making small talk. That was fine. She'd welcome getting out of her own head, worrying about what she was going to miss that wasn't real in the first place.

"Maybe not on a rowboat, but being in the water as much as possible. I'm not in the water much in Boston. Are you?"

"Not in town. But my family meets out at the vineyard fairly often. We have a compound there." A compound at

Martha's Vineyard. Of course, the Luss family has a *compound*.

She could only imagine, an enormous piece of property with both developed and undeveloped portions. A mansion with a swimming pool and tennis courts, maybe a private beach or dock. Outbuildings, guest houses and dedicated entertaining spaces, a band shell, gardens, animals.

Soon, he'd be returning to a life she could hardly conceive of. She wouldn't see him again unless they were invited to something by Melissa and Clayton. There was nothing between them except this week of fantasy and pretending. And not pretending.

What lay ahead for her when the week was over was quite something else. She had to get a job as soon as possible and find an apartment she could afford so that she didn't overstay her welcome at Shanice's. She had to build up again. That was okay. Her mission was clear. Once she found a job, starting as a barista or in lower management, she'd begin jockeying for a higher position. Maybe a night job, too, so she could start saving money for the big dream of ownership. On her own. As it should be. None of that was the problem.

She looked over to the problem. The cut of his jaw was tight, maybe even forced. His upright body was filled with tension. All muscle strength and posture. Fighting to not be the Ian who danced with her at sun up while the violinist played their song. *Their* song.

She choked back tears. Because in the time they'd shared together so far this week, there had been many shards of sunshine when he'd let her see not Ian Luss the billionaire who would find that serviceable marriage. No, in the wisps between dusk and twilight, between sips of morning coffee, between rowboats and New York and dancing foibles, he'd let her see who he really was. And she'd done the same. And now that she had, it wasn't something she ever wanted to stop doing.

This one man had the power to dissolve all the hurt she thought she'd carry with her for the rest of her life. Even if he could, would she let him? Would she take the chance? It was never to be, so the questions didn't need answering.

With seemingly nothing to provoke it, they exchanged a heartfelt smile as Hamilton came into view, neither saying any of what was going through their minds. Because, in a way, there was nothing to say. They both knew the laws. And to stop breaking them. Better that they just kept smiling and creating memories to hold on to. Why not continue to enjoy the grand masquerade when they got back to the resort? They held hands as the plane touched ground. She could do this.

The Bermuda day was glorious with sultry breezes. As soon as they got to the villa, they put on swimsuits and ran down those stairs that led straight into the water.

"I've got you," Ian growled as he grabbed her once they reached the bottom.

Picking her up, he flung her around until she could straddle his back and wrap her arms around his neck and her legs across his waist, piggyback style. He carried her farther into the water until he could swing her back again, this time cradling her in his arms. She sighed up at him as he held her, the sun behind his handsome face while he gazed down on her.

As long as she didn't let those thoughts of permanence blur the beautiful picture she was staring up at, of him looking down at her in warmth and approval and joy, there was no problem. She was just going to enjoy these last couple of days in paradise with him and then get on with her life. No problem. None at all.

"Good evening, Mr. and Mrs. Luss." Concierge Adalson waved to them as he passed by on a golf cart. "You're leaving us tomorrow?"

"Sadly, we are." Ian nodded.

"I hope you had a wonderful honeymoon."

"We did." Laney's voice was a little wobbly, but the concierge wouldn't have caught it.

They strolled the palm path near their villa, breathing in the early evening cool, admiring a flower here and there. It was their last night in Bermuda.

A housekeeper they'd seen a few times called out as she wheeled her cart, "Is there anything special I can leave in your villa for your final night with us?"

"We're fine, thank you," Laney answered.

Fittingly, they also saw the older couple they'd first seen on the plane from Boston. The two putted golf balls on a small green, and both waved as the Lusses went by.

Yes, they had become quite comfortable at Pink Shores. They were friendly and polite and were clearly in love. The staff had done everything they could to make sure their honeymoon was memorable and pitch perfect. Ian was certainly going to miss being here when they went home to Boston tomorrow.

He put his arm around his bride's shoulder, and she followed suit by wrapping her arm around his waist, motions they both performed automatically now. She wore a long and loose floral print dress that they'd picked up at one of the resort shops, her hair wild and free, her skin clean. Ian had on a simple blue T-shirt and jeans. His brain and central nervous system were still swooning from the encounter in the water a couple of hours ago, although showering and dressing for the evening helped him balance out. He was planning to appreciate every minute of their last evening together.

Besides, what had happened on the steps leading from the villa to the water didn't mean anything. When they'd first arrived almost a week ago, a wicked fantasy had overtaken him of laying Laney down on the bottom of the staircase and making love to her in a way that half of their bodies were submerged in water and half above it. With the private beach, the greenery and tall hedges giving them complete privacy, it was practically possible.

But at the beginning of the trip, he never could have imagined that they would have joined their bodies in rapture and rhapsody the way they had in New York. They'd agreed not to do it again, that it was an extra complication that they didn't need as the week came to an end. The resolve lasted for a couple of days and nights despite all the time spent romping in the water.

Then, earlier today, before he'd made a conscious decision to fulfill that specific fantasy, he was doing it, lifting her up again in his arms and laying her down at the bottom of the stairs, making short work of removing the black triangles of fabric covering the few inches of her body.

Hovering over her, he kissed every inch he could get his hands and mouth on before sliding into her and wrapping her legs around him. The cool waves that reached the stairs lapped over them, crashing gently onto their legs and across his back. Soon, they found the ocean's rhythm and joined it, moving along with the ebb and flow of each wave. He thrust into her as the sea crashed atop them and then he retreated, back arched, as the water receded. They repeated with the tide about a hundred times, because it felt that glorious. His lovely Laney, the Bermuda waters, all under the setting sun. For the last time.

The bartender put two cocktail napkins printed with the resort's logo in front of them as they entered the outdoor cocktail lounge. "What can I get you?"

"The other day we tasted the Rum Swizzle, the bartender mentioned another cocktail famous in Bermuda."

"Yes, the Dark 'n' Stormy."

"Two of those, please."

"Coming right up. This drink mixes ginger beer with dark rum. We pour it over ice and garnish with a slice of lime."

"It sounds wonderful," Laney said, approving.

"Ian Luss, we meet again." Connery charged toward them, the rail-thin Christie in tow. Oddly, a photographer trailed behind, a gangly young man with three cameras around his neck.

"Connery." Ian saluted with two fingers to his forehead, then pivoted back to the bar, hoping the bothersome man would go away.

No such luck in getting rid of him, of course. "I'm having some honeymoon shots done and figured it'd be cute to pose with a couple of the local cocktails. Bartender, fix us up something with lots of straws and umbrellas."

The bartender nodded and tried to conceal the speck of annoyance that washed over his face.

Ian had no choice but to rotate toward Connery again. "Nice idea." Maybe if he just responded to questions with short answers and didn't attempt to get a conversation going, Connery would move on.

The bartender presented the two drinks to Connery.

He grabbed them without any acknowledgment and handed one to his bride with such haste that a bit of it spilled over onto the ground, which he took no notice of. "Ian, let's get a couple of shots of the four of us."

"Oh, no, thanks, Connery. We're commemorating in our own way."

Ian didn't like Connery in general. In the few dealings he had with him, Ian found him too aggressive and unwilling to compromise. But what he really hadn't liked was when they'd run into each other a few days ago, he'd made some comment about assuming Ian would marry a *beauty queen type*. It was a slight at Laney that was in bad taste. Who would make a negative comment about a man's wife? On his honeymoon, no less!

What constituted a beauty queen wife, anyway? Purely beauty. And how was beauty defined, how was it not subjective? It was truly in the eyes of the beholder. From his view, Laney was absolutely lovely in her naturalness. Not to mention, it was her inner beauty that attracted him to her. It was a revolting thought that Laney's ex thought she should go under a surgeon's knife to add a *lilt* to her nose, to change an act of Mother Nature, who never made mistakes.

The way the sunshine reflected in Laney's eyes. Was there a measurement for that? And her kisses that took him to a jubilation he never wanted to return from. Did that have a numeric value? Not to mention the utter splendor of making love with her, feeling himself inside of her unimaginable lushness. Would that win a contest? To him, she was both a *beauty* and a *queen*.

In any case, Connery was so tactless that Ian couldn't wait to get away from him.

"Come on, Ian, what's the harm? Take a couple of shots with us," Connery insisted. He didn't wait for an answer as he grabbed Laney by the arm and asked, "What was your name again?"

"Laney." She forced a smile.

Ian was one move away from physically separating him from her. Meanwhile, Connery used his other arm to yank his wife over, which left Ian no choice but to join the foursome for the photo. He'd take a quick snap and then be done with it. At Connery's lead, they all held up their drinks and smiled.

"To happy marriages. Of course, mine is my third, but maybe three's a charm." He guffawed with a belly laugh. He turned to Laney and asked, "What was your name again?"

"We did it," Ian said as he held Laney's naked body against his own. "Our week as Mr. and Mrs. Luss comes to an end."

"In our marital bed." She laughed lightly against his chest. "I think we were quite convincing."

"Think of where we started."

"With the pillow fortress between us. Followed by you on the sofa."

"I was gentleman enough to not tell you how uncomfortable that was."

As Ian's fingertips traced Laney's breasts, she hoped he wouldn't stop the motion anytime soon. It was like he was painting her with the pads of his fingers, and she wanted to be covered by his color.

"Did the separation work for you?" Laney asked.

"No. I was thinking about what you were, or weren't, wearing," he said.

"Nothing."

"That's what I was afraid of."

"Yay for us, though."

"Yes, we were able to get to this," he said. "We explored what we wanted to together, and now we can part without wondering what might have been."

"And I would have, you know." She splayed her hand on his sturdy chest, letting the muscles underneath his skin imprint into her hand, solidifying another memory.

"I would have, too."

"Now we know."

"We took our masquerade to its ultimate conclusion."

"I came to relax and pull myself together after the fire and the creep."

"Did you?"

"I feel rejuvenated."

"Mission accomplished, then."

"And you? Are you ready to go find that proper wife?" Even though she was trying to be casual and cavalier, it hurt Laney to even say those words out loud. Because, in her heart—and she believed in his, too—the right partner for him had already been found.

He said only, "Now we'll part ways and get on with our lives."

"Exactly."

"Although, I bet we'll see each other again."

"Of course. Through Melissa and Clayton," Laney said.

"We'll be friendly at holiday parties," said Ian.

"Give each other a polite kiss on the cheek."

"After all, we were best man and maid of honor. That always makes a special bond."

"Everyone will laugh about the bride and groom and the bad oysters that launched the Great Bermuda Charade," said Laney.

"Maybe Melissa and Clayton will ask us to be godparents to their children someday."

"It could happen."

"But this will never happen again," Ian said.

"Neither of us would want it to," said Laney.

"It doesn't fit with our schemes."

"We knew that from the start."

"We are pointed in different directions," said Ian.

"Couldn't be more different."

"Couldn't."

And with that, Ian rolled on top of her, his magnificent weight bearing onto her, enclosing her. Sparking her yet again, *yet again*, with want.

Her arms circled his neck, hands feeling for his upper back, bringing him in closer to her, never close enough, sealing them together making sure they became one. Until...

"No more," she blurted suddenly.

He immediately moved off, not making her struggle.

"I can't do it anymore. I can't pretend this week didn't mean anything," said Laney.

His Adam's apple bounced as he resigned his back against the pillows beside her. "It meant everything."

"You've given me back the possibility of love. You've given me myself. You..." She couldn't say what came next. That part would have to stay in Pretend Land, a place that could never be.

They both knew that. Because he'd done more than just

show her that love would be worth fighting for. Something that she'd wanted and had recently convinced herself she wouldn't have.

She still wouldn't. Because the lucky woman who would get to spend her lifetime with him would never get to see what Laney had this week. He was determined that no one would see what he was capable of.

"This week will be inside of me for the rest of my life," Ian said.

She blew out her cheeks and then let out a slow exhale. "So where does this leave us?"

"Nowhere." His answer felt like a blow.

The rowboat on the pond and the carriage ride in New York. Scenes from movies or his imagination come to life. Bursting from the black-and-white screen in his mind into the here and now. Will that be how he'll remember her, as an actress in the play he wrote? Making her wonder if he'd really been with *her* this week, or would any willing woman have been able to assume the role? That was an unbearable possibility.

Instead, she'd remember the special rapport they had with each other. How precious he made her feel.

She'd mentally thank him every day of her life for helping her choose the right path out of the crossroads she found herself in. She could have fallen into a pit, let events of the past trap her and hold her down. He gave her the confidence and the hope to pull herself back up. She'd make him proud, tell him of her gratitude every morning when she woke up and every night when she went to bed. She suspected he wouldn't be far from her thoughts anyway.

Yet his march toward the future was clear. It couldn't include her. He'd remain loyal to his family and she respected him for it. It made him the noble and trustworthy man he was. Even if he was her destiny, she was not his. What a cruel twist of fate that was.

Still, she wouldn't have traded this week for anything in the world. Because she'd always have it. It would affect everything she did, said, thought and felt until her dying day.

CHAPTER ELEVEN

MULTIPLE SPARKS OF emotion were fighting each other for Ian's attention after the plane's wheels lifted up to fly him and Laney off Bermuda and back to Boston. The obvious one was that he didn't want to leave that pink sand and the sunrises and sunsets that touched him with their magnificent display of colors. Another was that he'd grown quite used to spending almost every moment with Laney, who stared absently out the window while holding the cup of coffee she'd been handed but had yet to bring to her lips.

They'd supposedly said all that needed saying to each other. That in an uncomplicated world, they might try to be together. She might be able to trust again. Ian might fulfill his heart's desire to truly be in love with someone and to display it in every way possible. Not just with anyone. With her. Those were all *mights*. That was talk; it wasn't what was going to be. Instead, they agreed to part smiling and cherish this unforgettable interlude forever.

Except that Ian wanted to toss all of that *should do* crap and smash it against a wall until it shattered into a thousand pieces!

And once the pilot made the plane's Wi-Fi available, things got infinitely worse. Numbly scrolling through a Boston news site, his thumbs froze when he saw the photo. He and Laney and Connery Whitaker and his wife Christie. From when they ran into each other last night and that buffoon Connery insisted they take a jolly photo together. He told Ian he was documenting their trip. In fact, he made a production of ordering tropical drinks and posing with them. A click-through button on the screen said Read More.

"Laney." Ian summoned her attention, as they might as well bite the bullet together. He hit the button. "Look at this."

"What is it?" She put her cup down on the tray and leaned in to him so they could both see the phone at the same time.

"Is Ian Luss, one of the city's most eligible bachelors, off the market?" he read aloud.

"Ick."

He continued: "It seems it won't be a daughter of society that will join the Luss empire. Apparently, Ian's independent woman eschews high heels in favor of wearing an apron and pulling espresso. Records identify her as last co-owning a small café in the Berkshires. Laney Sullivan isn't a name known in the upper circles, which has left readers dumbfounded as to how this seemingly odd couple got together."

"Oh my gosh."

"That's infuriating." Ian put his hand over his chest as his rib cage collapsed. "It's sick that people want to read trash like that."

He wanted to scream. Because gossip about him wasn't embarrassing enough. No, they had to drag Laney into it. With all she'd been through and that idiot Enrique making her feel less than. This perpetuated that exact same message. Who was worthy enough to marry. Who was acceptable to love. As if that was for someone else to decide. One of Boston's most eligible bachelors. Nauseating.

"Do you think…" Laney's spoke slowly because she was in shock, too "…Connery sent the photos to the site himself?"

"I wouldn't put it past him."

"It could have been some other onlooker who recognized you."

"Spilled milk at this point."

"I suppose."

The flight attendant returned, rightly oblivious to the shake-up he and Laney were reckoning with. She laid down a tray that had several compartments, all filled with snacks for the short flight. The dried fruits had a glisten, the nuts looked nicely roasted and seasoned, the grapes big and juicy.

Ian had no interest in eating. Laney looked the tray over with ambivalence as well. They sat in silence until it became unbearable.

"I'm so sorry, Laney. I failed to protect you."

"Was that your job?"

"It might have been."

Yes, he wanted to shield her from harm, both physically and emotionally. He wanted her surrounded only by people who supported her, who saw how smart and decent she was. How true to herself. He could still kick himself remembering when he'd suggested she might want to fix her hair at the wedding after it had gotten mussed. Not that she wouldn't have wanted to look her best, but why would anyone want to change someone as glorious as her? Her honesty shone in her face. He loved everything about her.

Wait…loved? Was this what being in love really felt like?

Pain and agony? He didn't know exactly how love informed the carrier. Was it the buzz he felt when he was near her? Or was it the burning, distracting longing when he wasn't? Was it the overwhelming impulse to defend her against any foe, including his family's and society's expectations? Was it in looking forward to the next day, sharing an adventure and discoveries made together?

Poets and painters had their ways of interpreting romantic love, of declaring it. Ian didn't know how to label it. Because all he'd ever known was that he was supposed to avoid it. Had it defied him, found him in the crowd anyway? Had it crept into the cracks of the cement wall holding him back?

He wasn't sure whether to lament or rejoice.

A limo met Laney and Ian at the airport in Boston. They slid into the back seat, the usual champagne and chocolates at the ready. She thought *the usual* because, remarkably, that's what the week had brought. Every single luxury imaginable at the resort, a private plane, the finest everything. She didn't know whether she could ever get used to so much opulence. At the moment, it didn't really matter. The driver was speeding them toward goodbye, and that would be that.

She kept her eyes looking out the window because she was at the point where being with Ian was stinging like a wound. They'd already expressed they wished that things could be different, that they could continue to explore the compatibility and bliss they felt toward each other. They couldn't. Period. She would be grateful to Ian for the rest of her life for showing her that a good man wasn't like Enrique. A good man wanted the best for his woman, accepted and nurtured her, didn't try to bring her down to inflate his own ego.

"I can't apologize enough for that ridiculous Connery and those photos and captions."

"Yeah." She pulled out her phone to torment herself with them again.

Just look at your face! she wanted to scream at Ian. He was so alive in those photos, with the most genuine grin as he held an arm around her. They were the perfect newly-weds, giddy in each other's company, the promise of a life-time together in their eyes. In a second photo, Ian looked at her with such awe, like she was the most heaven-sent thing he'd ever laid eyes upon. Didn't he see it, too, that by let-ting her go he was giving up on the very essence of who he was? How could duty make up for that? What his family was asking of him was too extreme, too unjust.

As requested, the driver brought her to Shanice's apart-ment building with the overflowing trash cans in front and the graffiti on the building next door. Three young men walking down the street stopped to gawk, as a limo was rarely seen in these parts.

"This is where you're staying?" Ian had obviously never lived in a neighborhood like this.

"I grew up a couple of blocks from here. This is me."

The driver pulled over to the curb and retrieved her lug-gage. It wasn't much, the small bag that she'd taken straight from the wedding onto the plane to Bermuda and the second containing what she'd acquired during the trip. The bathing suits. The navy evening dress. The heartbreak.

"Can I carry these up for you?" Ian pointed to them.

"No, I'm fine. It's only three flights of stairs." Her eyes pooled, and she battled not to let any drops out.

"I'm so sorry about…everything."

"Not your fault." Again, she wanted to yell at him, wanted to shake his shoulders. He was completely missing the point. She didn't care about the photos and being described with unflattering words by his colleague and the press. The way Ian made her feel was far more important than what some gossip website thought. He'd shown her that it was worth it to trust. That not only could she open her heart again, that she wanted to. She said softly, "I'll see you around sometime."

Even though she said she didn't need help, he swooped up the bags and headed toward the five-step stoop that led to the front door of the building.

Laney followed and used her key to open the door.

He elbowed it wide. "Sure you don't want me to come up?"

"No. I'll be fine." She took the bags from him.

"Laney, it was a time…" He couldn't finish.

"Yeah." She cracked a wry half smile. "It was a time." .

She headed up the stairs and didn't hear the front door click shut until she got to the third floor.

As soon as she let herself in, she rushed to the window to see him climb into the limo's back seat.

Come back! Follow your heart! Choose me! she pleaded, although she didn't really. She only silently mouthed the words.

Watching the limo drive away, she finally let the tears that had been waiting spill down her cheeks. She was hurt and she was furious. That he couldn't do it. He couldn't choose her. He couldn't choose love.

She spent the next week traipsing all over Boston. Streets

she'd known her whole life looked unfamiliar now. Dismal. Lonely.

She walked in Boston Common, the oldest park in America, and thought about the garden groves of the Pink Shores Resort with Ian. She ambled through the Freedom Trail, the path tourists always visited with its sights that tell the history of the United States. The harbor where Americans dumped hundreds of chests of tea into the water as a political protest.

She strolled on the Charles River Esplanade, thinking of when she and Ian fell into that pond and kissed for the first time. One day, she lingered in front of the Fletcher Club, where Melissa and Clayton's wedding took place, looking up to the windows as if there were something to see.

She spoke to Melissa on the phone and tried not to be too obvious in her probing to learn if she or Clayton had heard from Ian. Neither had.

Fortunately, after only a week, she was able to find a job as an assistant manager at a café a few blocks away from Shanice's apartment. It was a funky independent like she preferred, not part of a big chain that had a uniform way of doing everything. It was owned by a nice family.

Because she wasn't going to be making enough money to get a place of her own, Shanice agreed to let her share the rent for a couple of months. They reconfigured the living room with a standing divider so that Laney had a space that was her own. It would do for the moment. It was all fine.

Except that it wasn't. She missed Ian with every fiber of her being. Long nights were spent staring at the ceiling, wondering where he was, what he was thinking, what he was feeling. The truth was, it was never going to be fine without him. It was like she'd had hold of the best thing in the world. For a week. Until it slipped between her fingers.

Dutifully, Ian spent the next couple of weeks going on dates with unmarried granddaughters of his grandfather's world. Hugo accelerated the process to get Ian seen around town with other women in order to diminish interest in the gossip photos with Laney. They were women in the upper echelon, each and every one from wealthy families who were looking to make fortuitous matches that would increase their already high standings and statuses.

Abigail's lineage dated back to one of the original founding families of Boston. She had curly blond hair, an advanced degree and was fluent in five languages. Ian couldn't find words in any of the five to talk to her about. She devoted most of her time to charities that rescued kittens in need. Ian could tell from the get-go that she wanted children and would probably make a fine mother. It was also evident that she wanted to be in love above all else, which Ian couldn't offer.

With Jordana, he tried—he really did—to be interested in what type of granite countertops they'd want in the kitchen of the suburban estate they'd build, as she thought the *only way* to raise children was out of the city. Although she showed him stone samples on her phone, on the small screen, he could barely discern the difference between Caledonia and Santa Cecilia, let alone choose one. Yes, his kind of marriage would be about planning and organization. But he couldn't bear the shrewdness of picking out kitchen materials on a first date.

Morgan was the beauty queen that obnoxious Connery spoke of in Bermuda. On a scale of one to ten, she was a definite eleven. Groomed and poised. In her tiny red dress, she wrapped her arm in his as she tottered on high heels into the restaurant. Where she inserted a bit of salad from her fork between her teeth so as to not muss her lipstick. While Ian certainly appreciated a woman with a pleasant appearance, Morgan's lacquered lips made him think of Laney.

It was Laney who he thought was beautiful. Her and only her. Beauty wasn't a stationary thing that someone's outer shell was adorned with. Beauty was an energy that radiated from Laney and onto him, and it was with her that he felt normal, complete. Beauty was a way of living.

After every woman his grandfather chose for him proved to be an intolerable match, he simply couldn't stand any more wife *shopping.*

He loved Laney.

What he felt for her was necessary, like oxygen. It was not something he could do without. He was going to marry, all right. Even if it meant falling out of favor with his family. He hoped it wouldn't come to that, but it was a measure of his love that he'd do anything to have her. He would start by talking to his grandfather.

"Grandson," Hugo said from his padded chair behind the enormous mahogany desk that had been his throne and office for as long as Ian could remember.

Ian sat in one of the leather chairs opposite him. He finished explaining that he had fallen in love with the woman in those leaked photos, a woman who had no pedigree, and he could let nothing stand in his way.

Hugo steepled his two index fingers on the desk. "You know I don't make arbitrary decisions, Ian. Everything I do, I do for a reason."

"Yes, and I have the utmost respect for you, what you've

done for the company and, in turn, for our family. But I can't live without her. That is to say, I won't." He'd never spoken so demonstratively to his grandfather. Had never needed to.

"Then I'll have to be the wise one, as my own grandfather was."

Ian remembered the story of his great, great uncle being swindled by a dishonest woman. "And look at what happened to your uncle Harley, and that was with a baroness! Love cost Luss Global tens of millions of dollars in bad decisions because Harley was too distracted by matters of the heart to do his job."

"That's not the same situation, Grandfather. Harley and Nicole were wild. They drank brandy for breakfast. He never cared about Luss Global. She left him before they could have children, and now he's gallivanting around South America not doing a thing."

"That's all true. Which is why it's dangerous to make changes. When we don't deviate, our policies work, and have for generations. I'm trusting the future of the company to you, Ian. I need you to trust me back."

"I also need you to trust that I'm not one of my uncles. I will watch over and protect the company, just as you did. With Laney by my side, I'll be even stronger and lead Luss Global to even greater heights. I've seen how you and my father run your lives. You do it with singleness of purpose, and that has paid you back. But I'm different. I've always had a hunch that there was something else out there that I needed. Something that would not only inspire but would sustain me and allow me to reach my potential. And now that I've found it, I can't let it go. I'd be an empty shell without it."

His grandfather's face changed. He softened, making some of the deep wrinkles disappear. In an instant, he looked like a younger man. "I'd hoped to take this to my grave, Ian, but I'm going to tell you something."

So, his grandfather held a secret. And Ian had one of his grandmother's, one he'd never told a soul just as she'd asked.

"You think you're so different than I am? That I don't know what you're talking about? About emotion? About romance? I do."

Ian looked to him in question. "What do you mean?"

Hugo rubbed his chin. "I abided by the rules of my grandfather, your great-great-grandfather. My father chose my bride, your grandmother, the daughter of a financier from Philadelphia. We met only a couple of times before the wedding was arranged. Within a year, she gave birth to your father and then two years later to your uncle Harley. Two male heirs, plus managing the mansion we lived in with full-time staff, and my wife's work was done."

He paused for a moment and looked over to the photo of Rosalie he kept on his desk.

"You miss her, don't you?"

"Every day of my life." Hugo ran a finger back and forth along the top of the frame, almost like a caress. "As I was saying, within a couple of years, Rosalie's jobs as wife and mother were smoothly running operations, other than her worries about Harley always finding his way into mischief. I was ensconced here at the firm, to my father and grandfather's liking."

"Implementing your visions for what the company would become."

"One Sunday afternoon, after we'd been married for about six years, we were taking a walk in the formal garden. The sun was shining just so, creating what looked like copper flecks in your grandmother's hair. We were laughing about a comic drawing we'd seen in the newspaper. We laughed so hard and riotously, I took her hand and kissed the top of it. And...all at once... I realized that I was in love with her."

Ian's stomach jumped. He could hardly fathom what he was hearing! "You did?" That surely put a spin on his grandmother's secret.

"The conclusion almost knocked me off my feet. I suddenly saw my wife through the lens of someone who could never love anyone more, who could never obtain anything that made him feel as fulfilled as she did."

"Why didn't you tell her?" That was part of why his grandmother held her own secret, because she didn't know how Hugo felt.

"If she admitted to feeling the same, I was afraid I would get carried away spending time with her and not do my best for our company, just as my grandfather had feared. Or if she didn't love me that way in return, I would be heartbroken and unable to continue raising a family with her. It seemed the simplest and best decision to follow the Luss code of conduct, and conceal my true feelings. So, you see, I do know something about matters of the heart."

Ian balked at how difficult it must have been for his grandfather, if he felt like Ian did about Laney, to hold that truth inside of him. Especially not knowing the whole of it. Would his grandmother want Ian to act on her behalf and tell her husband what she'd buried all those years? Just so that he would know. And selfishly, might it help persuade him to let Ian and Laney pursue the future in open love? He silently asked his grandmother's spirit if he should reveal it now? Her answer was yes.

"She did."

"What?"

"Grandmother Rosalie did love you in return. Was in love with you."

Hugo's eyes became wet and milky, and a blush took over his usually pale cheeks. "How do you know?"

"Because she told me. Growing up, she was the only one who understood the person I was. She knew that going along with the family plan was going to be a hard path for me. So she told me because she thought it would help me not feel so apart from the rest of the family. That she was madly in love with you. But she didn't know if you were in love with her in return or if it would be acceptable to tell you how she felt, so she didn't. She also told me she'd meet you in heaven, although she didn't want you to rush to get there."

Hugo took an old-fashioned handkerchief out of his vest pocket and dabbed at his eyes. He touched the framed photo again, staring at it as if the smile on her face had new meaning. Ian got up from his chair and went around to his grandfather's side of the desk, where they had a long, tight, love-filled hug.

"Ian, you've confirmed what her actions always said to me. Still, it's beautiful to hear it out loud. Your grandmother and I were fools to keep those words from each other. I don't want you to miss out on what we did." Hugo patted him briskly on the back. "You and your Laney go forth in love. I'll trust you."

CHAPTER TWELVE

EMANCIPATED BY THE conversation with his grandfather and the admissions that love had played more of a role in the Luss empire than was commonly thought, Ian was ready to reclaim his lifeblood. The agreement was made that Laney's humble beginnings shouldn't prohibit their union. Only he didn't know where to find her. A call to Clayton led to a call to Melissa. They were making plans for their belated honeymoon, which they'd changed to the Florida Keys.

Melissa was surprised that he was calling to find Laney. He hadn't told either of them about what happened in Bermuda and New York, and if he had to guess, Laney wouldn't have let on, either, especially given how things seemed to end with such finality.

Melissa answered, "She's working at a café in Dorchester. Do you want me to call her?"

"No. Can you text me the info? I'll just stop by." Dorchester. Where Shanice lived and Laney had grown up.

Arriving at the café, he went through its wooden front door with the scratched-up etched windows. Inside, the furniture was rickety, with tables and chairs anywhere they could fit. The old place needed some work, but he knew Laney liked character.

At the counter, a young woman with blue hair was ready to take his order. Looking left and right, he didn't see Laney, so he asked if she was there.

"She's off today."

Disappointment deflated him. He should have called first. "Is she in tomorrow?"

"Yeah, at eleven. Do you want anything?"

Yes, he thought. He'd rather sit at a table for a while and try to feel Laney's presence than go home to his big empty bachelor pad. "Cappuccino, please."

He took a small table and sat with his back to the wall so he could people-watch the entire space. He surveyed the staff. They looked like a friendly bunch who worked well together. A very thin man whose arms were covered with tattoos looked like he might be the one in charge.

After Ian sipped his drink for a few minutes, the tattooed man passed by and asked him, "How's it going?"

"Is this your café?"

"No, I'm the manager, Theo. Is there a problem?"

"No, not at all. I was just curious who owns it."

"That's Mr. and Mrs. Giordano. But now the place is up for sale. They're retiring."

Ian's ears perked up. "Really. Would you happen to know which real estate agent is handling the listing?"

"I can find out for you. Give me a minute."

The smile that crossed Ian's lips had enough wattage to light up the city.

"Someone was in looking for you yesterday," blue-haired Cora blurted as soon as Laney came around the counter to put her bag away.

That was strange. Who would be looking for her? No one even knew that she worked here. It had only been a few days. "Who was it?"

"It was a he. He didn't leave his name, but if you have no use for him, you send him my way, okay?"

Laney chuckled. So an attractive man was looking for her. As mysterious as that sounded, she couldn't imagine who it was. Maybe it was a mistake. Or maybe it was a customer. It wasn't Enrique; he was back in Spain.

There's no way it was... No, she stopped that thought before it could go any further. Impossible. She shrugged her shoulders.

Her first task of the day was to inventory the paper goods and see what needed to be ordered. As she did, her eyes wandered around. This would be a nice enough place to work. For a while. She needed to make the best of it. In addition to the failure of the café in Pittsfield and the disaster that was Enrique, now she had yet another piece of emotional baggage to learn how to carry around. Ian. For the rest of her life, it would be Ian. Her one true love.

What was he doing right now, she wondered as she completed her task? Probably having a grand date with a refined woman from a prestigious family. Maybe he was taking her on a horse-drawn carriage ride in New York's Central Park.

No! That was only for her. She couldn't bear the idea of him doing that with someone else. That was hers. She swiped a couple of tears away with the backs of her fingers, then quickly washed her hands at the sink. There was no crying at work. No matter how much she missed the man she loved.

"Laney."

She heard a voice behind her so familiar she was sure

she was hallucinating. Wow, the mind was strong. Had she just been thinking so hard about him that now she was hearing his voice? What was next, having a memory of his arms around her? And as soon as she thought that, she did have the sense that his long and strong limbs were encircling her, pulling them into the private world that was each other's salvation.

"Laney."

She turned around. It hadn't been her imagination. Ian was standing right there, just like when they surprised each other by being on the plane to Bermuda. Here, the metal counter was the only thing separating them. Words came out of her mouth that didn't even sound like hers.

"What are you doing here?"

"What do you think? I came to find you."

"Why?"

"Because I love you."

Laney's heart thumped in her chest. Both of them knew they had fallen in love at Pink Shores but had never said the taboo words to each other. Now he was here saying them.

"And we're going to be together for the rest of our lives."

"I thought that wasn't possible."

"It's the only thing that's possible."

"What about your family?"

"It's time for a reevaluation. My grandfather and I are working it out."

"What do you mean?"

"I'll tell you all about it later. Meanwhile, I have a present for you."

He came bearing gifts. Laney was overwhelmed. This was so abrupt and so unlikely. Yet she wasn't going to deny that she wanted to be with him just as much as he was claiming to want to be with her. Could it be real? That love was in her cards of fortune, after all.

"What's the gift?"

Ian swept his arm from left to right across the café. "This."

"What?"

"The café."

"What about it?"

"I bought it for you."

"You what?" Now she really thought she was hallucinating. "How did you even know it was for sale?"

"Theo told me." He pointed to the manager, who gave them a thumbs-up signal. "I was here yesterday."

"Okay."

"Okay?" Ian read the displeased expression on her face. "What's wrong?"

"I want to own my own café!" she exclaimed. "I mean, it's beyond beautiful of you to offer, but I don't want to be in business with someone again. This is something I want to do for myself."

Ian's eyes became drawn and his face drooped into sadness.

Oh. She hadn't meant to shut him down like that, but he shouldn't have taken such a drastic action without talking to her about it first. She didn't want to be responsible to someone else if she failed, couldn't go through that again.

She watched inside his eyes as something bubbled. He swiped open his phone and did some furious tapping. Coming up for air, he announced, "Okay, Laney Sullivan. You are now the owner. You will make payments of—" he said and showed her a number on his phone's screen "—every month for five years, at which point you will own it outright. Do we have a deal?"

Laney's breath became fast and heavy. This was terrifying. "Ian, I…"

"There are two conditions of the sale."

Oh, here it comes. Everything always had a hitch. "What are those?"

"The first one is that you come around from that counter."

She slipped by Cora, who didn't even try to seem like she wasn't watching all of this take place. Same with Theo and a couple of other staff members.

"What's the other condition?"

"That no matter what happens with the café or Luss Global or any other business we might be in, that you'll be mine forever."

She threw her arms around his neck, and he wrapped his around her waist and spun her until her feet left the ground.

"You drive a hard bargain, Ian Luss. I accept."

She gave him a kiss to seal the deal.

* * * * *

Keep reading for an excerpt of
Just One More Night
by Fiona Brand.
Find it in the
Tropical Temptation: Exotic Seduction anthology,
out now!

CHAPTER ONE

ELENA LYON WOULD never get a man in her life until she surgically removed every last reminder of Nick Messena from hers!

Number one on her purge list was getting rid of the beach villa located in Dolphin Bay, New Zealand, in which she had spent one disastrous, passionate night with Messena.

As she strolled down one of Auckland's busiest streets, eyes peeled for the real estate agency she had chosen to handle the sale, a large sign emblazoned with the name Messena Construction shimmered into view, seeming to float in the brassy summer heat.

Automatic tension hummed, even though the likelihood that Nick, who spent most of his time overseas, was at the busy construction site was small.

Although, the sudden conviction that he was there, and watching her, was strong enough to stop her in her tracks.

Taking a deep breath, she dismissed the overreaction which was completely at odds with her usual calm precision and girded herself to walk past the brash, noisy work site. Gaze averted from a trio of bare-chested construction workers, Elena decided she couldn't wait to sell the beach villa. Every time she visited, it seemed to hold whispering echoes of the intense emotions that, six years ago, had been her downfall.

Emotions that hadn't appeared to affect the dark and dangerously unreliable CEO of Messena Construction in the slightest.

The rich, heady notes of a tango emanating from her handbag distracted Elena from an embarrassingly loud series of whistles and catcalls.

A breeze whipped glossy, dark tendrils loose from her neat French pleat as she retrieved the phone. Pushing her glasses a little higher on the delicate bridge of her nose, she peered at the number glowing on her screen.

Nick Messena.

Her heart slammed once, hard. The sticky heat and background hum of Friday afternoon traffic dissolved and she was abruptly transported back six years....

To the dim heat of what had then been her aunt Katherine's beach villa, tropical rain pounding on the roof. Nick Messena's muscular, tanned body sprawled heavily across hers—

Cheeks suddenly overwarm, she checked the phone, which had stopped ringing. A message flashed on the screen. She had voice mail.

Her jaw locked. It had to be a coincidence that Nick had rung this afternoon when she was planning one of her infrequent trips back to Dolphin Bay.

Her fingers tightened on the utilitarian black cell, the perfect no-nonsense match for her handbag. Out of the blue, Nick had started ringing her a week ago at her apartment in Sydney. Unfortunately, she had been off guard enough to actually pick up the first call, then mesmerized enough by the sexy timbre of his voice that she'd been incapable of slamming the phone down.

To make matters worse, somehow, she had ended up agreeing to meet him for dinner, as if the searing hours she'd spent locked in his arms all those years ago had never happened.

Of course, she hadn't gone, and she hadn't canceled, either. She had stood him up.

Behaving in such a way, without manners or consideration, had gone against the grain. But the jab of guilt had been swamped by a warming satisfaction that finally, six years on, Messena had gotten a tiny taste of the disappointment she had felt.

The screen continued to flash its message.

Don't listen. Just delete the message.

The internal directives came a split second too late. Her thumb had already stabbed the button that activated her voice mail.

Nick's deep, curt voice filled her ear, shooting a hot tingle down her spine and making her stomach clench.

This message was simple, his number and the same arrogant demand he'd left on her answerphone a number of times since their initial conversation: *Call me.*

For a split second the busy street and the brassy glare of the sun glittering off cars dissolved in a red mist.

After six years? During which time he had utterly ignored her existence and the fact that he had ditched her after just one night.

Like that was going to happen.

Annoyed with herself for being weak enough to listen to the message, she dropped the phone back into her purse and stepped off the curb. No matter how much she had once wanted Nick to call, she had never fallen into the trap of chasing after a man she knew was not interested in her personally.

To her certain knowledge Nick Messena had only ever wanted two things from her. Lately, it was the recovery of a missing ring that Nick had mistakenly decided his father had gifted to her aunt. A scenario that resurrected the scandalous lie that her aunt Katherine—the Messena family's housekeeper—had been engaged in a steamy affair with Stefano Messena, Nick's father.

Six years ago, Nick's needs had been a whole lot simpler: he had wanted sex.

The blast of a car horn jerked her attention back to the busy street. Adrenaline rocketing through her veins, Elena hurried out of the path of a bus and stepped into the air-conditioned coolness of an exclusive mall.

She couldn't believe how stupid she had been to walk across a busy street without taking careful note of the traffic. Almost as stupid as she'd been six years ago on her birthday when she'd been lonely enough to break every personal rule she'd had and agree to a blind date.

The date, organized by so-called friends, had turned out to be with Messena, the man she'd had a hopeless crush on for most of her teenage years.

At age twenty-two, with a double degree in business and psychology, she should have been wary of such an improbable situation. Messena had been hot and in demand. With her long dark hair and creamy skin, and her legs—her best feature— she had been passable. But with her propensity to be just a little plump, she hadn't been in Messena's league.

Despite knowing that, her normal common sense had let her down. She had made the fatal mistake of believing in the heated gleam in Nick's gaze and the off-the-register passion. She had thought that Messena, once branded a master of seduction by one notorious tabloid, was sincere.

Heart still pumping too fast, she strolled through the rich, soothing interior of the mall, which, as luck would have it, was the one that contained the premises for Coastal Realty.

The receptionist—a lean, elegant redhead—showed her into Evan Cutler's office.

Cutler, who specialized in waterfront developments and central city apartments, shot to his feet as she stepped through the door. Shadow and light flickered over an expanse of dove-gray carpet, alerting Elena to the fact that Cutler wasn't the sole occupant of the room.

A second man, large enough to block the sunlight that would otherwise have flooded through a window, turned, his black jacket stretched taut across broad shoulders, his tousled dark hair shot through with lighter streaks that gleamed like hot gold.

A second shot of adrenaline zinged through her veins. *"You."*

Nick Messena. Six feet two inches of sleekly muscled male, with a firm jaw and the kind of clean, chiseled cheekbones that still made her mouth water.

He wasn't male-model perfect. Despite the fact that he was a wealthy businessman, somewhere along the way he had gotten a broken nose and a couple of nicks on one cheekbone. The battered, faintly dangerous look, combined with a dark five-o'clock shadow—and that wicked body—and there was no doubting he was potent. A dry, low-key charm and a reputation with women that scorched, and Nick was officially hot.

Her stomach sank when she noticed the phone in his hand.

Eyes a light, piercing shade of green, clashed with hers. "And you didn't pick up my call, because…?"

The low, faintly gravelly rasp of his voice, as if he had just rolled out of a tangled, rumpled bed, made her stomach tighten. "I was busy."

"I noticed. You should check the street before you cross."

Fiery irritation canceled out her embarrassment and other more disturbing sensations that had coiled in the pit of her stomach. Positioned at the window, Nick would have had a clear view of her walking down the street as he had phoned. "Since when have you been so concerned about my welfare?"

He slipped the phone into his jacket pocket. "Why wouldn't I be? I've known you and your family most of my life."

The easy comment, as if their families were on friendly terms and there hadn't been a scandal, as if he hadn't slept with her, made her bristle. "I guess if anything happened to me, you might not get what you want."

The second the words were out Elena felt ashamed. As ruffled and annoyed as she was by Nick, she didn't for a moment think he was that cold and calculating. If the assertion that her aunt and Stefano Messena had been having an affair when they were killed in a car accident, *the same night she and Nick had made love,* had hurt the Lyon family, it went without saying it had hurt the Messenas.

Her jaw tightened at Nick's lightning perusal of her olive-green dress and black cotton jacket, and the way his attention lingered on her one and only vice, her shoes. The clothes were designer labels and expensive, but she was suddenly intensely aware that the dark colors in the middle of summer looked dull and boring. Unlike the shoes, which were strappy and outrageously feminine, the crisp tailoring and straight lines were more about hiding curves than displaying them.

Nick's gaze rested briefly on her mouth. "And what is it, exactly, that you think I want?"

A question that shouldn't be loaded, but suddenly was, made her breath hitch in her throat. Although the thought that Nick could possibly have any personal interest in her now was ridiculous.

And she was absolutely not interested in him. Despite the hot looks, *GQ* style and killer charm, he had a blunt, masculine toughness that had always set her subtly on edge.

Although she could never allow herself to forget that, through some weird alchemy, that same quality had once cut through her defenses like a hot knife through butter. "I already told you I have no idea where your lost jewelry is."

"But you are on your way back to Dolphin Bay."

"I have better reasons for going there than looking for your mythical lost ring." She lifted her chin, abruptly certain that Nick's search for the ring, something that the female members of his family could have done, was a ploy and that he had another, shadowy, agenda. Although what that agenda could be, she had no clue. "More to the point, how did you find out I would be here?"

"You haven't been returning my calls, so I rang Zane."

Her annoyance level increased another notch that Nick had intruded even further into her life by calling his cousin, and her boss, Zane Atraeus. "Zane is in Florida."

Nick's expression didn't alter. "Like I said, you haven't returned my calls, and you didn't turn up for our...appointment in Sydney. You left me no choice."

Elena's cheeks warmed at his blunt reference to the fact that she had failed to meet him for what had sounded more like a date than a business meeting at one of Sydney's most expensive restaurants.

She had never in her life missed an appointment, or even been late for one, but the idea that Nick's father had paid her aunt off with jewelry, *the standard currency for a mistress,* had been deeply insulting. "I told you over the phone, I don't believe your father gave Aunt Katherine anything. Why would he?"

His expression was oddly neutral. "They were having an affair."

She made an effort to control the automatic fury that gripped her at Nick's stubborn belief that her aunt had conducted a sneaky, underhanded affair with her employer.

Quite apart from the fact that her aunt had considered Nick's mother, Luisa Messena, to be her friend, she had been a woman of strong morals. And there was one powerful, abiding reason her aunt would never have gotten involved with Stefano, or any man.

Thirty years ago Katherine Lyon had fallen in love, completely, irrevocably, and he had *died.*

In the Lyon family the legend of Katherine's unrequited love was well respected. Lyons were not known for being either passionate or tempestuous. They were more the steady-as-you-go type of people who tended to choose solid careers and marry sensibly. In days gone by they had been admirable servants and thrifty farmers. Unrequited love, or love lost in any form was a novelty.

Elena didn't know who Aunt Katherine's lover had been because her aunt had point-blank refused to talk about him. All she knew was that her aunt, an exceptionally beautiful woman, had remained determinedly single and had stated she would never love again.

Elena's fingers tightened on the strap of her handbag. "No. They were not having an affair. Lyon women are not, and never have been, the playthings of wealthy men."

Cutler cleared his throat. "I see you two have met."

Elena turned her gaze on the real estate agent, who was a small, balding man with a precise manner. There were no confusing shades with Cutler, which was why she had chosen him. He was factual and efficient, attributes she could relate to in her own career as a personal assistant.

Although, it seemed the instant she had any contact with Nick Messena, her usual calm, methodical process evaporated and she found herself plunged into the kind of passionate emotional excess that was distinctly un-Lyon-like. "We're acquainted."

Nick's brows jerked together. "I seem to remember it was a little more than that."

Elena gave up the attempt to avoid the confrontation Nick was angling for and glared back. "If you were a gentleman, you wouldn't mention the past."

"As I recall from a previous conversation, I'm no gentleman."

Elena blushed at his reference to the accusation she had flung at him during a chance meeting in Dolphin Bay, a couple of months after their one night together. That he was arrogant and ruthless and emotionally incapable of sustaining a relationship. "I don't see why I should help drag the Lyon name through the mud one more time just because you want to get your hands on some clunky old piece of jewelry you've managed to lose."

His brows jerked together. "I didn't lose anything, and you already know that the missing piece of jewelry is a diamond ring."

And knowing the Messena family and their extreme wealth, the diamond would be large, breathtakingly expensive and probably old. "Aunt Katherine would have zero interest in a diamond ring. In case you didn't notice, she was something of a feminist and she almost never wore jewelry. Besides, if she was having a *secret* affair with your father, what possible interest would she have in wearing an expensive ring that proclaimed that fact?"

Nick's gaze cooled perceptibly. "Granted. Nevertheless, the ring is gone."

Cutler cleared his throat and gestured that she take a seat. "Mr. Messena has expressed interest in the villa you've inherited in Dolphin Bay. He proposed a swap with one of his new waterfront apartments here in Auckland, which is why I invited him to this meeting."

Elena suppressed her knee-jerk desire to say that, as keen as she was to sell, there was no way she would part with the villa to a Messena. "That's very interesting," she said smoothly. "But at the moment I'm keeping my options open."

Still terminally on edge at Nick's brooding presence, Elena debated stalking out of the office in protest at the way her meeting with Cutler had been hijacked.

In the end, feeling a little sorry for Cutler, she sat in one of the comfortable leather seats he had indicated. She soothed herself with the thought that if Nick Messena, the quintessential entrepreneur and businessman, wanted to make her an offer, then she should hear it, even if only for the pleasure of saying no.

Instead of sitting in the other available chair, Nick propped himself on the edge of Cutler's desk. The casual lounging position had the effect of making him look even larger and more muscular as he loomed over her. "It's a good deal. The apartments are in the Viaduct and they're selling fast."

The Viaduct was the waterfront area just off the central heart of the city, which overlooked the marina. It was both picturesque and filled with wonderful restaurants and cafés. As an area, it was at the top of her wish list because it would be so easy to rent out the apartment. A trade would eliminate the need to take out a mortgage to afford a waterfront apartment, something the money from selling the villa wouldn't cover completely.

Nick's gaze skimmed her hair, making her aware that, during her dash across the road, silky wisps had escaped to trail and cling to her cheeks and neck. "I'll consider a straight swap."

Elena stiffened and wondered if Nick was reading her mind. A swap would mean she wouldn't have to go into debt, which was tempting. "The villa has four bedrooms. I'd want at least two in an apartment."

He shrugged. "I'll throw in a third bedroom, a dedicated parking space, and access to the pool and fitness center."

Three bedrooms. Elena blinked as a rosy future without the encumbrance of a mortgage opened up. She caught the calculating gleam in Nick's eye and realized the deal was too good. There could be only one reason for that. It had strings.

He was deliberately dangling the property because he wanted her to help him find the missing ring, which he no doubt thought, since she didn't personally have it, must still be in the old villa somewhere.

Over her dead body.

Elena swallowed the desire to grasp at what was an exceptionally good real estate deal.

She couldn't do it if it involved selling out in any way to a Messena. Maybe it was a subtle point, but after the damage done to her aunt's reputation, even if it was years in the past, *and after her own seduction,* she was determined to make a stand.

Lyon property was not for sale to a Messena, just like Lyon women were not for sale. She met Nick's gaze squarely. "No."

Cutler's disbelief was not mirrored on Nick's face. His gaze was riveted on her, as if in that moment he found her completely, utterly fascinating.

Another small heated tingle shot down her spine and lodged in her stomach.

As if, in some perverse way, he had liked it that she had said no.

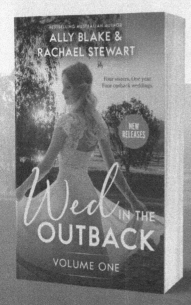
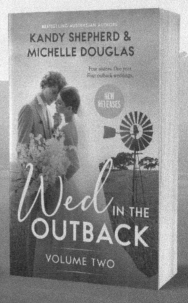

Subscribe and fall in love with a Mills & Boon series today!

You'll be among the first to read stories delivered to your door monthly and enjoy great savings.